Duets™

Two brand-new stories in every volume... twice a month!

Duets Vol. #49

Popular Harlequin American Romance author
Lisa Bingham will make you chuckle this month
with a wonderfully funny story about animal passions.
Joining her is Golden Heart finalist Susan Peterson,
whose *Everything But Anchovies* will leave you
smiling—and ordering out for pizza!

Duets Vol. #50

Bonnie Tucker leads off with a story to die for!
This writer always creates "wildly funny scenes
and memorable characters," says *Romantic Times
Magazine*. Reviewers at *RT* are equally pleased
with Lori Wilde, who "brilliantly weaves together
lovable characters, charming scenes
and a humorous storyline."

Be sure to pick up both Duets volumes today!

D0951507

Call of the Wild

"Oh, no," Alana whispered.

The uneasiness she'd been experiencing increased along with a sense of foreboding. "No, no, no."

Quickly she tabbed to the Maratonga Behavioral Institute's own search window and typed in the word *Nellie*. Her heart began to thud in her chest as her finger hovered over the enter button.

Biting her lip, she punched the key. Within seconds, an image flashed on the screen, fuzzy at first, then resolving into a crisp, clean picture that caused her heart to lurch, then skip a funny beat. There, staring back at her with dark, shoe-button eyes, was a fully grown female gorilla. And kneeling next to her was a man dressed in bush attire, his skin tanned, his blond hair glinting in the sun.

Alana didn't even need to look at the caption below the picture to identify the good-looking figure.

She knew him.

Knew him intimately.

Jake Grisham.

For more, turn to page 9

"Okay, now comes the fun part."

Quinby held the pizza dough in her hands and started turning it, tugging it, then throwing it up in the air.

Six-year-old Zach watched with rapt attention. "Can I do some, Quinby?"

"Sure, Zach, I just need some more dough."

Quinby tried to get by Josh, Zach's father, who had also watched Quinby with rapt attention, but for entirely different reasons. He held his position.

As Quinby reached for the dough, one jean-clad cheek bumped against Josh's groin, shooting a sharp message of need right through him. Immediately he shifted back, regretting his decision to make things difficult for her.

"Excuse me," Quinby mumbled, straightening up while brushing back a handful of warm brown curls, a tiny smile pulling at the corners of her lips. "I never realized cooking could get *quite* so cozy."

For more, turn to page 197

HARLEQUIN DUETS

ISBN 0-373-44115-0

CALL OF THE WILD
Copyright © 2000 by Lisa Bingham Rampton

EVERYTHING BUT ANCHOVIES
Copyright © 2000 by Susan Peterson

This edition published by arrangement with Harlequin Books S.A.

® and TM are trademarks of the publisher. Trademarks indicated with
® are registered in the United States Patent and Trademark Office, the
Canadian Trade Marks Office and in other countries.

Visit us at www.eHarlequin.com

Printed in U.S.A.

Call of the Wild

Lisa Bingham

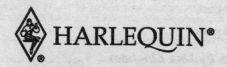

HARLEQUIN®

TORONTO • NEW YORK • LONDON
AMSTERDAM • PARIS • SYDNEY • HAMBURG
STOCKHOLM • ATHENS • TOKYO • MILAN • MADRID
PRAGUE • WARSAW • BUDAPEST • AUCKLAND

Dear Reader,

I'm so excited that *Call of the Wild* has finally found its way to the shelves. The book is very dear to my heart and was such fun to write.

The idea for the novel came from Bonnie Crisalli, one of my first editors at Harlequin. During a phone conversation she happened to mention that she'd never read a book where one of the characters was a sex therapist. Well...I've never been a person to refuse a challenge.

Nevertheless, I have to give credit for the addition of Nellie the gorilla as a secondary character to my middle school English classes. My students had been studying sign language, Koko the gorilla and Dian Fossey's *Gorillas in the Mist*. They became entranced by the humanlike behavior some of the gorillas displayed. When one of my students asked if the gorillas ever developed a crush on the humans who interacted with them...

The rest, as they say, is history.

I hope you enjoy *Call of the Wild*. It's my greatest hope that I can give you a few hours of laughter and whimsy with the antics of a jealous gorilla and her "keepers."

All my best,

Lisa Bingham

Books by Lisa Bingham

HARLEQUIN AMERICAN ROMANCE
692—THE PRINCESS & THE FROG
784—AND BABIES MAKE TEN
835—MAN BEHIND THE VOICE

To my ninth graders for finding
101 ways to make the class
stuffed gorilla sing
"Wild Thing!"

Prologue

"The Thwarted Seduction"

As a rule, blind dates were things to be avoided, but today, an exception had been made.

She'd been ready when her escort had arrived, her hair combed and a glaze of lipstick applied. Joining him in his vehicle, she'd been delighted by his impeccable appearance and polished manners. Nevertheless, she'd reserved judgment. Was he sincere in his compliments? Or was he merely another pretty face, another hard body, with little or no substance beneath the façade?

His choice of activities—a trip to the park and a romp on the swings—showed promise. Such an offbeat idea had a romantic innocence that charmed her. In the succeeding hours her suspicious nature melted away as he wooed her. So much so, that by the end of the evening, her defenses had fallen and there was no denying to herself that she was attracted. More than attracted...

She was aroused.

The shift in her mood was obvious, even to him.

The sexual tension became palpable and they couldn't keep their hands off one another. By the time they returned to her house, they were both too excited to pay much attention to the careful preparations that had been made—health-conscious foods, dim lighting and peaceful stillness. The meal was consumed in haste, but only because eating was expected and remained the last obstacle to the evening's true objective.

Sex.

The moment they finished dinner, a strained expectancy gripped the couple. A grape rolled from the table, making an audible plop in the silence, but neither of the occupants moved.

The male was the first to break the stillness. Rising from his seat, he analyzed the myriad expressions his companion displayed—excitement, fear, dread, curiosity.

Disturbed by his scrutiny, she assumed the haughtiness of a queen, but her reactions were clearly a front for her own confusing response to this stranger.

Well aware of his effect on her, the male grew more confident, his chest swelling, his body adopting an aggressive stance. Deliberately, he issued age-old signals of intent—his eyes narrowing, his body leaning toward hers.

The moment he touched her, she jumped as if jerked from a trance. Clearly irritated with her own skittishness, she attempted to slow the pace of his seduction with nonsensical chatter.

Grunting in annoyance, he again tried to touch her.

But the moment he took her wrist to pull her close, she balked.

He insisted.

She recoiled.

He demanded.

When she broke loose and dodged away, putting the table between them, he gestured to her emphatically, making it clear that he would not be dissuaded from his ultimate intent.

Ravishment.

1

JAKE GRISHAM watched as Nellie, a ten-year-old western lowland gorilla, bit her intended mate on the shoulder and then reached for his groin and squeezed. Wincing, Jake automatically crossed his legs as if his own family jewels were in jeopardy. It didn't seem to matter how many times he viewed the videotape, his body still tensed when Vance, a sexually mature silverback, sank to his knees, clutching his bruised *cojones*.

From her high, Louis XIV desk, Wilhemena Bush sniffed. As president and owner of the Maratonga Behavioral Institute and Zoological Park, she ruled her empire like a tyrant. She demanded implacable obedience to her edicts, and in return, provided funding and research facilities.

''That's it?'' she inquired as Nellie's image on the television screen marched to a nest of blankets in the corner of the gorilla's prefabricated home.

''That's it.''

Wilhemena leaned back in her overstuffed chair and peered at Jake Grisham over the tops of her cat's-eye reading glasses. A blue-blooded Bostonian heiress by birth, she dressed incongruously in a prim silk oxford shirt and a near-neon Samoan *lava-lava*. She was a slight woman, older than dirt, wizened, graying and as frail as a puff of air, but her piercing stare had been known to make grown men weep.

"As much as I admire your gorilla's gumption, it doesn't bode well for your experiment, Dr. Grisham. What do you intend to do now?"

Jake shifted uneasily in his chair. Then, in order to give himself time to formulate an answer, he jumped to his feet and strode toward the VCR and television set strapped to a beige media cart.

As he rewound the tape, he heard the rustling of papers from Wilhemena's desk and knew she was reviewing his file.

"This is the eleventh time you've attempted to mate Nellie, isn't it?"

"Yes, Ma'am." Jake cringed at his own meek reply—but Wilhemena Bush had the ability to make him feel like a schoolboy being reprimanded by his principal.

"I realize that we haven't yet been successful in mating Nellie—"

"Eleven tries, Jake. Eleven tries in two years. In my book, that strikes me as being more than patient."

The tape spit from the recorder, completely rewound, removing Jake's last opportunity to stall.

Sighing, he faced the president.

"I know it looks bad—"

She blinked. "It looks positively pitiful."

Okay. He'd try another tack.

"You must admit Nellie is much more receptive than she was in the beginning."

"Hmm." Wilhemena riffled through the pages on her desk. "Biff, mate number one, was sent to the infirmary with a broken rib. Mojo, mate number two, visited the clinic with contusions. Albert, mate number—"

"She *is* getting better," Jake insisted, already more than familiar with the statistics. Seven silverbacks had been allowed the opportunity to mate with Nellie. Five of them had received injuries extensive enough to necessitate a veterinarian's care.

Pushing the pages away, Wilhemena sighed heavily. "I know that your research is incredibly important, Jake. Of all the projects funded through our facility, yours has been one of my pets."

Jake fought the urge to snort in astonishment. Wilhemena Bush didn't have "pets." She was like a spider, carefully fashioning a web that would attract the most brilliant and media-attracting projects. But if she felt any of her researchers failed to attract the right sort of attention, she would pounce on the unsuspecting team and eat them for lunch.

Wilhemena slapped the folder marked "Project Mama" onto her blotter and leaned heavily on her desk, her rheumy gray eyes blinking intently.

Blink, blink. Blink, blink, blink.

"Dr. Grisham—"

Inwardly, Jake groaned. In the space of a few seconds, his relationship with Wilhemena Bush had deteriorated from "Jake" to "Dr. Grisham."

"—there comes a time in every project—"

He was about to become spider food.

"—when a person has to fish or cut bait."

"Ma'am, if you'll—"

She held up a hand, making Jake uncomfortably aware that he was rarely allowed to finish his sentences in her presence.

"Frankly, funding is tight at Maratonga. Government grants are drying up and private donations aren't as healthy as they used to be."

He waited, still feeling like a five-year-old deviant.

"As you know, primate research was inundated with money when *Gorillas in the Mist* was released—"

"Yes, I know that I—"

"—but frankly, Hollywood's latest hit, *Willy, the Wild-Eyed Ape,* had no such effect. Gorillas and their plight have become passé."

Jake gripped the tape so tightly the plastic creaked. *Passé?* Since when had trying to keep an endangered species off the extinction list become a whim of fashion?

He opened his mouth to offer a scathing rejoinder, then took a deep breath instead. If he argued with Wilhemena Bush, she would fire him just to prove who was in charge. Snapping his jaw shut, he waited for the final word by Her Royalness.

After several, interminable minutes, Wilhemena removed her glasses, allowing them to hang from a gilded chain. "I'll give you until the end of the summer. That gives you two chances at the most. Two chances. After that…she's out."

Jake still didn't allow himself to speak. He didn't trust any remark he might utter to sound suitably grateful—and after a decade of working with the White Spider, he knew full well that he must continue to adopt the posture and attitude of a grateful plebe in her presence.

And he *was* grateful. Frankly, after being summoned to her office, he'd expected Wilhemena Bush to pull the plug on the whole project and kick his fellow team members and him out the door.

"However, Jake—"

He was back to "Jake" rather than "Dr. Grisham."

"I insist that you add an expert to your team."

A slow irritation slid through his body and he clenched his jaw to keep from responding. After all, wasn't *he* one of the foremost experts in primate research? Weren't all of the men on his team at the top of their fields?

"I've noticed that the Project Mama research group is entirely male."

"That's because—"

She interrupted his explanation, saying, "I want a woman on your team. A psychologist or sex therapist. Such an addition would provide several new angles for media coverage. You'll need to bring in donations to continue your work even if Nellie manages to mate."

Jake bristled. A woman. The White Spider wanted a woman on his team. She wouldn't even allow Jake to explain that Nellie refused to work for women. She became agitated and aggressive whenever females were near. The all-male research team wasn't a silent statement of chauvinism, but a necessity.

Nevertheless, Jake didn't bother to argue. Unless he wanted to pack up his research and find another facility—and another gorilla—he would have to obey Wilhemena's bizarre commands.

But he didn't have to like it.

"I'll personally make the arrangements, Jake. Have no fear."

Oh-oh.

"Wilhemena—" he began.

She glared at him.

He cleared his throat and said more diplomatically, "Dr. Bush, I..."

He opened his mouth, intending to argue that if he were to be forced to hire an addition to his team, he wanted to handpick the new member. But how could he tamp down his own anger and frustration enough to keep from blasting?

"There's no need to thank me. Horace has already typed up a possible list of candidates. Since this is your project…"

Jack visibly relaxed. She had understood his wishes without his having to blurt them out.

"…I want you to narrow them down to three. If your selections prove similar to mine, I'll see what I can do. Otherwise…"

She lifted her hands in an "I'm-sorry-but-I-may-have-to-pull-rank" gesture. Then she offered him a shooing wiggle of her fingers. "You may go. Please see Horace on your way out for the list. He's already been whittling down the competition a bit."

Jake tensed even more at the news that Wilhemena's secretary had been pre-evaluating the latest addition. Was Jake the last man on the premises to offer his input on the idea?

Wilhemena grasped another colored folder and repositioned her reading glasses on her slim, bony nose. "Report back to me by the end of the day," she said sternly.

This time, Jake refused to utter his customary "Yes, Ma'am."

Summoning what inner control he still possessed, he offered Wilhemena a curt nod. Marching into the outer office, he snatched the slip of paper being held out to him by Horace Neeley—a ferret-faced little man that Wilhemena employed as her secretary and chauffeur.

Jake was in the outer corridor, storming toward the employee lounge with its rows of candy machines when he finally managed to glance down at the paper clutched in his fist. The first candidate leapt off the page as if it had been formed of neon.

Fifi D'Amour—Just Right Escort Service.

Jake stopped in his tracks, scanning the rest of the names and numbers. Growling in rage, he realized that the bulk of information given him involved at least a dozen call girls and escort services.

"Damn it all to hell and back!" Jake shouted, startling one of the janitors who was mopping the tile floor. "What kind of research does that old bat want me to do?"

DR. ALANA CHILDE rubbed the muscles kinked in the back of her neck from a long day of counseling and therapy sessions.

Generally, she enjoyed her work. She'd been a therapist for more than five years, and most of the time, she found her work incredibly rewarding. But there were days when her own sanity seemed tested to the limits. This afternoon, she'd been introduced to an elderly gentleman who believed intimacy made him invisible, a teenager who believed clothes were tools of the devil, two nymphomaniacs, and a Doberman pinscher with a thing for poodles.

Rolling her eyes, she straightened from the door. A

Doberman, she thought again in disbelief. What was she? A veterinarian? What did she know about dogs?

Unfortunately, the animal was part of a local drug canine corps, and since his human partner was suffering from a nasty divorce—and the resulting trauma seemed to be affecting his ability to work with the Doberman—the department had sought counseling for the pair.

"I've got to get rid of my column," Alana murmured under her breath.

For the first few years of her career, Alana had struggled to build a practice as a family therapist. But with the job market glutted with hundreds of newly graduated psychologists, she'd barely been able to make ends meet. Then, a year ago, she'd been approached by one of Los Angeles's leading newspapers about writing a human-interest column specializing in human sexuality.

Alana had been hesitant about taking the position. She was a family counselor, for heaven's sake—she had a certain image to maintain. But with car payments and office rentals coming due and a slow month in patient referrals, she'd reluctantly agreed to give the idea a trial run.

To her infinite surprise, her mix of professional insight, down-to-earth judgment, and blunt humor had created a cult following. Not long after that, she'd been invited to host a monthly call-in program with the newspaper's sister radio station. And only last month, she'd been approached about possible syndication for her column. If the negotiations became reality, she would be making more money than she'd ever imagined possible.

But the assignment had its drawbacks as well.

Such as attracting every bizarre, sexually active nutcase seeking help to her door.

Luckily, the column and her radio show allowed her the luxury of taking only a handful of special clients. She rarely stayed in the office more than once a week. Nevertheless, sometimes the eccentric nature of the cases that were referred to her was especially trying.

Sinking into her leather office chair, Alana made a few notations on the mysterious Doberman case, then dropped the file into her out box.

In all honesty, it wasn't just the odd clientele that made her nervous. What made her even more uncomfortable was the "character" she'd built for herself—especially after going on the air. During her first broadcast, she'd been so uncomfortable with her unaccustomed role as a sex expert that she'd unwittingly overcompensated for her feelings of inadequacy. The moment the microphone had turned on, she'd suddenly transformed into a sultry, sassy woman of the world.

And now she lived in fear that someday everyone would discover she was a fraud. A complete and utter fraud.

"Dr. Childe?"

The low, soothing tones of her receptionist floated

from the general region of Alana's speakerphone. In reality, Darlene Call was sixty, graying, and hard as nails, but her disembodied voice had the soothing drawl of a phone sex operator—a fact which Alana's patients continued to remind her.

Punching the intercom button, Alana said, "Yes, Darlene."

"I know you've finished for the day…"

"Thank heavens," Alana grumbled.

"…but you have a call on line one asking for a consultation. A Dr. Bush."

Alana frowned. A consultation. What kind of consultation? Police needing a psychologist's insight on a case? High society fund raisers? Wackos with imaginary impotent friends?

"I really think you should talk to her if you've got the time," Darlene said, using that I've-tried-to-get-rid-of-her-but-she-won't-go-away tone of voice Darlene occasionally adopted with particularly trying clients.

Alana squeezed her eyes shut and mentally gauged how many seconds it would take for her to hang up and run through the patient exit room, out of the building and to her car.

Too long.

Especially since she was wearing nylons and heels in an effort to live up to the "Love Doctor" image most of her referrals expected to see.

Allowing the air to leave her lungs in a rush, Alana capitulated.

"Fine. I'll take the call. But buzz me in fifteen minutes, just in case I need an excuse to get away."

"You got it, boss."

Tucking back a strand of hair that fell away from the smooth blond sweep cut bluntly at chin level, Alana reached for the phone.

"This is Dr. Childe."

"Hello, Dr. Childe. This is Dr. Wilhemena Bush. I'm the director of the Maratonga Behavioral Institute in San Diego."

There was something familiar about the voice, but Alana couldn't pinpoint where she'd heard it before.

The woman continued, "I have a matter of utmost delicacy I'd like to discuss with you. I'm an avid fan of your column and your radio program. That's why I thought of you."

Alana floundered for something to say, "I'm flattered, Dr.—"

"Please. Call me Wilhemena."

"Yes, Dr... Wilhemena. I'm afraid I don't understand what you need me to do."

"Oh, but you do," the woman insisted. "You see, I've been a regular call-in participant with your show and you've responded to several of my letters in your column."

"Oh?" Alana usually had a good memory for

names, but she couldn't recall a Bush having asked for help.

"I'm the 'Godmother.'"

Alana's eyes widened, her heart beating slightly faster. "*You* are 'The Godmother'?" Alana couldn't have hidden her astonishment and excitement even if she'd wanted to. 'The Godmother' had been one of the first callers asking for specific help. Her goddaughter suffered from an extreme case of frigidity—to the point of actually lashing out at the men who had dated her and attempted to involve her in a physical relationship. From what Alana could remember, she'd sent several of her companions to the hospital, her reactions had been so strong.

"How is Nellie?" she asked.

Wilhemena's tone tightened. "Not good. She attacked another one."

"Another date?"

"Yes."

Alana's delight faded to overwhelming concern. Even though she'd never met Nellie, she'd followed her case for so long she felt as if the woman were a regular patient.

"From what you've told me, she wants to consummate a relationship so badly," Alana murmured.

"That's why I've come to you for help. I think the time has come for Nellie to have some structured therapy."

"I couldn't agree more."

Wilhemena breathed a sigh of relief. "Good! Then you'll come see her in San Diego?"

"San Diego? Can't Nellie come here?"

"I'm afraid she's stuck in a...situation with her work which requires her to stay in San Diego. We were hoping you would agree to see her here. I assure you that if you arrange to spend a few weeks offering some intensive counseling, the Institute would be more than willing to make the assignment worth your while."

"The...Institute?"

"Nellie is a member of the Maratonga Behavioral Institute."

Alana thought the research facility must be quite forward thinking to provide sexual counseling for one of its employees.

"Please say you'll come," Wilhemena was saying. "I've got a little beach house where you could stay, and the Institute would provide for your meals as well as a healthy stipend, not to mention your fees. You could even look upon things as a working vacation."

"I have a broadcast next Saturday..."

"I'll arrange for a company helicopter to transport you there and back." Wilhemena's tone became urgent. "Please help. Please. If you don't, I'm afraid that Nellie's guardians may intervene."

"Guardians? I thought Nellie was of a legal age to make these decisions."

"Oh, she is. But Nellie is the beneficiary of an enormous trust fund. In order to ensure the proper disbursement of funds, Nellie is subject to the whims of her guardians—some of them board members here at the Institute—and I'm afraid they aren't too keen on the idea of therapy.''

Aha. The Institute was grudgingly paying for the therapy of an employee with family connections, but Nellie's guardians, who were board members of the establishment, weren't too happy about the idea.

A slow anger began to ease through Alana's veins when she thought of this woman—a delicate, emotionally fragile creature—who longed for love and physical fulfillment with all her heart, yet was beset by an overwhelming fear of men.

No doubt, her guardians were all male. Alana would bet the farm on such a fact. Otherwise they would have some empathy for the woman.

"Please say you'll help?" Wilhemena said.

Alana's mind was made up in an instant. "I'll do it."

"Really? You'll come to the Institute to see her? First thing tomorrow morning?"

"Of course."

"Thank you. You're her last hope, Dr. Childe. When I've been able to pass on your advice to Nellie, she's responded so much better. I'll have my beach house readied and the paperwork drawn up for your fees. In the meantime, I'll fax your office with instructions on how to reach our facility and the proper building. Visitors' credentials will be left for you at the front gate and I'll meet you at the entrance to the main office. From there, I'll offer you some background on her case. Then, we can visit Nellie and her guardians.''

''My son and his nanny will be coming along.''

''Marvelous. I'll look forward to meeting them. Good day, Dr Childe.''

As the line clicked, Alana thought she heard a small note of triumph in Wilhemena's tone, but she brushed the sensation away. Relief. It had been obvious relief she'd heard.

Hadn't it?

She'd barely hung up the phone when Darlene appeared at her door, ready to gather the files for the day.

Alana stood and stretched. ''Darlene, a fax should be arriving in a few minutes. When it comes, will you bring it to me please? Then contact Dr. Baird and let him know I'll be out of the office for the next two weeks, maybe three. Cancel what appointments you can. Those who don't want to cancel, refer to Dr. Baird.''

Darlene's brows lifted and her mouth spread into a smile. ''Are you finally taking a vacation?''

''I've got a patient to see in San Diego. Some emergency consultation work.''

Darlene was clearly disappointed. ''Don't you think you should take a little time off for yourself? You've been burning the candle at both ends.''

"It's a working vacation, of sorts."

The twinkle returned to Darlene's eyes. "Hopefully there's a man involved. You've been neglecting your social life lately. I can't remember the last time you had a date."

Alana shied away from that topic, saying, "Why don't you head home? I'm going to stick around here for a few more minutes. I've got the perfect topic for my next column and I want to e-mail it to my editor before the deadline."

The older woman's gaze was curious. It was obvious that Darlene knew Alana had purposely steered the conversation away from her personal life, but Darlene didn't press the issue. "Do you want me to lock up the waiting room?"

"Please. I'll leave through the patient exit."

After wishing Alana luck on her upcoming trip, Darlene disappeared and the office settled into silence. Flipping open her laptop, Alana quickly typed a scathing editorial about men who were insensitive to the emotional needs of virginal women. Then, she connected with the Internet and sent the text to her editor along with a quick explanation of her upcoming trip to San Diego.

It wasn't until she was about to log off that Alana began to get "the feeling."

For as long as she could remember, Alana had been plagued with an impulsive streak. Despite her degrees and her outward façade of cool professionalism, inside, there lurked a sense of self-consciousness that led to a need to prove herself. During such "relapses," she tended to act with her heart, not her head. And invariably, when she allowed her emotions to overrule common sense, she would get "the feeling."

Even now, as she began to anticipate a few weeks away from the office, Alana felt a twinge of disquiet. *A bad sign. A bad sign indeed.*

Alana couldn't imagine why she felt so uneasy. Yes, she'd accepted the consultation work with Nellie rather quickly, but it wasn't as if she didn't have a backup system when such emergencies arose. Dr. Baird was an old college friend who was new to the area and eager to build his own clientele. He would be more than happy to take her caseload for the next few weeks. And she really did need a break from her regular duties. She hadn't taken any time off in more than a year. No one could fault her desire to accept the offer of what amounted to a paid vacation.

So why was she suddenly so nervous...so anxious?

Sighing she was about to turn off her computer when she had a sudden thought. "I wonder..." she murmured to herself.

If there was one thing that had bothered her about Nellie's situation, it was the interference of Maratonga's board members in what should have been a personal decision to seek counseling. It didn't make sense.

Needing more information than she'd been given,

Alana connected with the Internet and typed the words "Maratonga Behavioral Institute" into the search engine. After only a few seconds, Alana had a hit.

Clicking on the first entry listed on the screen, Alana waited as the graphics and text arranged themselves in front of her.

"The Maratonga Behavioral Institute is dedicated to the preservation and study of animal behavior in…" Alana stopped. "Oh, no," she whispered. The uneasiness she'd been experiencing increased along with a sense of foreboding. "No, no, no."

Quickly, she tabbed to the Institute's own search window and typed in the word "Nellie." Her heart began to thud in her chest as her finger hovered over the enter button.

Biting her lip, she punched the key. Within seconds, an image flashed on the screen, fuzzy at first, then resolving into a crisp, clean image that caused her heart to lurch, then skip a beat.

There, staring back at her with dark, shoe-button eyes, was a fully grown female gorilla. And kneeling next to her was a man dressed in bush attire, his skin tanned, his blond hair glinting in the sun. Alana didn't even need to look at the caption below the picture to identify the good-looking figure.

She knew him.

Knew him intimately.

Jake Grisham.

''What have I done?'' she whispered in patent dread.

Not only had she unwittingly agreed to become a sexual therapist to a gorilla, but by doing so, she was about to come face-to-face with a man who thought he'd taken her virginity nearly a decade ago.

2

WITH ONLY a few months grace period before financial aid would be pulled on his project, Jake decided to push Nellie's comfort zone. Since she'd shown some progress with Vance, he had allowed the animal to be reintroduced into her daytime habitat in the hopes that familiarity might breed something other than contempt in Nellie's case.

Vance had been more than willing to oblige. It was obvious that his pride and his sense of virility had been badly dented on his previous encounter with Nellie. He was eager to show her just who was King of the Jungle between the pair of them.

But Vance had been reunited with her for less than twenty minutes before a fight had erupted. Before the animals could be separated, Nellie had injured the gorilla. Again. Bringing him to his knees with a powerful squeeze. Again.

In the observation area of the laboratory, hidden behind the two-way mirror, Jake Grisham winced.

"Damn," he whispered hoarsely.

In the habitat below, Vance, a captive-born lowland

gorilla, offered a series of guttural moans that quickly dissolved into high-pitched squeaks. Ever so slowly, the animal curled into a ball, clutching his groin, while Nellie stalked to her nest of blankets on the floor.

Obviously, she meant to nap alone.

"Get him out of there," Jake said to the team's zoologist.

Rusty Smithers cursed fluently under his breath as he marched out the door, leaving it open behind him.

"Get the other guys together and meet in my office for a conference!" Jake called after him.

"Will do, boss," he heard Rusty reply, his voice muffled by distance and exertion.

Returning his attention to the animals, Jake shoved his hands into the back pockets of his trousers to keep from striking his fist against the glass. The adrenaline that had been pumping through his veins since Vance's arrival quickly dissipated.

Damn it! Why couldn't they find a single gorilla capable of mating with Nellie?

"Dr. Grisham?" a hesitant voice asked from the doorway.

Recognizing the anal-retentive whine of Floyd Kingston, a security guard who manned the information desk in the lobby, Jake didn't bother to turn. Waving a vague hand in the man's direction, he said, "Just a minute, Floyd."

Rusty was stepping into Nellie's apartments, and Jake punched the intercom button.

"You might as well sedate Vance and put him out of his misery. Otherwise, he's likely to fight your efforts to help him."

"Right, *bwana*," Rusty responded. Obviously, he'd anticipated such a request because he took a tranquilizer gun from where he'd tucked it in the back waist of his pants. Aiming it at Vance's thigh, he said, "Help's a'comin', Big Boy."

Jake winced when the dart hit home. But as Vance's thrashing became minute twitches of distress, Jake breathed easier.

"Dr. Grisham?" Floyd said again. "I think—"

"Just another minute, Floyd," Jake interrupted.

Floyd was notorious for interrupting delicate behavioral experiments with "urgent business"—usually some form of busy-work sent to Jake's lab by the head office of the Maratonga Behavioral Institute and Zoological Park.

"But I was supposed to bring—"

"Leave it on the table and I'll get to it immediately."

"But…"

Ignoring the man, Jake watched as a pair of brawny intern students sent from UCLA struggled to lift Vance onto a gurney. Both of the men were ex-football players. Nevertheless Vance's bulk caused them to stagger. But judging by the care they took with Vance, the interns must have been watching the proceedings from the video booth. A distinct male empathy tinged every move they made.

"Watch his hand!" Jake warned, but Rusty was already catching the gorilla's hairy arm as it fell off the edge of the gurney.

Revealing how often the team had been faced with this same scenario, they quickly strapped Vance into place, checked his vital signs, then wheeled him from Nellie's apartments.

The instant the door closed behind them, Jake allowed himself a few quiet minutes alone. Filling his lungs with air, he willed the muscles of his jaws to lose their iron grip.

"Damn, damn, damn," he whispered under his breath.

Indulgently, he peered at the contented, sleeping gorilla. One would never know by looking at her that she had spent the past few minutes following Vance with hot, hungry eyes. Despite her display of passion, she'd felled the sexually mature silverback without a qualm.

Only a trace of Jake's irritation remained as he muttered, "You little tease."

"You always did blame the woman, didn't you, Jake?"

He froze, his mind grappling to identify the voice that was familiar, yet, oh, so...

He whirled to face the solitary figure standing in the doorway and his jaw unconsciously dropped.

No. Not standing. She *posed.*

The woman was limned with the light streaming in from the hall. The threshold framed her body as she rested her weight on one hip, an arm lifting over her head to rest on the molding in a way that made her breasts push against the soft silk of her shirt. Her suit was also silk, smooth and sensually tailored, with a skirt hemmed well above long, shapely legs. Legs that seemed to stretch forever.

"Alana?"

No. This...*creature* couldn't possibly be Alana Childe. She was far too svelte and sexy.

At his obvious confusion, her lips twitched in a knowing smile.

"It's been a long time, hasn't it, Jake?"

Startled, he peered at her more carefully. Alana Penelope Childe. Was it really the plump, impulsive, no-nonsense girl he'd once called "Al?" They'd been college study partners, even...

Damn it, he couldn't think about that now. He couldn't think about that last week in Mombassa after they'd finished a study-abroad stint among the Masai. They'd both been drunk and flushed with success. No wonder they'd...

Her husky chuckle drew his attention back to the present and the incredible woman who had appeared as if by magic.

"I'll take your reaction as a compliment," she said as she dropped her arm and took a step into the observation room. "Otherwise, I suppose I would have to be incredibly insulted."

"What are you doing here?" The words emerged in a husky rasp.

"My, my. What a welcome. And after all we've been through together."

Do not go there, his mind warned. *Do not go down that road.*

Alana's smile was coy, as if she knew exactly what he was thinking.

"Don't I deserve at least a hug? After all, I loaned you my paleontology notes during—"

"Will I never hear the end of a moment of weakness on my part?" Jake said, responding with words he'd said at least a hundred times. But this time, the banter felt far from familiar. Nevertheless, he refused to admit such a thing to Alana. Not when the devilish light in her cornflower blue eyes warned him of even more mischief to come.

"You are out of control," he muttered as he moved toward her and slid his arms around her waist. "As usual."

Closing his eyes, he willed himself to see Alana as she'd been the last time they were together in Africa— her hair pulled back in an unruly ponytail, her face burned and freckled, her clothes rumpled and frayed.

Unfortunately, the exotic, oriental fragrance she wore was in no way reminiscent of campfires or jungle growth.

She drew back far enough to study him, her eyes twinkling in a way he did remember. In large groups, Alana Childe often transformed into a classic extrovert, becoming the life of the party, the center of attention. What most people didn't know, however, was that her outward joviality was often a façade for a woman who was reserved, shy around strangers, and infinitely leery of any kind of male attention.

"You look awful," she stated bluntly.

"And you look great. What happened to you?"

She pulled a face, stepping out of his arms.

Jake had the strangest urge to pull her close again. To keep himself from surrendering to the outlandish idea, he tunneled his fingers into his pockets again.

"I'm serious, Alana. What happened to you?"

"You sound as if you think I've had major reconstructive surgery," she said as she prowled restlessly around the room.

"No, you just look—" He stopped himself before he could finish. Anything he said would probably open the door for further outlandish remarks on her part.

"What are you doing here?" he asked instead.

"I've been asked to help."

"Help?" he inquired vaguely. "With what?"

"Your monkey."

"She's a gorilla."

"Whatever."

"And how, exactly, do you propose to help?"

"I've been hired as her therapist."

"Oh?" The last Jake had heard, Alana had been pursuing a doctorate in anthropology and human development.

"I was told to start today since your matchmaking endeavors failed."

He shook his head. "You've lost me."

"Jake!" a shrill voice boomed from the corridor. "Isn't this a wonderful addition to your team?"

Jake whirled to see Wilhemena Bush striding into the room and gesturing in Alana's direction.

Wilhemena waited for Jake's response, obviously expecting some sort of effusive rejoinder.

"What's the matter, man? Have you buried your head so deep in your lab that you don't recognize a celebrity when you see one?"

Celebrity? Alana?

Jake met Alana's gaze, his brows lifting.

She merely grinned.

"Good heavens, Jake. You need to get out more. This is Alana Childe...The Love Doctor!"

THE LOVE DOCTOR.

In Alana's opinion, the title was absurd, but she didn't bother to refute it. After all, she made a great deal of money being the Love Doctor in print and on the airwaves. Her publicist could call her Little Bo Peep as long as Lancaster Communications continued to offer a six-digit salary.

Nevertheless, she couldn't control an inner squirm

of embarrassment. Jake Grisham had known her long before she'd changed her major in graduate school, highlighted her hair, and shed thirty pounds. He remembered her as the caterpillar she'd once been instead of the confident, vivacious, poised butterfly she'd become.

Yeah, yeah. Keep telling yourself you're confident and poised and maybe you'll believe it, her inner voice chided. *But admit the truth. With Jake Grisham around, you still feel like a gawky adolescent.*

"Isn't it marvelous?" Wilhemena Bush said, cutting through the thick silence. "Dr. Childe's services are in great demand, but she agreed to come here and help with our project."

"She has, has she? And how does she intend to help us mate Nellie with another gorilla?"

Alana chose that moment to interrupt. "Wilhemena, could you excuse us a minute? Jake and I are old friends, and I think he would react much more positively if I were to break the news."

Jake's eyes narrowed. "What...*news?*"

He was so openly suspicious, Alana nearly laughed. Poor Jake. He might look as if he stepped from the pages of *Men's Fitness,* but he was an academician through and through. As far as he was concerned, his projects were sacrosanct—pure science—and heaven forbid the human factor be included.

Wilhemena's eyes bounced from Alana to Jake then

back again. Then, with a small, satisfied smile, she said, "Fine. I'll leave the two of you to get... reacquainted."

It was obvious from her careful scrutiny that she had picked up on the vibes humming in the room around them and suspected that Alana and Jake had been more than mere "friends." But since Jake's expression was inscrutable and Alana kept her features bland, she withdrew, closing the door behind her.

"Damn it, Alana!" Jake began the moment the latch clicked. "I will not have you playing your games with my project!"

"I don't intend to."

He continued as if she hadn't spoken, growing more agitated with each word. He strode toward her—much as Vance had done during his seduction attempt—maneuvering her toward the corner.

"If you wanted to see me again, all you had to do is call."

"I don't have your number."

"I would have set up a tour of the Instit—"

"I'm not here for a tour—"

"You could have stayed with my mother—"

"Gee, thanks."

"But I will not—*not*—have you messing with Nellie and the future of this project!"

He was breathing hard. Somehow, in the course of his tirade, he'd pinned her in the corner and planted his hands above her shoulders on the wall. Leaning closer and closer, he grew suddenly quiet, his gaze fixing in the vicinity of her mouth.

Suddenly, the room seemed to shrink around them. The air Alana breathed grew thick. Her heart pounded in her chest.

Damn. She'd told herself she wouldn't let this happen. She'd told herself that she was over Jake Grisham, that he couldn't affect her any longer. Evidently, she'd been wrong.

Needing to put some distance between them, she deftly slipped free and moved to the window that looked down over what looked like a small classroom. If not for the gorilla sleeping in a nest of blankets in the corner, she could have convinced herself that she was looking into a normal preschool setting.

Jake touched her shoulder and it took all her will not to jump. She'd forgotten how silently he moved. And how he had only to touch her to make her feel completely alive.

Jake must have felt something as well—at least she salved her own weak conscience by thinking he did when he turned her to face him and stared intently at her face.

She stood rooted to the spot, praying that he wouldn't guess the way that point of contact shook her to the core.

You shouldn't have come, her conscience taunted.

You should have known you'd be in hot water within ten minutes.

And it was true. Alana had known that seeing Jake Grisham again would be a hell of a big chance. But she'd been determined to take a dose of her own medicine and prove to herself that she was over her brief fling with Jake Grisham. In the past few years, she'd grown older and infinitely wiser. At this stage of her life, it was time to let the adolescent crush die—and how better to accomplish such a thing, than to confront the object of her obsession?

But she'd underestimated the power he had over her. Seeing Jake hadn't doused those lingering feelings.

It had merely made her more keenly aware of them.

Silently, she grappled with her uncertainties even as Jake's eyes narrowed and his hand lifted. He slipped his fingers into her hair, drawing the tresses away from her face as if he were trying to see her as she'd been the last time they'd been together. Chubby little Alana with her ever-present ponytail.

Her breath hitched as he bent toward her.

Dear heaven, no. Not a kiss. She couldn't kiss him now. If she did...

If she did, she would be lost completely.

But even as the words flashed through her consciousness, he closed the space between them and his lips touched her own.

The passion was instantaneous, igniting from that sweet point of contact to spread through her body like wildfire, filling her with a long forgotten hunger.

It had been so long…so long since she'd been held by a man, so long since she'd felt this hot desire flooding through her veins and robbing her mind of all reason.

Of their own volition, her arms wrapped around his shoulders and her fingers dug into his flesh. When he pulled her tightly against him, she moaned, knowing that she had secretly been wishing something like this would happen.

Dear sweet heaven, was she that needy? That wanton?

Jake broke free, his lips moving to her cheek, her jaw. Alana gasped when his teeth found her earlobe.

"What are you doing here, Alana?" he breathed against her skin. "What are you *really* doing here?"

She knew she should find breath enough to assure him that he already knew, but she was able to do little more than sink her fingers into his hair and draw his lips back to her own.

Not now, a little voice whispered inside of her head. Now wasn't the time to deal with the realities of the situation. Instead, she wanted to wallow in this sweet, hot moment for as long as she could.

"Excuse me, Dr. Childe?"

Alana was wrenched back to reality in an instant. Embarrassment washed over her like a bucket of icy water as she looked beyond Jake's shoulder to see Wilhemena's assistant.

"Mr. Neeley," she said, then cleared her throat when the words emerged as a garbled croak.

She felt a heat seeping up her neck to her cheeks and knew that she must be blushing brightly enough for Neeley to see even from a distance.

"Dr. Bush asked me to come get you. She has those tapes you wanted to see of Nellie."

"I...uh, yes. Thank you."

Neeley gestured to the open door, making it clear that he didn't intend to leave without her. But when Jake moved to join them, Neeley stopped him.

"There's no need for you to trouble yourself, Dr. Grisham. Dr. Bush knows you'll want to spend all your time in the lab reviewing the problems with Nellie's last encounter. Therefore, Dr. Bush will take it upon herself to brief Dr. Childe on the particulars of your experiment. Then Dr. Childe will join you and your team tomorrow."

Alana glanced at Jake, but his features were inscrutable. If not for his rumpled clothing and tousled hair, she would never have known they'd embraced.

And you'd best remember that, Alana told herself as she briskly made her way down the hall. She might be older and infinitely more experienced in the ways of the world than she'd been the last time she'd seen Jake Grisham, but apparently her self-defeating attraction to Jake Grisham hadn't changed.

And despite what she'd just experienced, she couldn't surrender to the weakness he inspired in her.

Ever.

3

DUSK WAS BEGINNING to fall over the southern wing of the Maratonga Behavioral Institute when Alana finally decided she'd had enough for the day. A glance at her watch confirmed that Angel and Matthew would be here soon to pick her up in the rental car Maratonga had supplied for the length of her stay.

Lifting the remote, Alana turned off the VCR. Instantly, a plain blue screen replaced the image of Nellie and her most recent "beau."

What a nightmare.

Alana fought the urge to groan in despair. What did she know about the sexual habits of gorillas? And how had she allowed herself to become involved in all this?

She rubbed at her temples, watching the distant sway of palm trees and the glint of the ocean from the large picture window of a conference room that had been loaned to her as a temporary office.

Why, oh, why couldn't she learn to think things through? She'd been sure she could handle a meeting with Jake Grisham. She'd been so overcome with curiosity about what he was like after all these years that she'd ignored her own misgivings.

Alana grimaced at her own hubris. By the time she had installed her son, his nanny, and her own pile of belongings in Wilhemena's beach house, she'd actually decided that the meeting would be a healthy way to bring closure to her old romance. She would rid herself of her obsession once and for all.

Then she could stop comparing every man she met with Jake Grisham, a man who never would have tried making love to her at all if she hadn't made him drunk first.

But Alana had soon discovered that she'd been wrong. So very wrong. The moment she'd stepped into the same room with him, she'd felt electrified and alive. She'd grown nervous and anxious, overcome by the same twittering adolescent energy she'd experienced the first time she'd met him.

Alana flushed, realizing that she'd overcompensated for her feelings by being assertive and—

Brazen.

She'd done nothing at all to stop him from kissing her. In fact, if Neeley hadn't suddenly appeared, she probably would have...

What? What would she have done? Dragged him to the battered couch in the corner and ravished him?

Even as she chided herself for such foolishness, Alana was no longer so sure that such a thing could never happen. She had totally underestimated the remnants of her attraction to Jake Grisham.

Alana groaned and rested her forehead on her hands. When was she going to learn? When would she ever realize that rushing headlong into an uncomfortable situation wasn't always the best way to handle things? And now she'd put herself in an untenable situation. One which could ultimately be her undoing, emotionally and professionally.

Panic brought a halt to her thoughts in midstream. She would have to get out of the arrangement with the Maratonga Institute, that was all.

Grabbing her cell phone, she punched in the number for her editor. The moment she got Bill Munns's private line, she said, "Hi, Bill, this is Alana."

"Alana! I've been trying to get in touch with you. The reaction to the editorial in this morning's paper has been phenomenal! The guys at your radio station even picked up on things and began running an excerpt as a promo for your next broadcast. This is the best publicity any of us have had in years. We've had a flood of e-mail already, and from what I understand, the station has already got callers jamming the lines."

Alana swallowed against her own rising hysteria. "You've got to call Kevin and have him stop playing those spots."

"You're kidding, right? Those promos are a gold mine for the station and free publicity for the paper."

He quickly changed the subject. "Have you seen Nellie already? Is the situation as bad as it sounds?"

Alana groaned. "I've seen some footage of her. Bill, you've got to get Kevin to stop the spots."

"Why?"

She took a deep breath and said in a rush, "Nellie is a gorilla."

The silence on the other end of the line was deafening. Then, "Am I to assume that you aren't talking about the woman's personality traits? That by describing her as a gorilla, you mean she's a Tarzan of the jungle, 'oo-oo-ah-ah' gorilla."

Her sigh was fraught with her own conflicting emotions. "Yes. I was lured to the Maratonga Behavioral Institute under false pretences."

"I don't understand. You said one of your regular listeners, a woman who referred to herself as 'The Godmother' approached you. I've read some of your columns when The Godmother's appeals were featured. There were specific quotes made—supposedly from Nellie herself."

"Nellie has been taught American Sign Language. She communicates with the behavioral scientists. Her wish to consummate a relationship is quite real."

"But she's frigid."

"Quite. She's injured at least a half dozen male gorillas."

There was a beat of silence, then "This is incredible."

Relief surged through her body. "You're right. It's totally unacceptable. Get Kevin to cancel the sound bites and I'll make some sort of explanation in my next column—"

"No, no. I mean this is *incredible*. You're actually going to be a sex therapist to a lonely gorilla."

"No, Bill. I—"

"Man, if we think we're getting feedback now, I can't wait to see what happens when your readers find out about this!"

"No, I don't think—"

"I'll send a camera crew to the Maratonga Institute. Hell, that old bat, Wilhemena Bush, made a call this morning suggesting such a thing, but I put her off. After all, I thought it was a pretty sick idea to do a photo spread about some woman with sexual inhibitions. But this puts an entirely different slant on things. We could do a feature on your work there and include some background on gorillas and their similarities to humans. Man! I can hardly wait to tell Kevin what we've got going here!"

"Bill, I don't think that's a good idea."

"Why? It's a great idea! We're always being told that we're just a step away from the apes. Well, this is a chance to see just how close we are to our animalistic roots, and to get the information straight from the ape's mouth, so to speak." Alana could hear his phone ringing in the background. "Listen, I'm ex-

pecting a call from Atlanta that I've got to take. Are
you on your way to the beach house you're using?"

"Yes, but I—"

"I'll call you there in about an hour. In the meantime, you're a genius, Alana. A sheer genius."

But as the line went dead, Alana didn't feel like a
genius. She felt incredibly stupid and naïve for allowing herself to get sucked into this situation at all.

And now, it seemed she had no other alternative
than to see this project through to the finish. She'd
used every argument she'd thought would dissuade
Bill from continuing to pursue events as they unfolded
at Maratonga. Short of citing personal reasons...

Even as she considered backing out of the arrangement under such a pretense, she knew she could never
do it. If she did, she would have to explain to Bill that
Jake was at the root of her decision. She would have
to outline her past history. She would have to admit
she was still attracted to Jake. Worse yet, she would
have to confess that Jake was the only man who had
ever come close to being her lover.

Again, she groaned. No. It was too much. She could
never tell anyone, let alone her editor. She would
never admit that Jake was the only man to make her
feel passionate and sexy. Nor could she admit to her
editor that the great "Love Doctor" was probably the
oldest living virgin on the planet.

If only she'd been more careful all those years ago.
Inadvertently, she'd given Jake Grisham too much li-

quor. He'd passed out before their lovemaking could be consummated. Since then, she'd insisted to herself that she'd grown out of her stupid infatuation. She'd convinced herself that her obsession with him was an irrational reaction that would have fizzled out if they'd actually made love.

But as it was, she'd never been able to reconcile herself with what might have been. She'd unconsciously compared every succeeding man with Jake, and none of them had ever measured up. And for some reason, she'd been loath to make love unless she'd felt something more for her partner than a casual fondness.

"You're staying at work rather late, don't you think?"

She started when the deep voice slid into the darkness. Lifting her head, she froze when she discovered that Jake was standing in the doorway of her temporary office.

Instantly, she jumped to her feet. Then, afraid that he might somehow be able to read the gist of the thoughts that had been racing through her head, she sought something—anything—to hide her telltale reaction. Finally, she strode to the corner to turn off the television.

"I was just watching the last of the video footage Wilhemena gave me."

When she turned, it was to find Jake had silently closed the distance between them. His gaze was intent, his body tense.

"What are you doing here, Alana?"

She didn't even pretend to misunderstand him. He wasn't inquiring about her late hours, but about her presence at Maratonga.

Alana opened her mouth to cite her qualifications and her expertise in human sexuality, but the words died when she met the deep blue of Jake's eyes.

Suddenly, the office seemed far too intimate and the shadows far too inviting. She was reminded all too clearly of a dimly lit tent in Mombassa and a night filled with the heady beat of drums.

Too late, Alana realized Jake was still waiting for her response. She licked her lips to ease them of their dryness and watched in fascination as Jake's eyes darkened.

Was he remembering? Was he remembering that night long ago?

To her, the memory was overwhelming. So much so that she had to fight the urge to lift on tiptoe, grab this man by the collar and yank him down for a kiss.

Stop it! Was she so weak that even the thought of kissing him could turn her inside out?

"What are you doing here?" Jake asked again, his voice husky. But it was clear that the answer wasn't all that important to him. Instead, he focused his attention on her mouth. Before she knew what he meant to do, he put his hands on either side of the video cart behind her, effectively trapping her.

Summoning all her inner strength, Alana forced herself to resist him. If she didn't stop things now, she would merely make matters even more untenable.

"Is this the point where I'm supposed to take a lesson from Nellie?" she asked with more bravado than she felt.

Jake didn't react for several seconds. Then, when he remembered Nellie's favorite mode of defense, he sprang away from Alana as if burned.

She nearly smiled. Nearly. Then she decided not to put herself in a position where she could be misconstrued as mocking Jake Grisham.

"Are you ready to discuss Nellie's situation rationally?" she asked, praying that Jake wouldn't call her bluff and haul her into his embrace. If he did, she would be lost.

At the mention of Nellie, Jake scowled. "I still haven't been told why *we* should have anything to talk about. I fail to see how you'll be able to help matters."

"I'm getting to that." Needing to put some space between them, Alana went to the window. From where she stood, she had a clear view of the outdoor gorilla habitat and she wondered if any of the cavorting black shapes in the fenced enclosure were Nellie.

"First, tell me about Nellie and what you're trying to do here."

A beat of silence followed her request, but then she heard the rustle of Jake's clothes and felt him taking a place at her side.

"I still don't—"

"Jake, just give me the information I've asked for," she said impatiently. "Afterward, it will be your turn to interrogate me all you want."

"All I want, hmmm."

His tone and the sidelong glance he shot her way didn't bode well for the future.

Still watching her, Jake sat on the end of the conference table, propping his feet on one of the plastic chairs. She became infinitely conscious of the Indiana Jones-like attire beneath his lab coat. Damn. The sight of Jake Grisham in a pair of khakis and thick-soled work boots had always managed to make her knees shake.

Jake's expression grew pensive, and she thought she saw a ghost of a smile cross his features.

No. Not possible. He still looked grim.

"Nellie was six months old when she was given to me for my experiment."

That much Alana knew from what Wilhemena had told her. Nellie had been one of two infants born to the Maratonga Institute from a family of gorillas kept in the zoological section of the complex.

"You taught her American Sign Language," she stated when he hesitated.

Jake nodded. "She mastered her first two signs at nine months."

"She lived with you the whole time?"

"Yes. In essence, I raised her as if she were a human baby, until the age of two. Then, she was slowly reintroduced to the gorillas living in the naturalized habitat in the zoological section of the park. Since then, we've tried to help her to bridge both worlds— the wild and the scientific.''

''To what end?''

Jake inspected her carefully. ''Surely, Wilhemena has told you everything so far. You know exactly what I'm doing at Maratonga.''

''Yes, but I want to hear about the project from the horse's mouth, so to speak.''

He shrugged, but she thought his indifference was feigned. ''As you probably know, gorillas have been an endangered species for some time. The political upheaval present in their natural habitat combined with poaching and hunting has decimated the wild population.''

Warming up to his subject, he rested his elbows on his knees and leaned forward, causing a shock of sun-kissed blond hair to fall across his brow. In college, he'd been a free spirit, to be sure, but now, years later, Jake was positively rumpled, his stance loose. The effect was even more potent and appealing.

''Thanks to an outcry of public concern—and a little Sigourny Weaver film called *Gorillas in the Mist*—'' Jake continued and Alana was forced to yank her attention onto the matter at hand ''—we received a healthy dose of private funding soon after Nellie was born. Since the number of gorillas in Africa was dwindling and years of civil war made work within the unstable area all but impossible, scientists have been forced to turn their attention to those animals in captivity.''

Alana already knew that Jake was one such scientist. With degrees in zoology, anthropology, and primatology, he'd developed a reputation for being a *wunderkind* in animal studies. When his work in Africa had been curtailed, he had turned his attention to the gorillas in zoos. The numbers of the animals might be small, but if succeeding generations could be kept safe and alive, the animals could be introduced to their native homeland when the political climate improved.

''Unfortunately, helping the captive gorillas to survive and propagate isn't easy. As you may or may not know, very few gorilla infants can be raised by their mothers. When the babies are born, the adult female gorillas often lack proper maternal instincts. They have no idea how to nurse or nurture their offspring.''

''Which is how Nellie came to you in the first place.''

''Exactly. I had hoped to show that if one generation of gorillas could be taught *how* to care for their young—long before the infant is actually born—the cycle of neglect and ignorance could be broken. Through example, other female gorillas within the family units could begin educating one another, and such a cycle would hopefully continue throughout the succeeding generations.''

The plan was simple. A female infant gorilla would

be raised to cohabit the natural and the scientific worlds so that the best of both lives could be linked.

"I take it the project has been a success so far?" she murmured.

"More than we ever dreamed. Nellie spends several hours a day with me and my team. During that time, she's taught sign language and other communication skills. Then, by using a series of drills and planned playtime, we explore and document her natural ability to learn. In addition, for the past two years, she's been taught mothering skills—first with stuffed animals and dolls, and finally a puppy. In fact, when the puppy died of an infection, Nellie showed a very real grief to the loss."

"How is her interaction with other gorillas?"

"She has had no difficulties adapting to an alternate setting or to her peers. In fact, she has already displayed a penchant for attempting to teach the other animals a few simple signs."

What Jake didn't say, was that, for years, the experiment had been declared an unqualified success. Nellie had become the subject of scientific treatises, documentaries and even a PBS special.

"So why is the Institute threatening to cut your funding?"

Jake scowled. "Nellie is ten years old," he stated as if the fact explained everything. When Alana didn't respond, he said, "In essence, our darling little girl has entered puberty."

The information, combined with the futile seduction scene she'd seen on the video monitor in Wilhemena Bush's office began to make complete sense.

Jake stared down at his clasped hands, glaring at them as if they held the answers he sought. "Overnight, Nellie became obsessed with her appearance. She's moody, hypersensitive, jealous and stubborn. She fights with other female gorillas and teases the males."

He sighed, giving every appearance of being a concerned father. "An effort was made to curb her willfulness. Play therapy was intensified, her lessons were relaxed, then tightened, her privileges increased, then withheld. We even consulted a child psychologist—all to no avail. Since she was obviously sexually mature, Nellie was encouraged to mate with one of the gorillas at the Institute."

Jake shot her a look rife with remembered frustration. "Biff was alone with Nellie for less than fifteen minutes before he needed X-rays."

Jake joined Alana at the window, sitting on the sill in a way that drew her attention to the well-formed muscles of his thighs and the way the fly of his trousers bunched...

Stop it!

"If Nellie is capable of communicating with you, why didn't you simply have a gorilla to human chat?" Alana asked after clearing her throat.

"I tried that. But she refuses to communicate her

emotions or fears. If we try to push her into forcing a confidence, she throws a tantrum worthy of a three-year-old.''

The image of the fully grown gorilla dropping to the ground to pummel the floor with her fists and feet would have been comical if not for the fact that Nellie weighed nearly two hundred pounds and could revert to her wilder instincts if upset.

''I'd say you have a problem,'' Alana acknowledged dryly.

''In essence, we're baby-sitting the teenager from hell.'' He rubbed a spot between his eyes, making her aware of his weariness.

''We've spent two years trying to mate Nellie. Two frustrating years. In the past few months, the project has stalled completely. Unless Nellie somehow mates and becomes a mother, our experiment could be terminated completely. As it is, our funding has petered out to a trickle. We have barely enough to see us through the next two months.''

He shrugged, his eyes pinning her with their power. ''Which leads me to wonder why Wilhemena Bush has brought you here, and why she calls you 'The Love Doctor.'''

Alana grinned. Jake said the words as if he were pronouncing her ''The Empress of Whoopee.''

''I changed my major after returning from that study-abroad program we shared in Africa.''

She thought she saw the corner of his mouth tic.

"Oh, really?" he inquired blandly.

Alana squirmed a bit under his regard, well aware that Jake knew she'd changed her major three times *before* meeting him.

"Just how many times did you change it since we last talked?" His tone was wry.

"Once, Jake. I changed my major one last time."

"To what?"

"Behavioral Medicine."

He looked doubtful. "So you're a..."

"Therapist."

His gaze clouded with suspicion. "So you're working with my team as a..."

This time, her grin was genuine. Dropping her voice to the husky whisper she often used on the air, she drawled, "I'm your new resident sex therapist, Jake."

4

AT ALANA'S pronouncement, a hint of color tinged Jake's cheeks, and he pointed a finger in her direction. "Damn it, Alana, I don't have time for one of your elaborate practical jokes. You might not respect my work, but I assure you that I'm dead serious."

"So am I."

His expression was so filled with shock and disbelief, she felt a twinge of sadness. Granted, Jake had known her during a "flighty" period in her life. She'd been a career student with too much time and too little direction. She'd bounced from a major in history, to journalism, to biology.

It was her work in biology that had led to an undergraduate paleontology class, and from there to a study-abroad program. There she'd met Jake and had been astounded by his drive and focus. He knew exactly what he wanted from life and he wouldn't let anything get in his way—not even a woman who fell hopelessly, madly in love with him before the summer was through.

Unwilling to let Jake see how his comments had

wounded her, Alana decided to put him on the defensive instead. Inching toward him, she touched the placket of his shirt.

"What's the matter, Jake? Does my occupation disturb you?"

He didn't answer, so she continued.

"I suppose I should thank you for the career change. If not for that night in Africa..."

He dodged free, taking a deep breath and whirling. "Look, I apologized for that night. We were both drunk. The music, the drums..."

He still didn't know. He had never realized that she hadn't been drinking at all. Instead, she'd been intent on seducing Jake Grisham.

This time, it was her cheeks that grew hot. Not wanting to analyze her actions or the consequences she still lived with, she plunged on, "I'm not complaining, Jake. I found the whole experience rather liberating, as a matter of fact."

"Damn it, I—"

"Which is neither here nor there. My only reason for being at the Institute is Nellie. Wilhemena Bush felt that a sex therapist might be of some help."

"Help!"

"I can assure you that I've had a great deal of experience in the area. I have a private practice near Beverly Hills—"

"That figures."

"—a newspaper column and a very popular call-in radio show—"

"Dr. Ruth goes high-tech."

"The radio show was the source of my unfortunate nickname, but I don't suppose it will taint your standing in the scientific journals."

Jake planted his hands on his hips and glared at her. "Since you won't be involved with my research, the point is moot."

"*Au contraire.* I am an official member of your team. I have a feeling that your boss's reason for hiring me isn't altogether altruistic. My gut instinct keeps telling me that Wilhemena Bush is counting on my name, my column, and my radio show to attract fresh funding."

"That sounds like something she'd do," Jake growled. "Damn it, you are not working on this team, and you are *not* turning my research into a three-ring media circus."

Alana grimaced. Considering their past history and the awkwardness of seeing one another again, she hadn't thought her presence would be welcomed. But she had hoped that Jake would accept her credentials as being above reproach.

"Go home, Alana."

This time, it was her turn to glare. "Your manners haven't improved a bit in the last twelve years."

"Look who's talking. You walked in here as if you owned the place."

"I was escorted by a security guard."

"You barged into my research center as if it were some fast-food restaurant—"

"We tried to get your attention—"

"—not a research facility!"

"—but you were so involved in this…monkey business, you didn't notice a thing!"

Their voices echoed into silence at the same instant, and Jake took a deep, calming breath.

Alana Childe had been the bane of his existence from the moment they'd been paired up as laboratory partners in an undergraduate paleontology class. Throughout a year of college abroad, she'd dogged his heels like a devoted puppy—even going so far as to follow him in his career choices. He'd done his best to ignore her, discourage her, ostracize her.

Until Africa.

Then, in an unguarded, heated, erotic interlude, he'd made love to pesky, impulsive Alana Childe—and he'd felt guilty about it ever since. Although he had hazy images of hedonistic delight and sweat-slick limbs, he didn't remember much about the evening at all. He'd awakened to an empty tent to find Alana had already left for the States. Instantly, he'd acknowledged that he had just made the biggest mistake of his life—one which he knew had been responsible for the severing of their odd relationship.

Alana must have guessed the path of his thoughts, because she murmured, "Be honest, Jake. It's not the arrival of a sex therapist that has offended you. It's the fact that the therapist is none other than Alana Childe, your longtime nemesis. If the specialist happened to be anyone but me, you'd be turning cartwheels.''

''You certainly have a high opinion of your effect on me.''

She closed the distance between them again and he unconsciously took a step backwards, then found himself trapped by the table.

''It isn't my opinion. It's a fact. I still bug you.''

''Like malaria, maybe. You're always cropping up when I least expect it.''

She made a *tsk*ing sound, but it was clear that she wasn't offended by the banter. ''Happy to see me?''

''*Happy* isn't the word. Startled, wary, shocked would be better descriptions.''

''Come now, Jake. You were never shy with me before.''

She pressed against him, her thigh resting in the hollow created by his own, her hip bumping intimately against his arousal.

''Hmm. I'd say your list of reactions is incomplete, wouldn't you?''

Before he could answer, she stepped away, becoming immediately cool, professional and indifferent. ''Too bad I'm here on business. And I never mix business with pleasure. Still, I'd be happy to give you some pointers if you want them.''

Jake had barely absorbed her taunt when the sound of footsteps in the hall shattered the silence.

"Mommy! Mommy!"

The high-pitched call was followed by a blur of movement. Jake watched in astonishment as a boy of about two or three raced into the room and launched himself into Alana's arms.

In an instant, Alana's features transformed. Since meeting her again, Jake had found it difficult to reconcile the poised, sophisticated therapist with the same Alana Childe he'd known years ago. But the moment the child was hugged close to her chest, he saw the cool civility melt away to be replaced by a smile of sheer joy.

"Hello, Matthew!"

"Angel an' me saw the fish."

"Really? How exciting."

"An' I ate ice cream."

"My goodness. I hope you had some lunch along with all that ice cream."

The boy named Matthew dissolved into giggles.

Suddenly, Jake felt like he was an interloper in the scene.

A son. Sweet heaven above, Alana Childe was a mother.

Although the news shouldn't have been such a shock to him, it was. Over the years, he'd thought about Alana—more often than he should have done. But whenever the images of Alana had disturbed his ordinary routines, he'd always imagined her as he remembered her—a shy loner who took great care to keep herself free from all emotional entanglements.

He was suddenly doused with an icy wave of reality. Had he been kissing a married woman?

"Jake, I'd like you to meet my son Matthew."

Jake jerked back to reality. Too late, he realized he'd been staring at Matthew.

"Hello, Matthew."

The moment Jake spoke, Matthew scowled. Then, without warning, his face tightened into a mask of displeasure and he began to scream.

Jake was startled, not knowing why the mere sight of him had frightened the boy. With each passing moment, Matthew grew more and more frantic. He grabbed at Alana as if he could climb even more securely into her arms.

At the noise, a slight plump woman rushed into the room, offering a litany in Spanish in an effort to comfort the boy.

Feeling somehow chastened, as if he'd physically hurt the boy, Jake opened his mouth to apologize, but at a fresh scream from Matthew, he gave up.

"I'll talk to you later," he said to Alana. He doubted she heard him. She was too busy trying to calm the frantic youngster.

Striding into the hall, Jake beat a hasty retreat. What a rotten day. What a rotten, horrible day! And to top it all off, he'd just scared the wits out of a three-year-old kid.

JUST AS Alana had expected, Matthew's crying petered into hiccoughing sobs as soon as it became clear that Jake did not intend to come back.

"Feeling better?" she murmured against his soft, silky hair.

Matthew nodded against her neck.

Alana rubbed his back, feeling like a failure much the same way she usually did when Matthew had one of his episodes. She'd thought that his fear of men was merely a phase. Matthew had come to live with her when he was only nine months old. His biological mother had been one of Alana's childhood friends. When Debbie and her husband had been killed in a car accident, Alana had become his guardian and had eventually adopted him. From the beginning, he'd been leery of men, but lately any sort of male authority figure sent him into a panic.

"I thought he was getting better," she said to Angel when Matthew finally wriggled free and began to explore the office.

Angel offered a Latin shrug. "He *is* getting better—better at *acting*. That boy will get an Academy Award one day." She gestured to the way Matthew was happily playing with a swivel office chair. The boy's trauma was obviously forgotten.

Alana sighed, sinking into a chair by the conference table. "Why does he do that?"

Angel grinned and also sat down. "Perhaps it is something he learns from his mama," Angel said.

Alana eyed her in suspicion. "What do you mean?"

Again Angel offered a shrug. "Merely that Matthew is not the only one who seems to panic around men."

Alana gasped. "That's not true!"

Angel laughed and leaned on her elbows. "Tell me...is he the one?" She hitched a shoulder in the direction Jake had gone.

Alana's heart knocked at her chest. "The one?" she repeated.

"Is he the one who spoiled you for the others?"

Alana tried to convince herself that Angel was being particularly vague, but a heat spread uncontrollably up her cheeks.

"I don't know what you mean."

Angel giggled and clapped her hands. "I thought so. When we nearly burst in on you you were looking at him as if he were your long-lost soulmate."

"I was doing nothing of the kind!"

But Angel's eyes were sparkling in wicked enjoyment. "I'd say that was what caused Matteo to act out. As for me..." she sighed in patent enjoyment "...I haven't seen a look like that since my Antonio passed on. He and I could melt the polar ice cap."

"Angel!"

But Angel wasn't listening to her. Instead, she

crossed to Matthew and shooed him in the direction of the door.

Leaving Alana to wonder if her feelings for Jake had somehow become tattooed on her forehead.

THE FOLLOWING morning, Jake Grisham tapped his pen on the conference table and studied the hound-dog expressions of his staff. Clearly, the news that they would have a new team member arriving within the hour had filled them with the same weary resignation as it had in Jake.

Their close-knit group was about to be invaded by a sex therapist. A *female* sex therapist.

What Jake hadn't told them was that there was some personal history between Alana and him, and he wasn't about to do so. Even the thought of the months he'd shared with Alana was enough to cause his heart to thump against the wall of his chest.

In all truth, Alana had been a pest. From the beginning of the first semester, she'd watched him with adoring eyes, never losing an opportunity to spend time with him or hook up with him as her study partner. But in time, Jake had begun to see that her pushiness hid a deep well of insecurity.

It had been that vulnerability which had hooked him. He seemed to be the only person who saw the aching loneliness that often touched her gaze...or the blatant hunger.

Damn, it had been hot between them. Hot and passionate and intense. Yet the very vulnerability which had attracted him to her had also inspired a protectiveness that he hadn't known before or since. He'd been fully aware that Alana had wanted more from him, emotionally and physically. But he'd also known he wasn't ready for a commitment of any kind. He had his degree to finish, then a career in research to build. So he'd kept her at arm's length.

Until that last fateful night.

Damn it, why couldn't he remember? Time and time again, he'd tried to analyze that evening and what he'd done to make Alana leave so abruptly. He remembered the village celebration, he remembered kissing her, caressing her. He remembered returning with her to his tent, undressing, caressing…

Then his mind was a blank.

"Something wrong?"

Jake jerked, embarrassed at being caught woolgathering. Hoping the sensuality of his daydreaming would not be apparent to the other men present, he scowled and carefully schooled his features into a mask of irritation.

One by one, Jake studied each of his team members in turn, wondering what they would think of Alana Childe. William "Doc" Thompson, the chubby, elflike veterinarian fiddled with his pipe, even though policy prevented him from lighting it in the building. Rusty Smithers, a stocky, bighearted zoologist wearing his trademark Hawaiian shirt and fiddling with the tuner on his boombox, exchanged glum looks with Chen Tomeda, a Chinese exchange student with a Don Juan complex. Dino and Rudy Butrelli, twin intern students from UCLA with an amazing resemblance to Lewis Carroll's Tweedle-Dee and Tweedle-Dum, shook their heads like disappointed puppies. And Rueben Mott, Jake's personal assistant, had barely folded his seven-foot height into a chair. He seemed the most upset, especially since he was generally shy around unfamiliar women.

"When is she supposed to be here?" Rusty asked gloomily.

"Nine o'clock."

Sighing, Doc chewed on the end of his pipe. "I thought we had explained to Dr. Bush that Nellie won't work with the fairer sex."

"Bush is well aware of Nellie's temperament around females," Jake affirmed. "She just chooses to ignore it."

"This whole situation is ludicrous," Rudy blurted, his brother poking him in the arm to spur him on. "We're all trained scientists—specialists in our field. Why should we be forced to bring in an outsider in order to fulfill an old woman's whims?"

"Yeah," Dino echoed, nodding vigorously.

After another poke, Rudy continued. "What can a human sex therapist possibly have to offer to our study that we haven't already considered?"

"Are we sure she's really a therapist? For all we

know, she could be a call girl, or some kind of hook-her,'' Chen offered, his English heavily accented.

''Hooker,'' Doc corrected.

''That's what I meant,'' Chen offered. ''My vocabulary is still limited.''

''Not for long, bud,'' Doc added wryly.

Jake shot both men a stern look. ''She's not a hooker—so you'd better treat her with the utmost professional courtesy. She's a bona fide sex therapist, complete with all of the right credentials and degrees.''

Jake knew because he'd spent the evening investigating the ''Love Doctor'' to see what she'd been up to since their last encounter. Frankly, he'd been impressed—a degree in behavioral medicine from Stanford. Alana had been a busy, busy girl in the past twelve years.

Woman. She was a woman, not a girl.

''If Bush wanted us to get a sex therapist, why didn't she let us get our own guy?''

''Probably because she has her own motives for choosing this particular doctor,'' Jake said, thinking of Alana's radio show and her cult following. As much as he hated Bush's methods, even Jake had to agree that the mere mention of the study on the radio could mean hundreds of thousands of donated dollars.

''We could ignore Wilhemena's request,'' Rusty said, his eyes closed, the headphones to his boombox draped around his neck. The volume of his music was so loud that the whole room could hear the lively Mariachi music played by a local Spanish station.

"Ignore her request?" Rueben gasped, his expression revealing that Rusty had uttered blasphemy.

Rudy and Dino scowled.

Doc glared.

Chen merely poked Rusty and said, "Find some American jazz."

Rusty obligingly twisted the dial. "It's around here somewhere."

Doc slapped his hands on the table. "How can you talk about music when our entire project is in jeopardy? We've worked for nearly ten years—ten!—on shaping a mother figure for the park's captive-grown gorillas. Now, all that work is about to go down the drain!"

Jake held up a calming hand. The experts huddled around the table were more than aware of the stakes of teaching mothering techniques to a captive-born gorilla. They were all proud of the way she'd mastered the ability to nurture a baby. Now the time had come for her to care for her own infant.

But first, she needed to mate.

Rueben grunted, jerking Jake's mind back to the matter at hand.

"We can't ignore Her Royal Highness," Jake reminded them. "Wilhemena Bush keeps a finger in every pie at the Institute." Jake rubbed his finger against his temple. His head was already pounding.

"And if we don't play by *her* rules, the old bat will throw us out of her research center—if only to show us all she can."

The team became positively morose.

Rueben doodled on his pad.

Doc stared at a distant point.

Rudy and Dino rested their chins in their hands and stared pityingly at Chen, who would be forced to return to China. From around Rusty's neck, the shrill echo of a jazz trumpet sailed into the aura of doom.

"Off, Rusty."

"But—"

"Off."

Grumbling, Rusty reached for the power switch. In doing so, he accidentally hit the tuner. A second of silence quickly dissolved into...

"...you suffer from loneliness? Do you suffer from an inability to freely discuss your own sexuality? Have you had incidents when you found it difficult to perform? If so, tune in to The Love Doctor, Saturday evenings eleven to three..."

Without warning, a low feminine chuckle sifted into the room around them. "Wow. I've got fans already, and we haven't even been properly introduced."

5

JAKE FELT his heart skip a beat. Alana's silky voice slid through the room like a wisp of smoke, only to be followed by Wilhemena Bush's rasping, "Gentlemen..."

The members of Jake's staff stiffened at Wilhemena's greeting. They turned en masse to greet the president of the Maratonga Behavioral Institute, then caught sight of the woman standing next to her.

Jake reluctantly pushed himself to his feet.

"Don't let me interrupt." Wilhemena's tone made it clear that she didn't really care if she'd interrupted something or not. "I just wanted to let your men know that I've come to your rescue. Gentlemen, may I present...The Love Doctor."

The effect on the other men in the room would have been comical if Jake hadn't had a sinking sensation in the pit of his stomach. His team hustled to their feet, nearly tripping over themselves in the process.

"This is Dr. Alana Childe. Jake, I suppose you've already told your crew about the new team member."

"Yes, ma'am."

He caught Alana's amused look at his deferential tone. He opened his mouth intent on demanding to know why Wilhemena had hired this *particular* shock jock as their "visiting expert" but changed his mind. He knew why Alana had been hired. She had a name. She had a following. Her participation would be worth hundreds of thousands of donated dollars.

It was clear from the glint in Wilhemena's eye that she was expecting him to complain, but he wasn't about to do that. Not when Wilhemena's next best alternative might be Fifi D'Amour.

"Dr. Childe."

"*Dr.* Grisham." Alana's tone was mocking, daring him to pretend that they'd only just met.

Straightening, Jake explained to his men, "Alana and I have worked together before. Several years ago."

His men stared at him in open interest.

"Today's her first full day," Wilhemena said into the awkward silence. "You gentlemen should consider yourselves lucky that she was willing to rearrange her schedule to come help your little project. I trust that you'll offer her every courtesy and cooperation."

Jake's eyes narrowed at the glint of humor that he caught in Wilhemena's gaze.

Wilhemena amused? Why did that thought make him nervous?

The older woman's next comment was directed to

Jake. "Today, I expect that Dr. Childe would like to see Nellie and evaluate her for herself."

"You'd like to evaluate Nellie?" he repeated aloud. And just how did Alana mean to do that? Put the gorilla on the couch?

Alana eyed him knowingly. "Yes. And I'd like to see her right away, if you please."

Alana had always been a bossy little thing. A bossy little thing with long legs and snapping blue eyes. In the morning light, her hair appeared even more golden, its blunt cut brushing her chin. Her hair and makeup were understated, but coolly elegant. And the suit she wore...well, the suit was enough to make a grown man salivate, if his crew was anything to judge by. The tailored silk was fitted in all the right places. The men were staring at her as if they were dying of thirst and she was a cool glass of lemonade.

"Well," Wilhemena exclaimed. "This is already quite cozy. I'll just leave you all to your work. Good day, gentlemen."

"Good day, Dr. Bush," they all recited in unison as if they were prep school boarders and she the headmistress.

Alana waited until the door had closed behind Wilhemena Bush and her assistant before offering Jake's team a disarming smile.

"Hello. So nice to meet you all..." Her words hung in the air in an open invitation and the men quickly crowded around her to introduce themselves.

Jake watched the entire scene in disgust and something akin to discomfort. Alana fielded each man's attention with an effortlessness that he never would have envisioned in the woman he'd known. She laughed when they flattered her about her show and declared that they were her fans. She offered each man her hand and greeted them one at a time as if they were long lost friends. Even Rueben, who had hung back out of shyness, received the full-blown energy of her smile, making the giant of a man blush like a nervous teenager.

Jake didn't know why the sight filled him with a sudden, intense irritation. Alana was positively mooning over the men. Well, not really...

But this was a place of scientific research, not a sweethearts' ball.

"If I can have everyone's attention," he offered testily, then quickly softened his tone when Alana sent him an all-knowing look.

"I suppose we must get underway," she said.

Her legs moved with the grace of a runway model as she rounded the table and chose a chair to Jake's right. Sinking into place, she crossed her legs.

Jake could feel the testosterone level in the room rise a notch.

"Why don't you fill me in on some of Nellie's biographical data. That would probably be the best place to start."

Jake took his seat, his chest growing tight with ir-

ritation as the other members of his team nearly
tripped over their tongues to supply Alana with all of
the pertinent facts. By the time they'd finished, he was
tired of watching the display. He needed some coffee,
his routine and his work, in that order. And he was
more and more disgruntled at having his morning
schedule disrupted by Alana Childe.

"Is there something you'd like to add, Jake?" she
asked.

Her gaze conveyed to him that she'd read his displeasure and had taken secret delight from his reaction.

"No."

"So you have no other insight to offer me other
than what I've heard?"

He didn't answer.

"Then I suppose it's time I met Nellie."

She stood and the other men jumped to their feet.
Only Jake remained in his chair.

"Is something wrong, Dr. Grisham?"

She leaned forward, resting her weight on the table,
and for the first time that he could remember, Jake
noted that her hands were long and slender. The type
of hands favored for concert pianists and surgeons.
The type of hands that could trail along a man's back
from nape to spine and...

Jake tore his thoughts roughly into line. Alana's
presence this morning was a nuisance, a bother, and
he would do well to remember that fact. He had no
business thinking of her as a "woman." She was as

far from being his type as...well, she might be his type, but he didn't have to like working with her. And he certainly didn't have to admit to being attracted to her.

Alana sighed. "Is something wrong?"

Jake finally stood. "Look, Alana, I appreciate your being here. Really I do. In any other instance, I would welcome any insight you might bring. But we are at the crossroads of a very delicate study. I don't know what you've been told—"

"I've been told enough to make me think you're all a bunch of insensitive louts."

The teasing tone of her voice barely concealed the harshness of her words.

"Louts?" Jake drawled, his eyes narrowing in warning. "I don't think I've ever heard the word used in a sentence. Especially not by a medical professional."

She shrugged. "Frankly, I'm surprised Nellie has responded as well as she has, judging by the video footage Wilhemena showed me."

Wilhemena? No one called Dr. Wilhemena Bush by her first name alone.

No one but Alana Childe.

"It's obvious that your team has only taken her physical maturity into account, ignoring her emotional and psychological needs," Alana continued. "From what I saw, Nellie has never been completely comfortable with the mating arrangements made by you and your men.''

Jake opened his mouth to remind Alana that Nellie was a gorilla, not a human, and that she was about to be mated, not connected to her soulmate by a high-tech dating service. But he quickly changed his mind. So far, Alana had only seen Nellie through the eye of a video camera. Let her experience the gorilla first-hand—her moods, her unpredictibility, her sheer animalistic potential. Then, maybe Alana would realize that her presence on the team was superfluous.

''Would you like to meet Nellie now and ask her yourself?''

His sudden capitulation apparently unnerved her. But Alana quickly recovered. She tucked a strand of hair behind her ear, the only sign he'd seen so far of her own discomfort.

''Yes. Thank you.''

''Fine. You'll need to change first.''

Alana looked down at her suit. ''I can assure you I—''

''And I can assure you that you'll want to change.'' The statement was made in a way that brooked no argument.

Without giving Alana a chance to rethink her decision, Jake gestured to his office. ''I've got a set of coveralls hanging on the back of the door to my office bathroom. You can change in there.''

It was clear that she wasn't too pleased with the

idea. She probably thought he was lying about the need for coveralls, but when she happened to glance at the other team members and noted that they wore similar uniforms, she obviously decided to humor him—if only to expedite matters.

"Very well." She disappeared into the office and slammed the door.

For the first time that morning, Jake grinned, turning to share the smile with his team members. But one look at the way they stared at the closed slats of his venetian blinds had him scowling again.

"Do you think you could all stop salivating long enough to give me your attention?"

He didn't know why he bothered. It was obviously a strain for them to concentrate.

"Alana thinks Nellie will respond to her because she's a woman," Jake said. "Somehow, we've got to impress upon her Nellie's antifeminist tendencies."

Chen blinked. "Do you suppose she's single?"

Dino smoothed his hair. "I didn't see a ring."

"Gentlemen!"

They reluctantly gave him their attention. "Unless you'd like me to review Maratonga's guidelines on sexual harassment, I suggest you give the 'Love Doctor' a wide berth."

"I think he wants her for himself," he heard Rusty mumble under his breath.

Jake scowled. "I don't think you appreciate the situation developing here, gentlemen. That woman in there has just been hired as a temporary member of our team.''

Again, the men were staring at him in a way that clearly said, ''So what?''

''I think that we should all proceed carefully from here, otherwise, we could only worsen the predicament of this project.''

He received no response. At least none other than Rudy mumbling, ''She's such a babe.''

ALANA RESISTED the urge to curse under her breath as she stood behind the closed door and prayed for calm. Of all the infuriating, overbearing…

Although she'd expected some continued resistance from Jake, she hadn't thought that he would go so far as to show his skepticism of her contribution to the other members of his team. And then to insist that she change clothes…

Somehow, in the past twelve years, Jake Grisham had grown entirely too full of himself. He was pushy, didactic, rude and…

Lean.

Intriguing.

Attractive.

No. She wouldn't slip into that trap again. She had fallen under Jake's spell once before, only to discover that he was incapable of committing to any kind of long-term relationship. He was married to his work and he liked it that way.

Striding into the bathroom, she shut the door and stared at the shapeless jumpsuit hanging from a simple plastic hook.

Jake Grisham was up to something. There was no other explanation for making her wear this getup, and she wouldn't be at all surprised if he was intent on putting her in her place as little more than a token team member. But she wouldn't let his pettiness get in the way of her job. No matter what he thought, she intended to finish her consultation work as quickly and efficiently as she could. Even if it meant dressing up like a clown in a loose-fitting jumpsuit that had apparently seen better days.

Alana lifted the garment free with two fingers, frowning at the spatters of what looked like paint.

"I should have found another way to take a vacation," she muttered to herself. Damn, damn, damn. When would she ever learn to tame her impulsiveness?

THE MOMENT Alana emerged from Jake's office, she felt the heavy weight of seven pairs of eyes studying her from head to toe. But she couldn't ignore that it was Jake's scrutiny that caused a tiny frisson of awareness to skitter down her spine.

"Come here."

Jake issued the order in low tones that caused her knees to grow curiously weak. In a flash, she remembered the night of her seduction when Jake had drawn her into his tent with much the same words. His eyes had been hungry and his hands...

Abruptly, she wrenched her thoughts away from their forbidden track.

Think of your job. Only your job.

"You'll never get through to Nellie dressed like that," Jake was saying.

Alana glanced down at the baggy coveralls with its paint-spattered stains. Even with her height, she'd been forced to roll the sleeves and legs up to allow her to move. Taking the slender black belt from her own suit, she'd cinched up the waist, but she still felt as if she were swimming in the oversized garment.

"Is something wrong?" she asked, when it became apparent that Jake disapproved of her appearance. She might have thought he was throwing his weight around if the other men in the room hadn't looked equally troubled.

Jake reached out, and before she knew what he meant to do, he unhooked her belt and handed it to Rueben. "Put that away somewhere and get me a hat."

"A hat?"

No one paid attention to her squeak of protest. An old baseball hat with the Institute's logo was jammed down over her eyes.

"No, no. You've got to get rid of the hair," the one introduced as Rusty critiqued.

The hat was momentarily removed, her hair was piled onto her head, and the cap jammed on again.

"The makeup has to go or Nellie's going to feet," Chen offered.

"'Freak.' Nellie's going to 'freak,'" Rusty corrected.

"That's what I meant."

Before she knew what was happening, Doc had snagged a moistened towelette from the supplies on the counter and was wiping away her lipstick and blush.

"The eyes too," Dino advised.

"I know, I know."

Bewildered and slightly alarmed, Alana couldn't seem to get her wits about her until the men drew back. From a few feet away, Jake nodded.

"I guess that's the best we can do."

Alana didn't know why the men had worked so frantically to change her appearance, but she supposed she should be irritated since she'd gone to so much trouble to adopt the sophisticated elegance most of her fans expected to see in their favorite "Love Doctor." She opened her mouth to protest, but before any sound could be formed, Jake had grabbed her wrist and was pulling her from the room.

"Let's go."

She was led through a heavy steel door to an area outside of the main building. Briefly, Alana wondered if the men meant to usher her through the back gate, but then she saw a small mobile home surrounded by a chain-link fence.

"This is where Nellie lives?"

"Yup." The laconic reply was filled with another emotion. Something that sounded a little too much like barely concealed humor for her comfort.

"From the videotape, I assumed she lived in the main building."

"We just work with her there during the day or if we're trying to mate her. When she's not spending some time with the other gorillas in the outdoor habitat, she lives in her own house."

For the first time, Alana had some qualms about approaching an animal she had heretofore only seen on tape. Nellie had to be about the same size as a petite full-grown woman. And she was still an animal, after all. One that could be prone to fits of wild behavior.

Her gaze swung around the compound, taking in the heightened security measures. For the first time, she acknowledged that such provisions had probably been made to keep Nellie "in" rather than unwanted visitors "out."

"I see that you've taken lots of precautions with the fencing," she said, hoping she didn't sound as nervous as she suddenly felt. "Is Nellie dangerous?"

"Not usually."

Alana relaxed, but only until Jake added, "But she can be at times."

She wasn't sure if he had intended to spook her. If

so, he'd succeeded. Suddenly, she wished she was anywhere but here, about to confront a cantankerous, adolescent gorilla.

Jake abruptly stopped, turning to face the men that trailed after them like noisy puppies.

"Listen. I think this would work much better if *I* introduced Alana to Nellie." When the men didn't move, he added, "Alone."

The scientists mumbled to themselves and several disappointed looks were cast in their direction. Nevertheless, they filed away, muttering bits of explanations such as "charts to read," and "biofeedback results."

And then, all too soon for Alana's comfort, she was left alone in the sunshine with Jake Grisham.

Taking a deep, silent breath, she steeled her shoulders. "Thank you." At least if she was to make a fool of herself, the humiliation wouldn't be quite so public.

Jake's expression remained grim. "I didn't do it for you. I did it for Nellie."

Alana could have smacked him. It was clear he thought more of his gorilla than her. Nevertheless, she was too concerned about the upcoming meeting to do more than frown.

"Have all of your team members been here since the beginning of the project?"

"Most of them."

"They must resent my sudden inclusion."

His eyes were intent. "That's what I thought would

happen...but you seem to have bowled them over. They are obviously fans of the 'Love Doctor.'"

She grimaced. "I assure you, despite the title, I am a good therapist."

His expression remained unconvinced. "We'll see."

He studied her intently, pulling the hat even farther down over her eyes.

"A few words of caution. Nellie is very well behaved, for the most part, but there are a few things you should remember. No sudden movements, no loud voices, and when you smile, don't show your teeth."

Don't show her teeth?

"Ready?"

She nearly told him that she'd changed her mind and she would be on her way back to Los Angeles, but it was clear that he expected her to do just that. Straightening her shoulders, she said, "Fine."

"Stand back until I've greeted Nellie. She tends to be a little territorial around new people, so I'll want to introduce you."

"Fine."

Then her heart thudded in her chest as Jake turned the knob and opened the door.

6

"NELLIE?"

At his call, there was a grunt and a sudden blur of black.

Alana shrank back as the gorilla raced toward Jake, launching herself into his arms.

She was so big!

Although Alana had carefully studied the tapes, nothing could have prepared her for the strength and size of the real animal. Jake staggered beneath the gorilla's weight before finally depositing Nellie on the ground.

"Good morning, Nellie," Jack exclaimed, his hands moving in a corresponding greeting.

Alana watched as the gorilla signed something in return.

"This is Alan."

Alan?

Again, Nellie's hands moved.

Jake scowled.

"No, Nellie."

"What's she saying." Alana said out of the side of her mouth.

Jake shot her a silencing glance.

"Alan is a friend, Nellie."

Even without the benefit of an interpreter, Alana sensed that the masquerade was not going as well as Jake had hoped. Nellie regarded her suspiciously, then circled her, studying Alana from every angle. Then, without a sound, she presented her back to Alana and stalked to the corner of the room.

"I take it I've just been given the cold shoulder," Alana said softly, barely daring to move her mouth lest she show her teeth.

Nellie moved to the nest of blankets and faced the corner.

"Are you punishing her?"

Jake shook his head. "She's sulking."

"Why?"

He shrugged. "Stay here."

Alana had no intention of following him. She wasn't sure she could move even if she wanted to do so. Her feet were rooted to the floor and she prayed she wouldn't do anything more to irritate the gorilla that stared morosely at the wall.

"Nellie, what's the matter?" Jake asked.

Nellie tipped her chin higher in disdain.

"Nellie," Jake drawled in a singsong voice. "What's wrong with my pretty Nellie?"

Nellie offered a short, pithy sign that even Alana could interpret.

Jake frowned in reproof. "That's not nice."

Alana knew she should remain silent, but she couldn't resist whispering, "What's she saying?"

"Her language is…a bit unflattering."

Great. A gorilla was insulting her.

"Nellie, I want you to apologize to Alan."

The gorilla folded her arms and tipped her chin a notch higher.

"Nellie, you're being naughty."

A flurry of hand gestures followed.

"Nellie," Jake reprimanded sharply.

"What's she *saying?*"

Jake planted his hands on his hips and huffed in irritation. "She says you're ugly and smell bad."

Without warning, Nellie stood and whirled to face Alana. Alana's heart thudded in her chest as the gorilla studied her with a gaze filled with suspicion—and if Alana wasn't mistaken, pure feminine pique.

Nellie moved toward her, circling her again, her shoe-button eyes intent, a scowl creasing her forehead. Then, without warning, she pushed herself upright. Before Alana knew what she meant to do, she backhanded Alana's hat, sending it tumbling from her head.

The moment Alana's hair spilled to her shoulders, Nellie bellowed in outrage, her fingers flying in an apparent reprimand. Then, she loped toward Jake, grunting in displeasure as she came to a stop in front of him, resuming her tirade.

It was apparent that she was angry and growing angrier by the minute, so when Jake said, ''Perhaps you'd better leave,'' Alana needed no second bidding. Hurrying from the trailer, she closed the door behind her and leaned weakly against the panels.

Now what was she going to do?

THE MOMENT Jake exited the trailer, it was clear he'd just had a dressing down by a gorilla. His shirt was spattered with paint and what looked like smashed banana.

It was also clear that Jake expected Alana to turn tail and run, and he was looking forward to having her gone.

''That didn't go well, did it,'' Jake said, walking past her at a brisk pace.

Alana pursed her lips when it became equally obvious that he expected her to follow him like some obsequious lackey.

He stormed through the gate, holding it for her, then bellowing, ''Rusty!''

The portly zoologist appeared so quickly that it was obvious none of the men had gone too far away.

''Go in there and calm her down,'' Jake said with a nod of his head toward the trailer.

''Sure, boss. It's about time for her finger painting session anyway. She's been looking forward to it.''

He caught sight of the front of Jake's shirt and mumbled, "Guess we'll be needing more paint."

Jake didn't even pause. He strode back to his office, holding the door open for Alana and then closing it firmly behind them.

"As you can see, it's impossible."

Alana's brows rose. "'It'?"

Jake's hands spread wide. "This situation. You. Don't take it personally, but Nellie doesn't like you."

"Gee, Jake. Don't hold back your feelings."

His hands lifted to the front of his shirt and he began to unbutton the placket. Alana's eyes widened ever so slightly when she realized that he meant to change right in front of her.

He scowled. "I haven't got time for niceties, Alana. And since we're alone, there's no longer any need to pretend."

"Pretend?" she repeated slowly, her eyes following the wedge of hair and tanned masculine flesh being exposed to her view.

"It's obvious that you're here because Wilhemena intends to use you as a donor magnet. It's also clear that there's nothing that you can offer my team that hasn't been tried before."

He tore off his shirt and strode to the closet where several more identical garments hung from neatly spaced hangers. Alana hungrily traced the broad width of his shoulders as they tapered into lean, narrow hips. She was so engrossed by the sight, that it took a mo-

ment for Jake's words to sink into her head. When
they did, a slow anger began to build in her chest. He
was dismissing her. He was dismissing her expertise
and her credentials as if she were a stranger off the
street.

Her hands balled into fists. Granted, she wasn't a
primatologist. And granted she wasn't up to speed on
the psychology of a horny gorilla. But neither was she
completely incompetent.

"I'll understand if you want to head back to L.A.
tonight," Jake said as he buttoned the fresh shirt. "I'll
be more than happy to cover for you with Wilhemena.
As far as she's concerned, I'll tell her you're working
closely with us. I'll even keep you posted with enough
updates that you can include some material on Nellie
for your show. In the meantime, I'm sorry for the in-
convenience to your schedule."

By the time he was finished, she was fuming. She
might be completely out of her depth here. And she
might have agreed to this job under false pretenses.
But she was not, *not* about to bail out on the job now.
Not when it was so clear that Jake wanted her gone.

Suddenly, she had a need to shake his complacency.
More than that, she felt driven to make him look at
her, really look at her. Not as a nuisance, not as a
pest...

But as a woman.

The moment the thought raced through her head,
she knew she should curb such ideas. After all, only

yesterday, she'd been ready to ditch this assignment and get as far away from Jake Grisham as she could.

But now...

Reaching down, she undid the top button of the coverall, then the second one. When Jake's eyes suddenly latched onto the silk camisole she wore, she undid another button.

Finally, she had his complete attention.

He opened his mouth, but didn't immediately speak. Instead, he seemed to lose his train of thought as she sauntered toward him. The expression on his face was so intent, so suddenly sensual, that a sweet heat flooded through her body, settling low in the pit of her stomach.

"Have you finished?" she murmured.

When he didn't answer, she took another step closer, crowding him against his desk.

Reaching out, she touched a smear of green at the base of his throat. Growing bolder still, she swiped at it with her finger, then sniffed at the unmistakable scent of pistachios.

"What's this? Pudding?"

She watched in satisfaction as Jake's Adam's apple bobbed up and down.

"We use pudding for finger paint."

His voice was husky. Warm. Aware.

Alana knew she was playing with fire, but she couldn't resist putting her finger in her mouth and lick-ing away the pudding. Then she made a *tsk*ing noise with her tongue.

"Nellie must have been *very* upset."

"That's an understatement."

She took another half step, drawing close enough to feel the heat of Jake's body through the fabric of the coveralls. "What has her all worked up?"

"She doesn't like women."

She frowned as if she found the thought troublesome, then eased even closer. Her thighs pressed against his. "Why not?"

"She has never cared for the company of women."

Her lips twitched in a slight half smile. She was getting to him, and the fact was heady.

"Why not?" she repeated.

He was looking at her lips. "I...don't know. She, uh...has always preferred working with men."

"And yet, she doesn't seem to like male gorillas."

Too late, she realized her own machinations were beginning to backfire on her. Jake was shifting, his body leaning toward hers. As the distance between them closed, her thoughts scattered, then coalesced around one single idea—an overwhelming need to be kissed by Jake.

It had been so long. So very long.

Jake met her halfway, his hands sliding around her waist to draw her tightly against him, his lips covering hers with a hunger that she could scarcely credit as being directed at her. He lifted her on tiptoes, crushing her against him, his hands cupping her hips and pulling her even more firmly against him.

Her control vanished as her arms snaked around his waist. Needing more, wanting more, her hands spread wide, exploring the oh so familiar planes of his back and shoulders. If anything, Jake was leaner, fitter than ever before.

And entirely too intoxicating. It would be so easy to surrender to the moment and make love to Jake Grisham.

Whoa!

Wrenching free, Alana put several feet between them. Afraid that her hunger would be clearly written on her features, she turned her back to Jake as she tried to gather her equilibrium again.

What was she thinking? She couldn't let herself fall under this man's spell again. She had vowed to rid herself of her obsession with him, not...not...

Fan the flames of obsession higher.

Quickly schooling her features into what she hoped was a bland mask, she turned again, fixing Jake with an unconcerned stare.

"For your information, Jake, I don't give my name lightly. I will not be going back to Los Angeles, and I will not be spoon-fed your idiotic updates."

This time, when she strode toward him, she was careful to come to a halt well out of arm's reach.

"I've been hired as your gorilla's sex therapist, and I intend to do my job."

"Alana, be serious."

"I am serious, Jake. You may not like my presence here, but for the next few weeks, you're going to have to put up with it. Like it or not."

Sensing he was about to argue, she offered him a coquettish smile in an attempt to disarm him.

"Relax, Jake. I promise not to upset your little monkey."

"Gorilla."

"Whatever."

She knew she should back away now, that she shouldn't press her luck, but she couldn't resist reaching out a hand to smooth the rumpled cloth of Jake's collar. Then, just to make her point, she added, "Maybe if you're good to me, I'll see if I can't throw in a little advice for you as well, Jake. Free of charge."

MAYBE IF YOU'RE GOOD to me, I'll see if I can't throw in a little advice for you as well, Jake. Free of charge.

Funny, Alana. Very, very funny.

Jake was still fuming over her comment the following morning. Give him advice? *Him?* And who was she to tell him anything?

She was a sex therapist.

He squashed that thought the moment it appeared. It didn't matter what she was. Alana was history. He remembered the shell-shocked expression she'd worn soon after meeting Nellie. It was obvious that despite her bravado, she hadn't been completely prepared for the realities of working with a gorilla. She was finished. She wouldn't be back—no matter what she'd said.

Jake was so sure that he'd seen the last of Alana that when he looked up precisely at nine o'clock to find her striding through the door of the lab, he felt a pang of surprise.

At least he tried to tell himself it was surprise, even though the sensation was lower, sharper, more arousing than mere surprise.

To her credit, she'd learned something from the previous day's episode. Today, she'd worn jeans and a T-shirt. If anything, the casual clothes only heightened her femininity—as well as the long, slender length of her legs.

"You're back," he said lowly.

"Did you really doubt I would be?" she asked, her brows arching.

No, he supposed he hadn't doubted it. In fact, there was a part of him that had worried that she might call it quits, and if she had...

He didn't want to think about that. He didn't want to think about the sleepless night he'd had, or the way he'd been tormented time and time again with the fact that Alana Childe was a mother.

A mother to a child that was not his.

The moment the thought raced through his head, he squelched it. What did it matter to him if she'd had a dozen kids? For all he knew, Matthew could be the smallest of a whole brood of children.

"How long have you been married?" It was more of an accusation than a question. After all, she'd been kissing *him* without a thought to her significant other.

She seemed slightly amused. "I'm not married. I've never been married."

The information startled him more than he would have thought possible. He never would have pictured Alana as a single mother...and if that was the case, where was Matthew's father?

"I take it Matthew's father is here with you in San Diego?"

"No. Matthew's father is not a part of my life."

He frowned. "Why?"

"Because that's the way things are."

The answer gave him no insight into her situation whatsoever, but he had already revealed more to her than he'd intended.

"Rueben?" he bellowed. "Dr. Childe is here for her lessons!"

Alana frowned. "Lessons? I thought I would be working with Nellie today."

"You thought wrong."

Jake hadn't meant to be so abrupt, but the time had come for blunt honesty. Standing, he rounded his desk and sat on the edge. "Listen, Alana. I appreciate your enthusiasm and your willingness to provide us all with your expertise..."

He paused, realizing that the words had come out badly and were prone to a rather ribald interpretation.

"What I meant was…"

"I know what you meant, Jake, so why don't you spit out the rest of what you're trying to say? You want me to leave." A flush of anger touched her cheeks, and Jake was transfixed by the sight. She immediately transformed from a cool, poised professional to a vibrant woman filled with emotion.

Too bad it was anger she directed at him and not something far more intimate.

He scowled at his own thoughts, dragging his attention back to Alana as she lambasted him about his caveman techniques and his lack of professional courtesy. Through it all, he watched the flashing of her eyes and the vibrant play of emotion.

She was beautiful. Completely and utterly beautiful. And this entire display was turning him on.

To his relief, Rueben chose that moment to appear in the doorway.

Alana's tirade slowly petered away, leaving an uncomfortable silence in the room, one that was fraught with far more sensual tension than there should have been. It took all of Jake's will to tear his gaze away from her as she folded her arms across her chest, causing her breasts to push against her T-shirt.

"Alana, I'd like you to spend some time with Rueben today."

"Why?"

Damn, she was contrary.

"He's going to teach you some rudimentary sign language so that you can communicate with Nellie. Until then, I don't think it's a good idea for you to spend time with her. She is accustomed to signing with the team members and by translating to you, we would distract Nellie."

The information seemed to placate her. Bit by bit, her militant posture eased as the ire drained from her body.

"Very well." She leaned one hand on the desk, bending toward him so that only he could hear. "But I warn you...I'm a quick study and I won't be kept from my objective for very long."

7

ALANA WAS TRUE to her word. For the next two weeks, Jake did everything in his power to keep her out of the lab and isolated in the company of Rueben Mott under the pretense of learning sign language.

He knew the arrangement wouldn't last for long. Alana was willing to go along with his insistence that she learn to communicate with Nellie, but only if she were allowed to join Jake and the other team members for at least a few minutes every day.

Unfortunately, Nellie wasn't nearly so obliging. She still reacted to Alana with open hostility, making Alana's visits brief out of necessity. Yet, Alana refused to give up.

He had to give her credit for that, Jake thought as he strode through the early morning sunshine that streamed into the corridors near his office.

Alana had become as tenacious as a bulldog during the last two weeks. She seemed to have taken it as her personal crusade to help Nellie, so much so that Jake wondered what fueled her enthusiasm. So far, most of her columns had been dedicated to the plight of the animal, and the response from her readers had been phenomenal. She was flooded with mail, forcing her to spend several hours a day reading her fan letters. She had even arranged to take the rest of the summer away from her client load so that Nellie could be given her full attention.

Maratonga had also benefited from the exposure. Donations were pouring into the facility. The media had picked up the story, and the previous evening, the national news had played a sound bite discussing Nellie's plight.

Reaching the door of his office, Jake grimaced. As if he needed another reminder of the way his project had suddenly been thrust into the limelight, someone had taped a copy of Alana's latest column to the window. In it, she lambasted the team for refusing to allow Nellie to have a voice in picking her next prospective mate.

Jake snorted. As if Nellie would sit and view video footage of silverbacks. He crumpled up the paper in his fist. The idea was absurd. Clearly, Alana was beginning to chafe at having such limited time with Nellie and she was venting her frustrations in her column.

But what was Jake supposed to do? Let Alana have her way? Let her climb into the gorilla habitat unaccompanied by the other team members? Granted, she had memorized a wide variety of signs. She could probably understand much of Nellie's basic communication. But that didn't mean Alana had the skills to calm Nellie down if the gorilla flew into a snit over being in the same room as a woman.

Wrenching open his office door, Jake dumped his briefcase and his keys on the desk, then crossed to the window. Hands on hips, he stared sightlessly toward the employee parking lot, his mind racing over the day's tasks.

Another gorilla had been chosen by the team. Boris was a thirty-year-old silverback who had successfully mated dozens of times. He would be on loan to them from a sister research facility in Los Angeles and should be arriving in the next week. In the meantime, they were hoping to involve Nellie in more play therapy to prepare her for the intended assignation.

Jake scowled, knowing that Alana would want to help. But he couldn't get past his fear that she might get hurt.

As the thought stuck in his brain, Jake suddenly became aware of the fact that he was scanning the parking lot, waiting for Alana's arrival.

Swearing softly, he forced himself to turn his back and sit at his desk.

But even as he reached for the papers scattered over the blotter, his mind returned to Alana.

She was getting under his skin again, just as she had in Africa. It didn't seem to matter that they'd spent most of the past two weeks arguing over Alana's role in this entire affair. Even their arguments had the ability to make him feel more alive, more aware of her as a woman than ever.

Damn it, what was wrong with him? Granted, he'd spent a good deal of time with his work the past few years. What relationships he'd fostered had usually been brief and somehow lacking. Except with Alana.

Jake jumped to his feet. No. No, no, no. He was not going to fall for Alana Childe again. He'd been down that road before and the pleasure had been too often offset by her contrariness. He wasn't about to complicate his life any more than it already was. After all, hadn't he already decided that he was a confirmed bachelor? His work allowed for little else.

Or did it?

Too late, he found himself standing in front of the window again, his gaze scanning the parking lot.

Damn it! He would *not* fall under her spell. After all, he had more than just the two of them to consider this time. Alana had a son. A small impressionable son who went ballistic any time Jake was near.

No. He couldn't get involved again.

Jake sighed.

So why was he still looking out the window?

IN AN EFFORT to prove to himself that his infatuation with Alana was nothing more than that, Jake threw himself into his work. He brought Nellie into the indoor observation room, then left her with Dino, Rusty and Chen to complete her breakfast and morning grooming rituals. Then, he returned to his desk, intent on getting caught up on the paperwork necessary to transport Boris from Los Angeles to San Diego.

Today, when Alana arrived, he would see to it that everything was business as usual. He would be professional. He would be polite but detached. And he would not allow himself any more time to brood over the chaos she was bringing to his life.

But the moment Alana walked through the door, Jake knew he'd been overly optimistic to think that it would be business as usual for the day.

Despite the coveralls she'd been given since coming to Maratonga, she'd worn a loose, sleeveless sundress—one that tangled around her legs as she walked, yet revealed a good deal of leg through slits that ran up either side. Her hair was loose and tousled, her makeup much simpler than Jake had seen yet.

And if her appearance wasn't worrisome enough, in her arms, she held Matthew. The little boy had been dressed in similar play attire—shorts, a striped T-shirt and sandals. He was already gazing wide-eyed at the men who hurried through the door in Alana's wake. His fingers dug into Alana's shoulders as the team members quickly offered Alana coffee and teased her about her latest column. Yet, even with their jovial welcomes, Matthew gazed at them all in panic.

"Hello, everyone," Alana said, crossing to Jake without pause. Then, before he knew what she meant to do, she lifted Matthew and held him out in a way that clearly conveyed that she expected Jake to hold him.

"Alana, I don't—"

"Please, Jake."

Not knowing what else to do, he took the child, telling himself that Matthew was no different than all of the infant gorillas he'd held. The boy was small, somewhat helpless...

Suddenly, Matthew began kicking and screaming, transforming from a timid child to a squirming mass of arms and legs intent on escape.

"Matthew, remember our bargain."

In an instant, Matthew grew still. His lip trembled and he gazed at Alana in earnest supplication, but he no longer fought Jake's grasp.

"What's the bargain?" Jake asked.

"If he's good today, we'll spend the evening at the beach making sandcastles."

"Sounds fair to me," Jake replied, but when he looked down at Matthew, it was clear the boy was beginning to reconsider the offer.

"I'd like to see Nellie now," Alana announced to the room in general.

Jake scowled and stared pointedly at her dress. "Don't you think you should change first?"

"I know what I'm doing, Jake, and I'd like to see Nellie, please. The time has come for the two of us to be alone together."

Jake immediately felt the brunt of his team members' gazes. Clearly, they were waiting for him to argue. But this time, Jake had decided to let Alana have her own way.

"Fine." With a shrug of his shoulders, Jake made it clear to everyone that Alana could visit with Nellie if she wanted, but he washed his hands of the consequences.

The little boy squirmed and too late, Jake realized that he was still holding him and Alana was leaving the room.

"What about Matthew?"

Alana was already trailing after Doc and Rueben. "You'll have to watch him for me. Angel had an unexpected family emergency and had to return to Los Angeles and I haven't had time to make other daycare arrangements. He's a good boy, so I'm sure he won't be any trouble in the meantime."

Jake snorted at that pronouncement. He'd never seen any creature—animal or human—that wasn't a bother until they had reached the age of maturity.

As if sensing his thoughts, Matthew's eyes narrowed with apparent dislike and he pushed against Jake, wanting to be free.

"Be my guest kid," Jake said, setting the little boy on the floor. He had no sooner done so than Matthew drew back his foot and kicked Jake in the shin.

Hissing in pain, Jake bent to massage the sore spot, only to have the little boy slug him right in the stomach.

Taken unawares, Jake slipped on the tile and fell to the floor. Around him, the other members of his team snickered.

"Looks like you haven't lost your tuck, boss," Chen said.

"'Your touch.' Haven't lost your 'touch.'"

"That's what I meant."

ALANA KEPT UP a brave front all the way out of the observation room and down the short staircase to the door which would lead to Nellie's schoolroom. As far as she was concerned, no one would ever know how much that façade of cool complacency cost her.

Or how her trembling knees threatened to pitch her to the floor.

"You're sure you want to go in there dressed like that?" Doc said when they reached the thick metal door.

"I'll be fine." But her words didn't sound nearly as convincing as she had hoped they would.

"Remember the signs I've taught you," Rueben reminded her.

She nodded, clutching her purse even more securely. "Open the door, please."

The two men exchanged glances. Then, with a fatalistic sigh, Rusty opened the door.

Knowing that she would lose her nerve if she didn't act quickly, Alana strode inside. She'd barely made it three feet before a gob of green finger paint splattered the front of her dress.

Taking a deep breath, Alana forced herself to keep moving.

"You didn't expect any miracles," she muttered to herself as she took a seat next to Nellie and signed, *Hello, Nellie.*

Nellie seemed less than impressed with Alana's new language capabilities. She grunted in displeasure.

Go Away, Head Woman. Nellie No Like. Go Away, Away.

"Head woman" was the name Nellie had given Alana after the gorilla learned she was yet another therapist brought in to examine her. Even though Nellie had been told again and again to sign Alana's name, she refused. Alana had no doubts that Nellie's actions were a blatant snub meant to show just who was in charge between the two of them. Nevertheless, Alana didn't reprimand the gorilla on her lack of proper respect. Alana had more important battles to win.

Go Away, Head Woman. Nellie No Like, Nellie said again, when it became obvious that Alana hadn't moved.

"You don't mince words do you?" Alana said aloud, her own vocabulary allowing her to respond with little more than, *Alana Stay Here.*

Nellie jumped up from her chair and raced around the room, but Alana ignored her, having prepared herself for a tantrum. Instead, blithely ignoring Nellie, she opened up the large straw bag she'd brought with her and pretended to peer inside.

It was clear that she had piqued the gorilla's curiosity because Nellie paused and gazed at her with narrowed eyes.

Nellie Come Play With Alana.

No.

Shrugging, Alana pulled out a mirror and Nellie's head cocked. It was obvious that she didn't want to give Alana any attention at all but that she was intrigued by the appearance of the mirror.

When Alana withdrew a comb and began to primp, Nellie took a half a step toward her, stopped, then scowled and signed, *Give Me.*

No. Nellie Come Play.

Nellie shook her head and raced around the room again. But when Alana paused to reach into her bag again, Nellie stopped her antics so abruptly that she actually tripped and rolled over. When Alana took out a tube of lipstick, Nellie began signing.

Give Me. Give Nellie.

No. Come Here. Play With Alana.

Nellie shook her head, preparing to continue her pacing, but she froze when Alana removed the lid to the lipstick and applied the bright red color to her mouth.

The gorilla's fascination was clear. Nellie took a step forward, two, three.

Not wanting to lose what progress she'd just made, Alana set the lipstick on the table, providing a clear temptation to the animal.

Nellie began signing, *Nellie Want, Nellie Want, Nellie Want,* but Alana gave no outward reaction.

In a blur of black, Nellie shot toward the table, grabbed the lipstick, then retreated.

Alana had been planning on such a move, so she remained calm and still. She didn't even bother to turn and look at the gorilla, able to see in the glint of the observation glass that Nellie was smearing the red lipstick all over her face. Instead, Alana reached into the purse and took out a comb, a brush, and a plastic bag filled to the brim with hundreds of tiny, colorful plastic barrettes.

She heard a soft "oo" from behind her. Then, as if they had been friends for years, Nellie moved up next to her, nudging Alana with her hand and signing, *Nellie Play With Head Woman. Head Woman Play With Nellie. Nellie Like. Nellie Play.*

Resisting the urge to smile in triumph, Alana pivoted in her chair and began to comb Nellie's hair.

FROM THE other side of the window, Jake watched as Nellie settled on the floor and allowed Alana to begin plaiting a portion of her fur into tiny braids that were then fastened with bright plastic barrettes.

"I'll be damned," Doc said.

The other team members huddled close to the glass.

"It doesn't make sense. We've hired women before and they've never, *never* been able to get Nellie to respond like that."

"Maybe because they didn't try to appeal to her femininity," Jake said softly.

The other men stared at him and Jake explained, "In the past, the women we've hired have been scientists. They've tried to deal with Nellie from a position of authority. But Alana is appealing to her as a fellow female."

"Huh," Doc offered with something akin to wonder, chewing on his pipe.

From his vantage point high above, Rueben offered, "I think they both look kind of cute."

IF ALANA thought that she would receive a medal for the breakthrough she'd had with Nellie, she was sadly mistaken. Most of the team members had been enthusiastic in their congratulations, but Jake had been conspicuously absent. Although Rueben had explained that Jake had gone in search of someone to help her watch Matthew for the day, she couldn't help wondering if he was somehow angry with her.

Alana sighed and glanced at the clock. To her surprise, she found that nearly an hour had passed and she still hadn't seen Jake or her son.

Suddenly concerned, she berated herself for letting her preoccupation with Jake get in the way of her duties as a mother.

Hurrying into the outer room, she found Rueben working on his computer.

"Rueben, have you seen Matthew?"

Rueben removed his half-moon reading glasses and offered Alana a shy smile.

"He and Jake have gone to the day-care center."

"Day-care center?"

"It's on the ground level near the outdoor habitats. You've probably seen the playground equipment."

"I thought that was for the animals."

"Only the human kind. The day-care has a waiting list, but Jake was able to pull some strings and arrange for Matthew to be included for the next few weeks. He thought it might make things easier for you."

"Oh," she said softly, not sure how else to respond. She was curiously touched by Jake's efforts on her behalf. Granted, the arrangement was probably for his benefit as much as her own. He probably wanted to make sure that Matthew wasn't underfoot.

But it was still sweet of him to go to the effort.

"How can I get to the day-care facility?"

"It's a lot easier to find if you head outside and take the back walk to the playground. The main door to the classroom has been painted bright red, so you won't miss it." He glanced at the clock. "If you hurry, you'll probably catch the last few minutes of snack time. When the weather is like this, the kids eat on the picnic tables next to the playground. It's fun to watch the young gorillas pressing up against the fence to watch their human counterparts.''

"Thanks, Rueben."

Alana hurried down to the main level and from there through the lobby to the rear door. Following the directions that Rueben had offered her, she rounded the building, then stopped short at what she saw.

Two dozen children were scrambling around the grassy area, some finishing cartons of milk, cut vegetables and graham crackers, others cavorting on the playground equipment. But what caught her attention was the sight of a pair of figures sitting in the sandbox.

Jake Grisham.

And her son.

She paused, loath to interrupt what looked like a temporary truce. The two of them were bent close, examining the attributes of a battered yellow tractor that they were using to scoop mounds of dirt into a pail.

Even as she watched, Jake showed Matthew how to work the levers that caused the scoop to release the sand. Matthew scowled at him, but was clearly impressed.

Frowning, Alana wished that Matthew would be less antagonistic toward Jake. If only he would enjoy this moment of male bonding.

Alana pushed back a sigh. There in front of her was the one thing she couldn't provide for her son. A stable male influence. He needed that. As much as she might want to believe that she could offer him everything, she couldn't give him that. No matter how much she loved her son, she was still a woman and as such she could not offer him the masculine reassurances that he would need as he grew up.

It was a dilemma she had wrestled with before, especially during those frantic first few months as a single mother. When her dear friend Debbie and Debbie's husband had died in an auto accident, leaving Alana to care for Matthew, Alana had been dating an investment analyst. The relationship had begun to grow serious—at least from his vantage point. A conservative, moderately religious man, Rutherford Haynes hadn't questioned her wish to keep their relationship platonic for a while. Instead, he had urged her to consider a more permanent arrangement by way of a large spring wedding.

Alana had seriously considered the proposal—how could she not? By that time, she'd decided that her brief sojourn with Jake had damaged something in her psyche and she wasn't physically capable of feeling passion anymore. And Rutherford had been a good, kind man who would have been the perfect father for little Matthew.

But she hadn't loved him. Plain and simple. And Alana was realistic enough to know that a marriage without love was doomed to fall apart. If not right away, then eventually. So she'd broken off the relationship and had devoted herself to Matthew.

Until Jake had come along to awaken needs within her that had lain dormant for years. And now it was so hard to think of anything but wanting him. Needing him.

But even though she might be tempted to suggest they both indulge in a short-term affair so that this obsession with Jake would be banished from her system once and for all, Matthew's presence in the equation complicated matters. The little boy was already innately jealous of Jake. He seemed to sense that the man was a rival for Alana's attention.

So what was she going to do? Events and emotions were building up within her to the point where they could no longer be controlled or ignored. But neither could she allow herself to succumb to them.

At that moment, Matthew looked up and saw her standing at the edge of the play yard. Shouting "Mommy!" he jumped to his feet and raced toward her, spraying Jake with sand in the process.

Alana quickly scooped her son into her arms, chatting with him about the new day-care arrangements and how he liked the other children and the presence of all the animals.

But when she looked up to include Jake in the conversation, she discovered that he was gone.

8

LEANING BACK in her chair, Alana surveyed the stack of videos that had been left on her desk. Several days had passed since her breakthrough with Nellie. Since then, Alana had spent at least an hour a day with the gorilla for what Jake had dubbed "female bonding."

But even as her relationship with Nellie bloomed, her contact with Jake had become sporadic. She had a feeling that he was avoiding her, and she didn't know whether to feel complimented or insulted.

Only this morning, he'd stepped into her room, dropped the tapes on her desk and offered her a mocking smile.

"Since you're now so chummy with Nellie, we thought that you should offer some input on how to help her relax around her intended mate."

"I'm flattered."

"Boris will be arriving in about ten days and we're hoping to schedule a rendezvous between the two animals some time next week. You'd better get cracking. You've got more than sixteen hours of footage to preview."

Then he turned on his heel and disappeared.

Sixteen hours. As if anyone needed sixteen hours of "gorilla watching."

Suddenly, Alana smelled a rat. She was being given busy work. But why? For the past few days, she'd been given the impression that the team welcomed her efforts.

The team, yes, but not Jake.

Grimacing, Alana watched three of the tapes. But she soon grew bored...then suspicious.

Why was she watching footage of Boris? Boris's behavior wasn't the problem.

"The feeling" began to sink into the pit of her stomach. Something was wrong here. But what?

Standing, she decided the time had come for a long chat with Jake. At the very least, she needed more information on the proposed rendezvous with Boris.

But after an hour of trying to find Jake, the sensation that she was being kept away from something important grew even stronger. Especially when she happened to look out of the window and see a gorilla playing alone in the outdoor habitat.

Her eyes narrowed, and she grabbed a pair of binoculars from the sill where she kept them to watch Nellie's interaction with the other apes. Peering through the lenses, she couldn't doubt the evidence of what she saw.

Boris.

There was no mistaking the animal, not after she'd spent the last few hours studying him on tape.

That meant that the animal was already here. So why had Jake told her Boris wouldn't be arriving until next week?

A slow anger began to build within her when the answer became evident. She was purposely being kept out of the loop. Evidently, another attempt at mating Nellie was about to take place in the not-too-distant future. And while the rest of the team was doing everything possible to ensure success, Alana was clearly not to be included. Her attention was being kept diverted until after...

Tonight. Jake was going to mate Nellie this weekend while Alana went back to Los Angeles to do her radio show.

"Of all the—"

Alana bit off what she'd been about to say when a knock sounded on her door. Putting the binoculars on the sill again, she sank into her chair before calling out, "Come in."

The door opened and Jake poked his head around the edge. "I just wanted to wish you luck on your radio show this evening. Have a safe trip."

"I will, thanks."

Her tone was sweet, but her fingers curled so tightly around the arms of her chair that she could hear the leather creak.

Only when the door had closed again, did Alana's

grip lessen. Reaching for the phone, she quickly dialed the radio station's number.

She wouldn't be going to Los Angeles.

Not until she'd found out exactly what was going on.

IF ANY of the men responsible for Nellie's imminent mating attempt were to be interviewed and asked to define the ultimate goal for the evening, Jake Grisham was sure that the answers would be the same.

Sex.

Hot sex.

Jungle sex.

Stated so bluntly, Jake supposed that the average bystander would have been shocked at the single-mindedness shared by him and the other men. From the moment the romantic liaison had been proposed for that weekend, they'd done everything in their power to help Nellie lose her virginity. By evening's end, they intended to rouse Boris's interest, awaken his desire, and trap him into becoming crazy with passion so that he wouldn't allow Nellie much time to react.

As part of their plans, they'd made careful preparations to her mobile home this time, rather than the indoor observation area. The other team members had suggested the idea. Although Jake had openly doubted the validity of their research in regards to Nellie, the men had arrived early Saturday morning toting a copy of Alana's latest editorial—a guide to "Adding Romance to an Evening."

As per Alana's written instructions on creating the proper mood, the other men had put colored bulbs in the lighting fixtures, topped the wall lamps with silk scarves, filled the room with flowers, and arranged baskets of fruit and greenery in every possible location. Then, they'd concentrated their efforts on Nellie, fixing her hair, applying a light touch of makeup, and spritzing her with a perfume laden with pheromones.

Jake hadn't seen the necessity of the preparations. He kept reminding his team that Nellie was a gorilla, not a college prom queen. But the men had been so impressed with the rapport Alana had developed with Nellie, they'd decided to appeal to her feminine instincts.

For the most part, their efforts actually seemed to work—although Jake thought their latest choice of mates might have a great deal to do with it. Boris was older than most of the other gorillas and therefore slower and less threatening. In fact, Jake had been so impressed with the way the two gorillas had reacted to one another that he'd tried a new tack this time. Privacy. He'd sent the other men home with the assurances that he would call them if he needed them. He'd told them he would watch the proceedings from the television monitors in the lab and report to them all in the morning.

But less than twenty minutes after they'd left, he'd

been on his way to Nellie's mobile home. As much as
Nellie seemed to enjoy Boris's company, Jake still
didn't trust her to maintain her sweet deportment. He
intended to stay in the shadows and watch things
through a small gap in the curtains.

Jake still felt a twinge of guilt when he remembered
the way the men had mourned the fact that Alana
wasn't present to share in the fun. Holding a private
meeting with the men during the middle of the week,
Jake had insisted that it was important to the scientific
nature of their study that Alana be kept out of the
actual mating process—and it was true. Their work
was at a critical juncture and Nellie could not be upset
or distracted in any way. Alana Childe, with her barrettes and lipstick and feminine wiles was new to Nellie, and therefore distracting.

Just as she'd been distracting Jake more than he
would care to admit.

"What's happening?" a voice whispered from the
darkness.

Jake instinctively jumped, whirling away from the
window and flattening himself against the siding of
the mobile home. For one insane instant, he wondered
if he were about to be confronted by Security for being
a Peeping Tom. Obviously, his efforts to creep through
the night and check on the lovers firsthand hadn't been
quite as sneaky as he'd thought.

"Geez, Rusty," another voice said from somewhere
near the bushes. "You've got to whisper."

"Yeah!"

"Do you want somebody calling Security?"

"Or worse yet, the police?"

Judging by the rustling of bushes and the voices easing out from the darkness, Jake guessed the whole matchmaking crew was here—even though Jake had ordered them to stay away.

"Well?" someone prompted from the shadows. "What's going on in there?"

Sighing in resignation, Jake motioned for them to emerge from their hiding places. One by one, the men crouched beside him in the grass. As they huddled close, their expressions growing expectant, Jake knew they wouldn't leave until they'd been debriefed.

Doing his best to look stern, he glared at Rusty who wore a near-neon Hawaiian print shirt, Doc with his unlit pipe, Chen with his ever-present notebook, and Rudy and Dino with their own personal video equipment.

"With all of the hidden cameras, you brought your own as well?" Jake asked in disbelief.

"Yeah. Why not?"

Rolling his eyes, Jake became aware of one missing member of the team.

"Where's Rueben?"

"Here."

Jake looked up, up, up as the man melted out of the darkness.

"So what's the poop?" Chen demanded.

Dino jabbed him in the ribs. "Scoop. What's the 'scoop.'"

Ignoring the two men, Jake said quickly, "She's been very relaxed all evening."

"No signs of her usual frigidity?" Rudy asked, his eyes blinking behind thick glasses.

"None." For the first time, Jake allowed himself a pang of hope. "You were right about beginning the date with something quirky and unexpected, Rueben."

Rueben straightened even more, causing the moonlight to carve his features into a gaunt smug mask—a Frankenstein-wins-the-lottery kind of look.

"She enjoyed the trip to the beach," Jake continued. "They fed the seagulls. That's where he made his move."

Dino offered a knowing look. "What'd he do?"

Jake shrugged. "The usual. He began by touching her, smelling her. He even complimented her in sign language."

"And she didn't back away?" Doc asked, sucking on the stem of his unlit pipe.

Jake shook his head. "No, she actually seemed to…lean into the caresses."

As Jake tilted to define the motion, the group instinctively followed him, then breathed a collective sigh of relief.

"What then?" Rusty whispered.

"They came back here for dinner." Jake couldn't

prevent the grin that followed. "She even shared her food."

"Alana would be proud of our efforts."

Jake ignored them.

"What's going on now?"

Easing back into position, Jake peered through the tiny slit caused by a poorly fitting drape.

Thankfully, the noise outside hadn't disturbed the duo—if they'd even heard anything. They were still completely absorbed in their own company. Nellie was nibbling a slice of apple from Boris's fingers, lingering over the offering in a way that was completely suggestive.

Jake turned to offer his commentary to his companions, but his gaze met nothing but trees and bushes. A quick search told him that his co-conspirators had abandoned the "play-by-play" before it could resume. One by one, they'd positioned themselves near three other windows—all but Rusty, who had flattened himself on the stoop and peered under the slit of the front door.

"He's coming on to her," he whispered.

Quickly returning to his own peephole, Jake realized Rusty was correct. The male inside the trailer was obviously ready for some action.

Generally, it was at this point that Nellie would begin to show signs of unease, but this evening, she was clearly enjoying herself. She even flirted—smoothing her hair, tugging her ear, then pursing her lips and revealing the hint of color Rusty had applied.

"My gosh," Rusty whispered. "She's..."

Aroused.

No one said the word aloud. It didn't have to be said. The sexual energy present inside the trailer had increased to a point where even the witnesses outside began to shift in discomfort.

"Come on, come on," Doc groaned as the lovers-to-be stared at one another with hungry eyes. "*Do something.*"

A stark sensuality infused the trailer with a palpable tension. Sexual energy flooded the area with sweet, molten overtones—reminding the onlookers that it had been months since they'd forgotten Nellie's frigidity in order to tend to their own sexual needs.

"I gotta get a date," Rusty murmured.

"Amen to that," Dino agreed.

The air grew thick and charged, and Jake knew that the atmosphere for the couple within must be even more intense.

"Come on, baby, come on," he whispered, studying the female for any sign of rejection or fear.

There was none. It was clear from her expression that she wanted the wooing to continue.

Her anticipation was apparent to her companion as well. He was already aroused by her attention—painfully so. But he didn't move. He seemed to sense that his date would need to make the first move before she would allow the pleasure to commence.

"Do it," Chen whispered.

"I can't stand this," Rusty groaned.

"Take her already!"

Still, Boris waited.

Then, Nellie took a step toward the silverback.

The inconsequential movement shattered the last wisps of Boris's control and he lunged to his feet.

Swinging his arm, he backhanded the table that held the remains of their dinner. Plates and dishes and food scattered everywhere. Jake swore, sure that Nellie would flee as she had during the attempt barely a month earlier. But to his surprise, she became even more excited by the show of force. Her breathing was erratic, her body trembling.

"Easy, now. Easy," Rusty whispered.

The male took a step toward his quarry.

Nellie leaned toward him.

In three strides, Boris closed the distance, his body crowding hers against the wall. But when he reached to touch her, she jumped as if jerked from a trance and darted to the opposite end of the room.

Boris grunted, clearly irritated with her skittishness. Needing to assert his dominance, he began to bellow and grunt, clearly conveying that Nellie should submit to his authority.

Jake felt a twinge of unease. "Damn it. What's he doing?"

"Being a jerk," Rusty said, his voice dripping with disgust.

Inside the trailer, Boris stalked toward her, still bellowing. Nellie's eyes narrowed at the overt sign of male power and she bellowed in return.

"He's going to ruin everything," Rueben warned dourly.

"Do something, Jake. Break it up. Knock on the door. Interrupt them," Rusty urged. "Once they've calmed down, we can leave them alone again."

Jake shook his head. "You know I can't do that. This is the closest she's ever come to mating. We've got to give her a chance."

"I'm with Jake," Dino agreed. "He wooed her into trusting him once. He can do it again."

But it soon became clear that the mood inside the trailer had shifted irrevocably. As her date approached, Nellie recoiled, then swiped at the remnants of lipstick and scowled.

Boris, oblivious to her silent cues, continued to approach. As far as he was concerned, his patience had been stretched to the limits.

"He thinks she's challenging him," Rusty whispered.

"Maybe that's what she needs. Maybe he should just go for it and let her put up a token struggle," Doc whispered.

Obviously, the male had the same idea. His stance became cocky, his expression self-assured. Reaching out, he confidently caressed her cheek, her shoulder, and her breast.

Nellie shrieked in outrage, trying to dodge past him. Anticipating her reaction, he pinned her to the wall, his dense body crowding hers. Dipping his head, he nuzzled her neck, sniffing her own personal fragrance and the pheromone-rich perfume.

As his eyes closed in utter rapture, she grew still, stunned that she could inspire such a reaction in the silverback. Offering a sigh of wonder, Nellie inexplicably abandoned her will to fight. Surrendering herself to the moment, she wilted, her eyes drifting closed, her fingers curling into tight fists of need.

"That's it," Jake murmured under his breath. "Give in, sweetie. Give in."

A soft moan sifted into the darkness. Even with the walls between them, Jake could hear the strident breathing of the lovers—or was it his breathing?

"Come on, baby, come on," he whispered, straining closer to the window, knowing that everything they'd done that day—and for weeks in advance—hinged on this moment.

Shifting slightly, Nellie's resistance melted away and she dared to nip Boris's ear.

Come on, baby. Come on, Jake silently urged as Boris began to take over, initiating the first steps to lovemaking. Bit by bit, he urged her to the floor—and she went, willingly, sinking against the cool tile.

Then her eyes flickered open.

Swearing, Jake dodged out of sight as her gaze swung toward the same window he'd been looking through. Crouching low, he ran to where Rueben stood. But as he strained to see beneath the drapes, he instinctively knew that things had soured again.

"I think she saw you, boss," Rueben drawled, his tone rueful.

"Damn it, how could she possibly have seen me?"

But Rueben's comment had been correct. In that brief moment, Nellie's mental state had shifted from one of utter abandon...

To outrage.

"Here it comes!" Rusty shouted in warning as he jumped from his spot on the stoop and ran toward the bushes.

"Move, move, move!" Rueben added as incentive to Chen and Dino as they dove into the foliage.

Jake remained where he was, watching the romantic interlude dissolve into chaos. Inside, Nellie lunged to her feet, bellowing in fury. Her black eyes flashed in anger and her lips spread wide over gleaming teeth as she displayed a ferocity rarely seen in lowland gorillas—especially those raised in captivity.

Her hands raced in a series of motions. *You Beast! You Filthy, Bad, Bad, Beast! Bad, Bad, Fu—*

"All right, who's been teaching Nellie the profanity?" Doc demanded just as Nellie charged. Then, the gnome-like scientist ducked away from the trailer altogether as Nellie threw a chair out of her way, a vase, a crate.

"Watch out!" Dino cried as an oversized tricycle hit one of the windows, shattered the glass and sent the toy bouncing into the bushes.

Jake was already running toward the front entrance to the lab. "Rusty, get the tranquilizer darts!" he shouted as he frantically punched at the keypad, then wrenched the door open and lunged inside.

The shriek of an alarm was followed by a voice on the research institute's intercom announcing, "We have a code red situation in Auxiliary Lab One. All available personnel are to meet there immediately."

"Damn it, Dino. Get on the phone and tell everybody to back off!" Jake demanded. "This is our project and we'll handle things from here."

As his assistant dodged to the chain-link fence that separated Nellie's quarters from the workstations, Jake approached the combatant animals.

"Nellie!" he barked with as much authority as he dared considering her agitated state. "Stop, Nellie!"

He accompanied his orders with the appropriate signs, but the gorilla was beyond reason. All of her frustrations seemed to have become embodied in the furry presence of Boris. Slamming the silverback against the wall, she clearly demonstrated that she was no ordinary, submissive female gorilla. She was more than capable of defending herself.

Boris roared in pain and humiliation. Flailing his

powerful arms, he struggled to free himself just as Rusty darted into the trailer.

Steadying the tranquilizing pistol in two hands, he said frantically, "Which one? Which one do you want me to shoot?"

A clean shot of either gorilla was impossible, so Jake waved Rusty away. "Nellie, stop!" he shouted as the rest of his crew tumbled into the trailer. A part of his brain noted that each of the researchers had brought some means of subduing their favorite subject—candy, blankets, bananas, even the cast-off tricycle.

"Let Boris go, Nellie!" Jake ordered.

This time, Nellie apparently heard him. Pinning Boris to the wall, she twisted her head enough to see Jake easing toward her, his hands offering,

Come To Jake. Come To Jake, Pretty Nellie.

She cocked her head.

Come Here, Pretty Nellie. Leave Boris Alone.

Sensing she had an ally, Nellie signed, *Bad Boris. Bad, Bad Gorilla.* Then, jutting her chin out, her fingers flashed, *Punish. Must Punish Boris. Bad Gorilla.*

"No, Nellie. No!"

Jake dodged toward Nellie just as Rusty's pistol discharged and a dart whizzed through the air.

But both efforts to subdue Nellie and keep her from punishing Boris were too late. Nellie had already reached for the gorilla's groin, filled her palm with the most sensitive portion of his anatomy, and squeezed as hard as she could.

Blinking, Jake felt a stinging pain radiate from his right buttock. The floor beneath him shifted.

Stumbling, he turned in time to see Rusty's sheepish shrug.

"Sorry, boss."

Then everything went black.

9

"I SHOULD BE upset, you know. Really, *really* upset."

The voice came to him from somewhere far, far away, and Jake blinked, then blinked again as his vision seemed to seesaw for a moment before finally righting itself.

He groaned when he finally saw Alana sitting on a chair beside the couch in his office. Her legs were crossed, showing a good deal of leg—especially from his position.

Suddenly, his reasons for lying prone on his office couch came rushing back and he became conscious of the pain in his hip and the pounding of his head.

"How long have I been out?"

"All night and most of the day."

He winced at the note of satisfaction in her voice.

"When did you get here?"

"Actually, I arrived in time to see you and your crew peeking through Nellie's windows like a pack of puerile teenagers." She leaned forward, her gaze frosty. "What I want to know is why I wasn't told about this little love-fest. I'm a member of this team now—''

"You are not an official member of my team," he interjected, then winced when his own vehemence caused his head to throb.

"My contract with the Maratonga Behavioral Institute says otherwise."

"Listen, we employed some of your suggestions— hell, my crew has even been quoting from your articles—so you needn't worry that the Institute will demand anything more from you."

"That isn't the point. I signed my name on that contract. In my opinion, that offers me equal standing as any other member of your team. I should have been consulted before any of this."

He scowled, forcing himself into a sitting position. Then, as his head swam, he wished he hadn't. "What difference does it make? You have absolutely nothing to offer this group of scientists that can help our project in any way."

"Oh, really?" Her voice was silky quiet. "Including sharing with you the very reason why Nellie refuses to mate?"

Jake rubbed his temples. "There's no 'reason' other than her innate distrust of all male gorillas."

She snorted. "Bull. You've seen Nellie in the play yard. She doesn't differentiate between her playmates...only her mates. And you still haven't considered the most obvious reason why."

Jake scowled at her. "And after only a few weeks on the job, I suppose you know."

"I think I do."

"Then, in your expert opinion, why is Nellie so cantankerous?"

"Because she's infatuated with *you*."

For a moment, he was sure he hadn't heard her correctly, but when it became apparent that he had, he said, "That's absurd."

"Is it? Hasn't she always known you were watching her? At least until you arranged that little scenario last night? When she thought she was alone, she responded quite well to Boris. That is, until she saw you."

Finally, she seemed to take pity on him. Releasing him from her piercing gaze, she stood and crossed to the small refrigerator he kept in the corner of his office. Taking a bottle of cold water from the door and a package of individually wrapped aspirin from the first-aid chest bolted above it, she returned to hand them to him.

He eagerly swallowed the pills, then leaned back against the ancient, over-stuffed sofa and regarded her through half-closed eyes.

"As much as I respect your opinion and your credentials, I really think that your expertise in this matter is a little limited."

"Perhaps. But I might also be the only person on your team to see the situation with fresh eyes. And my credentials aside, I think I have a special insight into Nellie's condition that none of you will ever match.''

''And what's that?''

''I'm a woman.''

He dismissed that thought with a wave of his hand. ''Now *you're* forgetting that Nellie is a gorilla. Gorillas and humans might share some characteristics, even in the mating process, but she is *not* human.''

''No, but she thinks she is.''

He scowled at her. ''That's nonsense.''

''Not at all. She's been raised by human hands for the most part, she's been taught their language—''

''And she also interacts with her own kind.''

''But she doesn't *love* them. Not like she has grown to love you.''

''You're reading far too much into the whole situation.''

''I don't think so. Nellie doesn't have reluctance about working with women because of their gender in general. She dislikes them because she sees them as competition for your affections.''

''That's preposterous.''

''Why?''

He watched her from narrowed eyes. ''Nellie looks upon me as more of a father figure or a teacher.'' When she continued to look doubtful, he stood. ''Come with me and I'll prove it.''

''How?''

He grabbed her by the wrist and began moving to

the door. "We'll go visit Nellie in her trailer. Right now."

Alana eyed the short skirt and silk blouse she wore—and he realized she must not have gone home to change yet since he'd bid goodbye to her the night before. Jake knew what she was thinking. Nellie might have accepted her as an occasional playmate, but the ensemble would be pressing their luck.

"Out of the question," she said, tugging on his hand in an effort to stop him.

"I insist."

"This blouse is silk. My coveralls are at the beach house, so you've got to give me an hour to change."

"We do it now. Like that. If she throws something at you, I'll replace the suit."

Alana shrugged and fell into step, clearly deciding that it would be of no use to argue—and he was glad. His head was pounding, his butt ached, and before he passed out again, he intended to show her that her degree in behavioral medicine held little sway in the animal kingdom.

Jack was punching the key code to the security fence when his conscience began to prick him. What if Alana had a point? Jake knew that Nellie's bond to him was intense. He'd been with her since she was an infant; they'd spent more time together than even he would be able to count.

But surely, she didn't look upon him as anything more than her teacher.

No. It wasn't possible. And he would prove it.

"I'll go in first, then I want you to come in," he said, striding to the door of the trailer and punching in another series of numbers.

"What are you going to do?"

"Just follow my lead."

"But—"

He turned to find Alana staring at him with wide eyes and the effect of her gaze was like a sudden punch to the gut.

She was so beautiful. So incredibly beautiful. So filled with life and energy and warmth. How had he ever let her go?

Maybe it was the effects of the tranquilizer, but Jake suddenly needed to kiss Alana. Not just wanted, *needed.* His eyes traced the long length of her neck, the fullness of her breasts, her narrow waist and the flare of her hips.

And those legs.

"I think I could manage that," she said huskily.

Knowing that if he didn't move now, he would be hauling her into his arms, Jake forced himself to turn and walk away.

IT TOOK less than five minutes for Alana to prove Jake wrong. She waited until Jake had been in the trailer for the allotted amount of time, then knocked and entered. Nellie grunted in delight and scrambled toward her, signing *Hair. Hair Fix.*

Alana pretended not to understand. Instead, she signed, Hello, Nellie.

At that moment, Jake came up behind her and slid his arm around her waist. Before she knew what he intended to do, he turned her to face him and kissed her, a long, slow, sweet kiss that left Alana dazed and weak at the knees. Then he drew away signing and speaking, "Alana is very beautiful today, isn't she, Nellie?"

Nellie immediately stiffened. Her dark gaze jumped from Jake to Alana and back to Jake. Seeing the way Jake still held his arm around Alana's waist, she suddenly flew into a rage, racing around the room, dumping toys and supplies on the floor.

Normally, Alana would have offered Jake a smug smile at having her theories proved right, but the gorilla's distress was so real, so poignant, that it was blatantly clear that Jake had just broken Nellie's heart.

"Damn it, Jake," Alana whispered. "Just look what you've done!"

"What *I've* done!" Jake retorted. "You're the one who claimed she was infatuated with me."

"And you should have listened to my theory. Just because I'm not a high-and-mighty primatologist doesn't mean that I don't have a brain in my head." Her voice rose as Nellie began to work herself into a frenzy. "How could you? How could you break her heart this way? There were other ways to test the strength of her affection without being so...so heartless!''

''Damn it, she's a gorilla!''

''And therefore she doesn't have feelings? No wonder your own social life is such a disaster, Jake. You have absolutely no business having a relationship with anyone if you can't display a little empathy.''

He reared back as if slapped. ''Now, wait a minute—''

''How could you do this? How could you arrange this little scene without one thought for what it would do to Nellie—or to me? She had begun to look upon me as a friend. Now I'm a traitor.''

''I didn't think I—''

Nellie apparently sensed she had an ally because she rushed over to Alana, wound her arms around Alana's waist, and buried her head in Alana's stomach. Only once did she break away to sign, *Jake Bad. Jake Naughty.*

''Yes, he is, Nellie. Jake is very naughty.''

The gorilla hugged her even tighter, her body shaking.

Nellie Good. Nellie Not Bad. Why Jake Not Like Nellie?

''Oh, Nellie, Jake loves you. He loves you very much.''

No. Jake Not Love Nellie. Jake Naughty. Jake Mean. Jake Filthy Beast. Filthy, Filthy, Filthy Beast.

Whirling away from Alana, she began racing around

the room again, pulling over what few pieces of furniture and supplies she hadn't upended. It was clear that she was riding on a wave of anger and wasn't about to calm down anytime soon.

"I think you'd better leave," Jake said above the din.

Knowing that Nellie might charge in a fit of fury, Alana reluctantly moved to the door. But as she gave the animal one last glance, her heart ached in shared pain.

Then she glared at Jake. Nellie was right. He really could be a beast at times.

Closing the door, Alana stormed back into the Institute and made her way to her office. The time had come to write another column for her paper.

IT WAS LATE in the afternoon when Jake finally found Alana again. She was sitting at one of the picnic tables near the day-care center, sharing a snack with her son.

"Well?" She kept her tone purposely frosty.

Jake had the grace to look chagrined. "I think you've made your point about Nellie's feelings for me."

"So what do we do now?" she asked.

He sat down, resting his elbows on the table. "Well, I guess we're going to have to find a way to mend her breaking heart. It's been hours and she won't eat, won't sign."

He sounded so glum that Alana felt her anger begin to soften. "Maybe I should have a chat with her."

Jake opened up his mouth and she thought he would refuse, but he finally shrugged. "I guess it couldn't hurt.

"HELLO, NELLIE."

Knowing that Nellie might very well chase her from the trailer, Alana had come prepared. She'd brought Nellie a purse. Nellie's very own purse.

But Nellie was clearly not going to be so easily bought. She sat huddled in the corner, her head bowed.

Knowing that she was half of the reason for the gorilla's battered spirit, Alana crept closer.

"Nellie, can we talk?"

The animal kept her back to Alana, so Alana didn't bother to sign. She didn't know the signs for what she had to say.

Alana righted one of Nellie's chairs and sat just a few feet away from the gorilla.

"Nellie sad?" she asked.

She waited through a long silence before Nellie held up a hand and bobbed her fist in the sign for "yes."

"Alana knows you're sad. Alana is sorry."

Nellie didn't move.

"Alana is sad, too. Alana loves Nellie."

She didn't react.

"But Alana also loves Jake."

Until the words were said aloud, Alana hadn't dared

to think them herself. But by admitting the fact to Nellie, she was forced to examine the full meaning of her admission.

Suddenly tears pricked the back of her eyes.

Damn it. She'd allowed herself to fall in love with the man again. Hadn't she learned her lesson ten years ago? Didn't she know that nothing had really changed? Jake was no more in love with her now than he was then. He was attracted to her, yes. But that didn't mean that his feelings for her went any deeper than that.

She sniffed, the pressure of the past few weeks suddenly overwhelming her. Her breath caught in a sob...

And suddenly she was crying.

Alana didn't know how long she'd sat there sobbing, but she became aware of a soft, furry hand offering her a tissue.

"Thank you," Alana said in a choked voice, offering the proper sign.

Sad Alana.

She nodded. "Yes. I'm sad."

Alana Love Jake?

Alana felt her chin quiver. Lifting her hand, she offered the sign for "yes."

Nellie offered Alana a look filled with such sympathy and understanding that Alana found it difficult to believe that Nellie was only a "simple-minded animal." Although many people might think that Nellie was not capable of empathy, Alana knew for a fact that they were wrong.

Nellie moved to her nest of blankets on the floor and motioned for Alana to join her. Doing as she'd been bid, Alana settled on a pillow, wondering what Nellie meant to do. But when the gorilla pulled her close and began to groom her hair much the way gorillas in the wild did for their close family members, the tears threatened to fall again.

Alana had just gained a friend.

RAKING HIS FINGERS through his hair, Jake allowed the warm evening air to blow around him as he exited the freeway and made his way toward the tiny house he rented.

He'd noted that a definite shift had occurred in Nellie's relationship with the team members over the past few days. Although she continued to interact with Jake's crew on a fairly normal footing, she positively blossomed whenever Alana was present. But if Jake were near...

Nellie had perfected her snubbing techniques to an art form. If Jake visited her in her trailer, she huddled in the corner. If he came into her classroom, she would hide under the table. Then, for the rest of the day, she wouldn't eat or sleep until Alana managed to calm her down again.

Worse yet, something had shifted in Jake's relationship with Alana at about the same time. She'd become cool and distant. Alana seemed to have taken on the role of Nellie's guardian, growing as protective of the animal as any adoptive mother.

In doing so, she'd added a new dimension to the project. Nellie began to look upon Alana as a role model, mimicking many of her mannerisms and expressions. And perhaps even more importantly, Nellie had begun to watch Alana interact with her son.

Jake had been the first to notice the occurrence. Since Nellie's peevishness had made working with her difficult, Jake had allowed her extra time in the outdoor habitat with the other gorillas. And since the fenced enclosure bordered the day-care playground, many of the animals sat close to the bars, watching their human counterparts.

But while the other animals seemed to be entranced by the children's play, Nellie came alive when she saw Alana spending time with her son. She seemed fascinated by the way Alana would hug and kiss the boy and praise him over the slightest accomplishment. Soon, the hidden cameras in Nellie's trailer began to capture Nellie doing much the same thing with the stuffed baby gorilla they'd used to teach her nurturing techniques.

If the truth were told, Jake was feeling a bit out of sorts himself. Nellie's apparent anger and Alana's cool civility were beginning to wear on his nerves. He wanted things to be the way they'd been before, with Nellie eager to see him each day, and Alana—

What did he want from Alana?

Things were better this way for both of them. He was still a man who was determined to retain his bachelor status, and she was still a single mother. As such, he had no right to upset her well-ordered existence.

Even if he longed to be a part of her world. More than he ever would have thought possible.

Jake ached with weariness as he stepped from his battered Range Rover and locked the doors.

If he'd had his choice, he supposed he would have lived at Maratonga. His work was there, as well as everything he held dear.

No. Not everything.

He paused, staring into the darkness.

When had the shift occurred? When had he begun to care for Alana?

Then again, had he ever really stopped caring for her? Loving her?

It all seemed suddenly clear. In Africa, he had been so busy and so completely wrapped up in his selfish interests that he hadn't paid much attention to what was going on around him. He'd regarded Alana as being something of a pest, when in fact, he was never more alive than in those moments when she was with him. When she'd left, he'd tried to convince himself that his life was better without her and far less complicated.

But it had also been empty. So very, very empty.

He'd always blamed the fact that he'd never tried

to marry or start a family because of the demands of his job. But, in fact, he hadn't wanted to settle for second best—just as he hadn't wanted to admit to himself that he'd already lost a part of himself by letting Alana go.

So where did that leave him? He was still in love with Alana Childe, but his life was no less complicated. His work still demanded a good deal of his time, and...

No. He was making excuses again. Alana had shown him in the past weeks that she not only understood his work, but she also agreed with its value. And if he were honest with himself, he would also have to admit that she'd proven to be a very valuable part of his team. She might not have degrees in animal studies, but she instinctively understood the unique psychology of animals that had been raised in captivity. Moreover, she had an empathy that a formal education could not teach.

So why did he hesitate? Why didn't he storm into her office tomorrow morning and demand they begin a formal relationship?

Sighing, he realized it wasn't that easy. They still had a history together, one made even more awkward by that single night of passion. Added to that was the presence of Alana's son. The boy hated Jake—hated all men, it would seem. Jake didn't know if the boy's attitude was common to little boys or if Matthew was unique in that respect. But either way, the child would have to be figured into any plans Jake might make. He was a part of Alana's life.

A very permanent part.

For the first time, Jake was forced to admit to himself that he had never envisioned himself as a father. Raising Nellie had given him enough insight into parenting techniques for him to think that he was not particularly gifted in that area. He could change a diaper—or delegate the responsibility to one of his team members—but beyond that, he was better suited to the scientific world.

So that left him in a quandary. If he wanted to pursue a relationship with Alana and include her as a part of his life, he would have to make a place for Matthew as well. Was he ready for that? Was he willing to change that much? He was an old, stuck-in-his-ways bachelor. Was he really considering...

Marriage?

The thought sent a spear of panic through his stomach, but Jake didn't immediately dismiss the thought.

Maybe. Maybe he would be willing to go that far.

If he could reconcile himself to becoming Matthew's father.

With that thought firmly in his brain, Jake picked up his briefcase and rounded the Range Rover, heading through the clumps of trees that shielded his house from the detached garage.

He had barely stepped through the trees when he heard a shout.

"There he is! There he is!"

The pronouncement was made by a high feminine voice, and as he looked up, Jake focused on a gaggle of women carrying casserole dishes stampeding toward him.

10

"VERY FUNNY, ALANA. Very funny!"

Alana fought the urge to snicker as Jake stormed into her office and slapped a copy of the *California Expositor* on her desk. Plainly visible was the latest editorial she'd written for her column.

> Dr. Jake Grisham is obviously a man in need of a bit of feminine company. In all honesty, his Indiana Jones-like attire and rugged good looks are only slightly hampered by his caveman social skills. As one of his own team members admitted, "He's the sort who could use some home-style loving from a woman who can cook. Maybe then, he would treat women—and Nellie—with the respect they so richly deserve…"

"I'll have you know that last night I was accosted by at least two dozen women carrying tuna noodle casseroles."

Alana had to press her lips tightly together to keep from snickering out loud. She finally managed to control her mirth enough to ask, "Oh, really? Any of them good enough for me to request a recipe?"

"Damn it, Alana! I will not be made a laughing stock."

"Laughing stock? Everything mentioned in my column is well documented."

"Who the hell made the home-style loving remark?"

"I'm sorry. As a journalist, it's my duty to keep my sources secret."

"Alana!"

She stood and rounded the desk.

"What's the matter, Jake. I would have thought that you would appreciate the feminine companionship. According to your crew you aren't...'getting any.'"

She watched a hint of color climb his cheeks.

"I will not have you talking to my crew about anything but Nellie. As part of our crew, you should know better than to gossip.

Alana grinned. "Does this mean that I am now an official member of this project?"

Jake put his hands on his hips and took a deep, calming breath. "Yeah." He pointed a warning finger in her direction. "As long as my social life stays out of print."

She grinned. "Are you sure? Having me write about you could be as good as paying for a computer dating service."

Jake scowled. "I don't need a computer dating service."

"You're sure?"

"Yes, I'm sure!"

"And why's that?"

This time, it was his turn to advance. Before she knew what he meant to do, he pulled her tightly into his arms and bent his head to whisper against her lips, "Because I've already found you. So why would I want to look at anyone else?"

The words caressed her very soul and the kiss he offered her filled her body with a thrumming passion that she was growing addicted to. Standing on tiptoe, she wound her arms around his neck, responding to each touch, each caress with a hunger that threatened to consume her completely.

"Jake? There's a call for you on line three."

At the shout from the hall, the two of them reluctantly parted.

"I've got to go," Jake whispered, his voice raspy.

"I know."

"Look, I've got a busy day. With only a few weeks left before Wilhemena pulls our funding for lack of progress, I've got to make arrangements for another male gorilla. Then, I've got a project leaders' meeting until after seven."

"I understand."

"Can you free your schedule for later tonight? There are some things I'd like you to evaluate." He caressed her cheek and stroked the fullness of her bottom lip. "After everyone is gone, we could cozy up in my office, order some take-out."

Alana felt the warmth in the pit of her stomach radiate through her entire body. If she spent the evening with Jake in his office, there was a very good chance that work could be interrupted by passion. They could both end up entwined on the thick rug on the floor rather than concentrating on business.

She slid her fingers through his hair, drawing him down for one last kiss.

"I'll meet you at eight."

"SINCE YOU'RE GOING to be here for a while, I guess you'd better take a look at the possible candidates for Nellie's hot date," Jake said that evening as he pulled her into his office and shut the door.

Evening shadows were already beginning to cloak the room, but neither of them bothered to turn on a light. The soft glow of the television in the corner would offer them what illumination they needed as the night progressed.

Alana's lips spread into a smile. "Does that mean I'm being given a chance to help with the actual mating process?"

Jake had the grace to look chagrined. "Look, I'm sorry about how I acted when you first arrived, but you've got to understand that—"

"That your work is important and you were reluctant to taint the success you'd already obtained by delving into the unknown.''

His eyes were warm. ''Yeah.''

''Apology accepted.''

She sank into the seat next to him, curling one of her legs beneath her. When Jake didn't immediately start the VCR, she looked at him questioningly.

''Don't take this the wrong way, but you look so much more...relaxed than you did when you first came.''

She glanced down at her loose T-shirt, faded jeans, and tennis shoes in wry amusement.

''As a matter of fact, I feel more relaxed. Maybe it's the clothes. I always hated wearing suits.''

''So why wear them?''

She shrugged. ''Now that I'm a 'personality' people expect a certain image of me.''

''But you work on radio, not television.''

''The media still follows me around.''

''What do you care? Are they going to like you less if you don't dress like a sexpot?''

She laughed. ''A sexpot?''

''Yeah.'' His voice had dropped a notch. The awareness flooded through the room like warm honey. ''A sexpot.''

''I doubt my businesslike attire—''

''My entire team has spent the last few weeks with their tongues hanging out. They think you're a babe.''

Her brows rose. ''Someone actually said that?''

"Yes."

"Who?"

He grinned. "I'm not about to reveal my sources. Besides, the man who said it was right."

The words were as heady as any wine, flowing through her system like a potent aphrodisiac.

He set the remote on the table and bent toward her, his hands strong and firm as they slid into her hair, drawing her closer.

"I have missed you so much."

The words were a balm to a portion of her spirit that she hadn't even known was aching.

He was closing the gaps between them slowly, gradually, his eyes greedily searching her features.

"I don't know how or why I let you go the first time. When I woke up to find you gone, I should have followed you then and there."

Tears pricked behind her eyelids. Joy swelled within her like a budding flower.

"I'm so glad you didn't," she whispered.

"Why?"

"Because if you had, I wouldn't be the person I am today. I wouldn't know how to love you like a woman rather than an infatuated girl."

"You were no girl," he murmured, one hand dropping to skim her throat, her shoulder, then lower to cup her breast, one thumb skimming idly over her nipple. "You were all woman then, and you're all woman now."

She grimaced. "I was just thirty pounds heavier is all."

"You were beautiful then, and you are beautiful now."

"And you are my hero for saying that."

"But I mean it."

She took his hands, drawing him resolutely onto the rug at their feet.

"Which is why you are my hero. You make me feel beautiful and sexy."

"You've always been sexy."

She shook her head. "No. Being sexy is more a thing of the mind than the body. And I never really felt desirable—" her voice dropped to a whisper and she kissed the hollow at the base of his throat "—except when I saw myself through your eyes."

"Surely there have been other men..."

"No." She looked him straight in the eye knowing that the time had come for a true confession—and relishing the possibilities. "There have been no other men, Jake."

She waited until the full meaning of her words sunk in before saying, "I've dated. I've even entertained a few marriage proposals. But I could never bring myself to commit to anything more than a casual romance. In fact, until my work as the Love Doctor came along, I was beginning to get a reputation for being frigid, much like our lovable gorilla in there."

She laughed when Jake continued to stare at her,

obviously speechless. When he finally managed to gather his thoughts, he merely said in obvious disbelief, "You? Frigid?"

"Mmm-hmm." She stroked a finger over the hollow of his cheek, then traced the firm lines of his mouth. "You seem to be the only person capable of unlocking my wilder instincts, Jake Grisham." Her finger dropped from his lips to trail over his chin and down his throat. Then, she began to loosen the buttons of his shirt. "Around you, I can't seem to control myself. I'm hot, then cold. I can't sleep nights—and when I do, I have wild dreams of you…and me."

She would have continued, but he pulled her head down and kissed her hungrily, his hands sweeping over her body as he rolled over her.

She gasped in pleasure as the weight of his body pressed into her, one of his thighs slipping intimately between her legs.

"Don't say any more," he whispered when he finally managed to pull himself a hairsbreadth away. "If you do, I won't be able to control myself."

Her body pulsed in renewed pleasure at his words. She wanted nothing more than to do what he asked, to avoid the rest of her confession and surrender to the moment. But she had to tell him the rest. She wanted to tell him the rest.

"Just one more thing."

"Alana," he protested. Denied her lips, his mouth trailed over her cheek to the pulsing point beneath her ear. Then he nipped her slightly on the lobe and she jerked against him, a bolt of hot desire piercing her through.

She nearly lost the train of her thoughts. Nearly.

"Jake?"

"Hmm."

"Jake, there's still something you should know."

"What?" The word was only a slight puff.

"That night in Africa."

"Mmm. I remember."

His voice was filled with such fond remembrance, she offered a wispy chuckle.

"Jake, nothing happened."

He was smiling against her. "So you can't remember anything either?"

"No, Jake. I remember everything. You see, I purposely set out to seduce you that night."

His grin was indulgent. "You little devil. I'm so glad you succeeded."

He was pushing up the hem of her shirt, his hands sliding up her ribs to cup her breasts. Knowing that she had to keep her wits about her for one more second, she held his wrists, stopping him.

"No, Jake. I didn't succeed."

After a moment, he finally looked up, his brow furrowing.

"Jake, you passed out before anything could happen."

It took a moment, but he finally grew still and stared at her, his eyes dark with desire. Desire for her.

"What do you mean?"

Alana thought it was obvious, but she brushed back the lock of hair falling over his forehead and said, "Jake, I'm probably the oldest living virgin in the world."

He grew absolutely still.

"There's been no one but you. No one but you."

"But..."

She laughed at his expression. If ever she'd seen someone looking "poleaxed" this was the moment.

"But..."

This time, it was her turn to roll his back to the floor and rest her body over his.

"You see, unknowingly Wilhemena picked more of an expert than she thought. Not only am I professionally qualified, but I'm personally qualified as well." She kissed his jaw, the corner of his lips. "You see, Nellie isn't the only female who is frustrated and dying for the right man to consummate a relationship."

She kissed him fully then, her hand slipping low to slide around his hips and draw them more firmly against the part of her that ached for completion.

"And this time," she whispered when she finally drew breath, "I refuse to let anything get in our way."

"You're sure?"

"I'm very, very sure. I want to make love with you, Jake Grisham."

"We could go somewhere—"

"No. I want to make love to you. Here."

If she thought that he would balk again, she was mistaken. He, too, seemed to have only a slender thread of control left, and he was willing to trust in her assurances. Nevertheless, she couldn't help noting that there was a slight change to his lovemaking. He was slower, gentler, taking the time to savor each caress, each moment.

Having rid herself of the last of her fears that Jake would reject her, Alana willingly allowed the sensations to inundate her mind and body. Her own fingers grew bold, ridding Jake of his clothing, then eagerly helping him to do the same with hers. Time seemed to disappear as her body grew tighter and tighter, the sensations building one on top of the other until she knew she would disintegrate if Jake didn't do something.

Then, just when she feared that she would die of the exquisite sensual torture, Jake settled over her, his body pressing her intimately into the rug. Kissing her, he finally entered her, slowly, tenderly.

She gasped and Jake would have withdrawn but she held him tightly, wrapping her legs around him so that he would know by her silent urgings that it wasn't pain that had caused her to cry out. It was pleasure, sheer undiluted pleasure. Then, just when she caught a glimpse of his smile, her body exploded into a firestorm of passion and she closed her eyes, gasping again, her fingers digging into the strength of his shoulders to provide herself with a link to reality as the world suddenly spun out of control.

A part of her heard Jake offer a cry as he reached his own release, but she was too far gone to do anything more than clutch him close as her body was racked with spasms of unbelievable delight.

Then, as her body began to relax and a tingling warmth invaded her veins, she kissed Jake's shoulder, knowing that she would never love another man so completely.

Jake didn't just have the ability to unlock the passion within her...

He also had the keys to her heart.

LATER, much later, she found herself curled against Jake's side, a blanket from the couch tucked around them to ward off a chill caused by the air-conditioning.

"You let me go on thinking I was a bastard for not remembering that night." Jake's tone was indulgent.

"Since I never thought I would see you again, I didn't think there was much point in setting the record straight."

"You're cruel, very cruel."

"How was I to know that you would even give the event a second thought?"

His finger was idly tickling her shoulder. "You should have known."

She shifted to lie on his chest, propping her chin on

her hands. "Be honest, Jake. Until you saw me again, you hardly gave me a passing thought."

He shook his head. "I thought about you all the time."

"Really?" His answer pleased her no end.

"Really."

"So why didn't you ever do anything about it? Why didn't you try to find me and...renew our acquaintance."

"For the same reasons I didn't grab a Jeep and stop you from going to the airport as soon as I knew you'd left Africa. I couldn't remember what had happened that night, which was embarrassing. Added to that was the fact that I was so wrapped up in myself and my work that I didn't think I had the right to ask anyone to share my crazy schedule."

"It sounds like we both needed time to grow a little."

"Yeah, I—" He had been rubbing her back, but he suddenly stopped. Confused, he frowned, then stared at Alana. "Wait a minute. You're a mother. How did that happen?"

She laughed. "Matthew is adopted."

"Obviously."

Again, she laughed. "Matthew is the son of an old childhood friend. She and her husband were killed in an automobile accident. As Matthew's godmother, I was named as his guardian in her will. I've had him since he was nine months old."

Jake's features lightened again. "You're something, you know that? Journalist, therapist, mother and radio sex kitten."

"Sex kitten?"

"*My* little sex kitten."

She nudged him in the ribs in protest. "I will not have the term 'sex kitten' used in the same sentence as my name."

"Then what do you prefer?"

She grinned. "I've always been partial to the Empress of Whoopee."

They dissolved into laughter...which quickly faded into passion, so it was later, when they finally showered in Jake's office bathroom, then ordered take-out pizza and began watching the films of Nellie's possible mates.

In the end, they needn't have bothered to research the tapes at all. Only days later, Alana was joined by Jake as she made her way toward the day-care facility to pick up Matthew.

"How long has Angel been back?"

Alana grinned. "Since the night we made love in your office. Her sister broke her ankle, but she's doing much better so Angel arranged for a flight home earlier that day." She grinned. "Evidently there's some friction between the two of them stemming from an argument about a former beau nearly thirty years ago."

"Who ended up with the beau?"

"Neither of them. They both decided he was a bounder."

"So why the grudge?"

She shrugged. "I think it gives them both an excuse to make their visits brief. They enjoy each other's company in small bursts."

The sun was warm and Jake's arm was clearly territorial as it rested around her waist.

"I was hoping you'd join us for dinner tonight. Nothing special. Just barbequing on the deck and having a swim before Matthew's bedtime."

Jake's expression was carefully bland. "Are you sure Matthew will like the idea?"

She grimaced. Somehow, Matthew had sensed a change in Alana's relationship with Jake and he'd been especially trying. Alana was growing frustrated with her son.

Whenever Jake was around, Matthew grew more and more anxious. Those brief moments of hero worship Alana had thought she'd seen in his eyes had faded beneath a glare of pure resentment.

They were nearing the gorilla habitat when Jake suddenly stopped.

"I'll be damned," he whispered, drawing Alana to a halt.

Glancing at him, Alana saw that Jake had grown suddenly tense, his eyes widening in surprise.

"What's the matter?"

He pointed to the gorilla habitat. "Look over there, away from the others under the trees."

Alana quickly followed his gaze, then gasped.

"Well, bless her furry little heart," she whispered. There in the shade, Nellie was quite plainly mating. And she seemed to be enjoying it.

11

ALANA PREPARED carefully for the evening, knowing that Jake would be joining them for a celebratory dinner.

Soon after she and Jake had discovered that Nellie was mating, Alana had suddenly found her presence with the team superfluous, so she'd taken the rest of the afternoon off. Feeling enervated and slightly giddy, she'd gone to the toy store with Matthew and then to the ice-cream shop. After they'd gone shopping for a new summery dress for Alana, flowers for the table and an irresistible array of food. Finally, only an hour before Jake was scheduled to arrive, she and Matthew had hurried home to prepare.

Wilhemena's beach house was a beautiful structure, made of wood and glass and mere yards from the cerulean blue of the ocean. Taking advantage of the view and the balmy evening breezes, Alana laid out the table on the deck, using some of the pretty china she'd found in the dining room hutch. Then, she changed into the new clothes she'd bought, spritzed perfume behind her ears and the backs of her knees, and checked her reflection in the mirror.

Even to her own eyes, it was obvious that she radiated with an inner happiness that hadn't been there only a few weeks prior. Her expression was softer, her posture more relaxed, and the little lines of stress around her mouth and brows had softened.

Life in San Diego agreed with her—as did her relationship with Jake.

The thought brought a smile to her lips. Who would have thought that everything could turn out so perfectly? Nellie had successfully mated and Alana had entered into a romance of her own.

So where did she go from here?

Alana frowned, knowing that she didn't have the answer to that question. She'd been hired to come to Maratonga to help Nellie mate. With that task finished, her job here was over—no matter how much she might want to stay here in order to be close to Jake.

For a moment, the light in her eyes dimmed. There were still so many questions that had to be answered. But the time wasn't right to put any pressures on her relationship with Jake. The two of them were still just getting used to the idea of being lovers. The thought of anything more was premature, even though in her heart of hearts, Alana knew what she wanted of this relationship...

She wanted it all.

But tonight she wouldn't worry about such things.

She had planned a relaxing evening with the people she cared for most, and she wouldn't do anything to spoil it.

Hurrying into the kitchen, Alana wrapped an apron around her waist and checked on the garlic chicken roasting in the oven, then turned her attention to the vegetables that would accompany the meal. She and Angel were just finishing the last touches with the food when they heard the sound of Jake's Range Rover in the driveway.

Angel's eyes twinkled.

"So he's the one, eh?"

Alana felt the heat touch her cheeks. "The one?"

Angel shook a chiding finger in her direction. "There's no sense pretending. Your eyes give you away."

Alana's laughter was soft and rueful and Angel smiled at her like a doting mother. "It is good to hear you laugh, *menina*."

Anything else that Alana might have said was cut off by the ringing of the door bell.

"Go let him in," Angel said with a shooing gesture. "I'll finish putting things on the table, then get Matthew."

Matthew had been so tired when he'd returned from their shopping that he'd nodded off soon after walking through the door. If allowed to sleep too late, both Alana and Angel knew that he would be up all night.

Besides which, Alana wanted Matthew to spend

some time with Jake tonight. Somehow, her son needed to get over his fear of the man.

"Thanks, Angel," Alana said, quickly untying her apron.

She knew her cheeks were flushed as she hurried to the door. The mere thought of Jake waiting on the other side filled her body with an effervescent anticipation. Never in her life had she felt so alive, so beautiful, so...

In love?

Yes.

In love.

Jake smiled at her the moment the door swung open, the slow, heated smile of a lover.

"Hi."

The mere sound of his voice caused a quiver of excitement to skitter up her spine.

"Hi, yourself."

She motioned for him to come in and he brought his hand from behind his back to reveal a small bouquet of tulips and a bottle of wine.

"For you," he said.

He'd remembered. In Africa, she'd once told him that she loved tulips far more than roses, and that if a man wanted to impress her, he would offer her pale peach-colored tulips.

"How did you ever get peach tulips this time of year?" she whispered as she took the glossy blooms.

"Where there's a will, there's a way," he answered vaguely.

"Thank you."

Jake slipped his free hand around her waist, drawing her close. "Special flowers for a special lady," he said with a kiss.

What began as a simple brush of the lips soon dissolved into a fiery embrace, and it wasn't until they heard Angel clearing her throat that they parted.

"Dinner is ready," she said with a smile.

Angel took the wine and the flowers into the kitchen, giving Jake and Alana a few precious moments to themselves.

"Is Nellie okay?" Alana asked.

"She was sleeping like a baby when I left."

As they walked toward the deck, Jake kept his arm around her waist. "I take it congratulations are in order."

"Yes, I'm so excited that Nellie—"

"Not for Nellie, for you. Rusty said you'd received word about the syndication of your column."

Alana laughed self-deprecatingly when she realized that her involvement with Nellie and the plans for her evening with Jake had pushed the news out of her head.

"Yes, I received a call from my agent soon after you and I discovered Nellie mating. I have to go back to L.A. to sign the contracts and meet with my lawyers and my agent. It will take a few days to iron things out, but it shouldn't be long.''

She was about to ask Jake if he would consider joining her in L.A. the following weekend, but the thunder of little footsteps heralded Matthew's arrival.

''Mommy, Mommy, Momm—''

Matthew skidded to a halt as soon as he saw that Alana was not alone. Immediately his gaze dropped to the proprietary arm Jake had draped around Alana's waist.

''Let go of her!''

Alana offered a reproving, ''Matthew! You need to be nice.''

''No! Let go of her!''

Without warning, Matthew launched himself at Jake. Stunned, Alana watched as her sweet-natured little boy became a wild demon. Screaming, he began to punch and hit Jake, kicking him, clawing him with such force that Alana was momentarily knocked off balance.

By the time she righted herself, Jake had managed to wrap an arm around Matthew to keep him from striking out. But rather than calming Matthew down, the boy was growing red in the face he was so hysterical.

Alana had never seen Matthew in such a state and she was at a loss as to what had caused him to grow so angry and upset.

Angel came running in from the kitchen.

"What happened?" she asked rushing toward them.

"I don't know."

Alana tried to take Matthew, but as soon as Jake released him, the boy slapped her away, then turned and ran back in the direction of his room.

Tears came to Alana's eyes as she heard the door slam followed by her son's piteous cries. She wanted nothing more than to follow him and hold him, but since his anger seemed to be directed at her as well, she didn't dare.

"I'll go," Angel whispered, sensing Alana's distress.

Within seconds Jake and Alana were alone. In the space of a few minutes, their ebullient mood had completely dissolved, leaving a strange anxiousness.

Knowing she had to say something, Alana offered, "He's upset..."

The explanation was such an understatement that Jake's lips twitched in a smile. A sad smile that tugged at her heart. "That much was obvious."

She wrapped her arms around her torso, feeling suddenly chilled, knowing that their relationship had shifted in ways that she didn't want to examine.

"I think I'd better go," Jake said.

Alana opened her mouth, wanting to beg him to stay. But her first priority was to her son.

She followed Jake on wooden legs as he made his way to the door. Sadly, she realized that until tonight, they had been able to pretend that their relationship was just between the two of them, that any commitments they made weren't binding, that they were just exploring the depth and breadth of their feelings for one another.

But Matthew had shattered all that. They were suddenly confronted with the fact that any decisions they made would affect one little boy and his perceptions of security. Tears pricked at the back of her eyes, because she knew that their relationship was far too fragile to be dealt this blow. Once again, Jake wasn't ready to make a commitment and she couldn't accept anything less.

Alana bit her lip to keep from sobbing. How could she have found herself stuck in a situation so like her breakup with Jake ten years ago? Then, she'd left Africa and had never heard from him. Tomorrow, she would be going back to L.A. It would be so easy for them to drift apart before any binding ties could be formed.

Jake paused at the door. He seemed to study her features as if memorizing them for the future. Then, lifting a hand, he caressed her cheek with the backs of his fingers.

"I'll call you," he said.

Alana stood rooted, watching him descend the stairs and get into his car. She didn't blink, didn't speak as Jake backed out of the drive, then drove away.

But as soon as his taillights disappeared in the distance, the tears began to fall.

JAKE PUSHED away from his desk, seeking something, *anything* to keep his mind on work. With Nellie happily playing with Wally, her mate, and tests confirming the first signs of pregnancy, there was little for him and his team to do other than to review the mothering techniques they'd taught Nellie for the past few years.

For the first time in as long as he could remember, Jake actually found himself at loose ends. There were no late evenings scheduled at the lab, no conference meetings...

No Alana.

Sighing, Jake moved into the main laboratory, only to find his team members lounging about in a similarly glum fashion.

"You look like someone shot your dog," Jake said to the group at large.

He barely got a glance in return.

"It feels like it," Rusty said morosely. "I've spent years working with Nellie, teaching her, loving her, and now she only has time for that dope."

When Rusty hitched a thumb in the direction of the observation window, Jake crossed to see what Nellie was doing. Inside, the two gorillas happily frolicked with Rueben who was teaching them to play with silly string.

With a wry grimace, Jake realized they were all feeling a bit replaced. Ruefully, Jake supposed he was feeling the separation even more than the others. Until

Alana had pointed out Nellie's crush, he hadn't known how much he'd enjoyed the gorilla's unwavering adoration. It was the closest thing he'd ever come to being a father.

Until his stormy few weeks with Matthew.

"You should go get her," Doc said next to his shoulder.

"Nah. She's having fun."

There was a pause, then Doc said, "I wasn't referring to Nellie."

When Jake met the other man's gaze, he found Doc's expression sympathetic. "Good heavens, man, what are you waiting for? You love the woman. Go get her and bring her back."

"It's not that simple." Jake shoved his hands into the pockets of his slacks.

"Why not?"

"Things are complicated."

"In what way?"

"She has a job in L.A., a home, a life. My life is here."

Doc snorted. "You're grasping at straws. We both know Alana did her job just fine from here. What's really holding you back?"

Jake thought for a moment, trying to put words to the hesitation he felt—a hesitation that was eating at his heart.

"If it were just Alana..."

When he didn't continue, Doc prompted, "So it's the boy that's concerning you."

"He's already had a rough start to life and all with his biological parents dying. He deserves the best. The kid hates me, Doc. The last time I saw him…" He took a deep breath and exhaled it in a heavy sigh, not wanting to remember that night. "Even if he didn't scream at the sight of me, I'm not the right person to be a part of his life. He deserves a father with normal work hours and experience in raising human babies, not gorillas."

Doc laughed. "I didn't know that experience was a prerequisite for fatherhood. If so, no one would qualify their first time around."

Jake watched Nellie and Wally as they tumbled and rolled on the floor in play.

"I don't want to make a mistake that could end up hurting Matthew."

Doc sighed. "Do you love him?"

Jake carefully considered his answer, knowing that he had been dodging that issue himself since Alana had returned back home.

"Yes, I suppose I do," he offered slowly. Even saying the words was a relief.

"And do you love Alana?"

This time there was no hesitance, "With all my heart."

"Then it seems to me you'd be doing them a disservice by not telling them and letting them make up their own mind about their futures." He winked at Jake. "After all, you've been a great team so far." He gestured to the cavorting gorillas. "Just look at what the two of you have done. You've already created one family. Maybe now, it's time you started on another."

ALANA RECEIVED a page soon after her Saturday night radio show was finished. Looking at the number displayed on the screen, she immediately felt a wave of alarm mixed with anxiety.

The number was for the lab at Maratonga.

Quickly, she returned the call, her heart racing in excitement…only to plummet to the pit of her stomach when it was Wilhemena Bush who answered the phone, not Jake.

"Hello, Alana. We've got a problem here at Maratonga and we were hoping if you could come down here for the rest of the weekend."

"What's wrong?"

"It's Nellie. She's sad and morose. She won't sleep. She won't eat. She keeps signing that she wants to see you. With her pregnancy barely confirmed, we don't want her to be so emotional. If you could come, I'll send the company helicopter and get the beach house opened up for you again."

"That would be fine. I'll have to bring Matthew and his nanny."

"We were counting on it. Give Matthew and Angel

my best. A car will arrive at your home in about an hour to take you to the airport for the flight.''

Alana had to rush to make it home, pack bags, and be ready to leave in time. She instantly regretted having included Matthew in the trip. He was so excited about going back to Maratonga so that he could see the animals and his friends at day-care, she dreaded the moment when she would have to tell him that the visit was only a temporary one.

The flight to San Diego was uneventful Angel and Matthew chattered with the pilot over the headphones, but Alana only heard bits and pieces of their conversation. She knotted her fingers in her lap and stared out of the window, wondering what she would say when she saw Jake Grisham again. She hadn't heard a thing from him since returning to Los Angeles and she knew it was his way of saying that their relationship was over.

If only she could tell her heart it was over. But she loved him now more than she ever had—and she didn't know how she was going to survive without him.

All too soon, she recognized the coastline where Wilhemena's beach house was located. Then, in the distance, she saw the swaying palms and the sprawling buildings of the Maratonga Behavioral Institute.

Although Alana loved her work as a therapist, she couldn't remember a time she had felt so excited about her career as those few brief weeks working with Nellie. And who would have thought such a thing would happen? That she would enjoy working with a gorilla as much or even more than any of her previous patients. It was strange, but she didn't even think of Nellie in terms of being an animal, per se. She was just Nellie. Sweet, adorable, lovable Nellie.

The helicopter touched down on the roof and the noise slowly decrescendoed to the soft *whup whup* of the blades as they spun to a halt. With an unconscious cry of delight, Alana noted that the whole team was waiting for her—Doc, Rusty, Rudy, Dino, Chen, and Rueben. Even Wilhemena and Neeley.

But not Jake.

"You go ahead, Alana," Angel said over the headset. "I'll take care of Matthew and bring him down to the lab. You go see that poor creature who's been asking for you."

Unbuckling her seat belt, Alana stepped out of the helicopter and hurried toward the team.

"What's wrong with Nellie?" she said as she rushed toward them.

"See for yourself," Doc said, sweeping his hand wide for her to enter the Institute. "She's in the outdoor habitat."

Alana hurried through the door and made her way through the twisted corridors to the rear door. But when she reached the gated entrance to the outdoor habitat, she discovered Wally and Nellie happily playing in the grass.

At the sight of her, Nellie scampered toward the bars.

Alana Here. Alana Come Visit Nellie. Nellie Happy.

Alana quickly greeted Nellie, conversing with the animal with the limited signs she knew, flattering her, telling her how pretty she was. But the longer she spent with Nellie, the more Alana began to feel that she had been brought here under false pretenses. Nellie wasn't pining away for her. She wasn't sad or distraught. She was happy and healthy and pleased with her new companion.

Alana See Jake?

Her stomach suddenly flip-flopped like a teenager about to go on her first date.

Had Jake arranged this? Had he set up this scenario to bring her here?

Her heart began to thump wildly in her chest, and she forced herself to ignore it. No. She mustn't jump to conclusions. She had no reason whatsoever to think that Jake had arranged for her to be here. For all she knew, it was his men who were doing a little matchmaking of their own.

The thought was disheartening enough to still the wild flurry of emotions.

This time, matchmaking wouldn't solve matters. It was clear that Jake was not ready for any kind of long-term commitment. Just as she could never settle for less.

Suddenly eager to collect her son and put this place

behind her, Alana bid goodbye to Nellie and strode back to the main building. If she hurried, the pilot would still be around and she could be back in Los Angeles by nightfall.

She met Rusty as he was coming down the staircase.

"Have you seen Angel?"

He gestured above him with his thumb. "She's waiting in your old office. Wilhemena never got around to clearing your stuff out. I think she hopes you'll become a permanent member of our staff."

Alana let that remark pass without comment. A sudden lump in her throat made it nearly impossible to speak.

No. She would not cry. She would not embarrass herself that way. She would collect Angel and her son and make her way back to Los Angeles.

Then she would cry.

It was while she was passing Jake's office that she suddenly stopped. She could hear his voice, so deep and dark and intimate, and her heart twisted in her breast.

Was she so needy that even the sound of him speaking could bring her to her knees?

Unable to help herself, she crept closer to the door and peered around the door frame. But what she found there, rooted her to the spot.

Jake sat on the couch, cuddling Matthew while the boy sobbed, "I'm sorry, Jake, I'm sorry. I hit you because I didn't want you to leave my Mommy. I want a Daddy. I want a Daddy really bad. But every time Mommy finds one for me, he leaves." Matthew's chest shuddered in a sob. "They always leave." His little fingers clutched at Jake's shoulders. "But I missed you when we didn't see you anymore. An' Mommy missed you. An'…an'…." Matthew broke into fresh sobs and clutched at Jake's neck.

Jake held the boy close and whispered against Matthew's ear, "I'll never leave you. It's my fault and I'll make it right. Somehow, we'll all be together."

A small cry escaped from her throat and she lifted a hand to stifle it, but it was too late. In that instant, Jake looked up. In his eyes she saw the glint of his own tears. For one brief, aching moment, Jake's vulnerability was plain to see, and Alana knew that Jake loved her, completely, overwhelmingly, and that he was willing to do whatever necessary to be with her.

Alana gripped the doorway as her body became limp with relief. The last of her doubts and fears melted away to leave her with a radiant joy. He loved her. Jake Grisham loved her. And even more importantly, he loved her son.

Biting her lip, she stepped into the room.

Holding Matthew close, Jake stood as well. Before she could even speak, he said, "I love you. I can't live without you. Marry me."

Alana's knees threatened to give way and she felt the cool path of tears begin to course down her cheek.

Knowing that her voice would emerge as a croak, she quickly nodded.

And then, before she could take another step, Jake rushed to enfold her in a one-armed embrace, his other arm still cradling Matthew against his chest.

As she clung to him, Alana felt his lips moving against her ear.

"I've been so miserable without you. I wanted nothing more than to drive to L.A. and get you. But I thought that Matthew would never accept me in your life and I didn't want to do anything to upset him. I knew you'd think I was some kind of bastard if I did. I can't give you any promises that I'll be an easy man to live with. My schedule can be demanding, my—"

Alana placed her fingers against her lips. "Living *without* you would be difficult. Living with you will be heaven on earth."

Jake bent close for a kiss, and Alana clung to him, knowing there were still so many things that needed to be said, so many details they would have to discuss—where to live, when to marry. But for now, all they needed was each other. This moment.

And the realization that they were about to become a family.

"SO? WHAT ARE THEY DOING?"

Rusty shushed the fellow team members who were huddled in the hall waiting for a report. Peering around the edge of the doorway, he whispered, "They're kissing."

"What about Matthew?" Angel said excitedly.

"He's smiling. I think he's excited about the developments."

"Well, of course he is," Wilhemena Bush said from the stairwell, causing the men to jump and straighten into a comical form of attention. "Why else do you think I brought them all together?"

When the men didn't respond, Wilhemena glanced at her assistant and gestured toward them. "They still don't get it, do they Neeley? I was never going to cancel Nellie's project—not on such a flimsy excuse as her inability to mate in a timely fashion." She sniffed. "You would think that with all of these scientific minds they would have realized that it wasn't just Nellie who had a problem. Frankly, you would think that it would dawn on them that their own project leader didn't date much, that he could never seem to settle down, and that the only picture displayed in his office is one of a little village in Africa and a certain freckle-faced woman. Imagine my astonishment when I discovered that she was the one and only Love Doctor and that she too had suffered from an inability to maintain a lasting commitment. The temptation to bring the two of them together was simply too irresistible.

"Really, gentlemen. How could you be so blind to the obvious? Nellie was never going to mate as long

as she had all of you to dote on her.'' Her brows rose.
''If I were you, I'd follow your team leader's example.
Granted you don't have to get married right away,
but...'' Her expression filled with an unaccustomed
humor. ''You've just managed to mate a very recal-
citrant gorilla. The least you could do is get yourself
a date!''

Everything But Anchovies

Susan Peterson

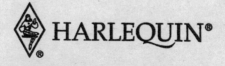

HARLEQUIN®

TORONTO • NEW YORK • LONDON
AMSTERDAM • PARIS • SYDNEY • HAMBURG
STOCKHOLM • ATHENS • TOKYO • MILAN • MADRID
PRAGUE • WARSAW • BUDAPEST • AUCKLAND

Dear Reader,

Romantic comedy has always been my favorite type of book or movie. The hilarious escapades of the hero and heroine as they fumble their way down the path to love are even better than chocolate...well, almost better. Humor is healing, uplifting and comforting.

In *Everything But Anchovies,* my heroine, Quinby Parker, is a lovable free spirit who is having a bit of a life crisis trying to decide what she wants to do with the rest of her life, especially since she's pretty much failed at everything she's ever tried to do.

Growing up in the Peterson household meant endless discussions about what each of us wanted to do with the rest of our lives. Every Peterson get-together has centered on the theme *What do you really want to do with your life?* Discussions have taken place over endless cups of coffee, with each sister taking her turn. I don't think I'll be taking my turn at our next reunion. I've finally found the thing I like to do best— storytelling.

I hope you enjoy Quinby's struggle to find her niche. Online readers can write to me at SPeter7836@aol.com and let me know!

Warmly,

Sue Peterson

To my mother, Beth, for your wonderful support and inspiration. You will never know how much your belief in me has meant. Thank you for being there and sharing in my struggles and triumphs.

1

QUINBY PARKER ALWAYS believed that making a good pizza was a lot like making love. Done right, it was slow and easy with a dash of spice and just the right amount of heat to melt things to a smooth consistency.

Unfortunately Quinby wasn't having much luck lately in the relationship department, and she had started to believe she'd lost her touch at weeding out the deadbeats and making a decent pizza.

She glanced up at the clock as she ladled another scoop of Mama Chen's secret pizza sauce over the dough. It was as if time had decided to crawl, leaving her with over an hour to go before Mama's daughter, Iris, relieved her.

This wasn't how she'd planned on spending her only day off. Tomorrow, she started the final two weeks of her field training, and filling in at the restaurant left her no time to prepare. Considering the poor quality of her two most recent job evaluations, Quinby knew she needed the time to get her head straight. If she didn't undergo some miraculous improvement, Quinby knew she was going to find herself kicked off the Brackett City Police Force.

She sighed and jammed the lid back on the plastic container. With one hip, she nudged open the door of the restaurant-size refrigerator and set the sauce on the middle shelf. As she slammed the door shut, she grabbed the heavy-duty lock off the counter and slipped it through the metal fitting. She snapped it shut with a firm click.

People always commented on the strangeness of keeping a pizza sauce under lock and key. But Quinby had learned early on that when Mama Chen told you to lock up the sauce, you locked up the sauce. Failure to follow Mama's orders put one at risk of getting a lecture, and Quinby would do anything to avoid one of Mama's lectures.

According to Mama, competing pizza franchises all across the city were after the secret of her sauce. Quinby was skeptical. She had a hard time believing that men with little plastic ladles waited around every corner, eager to rip off Mama's sauce. But over the years, she'd learned it was better not to question Mama when it came to pizza sauce.

Quinby paused, her hand hovering over the cheese bin. *Men hiding behind every corner waiting to steal sauce.* Interesting concept. Perhaps she should view this in a more positive light. Since finishing at the police academy and starting her six months probationary period with the Brackett City Police Department in upper New York State, Quinby's personal life had come to a screeching halt. After all, the sad reality of the situation was—no one wanted to date a cop. Especially one who was known to be somewhat of a klutz.

Quinby grinned. Maybe a few splashes of Mama's special pizza sauce behind her right ear would do the trick. If men were so all fired up to rip the stuff off, she might be able to snag a date or two with it.

Quinby dug some cheese out of the bin and sprinkled it over the sauce. Not much chance her best friend, Paige, would allow her to go anywhere smelling like a walking pizza. Unlike her, Paige, had standards.

Grabbing a wooden pizza paddle, Quinby slipped it under the pie and carried it over to the double stacked ovens. When she pulled down the door, a blast of heat hit her full in the face. She shoved the pizza in, slid the paddle under the bubbling pizza in the opposite corner of the oven and lifted it out.

"Is that for pickup or delivery?"

Quinby set the pie down on the cutting block and glanced over to see her former foster mother, Mama Chen, standing framed in the doorway leading to the main restaurant. Her small hands held open the swinging saloon style doors like she was entering a ballroom rather than a hot kitchen.

It never ceased to amaze Quinby. The woman was close to eighty, and she had the body of a forty-year-old. Her size and grace had always made Quinby feel like a blundering giant. In fact, the entire Chen family, all tiny, perfect humans, had the ability to make Quinby feel as if she was a lumbering elephant among a troupe of ballet dancers.

Quinby smiled and picked up the pizza slicer. "It's a delivery for Vito Bellini over on Eighth Street, Mama. Teddy is out on a run already, but Mac is due to report in—" she glanced up at the clock again "—at five."

Mama shook her head. "Mac just called in. He's sick and isn't coming in tonight." She reached behind her and pushed her fifteen-year-old grandson, Kenny, into the kitchen. "Kenny will finish the orders. You deliver the pizza."

Quinby slammed the knife down on the chopping block. "That's the third time Mac's called in this week."

Mama nodded. "He's finished. I'm finding a new driver."

Quinby groaned. With Mama's four sons out of town, her two daughters busy raising their families and the twenty or so grandkids too young to drive, it meant Quinby was left to fill in for the missing driver. Just what she needed to top off everything else wrong with her life right now.

Before all the parking and traffic tickets, she used to love doing the driving. It meant tooling around the city, racing the clock and the other drivers. Pure unadulterated excitement.

But those days were long over. Any more traffic tickets, speeding or otherwise, and Quinby knew she'd be cleaning out her locker down at the station.

"You sure we couldn't let Kenny do a few runs—just this once?" she asked hopefully.

Kenny's face immediately lit up. "Cool, Quin!"

Mama's wrinkles tripled as her expression settled into a disapproving frown. "Kenny's not old enough to drive. Don't be encouraging him, Quinby," she ordered. "I'll finish the pizza. You get your jacket. It's cold outside."

Grumbling under her breath, Quinby walked to the back of the kitchen to grab her battered leather jacket and beat-up old Met's cap out of the staff lockers.

As she headed out the door, she heard Mama say, "No tickets, Quinby. Drive slow."

QUINBY ROUNDED THE CORNER onto Macon Avenue and gripped the wheel so tight her knuckles turned white. The back tires skidded in the slush. She eased into the skid and straightened the car out. Darn but she was out of practice. She used to take this corner going forty-five on sheer ice.

The traffic was heavier, and she slowed to a crawl. A quick glance at the sidewalk revealed a good crowd of evening shoppers and the occasional loiterer. People were popping in and out of the stores, most likely returning unwanted Christmas gifts or cashing in their gift certificates.

In front of one of the city's less reputable clubs, a

group of men, clustered around the front door, were pointing and laughing. The object of their ridicule seemed to be an Amazon-size redhead in a short green dress pushing her way to the curb. She moved with a confidence and determination that contrasted sharply with the amusement of the men grouped out front.

Besides her size, the other startling thing about the woman was that she was the only one in the crowd without a coat. Seeing as the temperature was hovering at the twenty-degree mark, it seemed like a fairly off-the-wall thing to do. Curious, Quinby leaned forward to get a better look.

A flash of black fishnet stocking beneath the short dress forced a snort of laughter from Quinby. No doubt about it, the lady was an original. Fishnets had gone out with leisure suits.

She inched the car forward, trying to get a closer look.

The most impressive thing about the woman was the size of her calf muscles. Quinby figured someone should tell her to lay off the StairMaster for a couple of rotations. Either that or quit chewing steroids like they were after-dinner mints.

Looking up, she slammed on the brakes. She'd almost plowed into the back end of a taxi stopped for a red light. She could see the shift commander's expression now— *"And this makes how many traffic infractions this month, Parker?"*

Quinby shivered and tapped her thumb nail on the top of the steering wheel. The lady in green was standing just a few feet away, her arm raised to hail a taxi. Quinby smiled. *Good luck, sweetie. No one gets a taxi at this hour, especially looking like that.*

Cold air and flakes of snow slipped through the crack in the driver's side window. The rubber seal around the window was shot, making Quinby wish she could turn up the heat. But that was broken, too. She glanced in the rearview mirror and checked on the pizza. It sat squarely in the middle of the back seat. If it got any colder, she figured she could sit on Vito's pizza and warm herself. Of course, that meant forgoing the tip.

She grimaced. Who wanted a tip from Vito Bellini anyway. Two weeks ago she'd made a delivery at the meathead's apartment. Bellini had met her at the door buck naked and a wreath hanging from an appendage that wasn't on Quinby's wish list of things to see while delivering pizza.

Leaning down to coax another degree of warmth out of the wheezing heater, she jumped as the passenger door flew open and a pair of legs encased in fishnet stockings slid across the vinyl seat.

"Hey, what the heck—" Quinby sputtered as the car's springs sagged under the weight of the woman's bulk. Jeesh, she was built like a linebacker.

Quinby's protest didn't seem to faze the woman in the least. She pulled the door shut and glanced back over her shoulder toward the sidewalk.

Quinby frowned. Mama Chen had very strict rules about giving rides in the company vehicle. But when Quinby got a good look at the woman, she had to bite the inside of her cheek to keep from laughing. This was one butt-ugly-looking lady. She'd make the perfect *before* picture for electrolysis treatments. Obviously there was too much testosterone swimming around in this particular lady's bloodstream.

A ridiculous red wig, slightly askew, sat on her—his head. It dipped down in front to cover one very hairy, dark eyebrow. If her passenger ever plucked, it wasn't in this lifetime.

"I'm in no mood to argue. Just shut up and drive," her passenger said in a whiskey-smooth baritone.

Of course the voice confirmed Quinby's suspicions

that her passenger was a guy, and it certainly explained the five-o'clock shadow, the broad shoulders and the thick eyebrows. He extended a fishnet encased leg over the hump and a spiked heel slammed down on top of her foot.

"Hey, this isn't a taxi service," Quinby said as she tried to wiggle out from beneath the guy's foot.

"Too bad. I'm in a hurry, and don't plan on waiting another minute for one of those cabdrivers to pick me up. I need to get over to Beekman Street by five o'clock." He shoved a hand into an oversize purse and pulled out a fifty. "Get me there before five and this is yours."

Quinby swallowed. She still had her final $250 ticket to pay, and Vito's tip wouldn't even come close to this guy's offer. She looked up into his face. The most incredible brilliant blue eyes stared back at her from beneath caked on mascara.

"You might consider spending a little of that cash on a spa make-over? But if you're buying, I'm driving." She reached out to snatch up the bill, but tarantula eyes was too quick for her. He stuffed the bills down the front of his dress.

"*Oooo*, very clever," Quinby said. "Not much chance I'll be exploring the depths of that particular hideaway anytime soon."

"Pay attention to the road," her passenger warned.

She accelerated down Macon and beat the next light. Out of the corner of her eye, she watched him root around in his purse again. He yanked out a pair of well-worn jeans and a flannel shirt, tossing them onto the seat between them. A pair of beat-up work shoes followed.

"Having a bit of a gender identity crisis today, are we?" Quinby asked sweetly.

He reached up and pulled off the wig, revealing a

head of thick, black hair. The look he threw her was frosty. "Do you always have such a smart mouth?"

"Always."

Quinby turned onto the expressway, heading toward Beekman Street and suburbia. "Is there a reason we're trying to break a land speed record here or do you just like using strangers' cars as your own private dressing booth?"

He ignored the question and pulled the dress over his hips, struggling to get it up over his head. Quinby suppressed a giggle, taking in the odd sight of the pantie girdle with the padding to enhance his narrow hips and butt. A pair of falsies provided what he lacked up top.

Completely uninhibited, her passenger slipped the straps of the bra off his shoulders and peeled them downward. Quinby swallowed hard. Nice chest without the unnatural padding. He didn't seem in the least bothered by the cold air, his lean, hard body never shivering once.

Quinby sucked in a shaky breath of air. Lordy, she no longer needed the heater fixed. She'd gotten so warm, she could have slapped the pizza on her head to keep *it* warm.

The car swerved and hit the gravel at the side of the road. Never missing a beat, her passenger reached over with one hand, grabbed the wheel and steered them safely back onto the pavement. His other hand tugged the girdle down over his hips.

"I said keep your eyes on the road," he said.

"Not easy with you doing a striptease in the front seat," Quinby protested. "Shouldn't we at least be on a first-name basis?"

She tried without much luck to keep focused on the road, but her gaze kept wandering to the right. The guy was built. He buttoned the flannel shirt over a washboard stomach that would make one of the guys down at Tony's Gym weep with envy.

"The name's Reed. Sergeant Josh Reed. And you are?"

At the mention of his name, Quinby figured she might as well roll over and die. Things couldn't get any worse. Josh Reed was only the most decorated officer in the department. An icon. If she told him her name he'd probably recognize it as belonging to the idiot rookie on her way out of the department. Quinby didn't hold any illusions. People talked about her down at the station. He'd have to live in a cave not to have heard some of it.

In fact, she figured that on more than one occasion she'd been the talk of the locker room, and she constantly worried someone would find out she was the chief's illegitimate daughter. Now that would cause a few laughs. The great Chief Tennison's daughter washes out of the police department. Best to keep her mouth shut. The less he knew the better. She'd drop the guy off, collect her fifty bucks and forget about the whole thing.

Quinby watched him lift his hips up off the seat and slide out of the girdle. Now she was seeing a little too much of super cop Josh Reed. "Um… The lady in the car behind us looks like she's using her car phone to call the cops, and I think the guy next to us has swallowed his tongue. Is it really necessary to strip?"

Reed pulled worn jeans on over long, muscular legs and fastened the button. When he glanced up, he caught her stare. "I thought I told you to keep your eyes on the road."

He reached over and touched the wheel, his long fingers brushing hers and sending a blaze of heat up the back of her hand. Quinby jerked her attention back toward the road and overcorrected the van's drift toward the shoulder. As the van swung back toward the middle, the car next to her blasted an angry toot and accelerated past her.

Next thing she knew she saw blue and red lights flashing in the rearview mirror.

"Oh, shoot!" Quinby wailed. Now her goose was really cooked. The reflection of a Brackett City patrol car filled the mirror. The patrolman signaled for her to pull over.

"Go ahead and pull over. I'll handle this," Reed said.

Quinby flicked on her signal light and eased the van over onto the shoulder; the patrol car followed, pulling in directly behind her. She could see the driver leaning over to key in her license plate number into the computer, grab his hat off the seat and climb out of the car. He approached the driver's side window, but stayed slightly back out of her range of vision. Quinby was relieved he wasn't anyone she knew. She didn't need this one to get blasted all over the squad room tomorrow. The jokes would be unbearable. *Hey, Quinby, next time you try catching a little nookie in the front seat while on pizza delivery, you might want to pull over first.*

"License and registration, ma'am," the patrolman said.

Quinby jerked her wallet out of her jacket pocket and fished out her license. "Here," she said, shoving it into the patrolman's hand.

"Quinby Parker." His tongue turned her name over slowly, as if trying to remember where he'd heard it before.

Before he could continue, Quinby turned to Reed. "You mind digging the registration out of the glove compartment, Sergeant Reed?"

"Sergeant Reed?" The patrolman leaned closer, his

impertinent grin disappearing as quickly as it had appeared. "What the heck are you doing here, sir?"

Reed pulled the registration out of the glove compartment, leaned over and shoved it into the patrolman's hand. "Does it matter what kind of vehicle I choose to ride in, Officer Higgins?"

"No, sir." Higgins pushed up the bill of his cap and gave the documents a cursory glance before handing them back through the window. "Sorry I pulled you over. Your driver was all over the road. Not to mention that she was going at least fifty in a thirty-five zone."

Quinby glanced at her watch. Ten minutes to five, and they still had to get over the Plantation Bridge in the early-evening traffic.

Reed seemed to notice the direction her concern was taking. "She was going fifty at my request."

"She was driving erratically," Higgins said, obviously bent on defending his decision to stop her.

Reed scowled. "I was changing out of some undercover garb and knocked the wheel." He glanced pointedly at his own watch. "We need to make it across town before five."

Higgins jumped up, finally picking up on Reed's impatient tone. "Jeesh, Sergeant, why didn't you say so? Sorry I pulled you over. Forget I was even here."

Quinby closed her eyes and said a quick prayer of thanks. She'd dodged another ticket. Maybe her luck was changing. She snatched her license and registration back from Higgins and rolled up the window before he had a chance to change his mind.

"Thanks," Quinby said, pulling back out into traffic. "I can't afford another ticket right now."

"If you paid better attention to the road, you wouldn't get any." Reed pointed to a break in the flow of traffic in the left lane. "Squeeze in there. We're not going to make it at this rate."

Quinby could hear the tension in his voice. "Any particular reason that we're in such an all-fired hurry to get to Beekman Street? You late for a manicure or something?"

"My son is in a preschool program over on Beekman Street and parents are supposed to pick them up no later than five o'clock."

"I'll do my best," she said, taking a quick left onto Blake Avenue and heading for the bridge ramp.

Trying to brush off a stab of disappointment at the news that Reed had a son, Quinby guided the car up the ramp and merged with the other traffic. It figured. The best-looking guy she'd seen in a long time, and he had a son, which meant, given her luck, that he was married. She didn't hold out any great hope that he was interested in her or anything. That would be a little too much to expect considering her recent dry spell. But there was no denying her attraction to him.

Reed broke the heavy silence first. "Are you a student or something?"

When she shot him a puzzled look, he explained, "Well, most pizza delivery drivers seem to be students. They subsidize their incomes with a part-time job on the side. And half of them seem to be engaged in some kind of unofficial race to see who can deliver pizza the quickest. It understandably leads to a significant number of speeding tickets." He shot her an amused look. "I thought that might explain your rash of bad luck in the ticket department."

"Unfortunately I tend to drive fast whether I'm delivering pizza or not. Lead foot, you know." She hit the turn signal, accelerated and shot into the lane ahead of a Volvo coming up fast on the left. The driver hit the horn, but Quinby ignored him and sped up to avoid the long line of cars slowing for the next exit.

Reed slapped a palm against the dashboard. "What

are you doing? You're in the wrong lane. We need to get off at the next exit.''

"Not for long," Quinby assured him as she reached the head of the line of cars and aggressively nosed into the number two slot, ignoring the chorus of angry honks. They took the exit ramp a few seconds later. She shot Reed a triumphant look. "*Ta Da!* Sometimes driving like a maniac works."

"Sure, if you're looking to die young. Take the next left. The Standish Day School is the third block down on the right."

Quinby did as she was told, stealing a few glances over at Reed as she made the turn. His jaw was clenched, and he looked preoccupied. She wondered if now was a good time to tell him about the rouge and lipstick still on his face.

"Uh, you might want to—"

"There! Pull in behind that minivan," he interrupted.

"Okeydoke. Whatever you say." She pulled in behind the other car and jammed the stick shift into Park. She glanced down at her watch. "Ten minutes late. Sorry."

She watched him push open the door and untangle his long, lanky frame from the cramped front seat. She bit back a smile, trying to ignore the ridiculous red lipstick on the rugged-looking face. "Uh, I really think you might want to—"

"Hey, I'd love to chat, but I really need to get going. Thanks again, kiddo." He slammed the car door shut, effectively cutting her off.

Kiddo! He'd actually called her *kiddo*. Quinby slapped the edge of the steering wheel with the flat of her hand. Maybe she should have given him her name.

"Daddy! Hurry up, Daddy!" a small voice squealed.

Quinby glanced up to see Reed move up the walkway toward a little blond boy standing on the porch. The boy, dressed in an electric-blue snowsuit, jumped up and down waving.

The pinched-face woman standing next to the boy glared down at Reed with obvious disapproval. Reed seemed oblivious to everything but the boy. He bounded up the steps and gathered the little guy into his arms. A tall woman stood next to the boy, holding the boy's tiny, mittened hand tightly in her own. A decidedly unpleasant expression occupied her pinched face.

Quinby didn't doubt the woman would comment on Reed's bad makeup job. Hopefully it wouldn't cause him too much trouble. The guy seemed to have enough on his plate already. In any case, it wasn't her problem.

With a grind of gears, Quinby shifted into Reverse, backed up and pulled out. Time to get over to Vito's place with one stone cold pizza supreme.

2

JOSH PULLED OPEN THE FRONT door of Brackett City's police department and stepped inside. It had drizzled and snowed last night, creating an interesting mess on the streets. The salt pellets scattered along the front walkway by the janitor clung to the bottom of his well-worn work boots, crunching and crackling on the polished floor tile.

He stepped onto the heavy-duty, welcome mat and tried wiping the pellets off. No luck. Several kernels stuck stubbornly in the rippled groove of his soles. Josh shifted his gym bag to his other hand and tried knocking the side of his boot against the steel door casing. A few of the annoying pellets dropped onto the mat.

"Persistent little suckers, aren't they?" a voice observed.

Josh glanced up to see a tall woman with an amused twinkle lurking in the depths of her cinnamon-brown eyes standing directly behind him. She wore a beat-up leather jacket with the hem of her shirt hanging below the waist band. Her long legs were in a pair of faded jeans.

As she fidgeted under his scrutiny, two shapely knees poked between the frayed splits in the knees of her pants. She looked familiar, but Josh couldn't quite place her. It didn't matter because she was a pretty woman and well worth a second look. He straightened up and opened the door wider, standing back to allow her to enter first.

"If I try to walk down the hall with them on the bottom of my shoes, I'll take a header," he said. "They tend to act like little ball bearings."

The woman smiled and nodded, maneuvering around him. Her sleeve brushed his on the way past, and the light scent of fragrant soap wafted upward. Clean. Nice.

She stomped her sneaker-clad feet on the mat as she stepped into the entryway and turned to glance back at him. "Did you get into any trouble for being a few minutes late last night?"

Josh let the door swing shut. Of course. The pizza delivery girl. How distracted could a person get? Without the Mets cap, he hadn't recognized her. She was prettier than he'd originally thought. Great smile. Wide mouth. Full lower lip that she caught at one corner with her upper teeth.

Josh reached around her and opened the inside door leading to the lobby. "I caught a little heat from the head teacher. But it was worth it—Zack was happy to see me."

At the thought of getting chewed out by the uptight head teacher, Josh felt a flash of irritation. Definitely not the high point of his day. Especially on an evening when Zack was his and didn't have to be dropped off at his ex-wife's until bedtime.

"Can I ask a question?" she asked.

Josh grinned. "Curious about my outfit last night, right?"

She nodded, her curls bouncing up and brushing against her cheek. "You have to admit that it was a bit unusual."

"A perp I've been dogging for the past few weeks decided to hide out at The Purple Banana. I got tired of waiting for him to show his face, so I dressed the part and joined the crowd.''

''You get him?''

''Within fifteen minutes after entering the club.'' Josh answered her grin by widening his own, liking how hers played with one corner of her full lips. Sexy as all get out.

She stuck two fingers into the front pocket of her jeans and pulled out a crumpled fifty-dollar bill. ''You left the fifty bucks on the dashboard. I brought it in today, hoping I'd see you so I could return it. I didn't earn it.''

She pushed it into his hand, the touch of her fingers light against the side of his hand. A startling sizzle of heat shot up the length of his hand.

''I left it because you gave it a good try. It wasn't totally your fault that we were stopped.'' He laughed. ''I had a hand in that. Of course, if you hadn't been gawking at me while I changed you would have probably been able to keep the car on the road.''

''Hey, you were the one doing the flashing, cowboy. Besides, a girl's entitled to look.''

''See anything you liked?''

''Well, now that you mention it.'' She tilted her head to one side. ''I was going to ask you where you got that great push-up bra. I've been looking all over for one like it.''

He laughed and leaned forward to hand the bill back, but she backed away, holding up her hands to wave him off.

''I can't accept it. But thanks anyway,'' she said.

''You came all the way down here to the station just to bring it back?''

She shook her head. ''I work here, too.'' She held up a gym bag. The official emblem of the Brackett City Police Department was on one side. ''In fact, I work the next shift and need to get changed. Sorry again for making you late, Sergeant Reed.''

''No problem.'' As she turned to go, he reached out and stopped her, his fingers sliding into the crook of her arm. ''I remember Higgins saying your name was Parker. Parker what?''

The smile slipped a little, and she glanced away. ''Quinby...Quinby Parker.'' She gently pulled her arm out from beneath his.

Josh couldn't help noticing the slight tightening around her mouth. A definite sign of nervousness, as if she was suddenly apprehensive that the mere mention of her name was going to have a negative effect on him. He was sure he'd heard her name mentioned here at the station, but he couldn't remember in what context.

''Unusual name.''

The tenseness around her mouth seemed to relax again. ''My mother was a bit of a flake. She loved the rock song the 'Mighty Quinn.' Ever hear of it?''

He shook his head. ''Can't say that I have. I'm more the country type.''

He liked how her hair curled, the soft browns and gold twirling and corkscrewing all over her head in wild disarray. No wonder she wore a baseball cap—probably a failed attempt to tame the wildness. He wondered what her hair would look like caught up under a patrolman's cap. He suppressed a smile. Now that would be a sight.

''I've been pretty busy on a few cases so I guess we've missed each other up till now. When did you start?''

''A little over three months ago.''

''So you're still completing your field training?''

She nodded. ''This is my final two weeks.'' She smiled again and stuck several curls behind one ear. ''You've probably heard my name bandied about by some of the field instructors.'' Her nose crinkled a bit as she pulled a wry look. "You could say there isn't a mad rush to work with me."

But before he could ask why, she checked her watch. "Oops! I'm going to be late. Gotta go." She paused. "Maybe I'll see you around."

"Most likely," Josh said, thinking that he'd make sure they did.

With a quick wave, she turned and headed off down the hall, surefooted until she hit a particularly polished section of the floor. Josh watched as she skidded on the linoleum, and was jerked off balance. Her legs slid into a modified split, and she flailed outward with her arms trying to stay on her feet. No luck. She sat down with a hard thud.

Josh worked to hide his amusement and moved to help her up. But before he could reach her, Quinby jumped to her feet. She looked over at him, and Josh realized with surprise that she wasn't the least bit embarrassed.

Her eyes sparkled with merriment, and she burst out laughing, one hand rubbing her backside. "Not the first time I've ever been glad to have the extra padding back there."

He leaned down and retrieved her gym bag. "I could say something about nice padding, but it could be construed as sexual harassment so I'll just keep my mouth shut." He handed her the bag.

"Smart move, Sergeant. Don't ever comment on a woman's backside. Especially after she's just made a fool of herself."

Swinging her bag over her shoulder, Quinby ducked into the female locker room. The door swung shut behind her, cutting off his view.

Josh stood for a moment in front of the door, grinning like a fool. He liked how she hadn't turned into a trembling mass of embarrassment. She'd simply picked herself up, made a joke of it and moved on.

"You gonna hang around the women's locker room all day, Sarge, or do you think you have time to see the chief?" a voice interrupted his musing.

Josh turned to see Daley, one of the desk officers standing behind the reception counter and staring over at him, one eyebrow cocked.

"The chief wants to see me?" Josh said.

"He said to send you in as soon as you arrived." Daley jerked a thumb toward the hall leading to the administrative offices behind him. "He's been pacing the floor for the past hour."

Josh sighed. The chief's summons probably had to do with him leaving the scene of last night's arrest. Knowing the chief, he hadn't been too pleased to hear that a senior officer turned into Cinderella at the stroke of four-thirty and took off before all the reports were written. But then, Chief Tennison wasn't facing an irate ex-wife. An ex-wife bound and determined to move halfway across the country and thereby limit Josh's access to his son, Zack.

Josh stepped around the counter and walked down the short hall leading to the chief's office. Tennison's longtime secretary, Sandy, looked up from her typing and smiled sympathetically. She rolled her eyes behind her purple-framed glasses. From experience, Josh recognized the look. It meant Brad Tennison was in rare form.

"I hear he's looking for me," he said, resting his hand on the doorknob.

Sandy nodded, using one finger to poke at the bridge of her oversize glasses. "He started bellowing for you about thirty minutes ago. Go on in. I'll bring in some coffee and apple Danish. Maybe that will calm him." She grinned and stood up. "But don't count on it."

Before Josh could comment, she disappeared down

the hall toward the small kitchen off the reception area. Josh shrugged. No sense in avoiding the inevitable. He knocked and opened the door in response to the brusque command to "Enter."

QUINBY OPENED HER LOCKER and then ducked as something white catapulted out, hitting her shoulder as it sailed past. It bounced off the lockers on the opposite side of the narrow aisle and dropped to the floor. She leaned down and picked up the piece of elasticized material.

Quinby sighed. An oversize bra. From the looks of it, the thing had to be size 56 triple D cup. Where the guys had found one so big was beyond her comprehension. Probably someone's mother was going to be mighty unhappy when she found her bra missing from its spot on the shower rod.

Cautiously Quinby opened the locker door wider. A note, written in scrawling black letters, was taped to the back wall of her locker:

Next Time You And Sergeant Reed Decide To Do The Wild Thing, You Might Think To Try Lover's Lane Up By The Reservoir. It's Dangerous To "Get It On" While In A Moving Vehicle!

Quinby draped the bra over the top of the locker door and sat down on the bench to untie her shoes. Apparently Officer Higgins hadn't wasted any time letting his cronies in on the incident from last night. From personal experience, Quinby knew the jokesters weren't prone to let a minute go by without razzing someone, especially a hapless rookie like herself. Unfortunately Quinby knew she provided them with more than enough material.

"You forget to tell me that you were planning on implants?" a voice asked.

Quinby looked up to see her friend Paige tugging at the end of the gargantuan bra. "Yeah, it's for after I get fired from here and have to get a job dancing down at Sonny's Dazzling Dolls Club." Her grin quickly disappeared. "I'm worried, Paige. If there's one thing I don't need it's another job switch. My résumé is already too long to fit on one page."

"Stop that. You're going to make it through. You need to quit being so hard on yourself."

Quinby nodded. "You're right. I need to stop dwelling on the negative." She smiled again. "How was night shift?"

Paige sighed and dropped down next to her. "I'm beat. Riding around with Bull Michaels is not my idea of cutting-edge police work." She loosened the top button of her uniform. "All I've learned from the guy is which place sells the best Italian subs. And he's a slob." She rubbed the back of her neck. "There are so many sandwich wrappers on the floor of our car that we could open our own sub shop."

She used the toe of one foot to pry off her other shoe, and a smile of relief crossed her pretty face. "You and I could sell them out the side windows of our cars and make a fortune. We'd retire wealthy women."

"Yeah, and the way my luck has been running I'll be the one who gets caught, reprimanded and kicked off the force." Quinby stood up and unbuttoned her jeans, allowing them to fall around her feet. She left them there as she slid her shirt over her head.

For the first time, Paige noticed the note and leaned forward to read it. Her eyes widened with surprise. "You want to tell me what that's all about? Lover's Lane? You and the Iceman doing *the wild thing?* Obviously I've been living under a rock for the past few days. What have you been up to?''

"Nothing." Quinby bent down to snatch her jeans off the floor and shoved them into the locker, ignoring the fact that they missed the hook and settled in a heap at the bottom. "I played Good Samaritan last night and gave the guy a lift to pick up his kid. End of story."

She pulled the note off the locker wall, crumpled it up and stuffed it in her gym bag. "How was I to know the guy was going to disrobe in the front seat of my car. And considering the fact that I haven't been with a good-looking guy totally naked in…let me see—" she looked heavenward and then threw up her hands "—too long to even bother calculating, it was a wonder I showed as much restraint as I did." She resumed dressing.

Paige laughed. "*Sooo*, what's the verdict? Does he look as good out of clothes as he does in them?"

Quinby tucked her uniform shirt into her pants and pretended she didn't hear the question. She threaded her belt through the loops.

Paige poked her in the ribs. "I'm waiting…"

"For what?"

"For a detailed report on the Iceman's physique. Is he or isn't he as nicely put together as it would appear?"

"Oh for pity's sake! Is that all you ever think about— men's bodies?"

Paige's eyebrows shot up, and she burst out laughing. "And you don't?"

Quinby sighed and sank back down on the bench, her shoulders slumping. "He's built like a Greek god. An Adonis. It was all I could do to keep from drooling all over him." She dropped her head into her hands. "I was pathetic. So very very weak."

"Parker!" a voice bellowed from the other end of the locker room. "Officer Parker! Front and center."

Snapping to attention, Quinby stumbled over Paige's feet and rushed for the end of the locker aisle. She had no trouble recognizing the voice of her shift supervisor, Justine Cage.

"Here, ma'am," she said as she rounded the end of the lockers.

Cage stood at the other end of the room, hands on her hips and legs planted solidly apart. Every strand of her neat copper colored hair was in place. A pair of expensive shades hung by one stem from the corner of her front breast pocket—a pocket with a perfectly ironed crease down the middle. Quinby had yet to learn how to get that crease just right. Without fail, her crease always deviated slightly to the left.

"Don't bother rushing to make roll call, Parker. You've been placed on special assignment by the chief."

"I have?" Quinby glanced back down the aisle toward Paige who was peeking around the end of the lockers. Paige shrugged and ducked back. Unsure of what to say next, Quinby turned back toward Cage. "What kind of special assignment, ma'am?"

Cage frowned. "I'm not party to that information, Parker. I've just been instructed to tell you to meet downstairs in the garage. Your new partner, Sergeant Reed, will be filling you in on the rest."

"But—"

"I don't have time for this, Parker. Finish dressing and get downstairs. And you best be on your toes—Sergeant Reed doesn't suffer incompetence well." That said, Cage turned on one heel and left, leaving Quinby in the middle of the locker room more confused than ever.

IT WASN'T HARD FOR JOSH to see that his boss was having a hard time telling him what was bothering him. For several minutes after Sandy had delivered the coffee and danish on a small tray, the big man had made awkward small talk by asking mundane questions about some of Josh's recent cases without really showing interest in his answers.

"How's Zack?" Brad asked.

"He's good. We had dinner together last night at the Third Watch Grill. Zack entertained a few of the off-duty guys with his John Wayne walk."

Brad smiled and then sat forward, his expression serious. "Caroline still being uncooperative?"

Josh nodded, a sourness touching the back of his throat. Brad knew all about Josh's ex-wife, Caroline, and her intention to remarry and leave the state with her new husband. Josh was holding on to his rights as a father to see that Zack wasn't taken so far away that he'd only have the occasional vacations and summer visitation.

"She says that David has been offered a lucrative position with a large company in California."

"Good jobs are hard to come by," Brad said softly.

Josh nodded. "I realize that. But Zack is important to me. If he's thousands of miles away, our relationship changes. My influence on him diminishes. I can't accept that." The pain in his chest seemed unbearable. How could he explain to his friend and mentor that it felt as if Caroline was tearing his heart from his chest with the twist of her hand? He shifted uneasily. He couldn't, that's how. "We go to court in a few weeks to renegotiate custody and visitations."

"Her father meddling as usual?"

Josh snorted. "Meddling is putting it mildly. He's been pressuring me to back off. I'm surprised he hasn't come to you and tried to strong-arm you in some way."

Brad grinned, all teeth and steel. "Never said he

hasn't. I just know where all the bodies are buried so he isn't able to close the vise too tight.''

The sourness now felt like acid in Josh's stomach. Just what he needed. His ex-father-in-law, the mayor, trying to pressure his boss into getting him to comply with his spoiled daughter's selfish plans. ''I'm sorry you got dragged into this.''

Brad waved a hand. ''No need to apologize. I'm sorry I mentioned it. I can handle the mayor. You just concentrate on Zack.''

Josh shrugged and managed to paste a bitter smile on his face. ''I haven't laid down and rolled over yet. And I don't plan on it. Zack means too much to me to do that.'' For the first time, he noticed the distracted look in the chief's eyes. ''Enough about me. What did you really want to see me about?''

Brad took a quick sip of his hot coffee and then set it on his desk. ''I want you to take on a new partner.'' Before Josh could respond, Brad shifted his bulk forward in the chair, ignoring the creak. His well-worn face took on an unusual pleading look. ''I've got a rookie that needs your special touch.''

Josh shook his head. ''We've gone over this before, Chief. I've done my share of training new recruits. I'm not interested in baby-sitting at this point in my career.''

''I'm asking you to do this one as a favor to me.''

''Since when did I owe you a favor?''

''Since I've started giving you time off whenever you needed it to spend time with Zack.''

Josh's jaw tightened in anger. ''Don't even go there. I've put in more overtime than any other cop here in Brackett City with the exception of you.''

Brad held up a hand. ''Okay, okay. Forget I even said that.'' He took a deep breath. ''Look, Josh, I really need your help. Officer Parker is in danger of getting booted off the force. I think you're just the person to keep her on the straight and narrow.''

Josh sat back. Interesting. The pizza delivery girl with the wide mouth, sweet curves and wild hair. Now he seemed to remember a few muttered comments by a couple of officers around the station. Apparently Parker fit the mold of a classic problem rookie.

''If you have a screw-up on your hands, why are you scrambling around trying to keep her on the force?''

Brad sighed. ''Because she's my daughter.''

Josh sat back, not bothering to hide his surprise. He considered Brad Tennison a good friend, and as far as he knew, Brad and his wife, Peggy, never had any children. In fact, he seemed to remember hearing something about Peggy never being able to have kids. She had died two years ago from some type of cancer, and Josh knew for a fact that Brad hadn't remarried.

''Since when have you had a daughter?'' Josh asked.

Brad shrugged, his broad shoulders rolling beneath the freshly pressed creases of his uniform. He stood up and moved to the window, speaking with his back to Josh, ''Quinby's my daughter. No one here in the department knows that.'' He turned back. ''I had an affair with Quinby's mom back in the mid-seventies. When Peggy and I were going through a bad spell.''

Josh shifted in his chair, uncomfortable with the direction the conversation was going. Brad was his mentor. The man was like a father to him. In fact, the two of them had talked more than he had ever spoken to his own father. They had spent hours talking about their hopes. Dreams. Aspirations. But never about extramarital affairs.

He had always looked up to Brad Tennison. Saw him as *the Rock* when it came to marriage. In fact, Josh had sweated for weeks before telling Brad that things between himself and Caroline hadn't worked out, that they were getting a divorce. And now the guy tells him that he'd had an affair that produced an illegitimate child. This wasn't exactly the kind of conversation Josh wanted to be having with a man he thought of so highly.

"Look, Brad, none of this is my business. You don't have to explain anything to me." He stood up. "If you want me to take Quinby under my wing, I'll do it." Anything to get out of here.

"Sit down," Brad ordered. "I'm not finished."

Josh dropped back down into the chair and waited.

"I appreciate your loyalty, but you need to know a little bit about the situation." Brad grabbed his mug and took a gulp. "Quinby's done about every job a person can imagine—pizza delivery, data entry, dog groomer, jewelry store clerk, sanitation worker, plumber—you name it she's done it."

"Sounds like she's a tad confused about what she wants to do when she grows up," Josh said dryly. "She hasn't been so incompetent that she's been fired from all those jobs, has she?"

"Of course not." Josh could tell Brad was trying to hold on to his legendary temper. "She's just floundering. Trying to find her niche. I've been trying to help her get more focused—told her that being a cop is a good job." At Josh's raised eyebrow, he hastened to add, "It's not a bad job, Josh. It gives her security. Full medical insurance. A good pension. She could do a lot worse."

"Not if she isn't cut out to be a cop." He took a sip of his own coffee. "How much influence did you have on her decision?"

Brad spread his hands. "None. I told her outright that it had to be her decision. Quinby's the one who came to me and told me she'd entered the academy. She was adamant that I shouldn't cut her any special favors."

Josh rubbed the side of his face, trying not to let his

frustration show. "But from what you've said she's hanging by a thread. And now she comes begging for you to help."

Brad shook his head. "Not true. She doesn't even know I'm talking to you. She wouldn't be happy if she found out I was even thinking of interfering. Quinby has a bit of a stubborn streak." He ran a hand through his iron-gray hair. "But I'm desperate. I don't want her to fail at this."

"But maybe her failure is an indication that she isn't cut out for police work. You've told me a million times that not everyone can do this job, Chief. Why change your tune now?" Seeing the indecision on his boss's face, Josh pressed harder. "Are you sure it isn't because she's your daughter? That you feel guilty about all those years of neglect?"

As soon as the words were out of his mouth, Josh regretted them. The last thing he wanted to do was get involved in something that was obviously a personal issue. Hell, he had enough personal stuff on his own plate. The last thing he needed right now was to stick his nose into the chief's private anguish.

Brad pulled out his chair and sat back down. "You don't understand, Josh. The girl's got moxie. She's determined. She's bright. She did well at the academy, but now that she's out on the street, she's fumbling. I just want her to have a chance to straighten her life out."

Hating himself for backing off even a little, Josh asked, "What is she doing exactly that is getting her top billing on the termination list?"

Brad opened a file on his desk and shuffled through a stack of papers. "What hasn't she done might be the better question. She forgets to follow protocol while on call. She's insubordinate with her superiors and she's only passed her last weapon check by the skin of her teeth. Oh, and she keeps getting speeding tickets on her off-duty hours.''

Josh shifted in his chair and suppressed a grin, remembering Quinby's crazy driving last night and the close call that had almost garnered her another traffic citation. He glanced up at the clock and stood. "Look, I need to get going. I'll take her on after I tie up the Zander case. Put her on desk duty until I can free myself up. That oughta keep her out of trouble."

Brad closed his daughter's file and cleared his throat. "Sorry, Josh, I can't wait that long. I've taken the liberty of reassigning your other cases to Craig Branson. As of today, Quinby Parker is your one and only focus."

"What?" Josh snapped to attention, anger ripping up the center of his spine. "Do you have any idea how hard I've been working on the Zander case? Handing my cases off to someone else isn't acceptable."

Brad shrugged and sat back, apparently not in the least intimidated by Josh's anger. Instead he laced his hands behind his head, tilted his chair back and looked up at Josh with an unflappable expression. "Branson is perfectly capable of taking point on all your cases, including the Zander case. I'm more concerned about Quinby. And you're the only one I trust to do right by her."

"I'm honored," Josh said dryly.

Brad leaned forward and shuffled through the papers on top of his desk, pulling out a green file. "I'm assigning the two of you to witness protection. Apparently Oscar Pepper is giving his nurses the slip, and the district attorney is afraid he won't be available to testify when they need him on the Stanley case."

"Oscar Pepper witnessed a simple convenience store robbery—which I might add was a total joke as far as robberies go. The perp walked right into the arresting officer's hands. Why would Oscar need witness protection?''

Brad shrugged. "You know how these things are."

"No, I don't *know how these things are*. Explain it to me."

Brad's expression hardened, "Okay, fine. It's something you could do in your sleep. I'm not denying that. But the mayor of this city wants someone to make sure his father doesn't wander off and disappear before his daughter's wedding. And we're going to do what he wants."

Josh shook his head, not bothering to hide his disgust. "Why am I not surprised?"

"Look, Josh, all I'm asking you to do is check in on Oscar daily and make sure he behaves himself. You don't have to sit on the old man every second. Check in on him—make sure he doesn't wander too far. Patrol the neighborhood if you get restless. Just keep Quinby out of trouble."

Josh clenched his fist, struggling for control. "So essentially, you're asking me to baby-sit a bumbling cop and my ex-wife's grandfather?"

Red had begun to creep up the side of Brad's neck. "I'm not *asking* you to do anything. I'm ordering you to do it." He stood up, signaling there would be no further discussion.

"But I—"

"Can it! I'm done talking. Just do it." Brad waved off Josh's protest and stepped around the end of the desk to hand him the green file. "But whatever you do, don't let Quinby drive!"

3

QUINBY PACED THE NARROW aisle between two cars. Her thick rubber soles hit the cement floor of the department's underground garage with a resounding slap. As she passed the hood of her patrol car, she took a swipe at the antenna. An ounce of satisfaction shot through her as the thin wire twanged and vibrated back and forth in a wild arch.

"Of all the screwed up, asinine decisions! If he thinks for one minute that I'm going to—" She reached the end of the aisle, almost slamming into a wall of blue. Glancing up, she came face-to-face with the Iceman. He looked different in his uniform, intimidating. Solid. Immovable.

"Is this standard for you—stomping around garages and talking to yourself?" He spoke softly but with a touch of ice sliding along the edge of his tone. Gone was the easy humor with a light overtone of seduction he'd used on her earlier in the lobby. Obviously someone had filled him on what a screwup she was. Not hard to figure out who—her ever-loving father, who had all the faith in her that he did a captain of a sinking ship.

Quinby swallowed hard and lifted her chin. The Iceman's eyes were sharp blue stones of coldness. No big surprise there. Most likely he'd listened and bought the line of gossip about her, and now he was peeved at having to actually work with her. He was probably worried about tarnishing his perfect reputation.

"I was emoting. When I'm frustrated, I emote," she said.

Josh pulled a key chain out of his pocket and brushed past her, inserting the key into the door and popping the lock. "Well, don't." He nodded his head toward the opposite side. "Get in."

She shook her head. "I like to drive. I need the practice."

He turned slowly, one dark eyebrow lifting above his disturbing blue eyes. "You won't be sitting behind the wheel of any car I'm a passenger in until you pay off all your speeding tickets. And then you'll have to sufficiently convince me of your ability to drive safely. Are we clear on that?"

Quinby snorted. "Who do you think you are, my father?"

Josh laughed—a short, derisive sound, lacking even the smallest hint of humor or warmth. "Not by a long shot, Officer Parker. But I did promise the chief that I'd keep you out of trouble. So, for his sake, that's what I plan on doing."

Quinby's heart sank. Even though she had already suspected her father hadn't kept his side of the secret, Josh's comment confirmed that her father had broken his promise. "He told you, didn't he?"

"Yeah, he told me. Now get in the car." Without waiting for a response, he yanked open the driver's side door, slid behind the wheel and started a routine check of the equipment.

Quinby blew out her breath, feeling the hot flush of embarrassment flood her cheeks. So much for the strength of her father's promise. She had counted on him keeping that quiet. She didn't want her father getting accused of giving anyone special treatment.

Quinby turned and walked around to the opposite side of the car, pulling open the door and slipping into the passenger seat. She barely had her seat belt locked when the car slid into Reverse, and Josh backed out.

As he headed for the garage exit, Quinby asked, "I guess we'll be working your cases?" She had planned on keeping the hopeful note out of her voice, but it was there loud and clear.

He didn't even bother to glance over at her. "No."

Quinby sat silent for a few moments, hoping he'd fill in with an explanation. None was forthcoming. "Sooo, do you think maybe you could tell me a little about our assignment?"

"I've been yanked off all my cases. You and I are on special assignment."

Quinby perked up. Perhaps things were looking up. "Special assignment? Like an undercover operation or something?"

He shook his head and pulled out of the garage, steering smoothly into the flow of traffic heading downtown. "No. Nothing as exciting as that."

Again there was silence. Quinby waited until they stopped at the next light. "Are you going to tell me about it or am I supposed to guess?"

"We've been given the prestigious assignment of baby-sitting the mayor's father. Oscar Pepper is a witness to a holdup, and we're now his shadow."

"Wow. Must have been a big holdup, huh?"

"If you call some numb nut ripping off the local pawn shop with a Rocky Steller Laser Gun big stuff."

Quinby twisted in her seat to stare at him. "The suspect used a Rocky Steller Laser Gun as a holdup weapon? Would this be the same Rocky Steller Laser Gun they sell as part of the Rocky Steller Junior Space Warrior Kit?"

"That's the one."

She sighed and turned back around. "Don't get me wrong here, Reed, but this isn't exactly the kind of stuff

I expected to see you involved in.'' She shook her head in disbelief. ''Whether you realize it or not, you're the department hero. The cop we all look up to and want to emulate. Frankly, I'm feeling a bit let down here.''

''My heart bleeds for you, Parker,'' Josh said, his fingers tightening on the wheel. ''This is the mayor's way of getting the city to pick up the tab on an expensive baby-sitting assignment for his father. Oscar has a tendency to wander off, and the mayor is concerned the old guy won't make it to his daughter's wedding this weekend.''

He hit the accelerator as the light changed and sped through the intersection. Quinby jammed her feet against the floor of the car and braced herself. She shot a quick glance in Josh's direction, taking note of the tight muscle knot in his lean cheek. Apparently it was okay for him to take out his anger with a bit of fast driving.

Not that she could blame him for being mad. Quinby wasn't a fool. She knew the reason he was so angry. Her father had intervened, given him a directive to watch over her. Josh Reed had gotten the order to make sure she passed her final evaluation. And the special assignment he spoke about was a thinly veiled attempt on her father's part to make sure she didn't get into any more troublesome situations between now and the end of her training period.

It was almost laughable. The mayor was looking for a cheap way to make sure his father made it to a wedding on time, and Quinby's dad was looking for a safe way to make sure his daughter made it through her final few weeks of probationary period in one piece. It was a match made in heaven—two old warriors, who could barely say a civil word to each other, had struck a deal that benefited them both. Why even bother fighting it?

''Where are we headed?'' she asked, determined not

to sit in silence like some scolded child in the corner of the car.

"To meet with the mayor and our new assignment." He took the next corner with a sharp squeal of the back tires. "The mayor's waiting for us over at the Whispering Pines Retirement Community. His father lives there."

"We're really going to spend the next week watching some old guy?"

Josh nodded. "Technically we've been given the wonderful assignment of patrolling the retirement community and providing security for a witness to a crime. But since there's not a lot in the way of crime in the gated neighborhood, and no one is actually going to come after the mayor's father, I think it's safe to say that we'll become glorified sitters."

"Why doesn't the mayor just hire someone to watch his father? How come the chief is tying up two city employees with such a stupid request?"

"Good question. Perhaps the mayor can't afford to do something so rational." Josh seemed to push the words out from between clenched teeth. "Maybe the *wedding* of the century is costing our illustrious mayor more than he'd planned. Maybe the *wedding* of the century is eating into his reelection campaign."

Quinby glanced at her partner from beneath slightly lowered lashes. The way he'd spit out the word wedding twice made her think there was more to this whole thing than she'd originally thought. "Something tells me that I'm going to regret asking this, but who's getting married."

"The mayor's daughter." His fingers clenched the wheel again. "My ex-wife."

Quinby opened her mouth and then snapped it shut again. After a statement like that it might not be the best time for her to comment. Besides, what did one say after a revelation like that?

Of course, it did explain a bit about Josh's uptight attitude. Not only was he saddled with her, but now he had to baby-sit his ex-father-in-law's father while waiting for his ex-wife to get remarried. There was an interesting story somewhere in all that, but Quinby wasn't about to step into it without a flame retardant suit. Too dangerous. She sat back, content to wait it out.

LESS THAN FIFTEEN MINUTES later, Josh slowed the car as it approached the stone pillars and iron gate marking the entrance of Whispering Pines Retirement Community. A guard in a forest green uniform stepped out of the small booth to the side and approached the driver's side.

Josh lowered the window.

"Morning. You two the officers here to meet with the mayor?" he asked, bending down to look in.

Josh nodded.

The guard checked his clipboard. "He's at his father's place. Take the first right, it's the third unit on the right." He checked his watch and made a notation on his board, then stepped back and waved them on through.

"Pretty good security. I don't think we're going to have to worry about being overwhelmed by a crime wave," Josh said dryly.

He glanced over at his new partner. She sat facing straight ahead, her squarish chin jutted out just a bit, as if she was bracing for a lecture. She nodded but didn't comment or look over.

She'd been quiet since his little slip about his ex-wife. It would appear that he had inherited a partner who wasn't interested in prying. Unusual. In most cases, partners tried to glean every bit of information about their newly assigned co-worker. It was an attempt to understand the person who might someday hold your life in their hands.

Her silence was a relief, especially since Josh already regretted mentioning his relationship to Caroline. Or perhaps, previous relationship to her was a better description. In any case, talking about his ex-wife and the upcoming nuptials were not subjects he wanted to discuss with his new partner.

He pulled up next to a mailbox with the number 26 painted on it. They both stared at the neat little condo sitting next to a row of condos, which all looked exactly the same.

Pristine white siding with green shuttered windows. A small attached garage and a postage-size front lawn was the extent of home ownership for residents of Whispering Pines Retirement Community.

Most of the owners had attempted to put some mark of individuality on their unit by setting out an interesting array of lawn ornaments and seasonal decorations. Several front doors sported Christmas wreathes or some type of cutesy welcome signs. A few still had tree lights twinkling cheerfully in the window.

Oscar had gone for an interesting touch of originality with his own place. Josh had to stifle a laugh. A group of cute gnome figures were scattered across the snowy front yard. But Oscar had positioned the gnomes to look as though they were engaged in an activity not usually sanctioned by the local lawn and garden club. Josh figured that the old guy had irritated more than a few neighbors with the display, and he wondered how long before the owners' association was over to take it down.

Josh grabbed the door handle. "Okay, let's get this over with."

Quinby preceded him up the salted walkway, and Josh couldn't help noticing how nicely she filled out the back end of her uniform pants. He frowned, disturbed with the direction his thoughts were traveling.

Admiring his partner's backside was not okay. Maybe Oscar's gnome display was sending out some kind of subliminal message.

Josh's thoughts were interrupted by the front door opening. The mayor stood in the entryway, an impatient expression on his pudgy, boyish face.

His sharp gaze jumped past Quinby and hit Josh head-on. "You're late. What did you do, stop for doughnuts and coffee?"

A familiar irritation flashed through Josh. The man never let up. He gently shouldered Quinby aside and stepped into the entryway, using his size to tower over his former father-in-law. "Yeah, there's a dozen out on the front seat of the squad car. I figured we'd need them for this dangerous and all important stakeout of your father's house. Where is he?"

"He's gone," the mayor snapped. He brushed past Josh and Quinby and headed into the tiny living room off the hall entryway.

Josh motioned for Quinby to go ahead of him. When the mayor glanced at her for the first time, he said, "This is my partner, Quinby Parker. Quinby, our illustrious mayor, Sterling Pepper." He folded his arms. "Where'd Oscar go?"

The mayor ignored him and moved in on Quinby like a shark sighting its prey. The old goat hadn't changed one iota. He took her hand and held it between his, all the while making serious eye contact with her. "It's a pleasure to meet you, Officer Parker. I must say, you look a sight better than Josh in our city's new uniforms."

"Thank you, sir," Quinby said politely.

"Do you like the cut of the shirt? I ordered the designer to be especially sensitive to the needs of our female officers.''

Josh took great pleasure in the fact that Quinby's shoulders stiffened, and she snatched her hand back like a mouse running from the slam of the trap.

"A uniform is a uniform, sir." Quinby didn't hide the fact that she blotted the palm of her hand on the side of her trousers. "But it does remind me to ask, how are the new suits for city politicians? I hear they give them a special cut for those of you who lack a set of ba—"

"Perhaps, we could forego the fashion review and get down to business," Josh interrupted, trying without much success to hide his grin.

The mayor carefully smoothed over a look of irritation and moved to sit on the couch, motioning for them to join him. He patted the cushion beside him and glanced pointedly at Quinby. She ignored him and took the chair closest to the door.

Josh took the chair between them. "When did Oscar turn up missing?"

"He wasn't here when I arrived for breakfast this morning." The mayor picked a piece of lint off his gray slacks with two fingers and flicked it on the floor. "He knew I was coming. He does this just to irritate me."

"Is there some reason that your father wouldn't want to be here when he knew you were coming, sir?" Quinby asked, pulling out her notebook and resting it on one knee.

"He has good sense?" Josh quipped, garnering himself a hostile glare from Sterling.

Quinby didn't react. She sat on the edge of the chair, her back straight, her eyes alert. Josh figured the demonstration of unflinchable cop was for his benefit. Hard to believe she was having any difficulties getting through her rookie probation with an attitude like this. It was exemplary.

"As Josh will testify, my father is a bit of an eccentric. I've told the staff numerous times that they need to keep an eye on him. But as usual, they screwed up."

"He slipped out while I was showering," an indignant voice said.

Josh looked up. A middle-aged woman dressed in white stood in the doorway. Obviously the nurse who'd been given the slip. She folded a pair of muscular arms over an ample chest, her thick features composed into an irritable frown. Josh was pretty sure she wasn't the type of person who offered Oscar a pleasant back rub when bedtime came around. Or if she did, Oscar probably had the good sense to pass it up.

"This is Bea Crandall," Sterling said. "She stays with Dad and tries to keep track of him. She figures that he snuck out some time this morning or last night."

"We'll need a list of Mr. Pepper's friends—people he might have gone to see when he left here last night," Quinby said.

Bea snorted with ill-disguised disgust. "Any woman who glances in his direction is fair game. You might try the beauty shop or the bowling alley. He tries to pick up women in both those places." She glanced at the mayor, her face pinched. "Frankly, sir, that father of yours is depraved. He's like a dog in heat."

"You don't need to tell me," Pepper said. "The man is a total embarrassment. I can only be happy my sainted mother isn't here to see this disgrace."

Tired of getting nowhere, Josh stood up. "Look, we'll check some of these spots you've mentioned and get back to you. If Oscar shows up before we get back, call the station and let them know. They'll radio us, and we'll head back here." He nodded at Quinby. "Let's go."

She snapped her notebook shut, stood up and silently accompanied him out the door.

She waited until they were on the sidewalk outside before commenting. "Do you have any idea where to start looking?"

"Not really, but the thought of staying in there and hearing the old guy dragged through the mud didn't appeal to me. This way we can hit a few of his favorite hangouts, and knowing Oscar, he'll probably turn up at the Wrigley's Diner over on Rosemont by noon."

Josh rounded the hood of the car and pulled open the door. He glanced at her over the roof. "We'll head there around lunchtime and probably be in time to see him chowing down on a Philly steak smothered in onions."

Quinby nodded without comment and slipped into the car. Josh frowned and wondered why the sudden silent treatment. It wasn't as if he was the one responsible for getting them tied up with such a tedious assignment.

He ducked his head and climbed into the cruiser, surprised when he caught the scent of soap and vanilla wafting through the air trapped inside the car. Josh didn't think his squad car had ever smelled like vanilla. Sweaty socks maybe, but never vanilla. A man could get used to such a smell.

"SO HOW MUCH IS MY FATHER going to end up owing you for volunteering to do this baby-sitting job?" Quinby asked after a few minutes of silence.

"Baby-sitting? You mean you or Oscar?" Josh asked agreeably.

Quinby jammed her elbow up on the window ledge and with a stone face stared out the windshield. "Me of course. Oscar's eighty. At eighty you can afford the public embarrassment of having someone assigned to look after you."

She glanced over at him and immediately regretted it.

His profile beneath the visor of his cap was carved out of cool stone—classic male beauty. She swallowed hard and faced forward again.

"Even on a bad day, Oscar doesn't need anyone looking out for him," Josh said. "The old coot is slicker than grease on metal."

"Great. So that means this is all really an elaborate ruse to watch over me and to keep me from hurting anyone with my bungling attempts to be a cop, right?"

He turned to give her an assessing look, the sharpness of the stare so clear and pointed that it almost sucked the air out of her lungs.

"So it would appear," he said, facing forward again, the line of his jaw never loosening.

"At least you could have the decency to lie," Quinby snapped.

"Why would I do that?"

Quinby stared at him for a moment, opening and closing her mouth several times before deciding that it really wasn't worth the effort. She cracked the window a little before asking, "So why did you agree to do this? Couldn't be fear—I can't see you worried that my father might ruin your career. And you're not the kind of guy who would do it out of the goodness of his heart."

He turned his head toward her again. A mild look of amusement played with one corner of his mouth. "You wound me, Parker. What makes you so sure I'm not doing this because I believe in helping hapless rookies and old men?"

"Because Dudley Do-Right you're not. There has to be something in all this for you or you wouldn't be doing it."

"You're pretty sure of yourself, aren't you?"

"I might be a bit of a screwup, but I pride myself on my ability to figure out my fellow man."

"Your father has always stood by me. I'm doing this for him." He pulled up to the curb.

Two women standing on the corner shifted positions from a half-slouch to attention and glared at the patrol car. The closest, the one wearing a tube miniskirt, mid-thigh shiny black boots and a well-worn leather jacket, scowled, and then, just as quickly, a wide smile broke across her elegantly made-up face. She hitched her over-the-shoulder bag higher and sashayed over to the car with a hip-swinging swagger that would put out the eye of a gawker within two feet.

"Roll down your window," Josh ordered.

Quinby did as she was asked.

The woman rested her hand on the top of the car and leaned down. "Well, well, well, if it isn't the devastatingly handsome and infinitely braver, Sergeant Joshua Reed." Her breath smelled of cool mint and cigarettes. "Reed, honey, you really need a fashion consultant. I heard you were racing around downtown last night in full drag. Word is your jewelry clashed with your outfit. A man could ruin his reputation with a review like that."

Josh smiled, a genuine twinkle splintering the blue ice of his stare. He leaned across the seat to greet their visitor. Quinby wedged herself closer into the corner of the seat, unsure how she was going to handle him leaning so close that he was practically on top of her.

"How's it going, Alice?" Josh said. "You and Caro staying out of trouble this early in the morning?"

"We're headed over to Wrigley's for a cup of Joe and a plate of his fatty bacon. Care to join us?" Alice flicked a look in Quinby's direction, and the contempt in the look told Quinby she wasn't included in the invitation.

"Maybe later. I have a few things to do first. Have you seen Oscar during your travels this morning?"

Alice laughed. "Not since Saturday when he hobbled past and hit some jerk with his cane. The guy was hassling Caro, and Oscar gave it to him right between the slats. You should have seen that creep scream." She reached up and wiped the corner of one eye. The twenty or so silver bracelets on her arm jangled merrily. "Caro gave Oscar a good smack on the lips, and Oscar toddled off as happy as a clam, a dazed look in his eyes."

Josh nodded. "Okay, just checking." He sat back up and Quinby wished he'd stayed leaning across her. His aftershave was a definite improvement over Alice's perfume.

As if she knew what Quinby was thinking, Alice braced an ample hip against the side of the car and gave her the once over. Her red lips and white teeth moved diligently around a wad of green gum. It snapped and crackled. "I thought you were the proverbial Lone Ranger, Reed. Who's the new blood?"

"This is my new partner, Officer Parker. Quinby, this is Alice. She's the chief distributor of love over here on Stiller and Vine."

Alice threw back her head and roared, giant puffs of vaporized air floating upward out of her red mouth. "Oh, that's rich, Reed. I'm chief distributor of love." She glanced over at the other woman, leaning against the telephone pole, a bored expression on her artfully made-up face. "You hear that, Caro?" Alice called. "Reed called me the—"

"I heard him, Alice. You're only two feet away." Apparently Caro wasn't in the same friendly mood as her friend. She threw her cigarette down and ground out the glowing tip with the heel of her three-inch spiked shoe. She turned her back to them.

Alice shook her head. "Girl's got a bad attitude. Gonna get her in trouble one of these days." She pushed off the side of the car and it rocked gently on its springs.

"Nice to meet you, Officer Parker. Don't let the Iceman scare you, girlfriend. He tries to hide it, but he's got a tongue so sweet that a girl could die of sugar shock before she hit the pavement in a swoon." She blew Josh a kiss and sashayed off.

Quinby rolled up the window. "Seems you're a real favorite with the working girls."

Josh eased the car away from the curb and into the flow of traffic. "A good cop needs to know everyone on the beat. Alice has given me more than one good lead during the time I've known her."

"Where do we go now?"

"We'll try the Sweetness Salon over on Reilly Avenue. Sometimes Oscar goes over there to entertain the ladies."

"Your ex-grandfather-in-law hangs out in a beauty shop?"

"Oscar fancies himself as a bit of a ladies' man. Wherever there are women, you'll find Oscar."

"Sounds like the apple doesn't fall far from the tree."

Josh quirked an eyebrow. "Meaning?

Quinby shrugged. "I'd hazard a guess that the mayor fancies himself somewhat of a ladies' man too."

Josh reached over and adjusted her visor, blocking out the late-morning sun, which had started to hit her face. She nodded her thanks, and she could immediately tell that Josh had done it absently, without even realizing he was doing a good deed until it was over. Perhaps he wasn't as hard-nosed as everyone seemed to think.

"Oscar isn't anything like his son," Josh said gruffly. "Oscar's got actual charm. That's something our illustrious mayor hasn't got on a good day."

4

WITH A QUICK FLICK OF HIS wrist, Josh sent the car into a quick, tire screeching U-turn in the middle of the street. Out of the corner of his eye, he saw Quinby brace herself with a hand against the front dash. She shot him a look of annoyance. Obviously she didn't appreciate being caught unawares.

He suppressed a smile. He couldn't help but like the flash of anger in the depths of her warm brown eyes whenever she was ticked off.

A few minutes later, he pulled into a parking slot right in front of the Sweetness Salon. Josh glanced over at Quinby as he unbuckled his belt. She studied the sign, looked at him with a raised eyebrow and then sighed and climbed out. Josh reached into the back seat and pulled out a canvas bag. A quick glance at the shop window told him that the salon was packed.

As he climbed the steps to the entryway, he smiled. He wondered how Quinby would react to Sweetness and his partner Jeb. Pushing open the door, he stood aside to let Quinby step inside. She came to an abrupt halt right inside the door.

As usual, Sweetness stood at the first station in the front of the salon. It was the most visible spot, allowing anyone and everyone entering the establishment to lay eyes on him first. Josh knew Sweetness liked it that way. It gave Sweetness a chance to get a look at anyone coming in, and even more importantly, it allowed the customers to get an eyeful of Sweetness before they saw anyone else in the salon.

As soon as he spied Josh, Sweetness threw down the curling iron he was using on his customer and clapped his thick-fingered hands to his lips. A collection of gaudy cocktail rings glittered on every finger. "Joshua!" he squealed.

Every head in the shop turned to stare at them.

"Mornin', Sweetness," Josh said. "How's the hair business?"

Sweetness threw back his huge head, his curly hair a brilliant red this week. He cupped a hand to the corner of his mouth and glanced over his shoulder in the general direction of the back of the shop, looking as if he was getting ready to tell some deep, dark secret. "Things are so good, Josh, that Jeb and I are getting ready to open another shop up in Lake Placid. A hoity-toity shop this time."

Out of the corner of his eye, Josh saw Quinby's eyes widen in surprise, her shock probably coming from the fact that she was face-to-face with a seven-foot drag queen. Josh didn't bother to hide his amusement.

He loved watching the reactions people had to Sweetness, almost as much as Sweetness did. And while he was at it, Josh had to admit that the fact that it was Quinby standing there gawking made the surprise all the more fun. Unlike others, Quinby didn't seem the least put out by Sweetness's uniqueness. Only curious.

As if on cue, Quinby turned and whispered out of the corner of her mouth, "Looks to me like you've got some serious competition, Josh. He looks better in a dress than you do."

"No way," Josh said. "When did you become a fashion critic?"

"Since I witnessed your legs in fishnets."

Oblivious to their side comments, Sweetness sauntered over, his huge bulk straining and bulging every inch of his purple sheath dress. "Did you bring back the wig I loaned you?"

Josh handed him the bag. "The dress and the other…um…items are in there, too."

Sweetness took the offered bag and beamed. "I can't wait until I wear the wig to my next party. I'll be able to tell everyone it's *the* famous wig. The one that was used to catch some scumbag." He reached out and patted Josh's cheek. "However, I got word back from a few people that your walk was entirely too butch. We really are going to have to work on your presentation, Josh honey."

He pranced, showing off an astounding amount of gracefulness for such a large man. "This is how it's done, honey." Sweetness paused, sashayed back and slapped a hand on Josh's shoulder. "But not to worry. You weren't a total flop. All the boys were calling or stopping by this morning to see if you were available and what your phone number was. Of course I pumped you up big time—told them they needed to get a look at you in your uniform."

Beside him, Quinby burst out laughing.

Josh smiled amicably back at Sweetness. Although the conversation had taken a rapid turn for the worse, he knew better than to give the big guy any indication that he was bothered by it. "Well, I wish I had time to exchange phone numbers, but we're here looking for Oscar. Has he stopped by today?"

Sweetness pursed his lips. "I haven't seen him, but let me check." He headed for the back of the shop, bellowing as he swayed on his heels, "Jeb! Have you seen Oscar this morning?"

Quinby leaned closer and whispered, "Sounds like you were a real hit at the club last night, Josh. Ever think about doing a bit of moonlighting?"

"I'll bet the tips beat delivering pizza any day," Josh shot back. "Maybe you should give it a try. You'd have those speeding tickets paid off within a week." He smiled, putting a bit of the shark into it. "Want me to ask Sweetness if they allow skinny women to dance there?"

Quinby snorted. "That'll be the day that I'm described as skinny. But if there are any openings—" she grinned back with a touch of sass "—let me know. You never know what I might do."

Josh groaned. "That's exactly what your father is afraid of—more jobs to flesh out your already overdone résumé."

Quinby's eyebrows lowered a touch over her brown eyes. "When you've scrounged around for money as much as I have most of my life, any job is a blessing." She tilted her head up and smiled again. "Although I haven't tried exotic dancing…yet."

Even though she quickly hid it, Josh was surprised at the flicker of hurt he saw dart across Quinby's face. There was more to this issue of Brad Tennison having an illicit affair than he'd originally thought.

"Sorry, I hadn't realized things had been so tough for you," he said quietly.

"Yeah, well maybe your good buddy, Chief Bradford Tennison, doesn't belong up on the pedestal you've put him on." Quinby shrugged the incident off as if angry at herself for putting a voice to her resentment. She moved away to talk to a few of the women sitting in the waiting area, checking to see if any of them knew about the location of a man named Oscar Pepper.

Although she spoke in low tones, Josh could see that she held her spine ram rod straight. He couldn't see her hands, but Josh had a strong feeling they were clenched in tight fists. An unmistakable tug of appreciation for her toughness pulled at him as he stared at her, but he quickly pushed it aside. She was a screwup. He didn't need to get involved with a screwup.

"Pretty little thing."

Josh turned to see Sweetness standing beside him. He'd been so involved in staring at Quinby that he hadn't even heard him return. "She's my new trainee."

Sweetness raised an eyebrow and then winked. "Trainee? Is that what they call them now. Well, from the sauciness of her tongue, I'd hazard a guess that she's keeping you on your toes." Sweetness nodded his head toward the back of the shop. "Jeb says howdy. He's in the middle of a full-body massage—some stressed-out magazine editor. But he says he hasn't seen Oscar in days."

"Any idea where he might be hanging out? The man's supposed to be in protective custody, and he's out running around."

Sweetness shook his head. "Oscar don't like no one messing with his freedom. Did you check out the Diner?"

"We're headed over there next."

"Where's that?" Quinby asked, walking back over. She nodded toward the women. "None of them have seen Mr. Pepper."

"Are you going to show some class and actually introduce me to your new partner, Josh?" Sweetness asked, shoving a hand on one meaty hip and thrusting his pelvis forward as if he was some rail-thin runway model.

"Quinby, this is Stephen Sweet aka Sweetness. He and his partner, Jeb, own the place."

Quinby stuck out a hand. "Nice to meet you, Sweetness."

Sweetness's huge hand engulfed hers, and she stumbled slightly as he yanked on it and pulled her in close. "*Oooo,* girl, I could make you sparkle," he cooed.

Unsure how to react, Quinby stuck an errant strand of hair behind her ear and stepped back. The big guy had pulled her in really close. "Thanks, but there isn't too much call for cops to sparkle."

"And that is a shame. From the looks of the few lady cops I've seen driving around town, it isn't hard to see that you all need a little help. Nothing worse than a drab-looking lady cop. Men—they're hopeless." Sweetness reached out and patted Josh's right biceps. "All except Josh, of course."

"Leave her alone, Sweet. She looks just fine," Josh said.

"Sure she looks fine, but I could make her glitter." Sweet wrinkled his nose and reached out to tug on several strands of hair that had escaped from beneath Quinby's cap. He shook his head. "Dry as a desert bone, girl."

Quinby shrugged, not sure how to respond to a comment based on the dryness of her hair. "Uh…it must be hereditary. My mom had dry hair."

Sweetness rolled his eyes and then turned to study the shelves of beauty products behind him. "Nothing is unfixable, honey. Just think if I'd settled for what I'd been stuck with." He smiled and smoothed a big hand down along the sides of his bulky body. You can't imagine how hard I've worked to create this image of loveliness."

"Too scary to even contemplate," Josh said. He ignored Sweetness's glare and asked again, "We're not here for a beauty consultation, Sweetness. All we want to know is whether or not you've seen Oscar lately?"

"That eighty-year-old Casanova usually hangs around here hitting on all my customers." Sweetness reached up and pulled a white plastic bottle with a silver domed top off the shelf. "He gets the ladies giggling so hard that no one ever gets anything done. But he's harmless.''

He tapped a claw-shaped red nail against his top teeth, a frown popping up between his perfectly plucked brows as he contemplated the back of the bottle. Quinby wondered how he got them so perfect. Whenever she tried to pluck, she ended up writhing on the bathroom floor. Paige called her a pathetic wimp and was forced to hold her down in order to pluck.

''Here. This is what you need,'' Sweetness said, trying to shove the bottle into Quinby's hands. ''Otherwise you're going to be bald by the time you're fifty.''

Quinby tried to shove the bottle back into the hands of the bear-sized hairdresser. ''I can't take this.''

''Sure you can, honey. I'm givin' it to you.''

''You don't understand, I can't accept anything—''

''Just take the bottle, Quinby,'' Josh said wearily. He pulled a twenty-dollar bill from his wallet and plunked it down on the counter. ''Could we just get out of here? We still have a few other places to check.''

Sweetness grabbed a silver bag out from beneath the receptionist's counter, artfully stuffed a sheet of white tissue paper in it and set the bottle of conditioner into the center of his creation.

He paused and glanced at the two of them, a small smile curling the corners of his rosebud mouth. Nodding to himself, he reached under the counter and slipped another tiny bottle into the bag. Extending an elegantly manicured hand, he handed the bag to Quinby.

''I've added a few ounces of my favorite massage oil in case Josh ever stops by your place for a little after-duty instruction.''

Quinby grabbed the bag and tucked it under one arm, trying to ignore the fact that her face was heating up to the temperature of the midday sun. She didn't dare look at Josh.

"Thanks," she mumbled and headed for the door and some much-needed cool air.

THE MIDDAY SUN HIT THE metal skins of the cars parked out front of the beauty salon and threw up sparkles of light that was almost blinding in their intensity. Josh reached up and slipped his shades into place.

In spite of the sun, the temperature still hovered around the thirty-degree mark. He zipped up his jacket and glanced over at Quinby. She was taking deep breaths of cold air. Either trying to clear her nose of the smell of perm chemicals or attempting to forget the fact that she'd turned the shade of a ripe tomato in response to Sweetness's comment about the massage oil.

Josh grinned. "You left too quickly. Sweetness wanted to make an appointment for you to come in on your off hours for a color treatment."

Quinby squinted in the bright light and shook her head. "Are you nuts? I wouldn't let that guy color my worst enemy's hair."

"So now you're an expert on hair coloring?" Then with an exaggerated groan, Josh hit his forehead with the palm of his hand. "Oops, I forgot—you are an expert on hair, too, aren't you? How long was it exactly that you worked as a hairdresser? A week? Two? A month?"

Quinby's jaw tensed, and her stare sliced through him. "I worked as a shampooing assistant for a month when I was nineteen. I never claimed to be an expert."

"Stamina, Parker. Life is about stamina and endurance. Learn that and you'll last at this job a lot longer than you have in any of the fifty or so jobs you've held over the years." Josh shot her a tight smile and then, stepped off the curb. As he opened the driver's side door, he said, "Get in. We'll get some lunch, and if we're lucky, we'll run into Oscar."

Quinby nodded, her cheeks still suspiciously pink and climbed into the car.

A short time later, they pulled up to the Wrigley Diner. It sat on the corner of the intersection of Belmont Avenue and Main Street. At one time, it had sat smack dab in the middle of a bustling residential area. Nowadays, it was considered to be on the wrong side of the tracks. It hadn't always been that way.

Josh's memories of the diner were long-running. Even as a kid of seven or eight, his father had brought him down to the greasy spoon every Saturday for breakfast. It had been the highlight of Josh's week. Breakfast with Dad.

Not that his father had really paid all that much attention to him. Dek Reed was more interested in the other guys who haunted the diner during the early Saturday morning hours.

Dek would lift Josh up with his big hands and plop him on top of one of the red cushioned stools at the counter. The waitress, the one with the blond, beehive hairdo under a hair net and a tendency to tweak Josh's cheeks every time she passed, would slap down two oversize platters of fried eggs, bacon and toast with jelly.

As his father laughed and joked with his pals, Josh would sit on the stool, his legs swinging back and forth, hitting the counter wall and bouncing back off while he watched the people come and go.

Mostly Josh watched the people coming because he was waiting. Waiting for the man in the blue uniform who came through the doors at exactly 8:15 a.m. every Saturday morning. The big policeman who never failed to sit down next to him, dropping his hat onto Josh's head as a way of a greeting.

The big cop would nod and greet the other customers before ordering a cup of black coffee and a sugar doughnut. Always the same. Always in the same deep, gruff voice that rumbled its way to the tip of Josh's toes and made him feel strangely safe and secure.

Josh shook off the memories and pulled into the tiny parking lot. He glanced over at Quinby. Little did she know that Josh's favorite person as a child had been none other than her father, Bradford Tennison. A man who had sat next to a lonely seven-year-old boy and filled him with stories of honor, integrity and police work.

He got out of the car, climbed the steps to the back door and led her inside. As usual, the place was filled to capacity. The noise level was high with laughter, and the clatter of cutlery on heavy ceramic plates and the low drone of voices. The smell of French fries, burnt coffee and onions permeated the air.

"Smells good," Quinby said, stepping up beside him. She surveyed the crowd and whistled softly. "Sure looks like a popular place."

"Just don't order the chili," Josh warned as he moved toward the only two empty stools left at the counter.

A quick survey told him that Oscar wasn't seated at the counter or at any of the booths lining the outer edge of the diner. Unless the old guy was hiding in one of the rest room stalls, he wasn't in the diner.

"Hey, Josh, long time, no see," one of the waitresses said as she brushed past him with four plates cradled in her arms, trying to reach the group seated at one of the booths in the corner.

"Been on a diet, Cammie." Josh called over his shoulder, settling himself on the stool. "Can't take all this grease and stay fit and trim."

Cammie set the plates in front of her customers and laughed. "Yeah, right." She glanced at Quinby and winked. "Men. They joke about getting fat while scarfing down wings, beer and chips. Me? I look at a potato chip and the fat jumps on my hips.''

"I hear you," Quinby said, sitting down next to Josh and setting her hat on the counter. She nudged him with an elbow. "You a wing man?"

"Been known to eat them," Josh said laconically.

"Then you'll have to stop by Mama's some Sunday or Monday night. I whip up a mean batch of wings for the gang on football night."

She grabbed the plastic menu from between the sugar dispenser and the ketchup bottle and sat looking over the selection. Josh watched her wrinkle her forehead and gnaw at the corner of her bottom lip.

He wondered about her invitation for wings and football. It was possible that she'd thrown it out just for the heck of it. But then again, there might be some deeper, hidden meaning. He wondered which one it was.

Invitations for a lazy Sunday afternoon watching the game and throwing back a few beers was a pretty common thing between partners, but somehow Josh couldn't help feeling differently about this one. At least it *felt* different to him.

He'd had female partners before. Heck, he'd even been attracted to one or two of them. But he'd always been able to put the feelings aside, to wrestle them into submission. He'd never acted on them. But here he was the first day with Quinby Parker, and he couldn't deny the overwhelming pull. The undeniable attraction to someone definitely *not* his type. Besides, a smart cop didn't get romantically involved with his partner—end of lecture.

The counter waitress, Bea, slapped two white ceramic mugs down in front of them and stood with one large hand sitting squarely on her broad hip, an order pad held at the ready in her other hand. "What'll it be, folks?"

"I'll have the grilled cheese with bacon, Bea. And

tell Ernie not to put any of those fatty pieces he keeps back there on it. You seen Oscar lately?''

Bea pursed her bright orange colored lips. ''Seem to remember him being in here two or three days ago. He spent the whole time complaining that his oatmeal had lumps in it. Charlie finally got tired of him and threw him out. Knowing Oscar, he'll be back in a few days. He and Charlie squabble like that all the time.'' Bea scribbled a note on her pad and then looked up again. ''You want tomato soup with that?''

Josh smiled up at her. ''Of course. Why do you even ask?''

Bea grinned and glanced at Quinby. ''I could pour tomato soup down this boy's throat morning, noon and night and he'd never get tired of it. He drinks it like he owns stock in it.'' She reached behind her and grabbed a coffeepot off one of the six burners and expertly poured two cups of thick, black coffee, never spilling a drop. ''What can I get you, honey?''

Josh watched her out of the corner of his eye, curious as to what she'd order.

''I'll have the chili,'' Quinby said as she shoved the menu back where she had found it.

Conversation at the counter stopped and every head turned to look at Quinby. Josh smiled to himself and took a sip of coffee. Just as he'd expected. She'd gone for the very thing he'd warned her not to order.

Bea glanced over her shoulder toward the kitchen and then whispered, ''I ain't trying to tell you what to order, honey. But are you sure you really want the chili?''

''Bea!'' a voice bellowed from the kitchen. ''The customer ordered chili. Don't be trying to talk the customers out of my prize-winning chili.''

Josh looked up to see Charlie Wrigley framed in the window cut out of the wall between the kitchen and the serving area. His tough, craggy face was scrunched up into a frown.

He slammed a white, blue rimmed bowl down on the shelf with an attention-getting clunk and glared meaningfully at Bea. Josh couldn't help but wonder whether the chili was already eating its way through the bottom of the bowl.

Shaking her head, Bea went over to collect the bowl of chili and set it down in front of Quinby. She reached below the counter and laid four packets of crackers next to the steaming chili. "Pace yourself, honey, and use the crackers to mop up some of the heat." She moved off to fill Josh's order.

Josh reached over to lift a small package of antacids off the display rack next to the cash register and set them next to Quinby. "I think you might need these later." He smiled. "And just so you know, once we're back in the car, there won't be any unscheduled stops."

"What's the matter, Josh? Can't handle the hot stuff?" An answering grin stretched Quinby's perfect lips, and the brown eyes twinkled with amusement.

"Oh, be assured, partner, I can handle the hot stuff. It's just that I'm not too partial to creating an inferno in my stomach. I like my heat elsewhere."

Josh prevented her from responding by swiveling forward and digging into the soup Bea had set in front of him. He could tell she was staring at him, a look of defiance sparking in the depths of her eyes. She was almost too predictable. Out of the corner of his eye, he watched her scoop up a hearty spoonful, open her lips and tuck the mouthful neatly in with a flourish.

As Quinby slid the warm metal spoon out from between her lips and started chewing, she tried to ignore the tiny flare of triumph that flickered to life in the back of her brain. Who did Josh Reed think he was that he could tell her what not to eat. Jeesh, the guy's arrogance was unbelievable.

The chili was hot. But not unbearable. In fact, it was pretty darn good. Spicy and filled with interesting tastes. She shot a smug grin in Josh's direction and scooped up another mouthful. Delicious. Absolutely scrumptious.

She delivered three more hearty bites and reached up to loosen the collar of her shirt. Warm in here. Must be the large crowd packed into such a tiny space. She used the back of her hand to wipe a bead of sweat off her forehead. Whew. She wished someone would turn down the heat.

Then out of nowhere, a four-alarm fire scorched the back of her mouth, spread to her throat, and then up her nose. It was as if she'd taken a mouthful of hot chili peppers, chewed on a dozen jalapeño peppers and washed it all down with Texas Hot Sauce. Tears filled her eyes, and she gripped the edge of the counter with both hands.

Bea appeared in front of her—at least Quinby thought it was Bea as she couldn't see very clearly through the veil of tears filling her eyes.

"Here you go, honey," Bea said sympathetically, setting a pitcher of something in front of her. "Don't bother with the glass. Just chug it right out of the pitcher."

Ignoring the laughter coming from around her, Quinby picked up the pitcher and drank deeply. Cool water washed over her burning tongue and down the back of her throat. Finally she set the pitcher down, wiped her eyes with the edge of her sleeve and glanced over at Josh.

Of course, he was chewing on a corner of his sandwich as if nothing had happened, watching her with an amused look on his handsome face. "Feeling okay, Parker? You're looking a bit red in the face."

"Very funny," she managed to sputter before picking up the pitcher for another deep drink. It seemed as if the fire in her mouth had only decreased a measly degree. She set the jug back down. "You knew I'd order the chili, didn't you?"

Josh shrugged, his broad shoulders moving easily beneath his jacket. "I was pretty sure you would."

"So why did you set me up?"

"One of the things I've learned over the years is that the trainee who consistently resists helpful hints from her trainer is the one who isn't going to make it. You fit that prototype, Parker. I was simply testing out my theory."

Quinby used two fingers to fish a chunk of ice out of the pitcher and popped it into her mouth, sucking on its comforting coldness as she contemplated what Josh had just revealed.

No question that it was a bit disconcerting to know she had a field training officer who didn't hold out a lot of hope that she'd successfully finish her probationary period. But then, it wasn't as if the phenomena was new to her. None of her F.T.O.s had been very encouraging. One more wasn't going to make that much of a difference.

She hitched forward on her stool, pushing the offending bowl of chili out of the way with one elbow. "Look, I really want this, Reed. Are you planning on helping me or tripping me up?"

Josh swiveled to face her, his long legs bumping the sides of her thighs as he turned. A dark, serious look lurked in the frozen depths of his blue eyes. Quinby shivered. Perhaps she had overstepped her bounds with that question.

"I don't set out to flunk anyone, Parker. Trainees do

that all on their own. If you're interested in getting through these next two weeks, I have two suggestions—put your ego on hold and listen carefully to all I have to offer. You do that, and we'll get along famously.''

Quinby swallowed hard and tried to ignore the ball of fire sitting in her belly. The one attempting to burn through her stomach lining. "I'm sorry. I didn't mean to infer that you'd try to purposefully get me booted off the force.''

Josh leaned forward, warmth radiating from him like a furnace. "Oh, you misunderstand, Parker. I will most definitely boot your butt out of this department. But it will be because you didn't listen to the advice you're given, and you acted with blatant disregard for your own or someone else's safety. Do we understand each other?''

Quinby nodded, smart enough to know when *not* to say anything. After all, there was too much of a chance that she'd say something that would turn up the heat on the hot water she was already bathing in.

Josh smiled, a tight, formidable smile, and Quinby felt pretty close to the same way she used to feel when called down to the Brackett City's high school principal's office.

"Don't be too eager to write me off, sir. I might surprise you," Quinby said softly.

"I'm glad to hear that," Josh said around a mouthful of grilled cheese sandwich. "I'll be looking forward to being proven wrong.''

Quinby pushed two antacid tablets out of their foil package and popped them into her mouth. She chewed them while making a vow to knock Josh Reed's socks off with her competence. Now, if she could only put her natural klutziness on hold for the next ten days.

5

QUINBY SLAMMED THE DOOR of her locker shut, spun the lock and brushed past the two women sitting on the benches chatting while they finished dressing. She'd practically thrown her civilian clothes on in an effort to get out quickly. She glanced over her shoulder at the oversize clock hanging over the entrance to the shower room. She grinned. Done in record time—less than ten minutes.

As she headed for the door, Quinby glanced at the mirror running along the wall and scowled at her reflection. The tangled mess of brown curls crowning the top of her head and falling to her shoulders reminded her of an osprey nest on the top of a telephone pole. A familiar sight, but a frightening one nonetheless.

She knew she owed Josh some show of appreciation. Following the fiasco at the diner, he had actually taken the time to help her. He'd been patient and painstaking in his approach to begin teaching her the skills she lacked.

It was as if he'd known that she was finally open to receiving the information—it flowed over and into her like a pure water spring, seeping into every pore. She'd become a virtual sponge. The least she could do was thank him.

Slightly out of breath, Quinby pushed open the locker room door and rushed out, tripping over the door frame and almost taking a header into the hallway.

She pulled herself up and tugged at the hem of her rumpled shirt, checking out the other end of the hall. Nothing. The door to the men's locker room was closed, the hall empty.

Perhaps Josh had already changed and left. An undeniable sense of disappointment washed over her. She walked out into the lobby area, affecting a casual look. The only one around was the desk officer. He sat at his computer, the phone receiver pressed against his ear. He nodded to Quinby but didn't pause in conversation. For a moment, she considered asking him if Reed had passed through already, but then the thought of being too obvious made her hold back.

The fact that she rushed getting dressed in the hopes of getting out in time to see Reed one last time before heading home hadn't escaped her. If Paige was around to witness this she would have laughed herself to tears—*sure you wanted to thank him, Quin. Tell me another good one.*

Quinby stiffened. Was it a crime that she actually liked being partnered with Josh? That she enjoyed talking to him? Spending time picking his brain and learning all that he knew about policing? Hardly.

Quinby paused. Well, maybe she was acting a little weird. How often did she hurry, dress and run out into the lobby so she could meet her other field training officers? Never.

Shaking her head, Quinby zipped up her jacket and turned toward the front door. Obviously loitering in the lobby was a little too over the top. Better to leave. She'd see Josh soon enough tomorrow, and no doubt he'd do something to irritate the heck out of her. Hopefully it would be enough to jolt her and make her realize that waiting in the lobby for some uptight, anal-retentive guy was a bit too weird even for her.

Quinby walked out of the building and was halfway

to her truck before she noticed a small group clustered around a souped-up Camaro at the back of the lot. About six men and one woman stood in a tightly packed group, laughing and talking. It was the usual goofing off people exhibited once their shift was over.

Quinby paused for a moment, considering whether or not she wanted to amble over to join the group. But then she noticed Cal Tripp standing in the middle of the group. The sight of Tripp and a few other of his cronies was enough to make Quinby wish she'd decided to loiter a bit longer in the lobby. Cal and his crowd didn't miss a trick when it came to getting on her case about her recent work related difficulties.

Quinby tightened the jacket around her and headed for her truck, hoping that the group wouldn't notice her. She stuck the key into the lock and the button popped up. Her luck ran out as she pulled open the door.

"Hey, Quin!"

Quinby froze. It was Tripp's voice.

Taking a deep breath and forcing an easy smile on her face, Quinby turned around. "How's it going, Tripp? Bit cold to be hanging out in the parking lot, don't you think?" she said and then winced. Her voice cracked right at the end. If Tripp didn't know before how nervous she was, he did now.

He stepped out of the circle of cronies and moved toward her. "We were just admiring Roselli's car. She's been doing all the restoration herself."

Quinby glanced at Karen Roselli, Tripp's partner. The two of them had been classmates at the police academy. A natural athlete and a brain, Roselli seemed to take great pleasure in rubbing Quinby's nose in the fact that she had to struggle and study to successfully pass every test—physical as well as academic.

"I noticed it when I came in this morning," Quinby said. "Nice job, Roselli."

Roselli sauntered up next to Tripp, and Quinby tried to ignore the smug smile that tugged at the corner of her mouth.

"You a car buff, Parker?" Tripp asked, his tone conversational. He moved to stand in front of her, and the small crowd shuffled after him, forming a ragged semicircle behind him.

Quinby shook her head, pressing the tip of her key into the center of her palm. She needed to stay calm. No one was going to get hurt. They were just looking to harass her a bit. She'd handled worse.

"Too bad," Tripp said. "I was thinking that you might be able to get a job at a local grease shop once you got your butt kicked off the force."

"Thanks for the concern, Tripp. I'll definitely keep it in mind, right after I remind the chief to put out a memo informing everyone that you've opened a career counseling service here in the parking lot."

A ripple of laughter rolled over the group. Tripp's expression hardened. Obviously he wasn't too keen on hearing any mouthy responses. Actually, Quinby knew she'd be a lot better off if she learned to keep a muzzle on it. But when she was nervous, the smart-aleck remarks seemed to roll out all on their own.

Tripp leaned a hip up against her truck and smiled, but Quinby wasn't fooled. It wasn't a pleasant smile. It was the kind of smile a shark had when it eyed one of the pretty little reef morsels swimming among the coral. She braced herself, unsure what kind of ammunition he could use against her.

"I was talking to one of the old-timers the other day, and he said you were a real pistol when you were a teenager, Quinby. A certifiable punk. Said he had picked you up a time or two joyriding with some of the local thugs." He glanced back at the group. "It's a crying shame that the department is reduced to recruiting former teenage punks. It messes with our public image."

Quinby stifled a smile of relief. If that's all he had she was home free. "We can't all be jock-heads, Tripp—all muscle and no brain. Besides, my record is clean. You know that because I would have never gotten into the academy if I had any marks on my record."

Tripp came up off the side of her truck and stepped in close, his expression bitter. Quinby stood her ground.

He hit her shoulder with the flat of his hand, a psuedocomradely nudge that was meant to provoke. "Guess we shouldn't be too surprised that you turned out the way you did, Parker." He glanced back at the crowd. "My source tells me that Parker here had a tramp of a mother. The *lady* got picked up more than a few times for public intoxication and disorderly conduct. No big surprise that Parker doesn't even know who her daddy is."

Quinby started to laugh. She couldn't help it. Put her in a tense situation and she started to laugh uncontrollably. It had been that way for as long as she could remember. And to make matters worse, she hiccuped at the end.

"You're such a putz, Tripp. My mother was an alcoholic. So what? She was harmless. And my father didn't hang around. Big deal." Quinby shrugged. "No story in that. Plenty of people have problems. Speaking of which—why don't you go home and inflate your date?"

The tiny lines around Tripp's eyes tightened, and his eyes narrowed. No appreciation for her wit there. He laughed, a harsh, forced sound. Apparently he wasn't going to be put off so easily. The flat of his hand nudged her shoulder again, pushing her back another step.

"Step down, Tripp," a soft voice said.

Tripp glanced beyond Quinby's shoulder and backed

off. Quinby didn't need to look. She recognized the voice. Josh Reed.

"Trying to incite a riot, Tripp? Or are you just using your natural charm to initiate another rookie?" Josh asked.

"We were just chatting with your new partner, Reed." Tripp spread his hands wide. "No harm done."

Quinby glanced over her shoulder. Josh stood about two feet away, his weight resting casually on one leg, his arms folded. Strands of dark hair, lifted by a light breeze, fanned across his forehead. His face was expressionless. Empty of emotion. Every line hardened as if carved from ice. No doubt about it, the nickname fit him like a glove.

Others in her position might feel a sense of relief that he was there to intervene, but not Quinby. In fact, she was annoyed. Heat flooded her cheeks. If he stepped in now, everyone would think she couldn't handle Tripp's hassling herself. It would only make matters worse.

Oblivious, Josh moved up to stand next to her. "I'm not blind, Tripp. I know exactly what was going on here, and it's going to stop now. Shove off."

"No. You shove off, Reed," Quinby hissed out of the corner of her mouth. He looked over at her, surprise and amusement tugging at the corner of his mouth. Apparently he hadn't expected that kind of reception from her.

Quinby stepped in closer and gave him a little push with her shoulder. "I'm handling things. I don't need your help."

Josh shook his head and stood firm. "I'm not going anywhere, Quin. We're partners, and partners stick together."

He used his elbow to nudge her, as if he wanted her to step behind him. Irritated, Quinby elbowed him back. Who did he think he was, pushing her behind him like some fragile piece of fluff? For a moment, their elbows jabbed at each other, struggling for dominance, locked in a silly battle to win.

Tripp burst out laughing. "Well, when you two *partners* decide who's going to take care of this little incident, just let me know. But for now, we're headed over to O'Sullivan's for a few cold ones." He nodded to his crowd of hangers-on. "Let's go, gang. We'll leave the kiddies here to discuss what is and isn't a partnership."

They walked off. Quinby scowled at Josh. Bully was too good of a name for him. She turned to leave, angry that he'd thought so little of her ability to deal with the situation that he had come running to get her out of trouble.

He'd bought the same assessment of her that everyone in the modern world seemed to share. Big, klutzy Quinby Parker. Lovable, but a real screwup.

"Where are you going?" he asked, his voice low and deadly.

"Home," she said, not even bothering to watch as several cars roared out of the parking lot, the night air punctuated with several mocking blares of a horn.

"We're not done discussing this incident," Josh said.

"Well, stick around and discuss it to your heart's content." Quinby yanked open the door of her truck. "But you'll be talking to yourself because I'm going home."

His eyes narrowed in anger, and she watched a tiny muscle in his jaw tighten. Shrugging, Quinby threw her gym bag onto the front seat and started to climb into the truck. Forget all the good feelings she'd had about their partnership earlier. Josh had dampened those feelings pretty effectively.

He came up fast on her right, pushed the door shut and blocked her from getting in. "I said we're not done talking."

"Tomorrow will be soon enough for one of your lectures."

Quinby tried to ignore the strange flutter in the pit of

her stomach—probably a leftover reaction to the chili at lunch. Only problem was, Josh was now so close that she could reach out and stroke the side of his face. She closed her hands into fists. "I'm tired, and you're frustrated. Let's call it a night."

Josh leaned in and rested one hand on the roof of the car, blocking her exit to the right. When Quinby turned to the left, his other hand settled against the car. He had effectively hemmed her in.

Muted light from the street lamps sliced down to illuminate one side of his face, and its clean beauty almost made her weep. Why was he doing this to her? Didn't he realize the effect he had on her? Had he no pity?

"I—I need to get home," she stammered, her voice sounding thin and uneven. She bit the corner of her bottom lip, angry he didn't see or hear that she was close to the edge. Couldn't he see that he was pushing too hard? Apparently not, because there was no sign he was going to back off or leave.

Instead he stared down at her, the color of his eyes muted in the light. Quinby shivered and knew it had nothing to do with the cold air whispering against her cheeks.

"I already told you, I'm not finished discussing this." His voice was pitched low and strummed her nerve endings like the touch of a feather.

Quinby shrugged again, her shoulders brushing against the sides of his jacket, the rustle of nylon soft and whispery in the night air. "Look, they're gone. I appreciate your help, but it's too cold to stand out here talking."

"You're not getting the idea of what a partnership is," he said.

She had to tilt her head back to see him. "What are you talking about, Josh? You and I sit in a patrol car together and drive around looking for a little old man. What's so hard to understand?"

"Is that what you think policing is? Because if it is, I can tell you now that you're not going to make it."

She flinched. That one hurt.

He seemed to notice the hurt he'd inflicted, and the tone of his voice softened. "You need to understand, Quinby. It's not a good sign that you don't know how to work cooperatively with your partner. It's good basic policing to understand the need to work with your partner in difficult or confrontational situations."

"For pity's sake, Josh, I wasn't in any danger. A couple of workplace bullies thought they'd take a shot at pushing me around. It wasn't any big deal."

"I see it differently, Quin. I see this as a perfect example of the trouble you're having making it as a cop. You don't know how to work as part of a team. You're bullheaded and have a stubborn streak as wide as the Grand Canyon."

"Jeesh, Josh, don't hold back. Tell me what you really think of me." His assessment stung, but she hid her feelings behind an amused smile.

"Things aren't going to get any better for you, Quin, unless we talk about this and figure out a way for you to make some changes."

Quinby laughed. "It was a simple teasing incident, Josh. You're acting like I shot my firearm into the crowd or launched myself at them and wrestled them to the ground. We had a few angry words. No big deal."

"You're treating this too lightly."

Quinby reached out and laid the palm of her hand against his chest. She pushed, but he didn't budge. "You're just ticked that I didn't back off and act like a scared little rookie—that I didn't stand down and let you handle everything."

She wanted to drop her hand but didn't, fearing he'd move in even closer. But she couldn't help but be bothered by the rise and fall of his chest beneath her hand.

He seemed to sense her discomfort and he leaned forward, resting his weight on her hand, seeming to test the firmness of her resolve to keep him at a distance. "You should have stepped back when I came over. I thought you understood that your job is to get through this probationary period without another write-up."

Quinby sucked in a breath of cold air, hoping it would cool down the flash of heat rushing through her. "You're not getting this. I was off duty. The guy tried to push me around. Do you expect me to just stand there and take it without saying anything?"

"You're the one not getting it, Quin. Being a cop is about holding your temper, dealing with difficult situations and coming out a winner because you're able to defuse a hot situation, not because you ratcheted it up another twenty or thirty degrees with a bunch of sarcastic remarks."

"Oh, so now you're accusing me of being a hothead?"

"Are you?"

"No. I—I happen to be a very cautious and thoughtful person. I don't shoot my mouth off, and I don't have a short fuse."

Quinby stared defiantly back at him, but as much as she tried to ignore it, a tiny bubble of laughter pushed at the back of her throat. Who was she kidding? It was a miracle that a bolt of lightning hadn't ripped across the sky and split her in half for that little lie.

Quinby's lower lip quivered as she started to lose the battle to keep from bursting into laughter. She turned her head away in an attempt to keep it hidden from Josh.

"Don't even bother to try to hide it," Josh said, his own amusement now obvious in the light tone of his voice.

Quinby dropped her hands down and tucked them behind her. Josh reached out and took hold of her chin, and gently turned her face toward him.

In a heartbeat, the air around them seemed to change.

One minute, they were both laughing, and the next, they were staring at each other, the air crackling between them.

Quinby could see Josh's face clearly—the slightly tousled locks of his dark hair, and the cold vapor spilling between his lips. He shifted, moving closer, his tall frame crowding into her space.

Quinby pressed up against the side of the truck, her hands trapped behind her. The cold metal seeped through the warm wool of her mittens and chilled the palms of her hands.

Somewhere off in the distance, she could hear the hiss of tires on the slick pavement. But here in the parking lot it was dark and quiet.

"Why is it so hard for you to listen?" he asked softly.

"It's not hard. I'm listening. Tell me again."

"I think I'd be wasting my breath."

"No, I promise that I'll listen this time," Quinby said, suddenly afraid that he was going to leave her here in the cold. Alone.

She wanted to reach out and slide her hand along the side of his cheek and around to the back of his head. She wanted to feel his hair and run her fingers through it. To touch his warmth in the cold night air. But instead, she pressed harder against her rebellious hands, keeping them securely in place.

Confusion seemed to cloud his features, and Quinby wondered if he was struggling with the same feelings. A sensation struck her that the world had suddenly tipped upside down and was trying to suck her down along with it.

He leaned closer, the coolness in his eyes warming, and the heat of his breath welcome on her cold skin. Quinby knew what he was going to do even before he did it, but it was still a shock when his lips settled over hers, first soft and tentative—as if he was testing hers, and then hard and decisive. Demanding.

An overpowering heat engulfed her and wrapped her up in its strange warmth. But as she leaned into the kiss, suddenly eager to leap into the center of the fire, Josh pulled back. He simply lifted his mouth off hers and straightened up.

Saddened by the sudden loss, Quinby ran her tongue along the inner edge of her bottom lip. Unable to say anything, she stared up at him.

He stared back, a puzzled look swimming in the blue of his eyes. Quinby pressed her hand to her mouth, the wool of her mitten damp from the frost on the side of the truck. What was she supposed to say? Did he want her to say anything?

"So this is what you meant when you said partners should cooperate?" As soon as the sarcastic response passed her lips, Quinby knew she'd said the wrong thing.

Josh shook his head and jammed his hand angrily through the thickness of his hair. His other hand clenched tight in a fist. "No... It has absolutely nothing whatsoever to do with that. It was a mistake. A stupid mistake."

He turned as if to walk away and then stopped, his back to her. He stood there for several seconds. Quinby figured that if he was as shaken as she was, then he was uncertain about what to do.

He turned back around. "I'm sorry, That should never have happened. If you want to write out a report charging me with sexual harassment, you have every right to do it. I won't deny it."

He turned and walked to his truck. Quinby stood watching his long legs eat up the snow-covered ground. She was shaken, unsure of what to do or say. Sexual harassment? Heck, the guy didn't know how close she'd been to wanting to go home with him.

He didn't look back but instead, yanked open the truck door, climbed in and slammed it shut. He stared blankly over the dash and out the frosted windshield. Quinby wasn't sure he even saw her standing there in the almost empty parking lot. He was obviously too stunned by what had happened.

Struggling to understand it herself, Quinby opened her own door and got in, still flushed and struggling to breathe. That man could kiss! Who'd have thought.

She fumbled to get her keys in the ignition, dropping them twice. With numb fingers, she finally managed to get the engine to turn over, the entire truck shuddering and shaking in response to the cold.

She backed out, shifted into first and stomped on the gas, shooting across the parking lot with a soul-satisfying roar. As she passed Josh's truck, she glanced quickly to gauge his reaction. But he seemed unimpressed, still sitting like stone in the front seat—staring blankly out the window.

JOSH SAT IN THE DAMP CAB of his truck, the keys dangling from the ignition. He watched Quinby back out of her parking slot and drive off in a cloud of vapor.

He hit the outer edge of the steering wheel with his closed fist and swore softly. What the heck did he think he was doing kissing a field trainee? A field trainee assigned to him so that he could straighten her out, no less.

Kissing Quinby Parker and practically mauling her in the department parking lot was not what the chief had in mind when he assigned Josh to work with her.

Reaching down, he turned the key, starting the truck. The engine was a low, smooth rumble. He flicked on the heater, waiting in the dark cab for the cold air to change to hot.

He rubbed the side of his jaw. How was he going to handle this? He couldn't deny his attraction to her. Hell, he had to admit that there was a sizzle of attraction between them from the moment they'd met. But he needed to push it aside.

Easier said than done. Seeing her standing there in

front of him, her smooth skin cooled by the night air
and her chocolate-brown eyes looking up at him from
beneath a fringe of dark lashes had been more than he'd
been able to resist. Her hair had shimmered in the soft
light from the street lamps, and a few flakes of light
snow had sat cradled in the curve of her curls at the top
of her head.

He had caved like a randy eighteen-year-old on a date
with the prom queen. Just the thought of her standing
there in the darkness, her lips parted in anticipation of
saying something sassy and stubborn brought back a
yearning so intense Josh shifted in discomfort. How
long had it been since he'd experienced such a feeling?
Too long.

Josh lifted his head. That was it. He'd simply been
out of circulation too long. The separation from Caroline. The divorce and all its nastiness, and then his intense concentration on Zack, making sure the little guy
was secure and happy. It had all combined to cause him
to forget that part of himself that needed companionship—intimacy.

Unfortunately there was no way that Quinby Parker
could be the person to satisfy that need for companionship. She was his partner, not his lover. Josh shoved the
gear into Drive and stepped on the gas, taking a juvenile
sense of pleasure in the sound of the tires spinning in
the snow. The truck's body jerked forward, and he
pulled out of the lot.

It was time to tuck his silly adolescent thoughts away
and concentrate on his job—getting Quinby Parker
through her final two weeks of field training.

6

EARLY THE NEXT MORNING, Quinby found Josh waiting for her in their squad car, a clipboard balanced on his knee and an impatient scowl on his face. It wasn't hard to tell from the set of his jaw that he was feeling uncomfortable about what had happened last night. Obviously it had thrown them both off balance.

As she opened the door and slid in next to him, he glanced up. No welcoming smile. No greeting. He shoved the clipboard into her hands and started the car.

"I called Oscar's house this morning. He didn't come home last night." He backed the car out of the narrow spot and headed for the garage exit. "The nurse told me that he hasn't checked in, either."

"Do you think something could have really happened to him?" Quinby asked, stowing the clipboard next to her as she buckled up.

"Doubt it." Josh pulled out into the light traffic and headed downtown. "He's just lying low because he knows it irritates the heck out of his son. He has to come out of his hiding spot at some point—it might as well be today."

Silence settled around them.

Quinby shifted in her seat and moistened her lips. Josh might be trying to ignore what had gone on between them last night, but she couldn't.

"You're not still mad about last night, are you?"

He shook his head, keeping his eyes straight ahead. "Not in the least."

Outright lie. Obviously he was still brooding about her reaction to Tripp and the flash of mutual attraction that had reared its ugly head at the end of their conversation. Not that she blamed him. Quinby had spent the majority of her night tossing and turning while her mind played and replayed the incident.

"Look, I know last night was a mistake. I'm sorry about the scuffle with Tripp, and I really apologize for coming on to you." She shot a sideways glance in his direction, trying to gauge how he'd react to her willingness to take the blame for their little indiscretion.

He grunted noncommittally and she tried again. "I know my father has put a lot of pressure on you to make sure I make it, and I appreciate that you haven't taken it out on me. But you have no idea what Tripp and his cronies have put me through these past few months. I don't like backing down."

He didn't look at her, instead he kept driving.

Quinby leaned forward and waved a hand. "Hey! I'm apologizing here."

He glanced over at her, the ice-blue of his eyes slicing through her with ease. "There isn't any need to apologize, Parker."

Quinby's heart sank. He was back to calling her Parker.

He stopped at the light, exhaled softly and said without looking at her, "I'm to blame for that mix-up last night. It's a mistake that won't happen again."

Quinby opened her mouth to agree, but Josh stiffened, leaned forward to switch on the cruiser's flashing lights and headed for the curb.

"There he is," he said.

Quinby searched the crowded sidewalk for their target. Finally she spied him, a little man, a tad over five feet. He wore a dapper, charcoal-gray overcoat and walked with a noticeable limp. A green bombardier's cap was pulled down low and the fur-lined earflaps flopping loose in the breeze.

Oscar used a sturdy wooden walking stick, and he leaned on it heavily when stepping out with his right foot. Whenever anyone got in his way on the crowded sidewalk, Oscar used the tip of the stick to nudge them aside, ignoring their annoyed glances or angry comments.

"Roll down the window," Josh said, guiding the car to the curb.

As they came up alongside, Oscar turned and glared at them. Irritation flashed across Oscar's craggy face as he tried without much success, to hobble away.

"Slow down, Oscar," Josh said, allowing the car to coast along the curb. "For crying out loud, Oscar, I'm in a car. You can't outrun a car."

Oscar stopped so fast that Josh had to slam on the brakes, throwing Quinby forward against her shoulder belt. She glared at him.

"Get lost, Josh. I'm not interested in hearing anything you have to say." Oscar hauled off and hit the side of the car with the cane. It rattled against the door panel and nearly pulled the old guy off balance. He teetered for a moment, almost taking a nosedive into the gutter. But somehow he managed to regain his footing.

Obviously angry, Oscar glanced back at the crowd. "Did you see that? Did anyone see that police car hit me? I need witnesses. I'm going to sue."

No response. The crowd surged past with hardly a glance.

Josh shook his head and jammed the gear into Park. "Open the passenger door," he said to Quinby. "Get in, Oscar. I'm not in the mood for any of your usual shenanigans."

Oscar seemed to sense the kind of mood Josh was in and opened the rear door, settling into the back seat with a grunt.

"Where have you been?" Josh asked, putting the car into gear and pulling back out into traffic. "We've been looking all over for you."

"Been around," Oscar said laconically.

"Where exactly is around?" Josh asked.

Oscar laughed, a short derisive sound. "You thinking I'm some kind of fool, Josh? I'm not so old and senile that I'd tell where my hidey hole is to some copper and his sidekick. I might need it again."

Quinby cringed and glanced over at Josh, trying to gauge his reaction. Some copper? Now that was a cruel shot. Josh didn't seem the type to be average—not even a little. The guy was a rock.

She considered the insult. If Josh was supposed to be just some copper, who did that make her? Jeez, could this get any worse?

Josh seemed oblivious to the insult. "Okay. Let's try a less threatening line of questioning. Where were you headed just now?"

Oscar leaned forward and hooked an arthritic finger through the metal mesh separating the back seat from the front. "Sadly I was on my way to pay my last respects to an old and very dear friend."

Quinby turned slightly so she could see the old guy and still keep an eye on Josh. Josh stared at Oscar in the rearview mirror. "You were on your way to a wake?"

Oscar nodded. "Sadie Dunn passed on two days ago. She's an old friend of mine. You going to give me a ride over?"

Josh sighed again. "Sure. Where's she at?"

"Boomer Racette Funeral Home. Sadie is first-class all the way." He cocked his head and considered his response for a moment, and then said, "I guess I should change that to say her husband believes in sending Sadie off in first-class style."

Quinby kept her mouth shut, but she wasn't sure what bothered her more, the fact that the old guy wasn't in the least remorseful that he'd led them on a wild-goose chase for two days or that he was planning on attending a funeral at a place owned by a guy named Boomer. Somehow the name Boomer didn't evoke the usual feelings of sadness and melancholy one frequently experienced when forced to deal with a funeral director.

Within a few short minutes, Josh pulled the patrol car up to the curb in front of the funeral home. The cruiser had barely rolled to a stop before Oscar had the rear door open. He climbed out and moved up to the front of the car, bending down to check his bow tie in the side mirror. Quinby rolled down the window.

Oscar turned his head and smiled at her, his top choppers coming loose, forcing him to jam a thumb up against the roof of his mouth to secure them back in place.

"Got any adhesive stuff on you, sweetie?" he asked.

Quinby shook her head wearily. For this she wanted to be a cop? Who'd have figured? She considered the advisability of stopping back over at Sweetness's shop and seeing if he was in need of a shampoo assistant.

Oscar seemed oblivious to her career crisis. He straightened up and adjusted the flaps on his bomber hat. "I'll meet you two in about an hour or so—depending on who's hanging around to say good bye to Sadie." His expression hardened. "Don't come in. You'll cramp my style."

Giving them a quick wave, he took off up the sidewalk to the main entrance of Boomer's establishment.

"We'll cramp his style at a funeral. No doubt he's

planning on trying to pick up a few lovelies while paying his respects to his deceased paramour.''

Quinby glanced over her shoulder to see the line of cars behind them, waiting to let out more mourners. ''You think he'll try to give us the slip?''

Josh nodded. ''You can count on it. Go on in and take a look around. Don't let him out of your sight. I'll drive around back and keep an eye on the rear exit.''

''What if he sees me?''

Josh shrugged. ''Doesn't matter. He knows that we aren't going to back off now that we've spotted him. Give him room to operate otherwise he'll get testy. We definitely don't want a testy Oscar swinging that cane of his—trying to take out one of Brackett City's finest in front of some of our loyal and most upstanding citizens.''

Quinby grabbed her hat off the seat beside her and opened her door. ''Hopefully, Oscar doesn't plan on sticking around too long. Funerals and wakes are not my idea of how to spend my day.''

''Well, if you get bored you could always wander out back and see if old Boomer needs a hand.''

Knowing what was coming next, but unable to dodge the dig, Quinby leaned down and looked across at her partner. A small smile played at the corner of his mouth, giving him a light, teasing expression. His eyes showed none of the humor playing around his lips. Quinby tightened her grip on the door and sucked in a lungful of cold air.

''Okay, I'll bite. What's that supposed to mean?'' she asked.

The smile turned into an outright grin, making Quinby's stomach do a strange flip-flop. How did he do that, she wondered.

Josh shifted the car into Drive. ''Heck, Parker, I just thought you'd be happy to give old Boomer a hand.

With that list of jobs you've done, working in a funeral home must be in there somewhere." He started the cruiser rolling forward.

Quinby straightened up. "Funny, Reed, real funny." She slammed the door, but not before she heard him start to chuckle.

Turning away, she started up the wide walkway leading to Boomer's funeral home. Maybe this policing thing wasn't going to work out, and she should keep an open attitude toward this funeral home thing. Could be a brand-new career path was opening up for her.

BOOMER'S PLACE WASN'T MUCH different than any other funeral home Quinby had ever visited. Not that visiting them was a favorite pastime of hers.

It was a bit more pretentious than your run-of-the-mill funeral home. The front lobby was lined with dark green, seven-foot ferns. The ferns shaded several elaborately covered Victorian couches dotting the hall, and strategically placed brass spittoons sat to the right of each couch. Quinby couldn't help wondering if anyone actually used those things anymore.

A tight cluster of people stood in front of double doors opening to a room on the left. Eight or nine weathered, wrinkled faces turned to look at her, surprise apparent from their expressions. Quinby was sure none of them had expected a city cop to show up to pay her respects to poor Sadie Dunn.

Quinby smiled and held up a hand. "No one panic. I'm just waiting for a friend."

Since the doors on the opposite side of the hall were closed, she figured that Sadie's wake was in the room just beyond the crowd. As she stepped forward, the crowd broke apart and split, moving out of her way.

Of course, Oscar had already taken center stage. He stood at the front of the room waving his cane and bellowing, "You old goat. You don't deserve her! You never deserved her."

Behind him, on a raised platform and covered with flowers lay Sadie, looking lovely in a blue chiffon dress and a better than average makeup job.

Oscar's attention was focused on a barrel-chested man in an ill-fitting black suit. He stood a few feet away from Oscar, his face flushed an interesting shade of red, and his oversize nose a startling shade of purple.

"Sadie wasn't interested in you," Oscar's rival shouted. "She was playing you for the fool while planning to go to Vegas with me."

Someone grabbed onto Quinby's arm. "That's Buzz Bradley. Sadie was stringing him along, too."

Startled, Quinby glanced down. Way down. A tiny, birdlike woman who came only as high as Quinby's belt clutched her forearm with skeletonlike fingers. She smiled up at Quinby, her dentures a blinding flash of white enamel.

"And you are?" Quinby asked.

"Oh, I'm Buzz's wife, Grace." Quinby blinked and Grace patted her arm. "No scandal, honey. Sadie was quite a woman. She had every man at Whispering Pines panting after her like dogs in heat." She shook her head, blue tinted curls shimmering in the subdued lighting of the viewing room. "Men. You have to love the poor dears. They're incapable of rational thought when it comes to issues about sex. Absolutely everything revolves around their—"

"Whoa, Grace. No need to fill me in on the little details," Quinby interrupted. "I'll take your word for it."

Somehow Quinby didn't feel fully equipped to deal with a woman, who looked like someone's sweet old grandmother, casually discussing the anatomy and sexual habits of men while attending a wake.

Grace patted her arm. "A bit uptight about sex, aren't you, honey?" She shook her head again. "You young girls need to loosen up." She turned back to consider the two men on either end of Sadie's coffin. "Buzz might have a lot to be desired as a lover, but he's no slouch when it comes to a fight. Oscar might get his clock cleaned this time. But I'm going to put my money on Oscar. I'm going to Vegas next week and a win could get me some quick change for the slots." She smiled sweetly at Quinby.

"I'm hoping no one gets his clock cleaned," Quinby admitted. She could almost read her evaluation now—*Officer Parker failed to prevent a knock-down-drag-out brawl between two, frail, elderly gentlemen at a local funeral.*

She raised a hand to her belt and flicked on her radio, turning her head slightly so she could speak into her shoulder mike, "I've got a small problem brewing in here, Reed. Stand by because I might need some backup."

Josh's curt assurance that he was ready for the word crackled through the mike.

Oscar sensed the possibility of his moment of glory drawing to a premature close, so he moved around to the top of Sadie's final resting place. He grasped the corners of the coffin with both hands, putting on a show of guarding Sadie.

Quinby wasn't sure what Oscar thought he was guarding Sadie from—maybe he was suspicious that old Buzz might try jumping into a spot right there next to Sadie. Whatever he was thinking, the scowl on his face was enough to scare off the Grim Reaper himself.

Unwilling to back down, Buzz hobbled up to confront Oscar. His face was flushed a bright red, a tiny vein between his iron-gray eyebrows standing out in stark relief.

"Take your hands off my Sadie, you gas-bag Romeo," Buzz shouted. "Sadie wasn't in her right mind when she took up with the likes of you."

"Sadie knew exactly what she was doing when she took up with me, you Viagra-deficient Casanova," Oscar taunted.

Sighing, Quinby stepped up to the coffin and held up her hands. "All right, that's enough. The two of you should be ashamed of yourself. You're grown men acting like two teenagers with raging hormones."

Both men stared at her with slightly dazed expressions. Quinby knew she needed to defuse the situation as quickly as possible. Things were spiraling out of control at an alarming rate.

"I want the both of you to step back away from the coffin and sit down," she said. "This is no way to treat a loved one."

"And we all know how loved Sadie was!" Grace shouted from the peanut gallery.

Quinby shot the elderly woman a look that told her not to make matters worse.

Grace smiled sweetly and shrugged her bony shoulders. "Well, no one can argue that Sadie wasn't a busy woman," she said, glancing around for support from her friends.

Sighing, Quinby turned back to the two combatants. Oscar leaned down and yanked the skirt from around the coffin. Using his foot, he unlocked the wheels of the bier and then, started to push the coffin toward the side door. Enraged, Buzz scooted down the opposite side of the box and grabbed Oscar. The two fell into each other's arms.

As they wrestled, all grunts and creaking joints, they fell back against the front end of Sadie's coffin. The impact sent the coffin sliding off the opposite end of the bier, tipping it up on one end, half-on half-off the stand.

The force of the fall was enough to send Sadie swinging into a sitting position. Or maybe Sadie just decided she'd put up with enough fighting between her two former lovers and wanted to join the festivities.

A shocked silence settled over the crowd. Every head turned toward Sadie, who sat pressed up against the lower half of the lid, looking pretty as you please in her blue chiffon dress.

"Holy Toledo! She's come back. Sadie's come back," Grace said.

The announcement triggered a mad rush for the exit at the rear of the room. Quinby watched as sixty or so people tried to squeeze out the double doors all at the same time. She figured that the stampede out the front door of the funeral home was going to attract more than a little attention.

Once the crowd hit the front walkway, rumors of Sadie Dunn sitting up in the middle of her own wake was going to spread like wildfire. And the fact that her two lovers were engaged in a wrestling match during the resurrection would only add to the juiciness of the rumor. Quinby wondered if now was the time to wander out back and check to see if Boomer Rachette was looking to put on a little extra help.

JOSH WAS OUT OF THE CRUISER and through the back door as soon as Quinby called over the radio. He found Boomer standing in the center of his lobby, a tide of guests streaming through the viewing room and out the front door.

Boomer was trying to shout reassurances, but no one seemed interested in listening. They flowed around him like lemmings headed over the cliff into the sea. It was an odd scene, especially when coupled with the melancholy classical music being played over the intercom.

"Where's Oscar?" Josh demanded.

Boomer scowled and pointed toward the viewing room. "Arrest that old fool. He's ruining my business."

Josh gently shouldered his way through the exiting crowd and entered the now almost empty room.

Oscar and some other elderly guy sat side by side on a couch, handcuffed together and glowering up at a little old lady who stood over them with a cane.

"Come over here and help me get this coffin back where it belongs," Quinby said, standing at the front of the room, with her hands on her hips. She looked peeved. On second look, Josh decided that peeved might be too mild a description.

Several curls had pulled free from her ponytail, and coiled along the side of her face. Her eyes flashed with irritation as she blew them aside. Josh struggled not to grin.

"You sure do know how to liven up a wake, Parker. What happened?" he asked as he walked over to help her lift the heavy box back into place.

"You wouldn't believe me if I told you. Do you think we could just call it a day and take Oscar home? I'm sure Sadie will understand if we don't stick around for the rest of the wake," she said.

"No doubt you're right." Josh went over and unlocked the two men, and the three of them headed for the back door. Josh could only hope that they'd get out before Boomer started shouting something about filing for damages.

LATER THAT AFTERNOON, Quinby inserted the key into the ignition of her truck and said a little prayer. She pumped the gas pedal twice and turned the key. Nothing. Not even a grind. It wasn't a good sign.

She really needed a new vehicle. As much as she loved the old pickup, it was on its last wheeze. She turned the key off and sat back. It was too cold to walk, and she knew Paige had a date tonight so she wasn't available to come pick her up. If Quinby called the restaurant, Mama would have to leave to fetch her. Better to just call a cab.

A knock on the window startled her out of her reverie. Glancing up, she saw Josh standing on the other side of the frosted glass.

"Won't start?" he asked as she rolled down the window.

"Yeah, I think the battery is dead. I've been meaning to get a new one put in."

Quinby could see the indecision on his face—did he stick around and help or did he take off, figuring she'd find a way to get home. She was pretty sure he was remembering his last attempt to play the Good Samaritan in the department parking lot.

"Look, don't worry about me," she said. "I'll get one of the guys from inside to come out and give the truck a jump."

He leaned on the windowsill, poking his head through the open window. "Try the ignition again," he ordered.

His warm breath brushed against the side of her face, and she tried to ignore the silly flutter in the pit of her stomach as she leaned forward to try the key again. Nothing.

Josh straightened up and pulled the door open. "Forget it. It's dead. I'll give you a ride home."

Quinby shook her head. "You don't need to do that. I'll call a cab." She climbed out of the vehicle and slammed the door. The whole truck shuddered, and a piece of rust fell off the front end. "No need for me to tie you up. I know you have to pick up Zack."

Josh glanced down at his watch. "I do, but that doesn't mean that I can't give you a ride." He nodded toward his shiny, black, much newer truck sitting two slots down from her beat-up piece of junk. "Get in.

We'll swing by and get Zack first. Then I'll drop you off. That way I won't be late, and it won't give my ex a reason to jot down a note about my mess-up. I try not to give her anything to complain about.'' He started toward his truck, but Quinby hung back. When he realized she wasn't following, he swung around, a frown springing up between those magnificent dark brows. "Come on, Parker. I don't have all evening."

"You really don't have to do this," Quinby protested.

"Of course I don't. Now quit stalling or you're going to make me late."

He turned and walked over to his truck. Sighing, Quinby trudged after him.

As she climbed into the cab and settled into the passenger seat, he asked, "Where do I drop you?"

"Chen's Pizzeria."

"You working tonight?"

"No. I live over the pizzeria."

"Doesn't the entire Chen family own and occupy those apartments over the restaurant?"

"Yes."

"So how did you manage to wrangle a spot in among the Chen family?"

"Because I'm one of the family."

Josh snorted. "I don't mean to burst any bubbles here, Parker, but I'd stake my reputation on guessing that you're *not* Chinese-American."

Quinby snapped her seat belt on. "Very funny. The Chens were my foster parents when I was a kid. I just never left, so they were kind of stuck with me."

He paused, his hand on the shift. His gaze softened a tad. "I'm sorry. I didn't know that you were raised in foster care."

Quinby shrugged. "No big deal. I went to live with the Chens when I was fifteen. My mom was pretty sick, and when I got into some trouble with the law, the powers-that-be decided that foster care was the best place for me.''

He nodded, studying her face for another second before, shifting into Reverse and backing up. As he headed out of the parking lot and entered the flow of traffic, he was quiet. Contemplative.

Quinby had the feeling that he was mulling over the information she had just revealed about herself. Strangely enough, the fact that he seemed to be considering it so seriously didn't really bother Quinby. There was no concern on her part that Josh would use the information to hurt her.

Within a few minutes, Josh pulled up in front of the day care. He left the engine running and jumped out. Cold air rushed into the cab of the truck.

He reached behind the seat and pulled out a child's booster seat. Shoving it up on the front seat next to Quinby, he said, ''Do you mind getting that secured while I get Zack?''

''Sure'' Quinby said.

She bent over to pull the middle seat belt up through the brackets on the seat. The cloth snagged on the metal and twisted. Quinby swore softly and tugged. The heater threw hot air on her face, and her own seat belt rubbed against the side of her neck.

She reached down and unsnapped her own belt. How did parents do this while holding a squirming kid in their arms? Finally managing to untwist it, she snapped it shut and sat back up just as Josh was coming down the front steps of the day care with Zack in his arms.

7

QUINBY WATCHED AS JOSH pulled open the door and set his son on the running board of the truck.

"Get in your seat, Zack," he said.

"No." Zack stuck out his lower lip and jammed his small hands up against the door frame, preventing Josh from moving him any further into the cab.

Quinby gave the little guy a soft smile and received a suspicious glare in return.

"I don't wanna sit in no baby seat," Zack said.

Quinby struggled to hide a grin. The full lower lip and blue eyes looked remarkably familiar. It was like looking at a miniature version of Josh, which made Quinby fairly certain the little guy was going to rival his father as a babe magnet by the time he was fifteen.

What was she supposed to do now? The little guy was stuck in the doorway, refusing to come in because she was sitting there and his father expected him to sit in the booster seat. She could always offer to get a taxi from here. Seemingly oblivious to the tiny tantrum brewing, Josh lifted Zack onto the front seat. Zack stared defiantly down the length of the cab, his feelings about finding Quinby sitting there more than obvious.

Quinby glanced at Josh. He shook his head, a small muscle in his cheek jumping into a noticeable knot. Apparently the booster seat was a frequent bone of contention between father and son. It wasn't hard to see that in addition to hating the *baby* seat, Zack wasn't too happy about finding an intruder sitting in the front seat of his father's truck. No doubt Zack had expected to have his dad all to himself.

"I'm not in the mood, Zack," Josh said. Zack's scowl got darker. "Just get in the seat and buckle up. I'm cold, tired and I don't want to argue."

Zack folded his arms. "No."

Quinby could see Josh's lips tighten in exasperation.

"Come on, big boy, do me a favor and get in the seat." Although Josh's voice had softened a bit, Zack still seemed bent on pressing the rebellion. He shook his head, the bright red and green pompom on top of his hat bobbing merrily.

Quinby held up a hand. "Hang on. Everyone relax. I'll take the booster seat." She shifted herself toward the middle of the cab. "Gotta admit, Zack, I don't think I can get my big rear end in that tiny seat but I'm willing to try."

Zack watched her, his blue eyes widening in surprise.

"Quin…" Josh said, his voice trailing off helplessly as she tried to wiggle her rear into the tiny booster seat.

She squeezed her eyes shut and pretended to push hard to get it past the sides. She peeked out of one eye and smiled at Zack. He grinned hesitantly, the corner of his mitten finding its way up to his lips to be gnawed on.

Quinby was pretty sure he was wondering who the nut case was sitting in his father's truck and trying to get into his booster seat. But he wasn't about to stop her at this point in the game.

"Zowie. Sure is a tight fit," she said, pretending to push even harder.

Zack started to giggle.

"Might get stuck," Quinby said.

Zack was laughing outright now, his mitten forgotten. "You're too big." He pushed playfully against her arm.

"You sure, Zack?" Quinby grunted and pushed harder. "I think I'm almost in."

"No way," Zack said, leaning against her and pushing harder. "You're gonna get stuck."

Quinby put her hands on either side of the chair and pushed as if trying to get out. "You're right. Now I'm stuck."

"Uh-oh," Zack said, suddenly serious. He maneuvered his small hands behind her and started pushing. "I help you."

Quinby allowed herself to pop out of the seat. "Whew. Thanks, buddy. I thought I was stuck in the front seat of your dad's truck forever and ever." She settled back into the passenger side of the cab and beamed at Zack. He beamed back at her.

"What's your name?" Zack asked as he climbed into the vacated booster seat.

"Quinby Parker. I'm your dad's new partner." Quinby said, glancing over to check Josh's reaction to her antics. He grinned at her, shook his head in disbelief and climbed behind the wheel.

Zack turned and looked at his father. "That true, Daddy?"

"Is what true, Zack?" Josh asked, his attention obviously focused on getting his son buckled in before he staged another protest.

"You work with her?"

Josh sat up and put on his own belt. "Yeah, Quinby's my new partner, Zack." He put the truck into drive and pulled out into light traffic.

Quinby clicked on her own seat belt and settled back in the seat, surprised by the little flutter of contentment that passed through her in response to Josh's confirmation that she was indeed his partner. It felt good. Mighty good.

A FEW MINUTES LATER, they pulled up in front of Chen's Pizzeria. Josh squeezed the big truck into the only empty spot directly in front of the massive oak door leading to the eat-in portion of the establishment.

"Pizza? You live at a pizza store?" Zack squealed, awe infusing every fiber of his small frame. He wiggled in his seat, straining against his seat belt in an attempt to see out the window. "You must eat pizza every night?"

Quinby glanced over his head at Josh. "Quite the talkative little guy, isn't he."

Josh laughed. "You don't know the half of it."

"I don't exactly live *in* the pizza place, Zack. More like over it." Quinby pointed up to several small windows on the second floor. "I live up there. And no, I don't eat pizza every night." She smiled and nudged Zack with her elbow. "Sometimes I eat a meatball sub."

Zack bent forward and looked up. "I wish I was you."

Quinby grinned and resisted the urge to lean forward and kiss his pink cheek. Instead she opened the door and stepped out. "Thanks for the ride, Josh. Nice meeting you, Zack."

"I want pizza, Daddy," Zack said.

"Not this time, big guy. We need to get home," Josh said.

"But I want pizza," Zack whined. "I'm tired of plop pies."

Quinby laughed. "Plop pies?"

Josh shrugged and shot her a sheepish grin. "I'm not known for my culinary skills. One of Zack's favorites is chicken pot pies. When he was little, he thought I was saying plop pies." Josh shrugged. "The name stuck."

Quinby nodded toward the restaurant. "Don't mean

to interfere, but if you guys want to come in, I'll make up a pizza for you to take home.'' She shifted her feet, her smile hesitant. ''Or you could eat it here. It's the least I can do to thank you for rescuing me from a cold cab ride home.''

Josh paused. He knew he should say no thanks and drive home. But he couldn't. And even more importantly, he didn't want to. The thought of a few more minutes in Quinby's company was too good to give up.

She stood on the sidewalk in front of Chen's Pizzeria, leaning casually on the door and smiling into the cab at them. He was struck again by her unique beauty. It was a different beauty, not something that he could easily describe. Something that pulled at him and made him want her. Made him want to spend more time with her even though a small voice inside his head told him to put the truck in Drive and get out of there.

Zack pulled at his sleeve. ''Can we, Daddy? Can we eat pizza with her?'' His eyes pleaded in a way that never failed to get to Josh.

''Come on, Dad, bend a little,'' Quinby teased, her grin widening as she seemed to sense that he was weakening.

Josh unbuckled. ''Sure. Why not.'' He reached over to help Zack, and as soon as he was free of the seat, Zack scooted out the door on Quinby's side. Obviously he wasn't going to take any chances that Josh would change his mind.

As Josh rounded the hood and stepped up on the curb, he found Quinby crouched down on the frozen sidewalk, using one hand on the cold cement to balance herself as she allowed Zack to climb on for a piggyback ride. He squealed and wrapped his arms around her neck.

Quinby hitched him up higher on her back and turned to smile at Josh. ''Ready?''

He nodded and couldn't help but envy the fact that Zack had his head pressed into the thick curls of Quinby's hair, and his mittened hands clasped tightly around her slender neck. He wouldn't mind occupying that position himself—but he'd have less innocent plans for where his hands would wander. Touch. Explore.

He blinked, and checked Quinby's expression to gauge whether or not she had any inclination of the direction his thoughts had taken. But she simply smiled up at him, a puzzled look on her face.

"You okay?" she asked.

"Sure. Sure. I'm fine." He motioned them to go ahead and followed the two of them through the front door of the restaurant.

Mama Chen's was decorated like a traditional Italian restaurant. Small tables with red-and-white checkered tablecloths lined the wall, divided and made more intimate by small brick partitions. The center of the room had larger, more family-size tables. Tiny lanterns sat in the middle of each table and gave a warm, flickering glow.

The Chen's obviously did a brisk business because in spite of it being a Thursday night, the place was fairly crowded with couples and families. A tiny Asian woman stood behind the reservation desk, and as they entered, she looked up. Her delicate, well-wrinkled face broke into a welcoming smile.

"Quinby! You're home for dinner and you've brought guests." She stepped out from behind the desk and moved to greet them. Her gaze was drawn immediately to Zack, her dark eyes twinkling with the look of a woman who adored children. "And who might this be?" She reached up and lightly touched Zack's shoulder.

"Evenin', Mama," Quinby said. She grabbed Zack's forearm and swung him around to sit on her hip. He seemed completely at ease with her, sitting there looking at the Asian woman with suspicious interest, his sturdy legs wrapped tightly around Quin's slim waist.

"This is my new partner, Josh Reed and his son, Zack. They gave me a ride home." Quinby crinkled her nose in disgust. "The truck died on me. I'm repaying their kindness with one of my junk pizzas."

Zack leaned forward and whispered loud enough for them all to hear, "No anchobies, Quin. I hate anchobies."

Quinby smiled down at him and slid his hat off the back of his head. "You got it, buddy. Everything but anchovies."

Mrs. Chen offered Josh her hand. "So you're the new partner Quinby can't stop talking about?"

"She talks about me, does she?" Josh said, shooting a smart-alecky grin in Quinby's direction.

Quinby raised an eyebrow and poked Mrs. Chen. "Don't say that. I *do not* talk about him all the time."

"Oh, hush, you do, too," Mrs. Chen said.

"She's going to make a fine officer, ma'am," Josh said, shaking Mrs. Chen's hand gently.

Quinby scoffed. "Don't be lying to Mama. She's got a built-in radar to pick up a person's creative little lies." She grinned affectionately at the older woman. "I should know—she caught me in enough of them over the years."

Mama Chen reached up and patted Quinby on the cheek. "You're always so full of it, Quinby. But you're a good girl." She turned back to Josh. "Don't listen to her talk about being a bad girl. She works hard, and she makes the best pizza of all my kids."

Josh watched Quinby's pink cheeks deepen in color, her brown eyes shinning with obvious appreciation of the compliment.

"Jeesh, Mama, don't embarrass me with all that

goopy mother talk.'' She glanced at Josh and smiled apologetically. ''Come on. We'll go out in the kitchen, and I'll make you both that pizza.''

''Mothers are allowed to talk like that, Quinby—it's our job. If you make a mess of the kitchen, make sure you clean up,'' Mama Chen ordered, moving to greet a couple who had come through the front door behind them.

Quinby glanced at Josh and shrugged, her expression amused. There was no doubt she loved the woman. No wonder she had never left the shelter of the Chen family. Apparently she felt as if she belonged. And considering Mama Chen's reaction to Quinby, it was obvious that the feeling was reciprocated. He followed Quinby and Zack through swinging double doors at the back of the restaurant.

Leaving the intimate lighting and soft dinner music of the dining room, they entered a brilliantly lit kitchen filled with delicious, exotic smells. Several cooks shouted a greeting to Quinby, but none of them left their posts next to the huge ovens.

Within minutes, Quinby had both Josh and Zack situated in front of a massive wooden island counter, pristine white aprons on and a ball of pizza dough in front of them.

Zack, comfortably perched on a high stool, poked his finger into the dough and giggled. ''Pizza's flat, Quinby. How we gonna make a pizza with this?''

Josh watched Quinby finish putting on her own apron, her quick hands nimbly wrapping the string around her waist and then tying it in a neat bow in the front.

''You're right, Zack. First we have to flatten the dough out. And I'll need your help to do that.''

Quinby stepped in between the two of them, her shoulder brushing up against Josh's, her soft scent wafting upward and invading his senses, reminding him of her softness when he had kissed her. He fought against the surge of attraction pulling at him.

As Quinby leaned down to show Zack how to spread the dough from the center out, her shirt tightened across her shoulders and back, and Josh found himself following the clean indented line of her spine stretched down the length of her back. He fought the sudden urge to reach out and trace the line from top to bottom—to run the tip of his finger down the narrow column to the frayed waistband of her worn jeans.

He shook his head and tried to concentrate on what Quinby was saying to Zack as they giggled and spread the dough out on the countertop. Josh wondered what her reaction would be if she noticed him staring at the sweet line of her back.

"Okay," Quinby said, picking up the dough and settling it over her fists. "Now comes the fun part."

She lifted the dough and started turning it, tugging and spreading it outward before throwing it up in the air and allowing it to land back down on her fists. She continued working it outward, twirling it and then throwing it up again.

Zack watched with rapt attention, his mouth a perfect circle of awe as she threw the dough higher and higher. "Wow! Can I do that?"

Quinby smiled at him and slid the fresh dough onto a well-oiled pizza pan. "Sure, Zack. Let me get you some dough." She reached past Josh, her arm brushing against his chest.

She jumped slightly and glanced up at him from beneath thick brown lashes. "Sorry." She pointed to a large bin situated next to the counter. "I just need to get another ball of dough out of the bin."

Josh wasn't sure why, but he held his position. "Go right ahead."

A slightly flustered expression flashed across

Quinby's face as she stretched around him. She was making an obvious effort not to come in direct contact with him, but considering their close proximity to each other, not touching was an impossibility. As she dug down into the bin, one jean clad cheek bumped against his groin, sending a sharp message of need shooting straight through to his brain.

Josh shifted back, immediately regretting his decision to make things difficult for her. He had only succeeded in making things harder on himself—hard in a very prominent place on his own body.

"Excuse me," Quinby mumbled, straightening up and brushing back a handful of warm brown curls. A dusting of flour smudged her right cheek, and as she glanced up at him, a tiny smile pulled at the corner of her lips.

"I never realized cooking could get quite so cozy." Her innocent tone was disrupted by the wicked twinkle in her eyes.

She divided the dough into quarters and gave one quarter to Zack. "Here you go, buddy. You can make your own little pizza with whatever you want on it."

Josh watched as she guided Zack's hands, helping him spread and work the dough. Getting it up in the air was a bit less successful, but Zack really wasn't disappointed. He got to choose his own toppings, and he sat comfortably in Josh's arms as Quinby slid their pizzas into the huge oven. Within a short period of time, they were all settled at a cozy table in the main dining room eating their delicious creations.

AN HOUR LATER, with the pizza devoured and their stomachs sufficiently filled, Quinby sat back and glanced over at Zack. He had a ring of tomato sauce circling his mouth and a red stain down the front of his shirt. But he had a contented smile plastered across his mischievous face, and from experience, Quinby knew there was nothing better than eating your own creation. The width of Zack's smile was proof of that.

It was when Quinby started to pour Josh and herself a cup of coffee that Mama chose to appear. Quinby had been waiting for her, knowing that Mama couldn't resist the pull of little Zack. Her love of small children was legendary, and sure enough, within minutes, she had charmed Zack out of his seat and had him begging to go upstairs with her to visit her pet parrot Zale.

"She's like the Pied Piper," Quinby said with affection as the two disappeared toward the back of the restaurant.

"She seems very fond of you," Josh said.

"I don't think I ever felt safer than when I was sitting with Mama, drinking tea and getting a lecture about something or other I'd done wrong." Quinby could see the questions just waiting to burst forth from between Josh's lips, but she was tired of talking about herself. Time to be a little more assertive for a change.

"How long—" he started.

"Not so fast," Quin interrupted. "It's my turn to ask the questions."

Josh laughed, but he didn't protest. He simply leaned forward, resting his forearms on the table and waited.

"Why did you and Zack's mom break up?"

Josh nodded, as if he knew that she'd ask this question. "It was as simple as two people getting together who should never have married in the first place."

Quinby frowned. "That's pretty sketchy. What happened?"

He shrugged. "Too young. Too selfish. Too immature. Too stubborn. Take your pick. Any one of them fit."

"That's pretty harsh, Josh. There had to have been something that drew you to Caroline."

"Sure, raging adolescent hormones. If we had waited,

we would have quickly found out we were completely unsuited to each others temperament. Complete opposites.''

"But something good must have come out of it.''

Josh's gaze softened. "That would be Zack—he's the best thing that's ever happened to me." The corners of his mouth turned up in a bittersweet smile. "For Caroline, too, for that matter.''

Quinby waited, silently soaking in the picture of Josh in the candlelight. It scared her how much she liked looking at him—being with him. As if he had gotten under her skin and connected with her on a level she didn't want to admit existed even to herself. She liked the way his long fingers toyed with the salt shaker, the square nails neatly trimmed and the blue trace of veins beneath his tanned skin.

Quinby liked how the glow of the flame touched one side of his face, creating tiny flashes of light in his dark hair. An unfamiliar longing washed over her, and Quinby forced herself to fold her hands in front of her—to clench them tight together in a pathetic attempt to escape the overwhelming urge to reach out and touch him.

She dipped her head, gathering her strength. It was all she could to keep from pulling him to her and kissing him long and hard, just as he had kissed and held her last night.

Josh sat silent, seemingly lost in his thoughts.

Finally Quinby asked, "So if the both of you agree that Zack is the best part of your marriage, why is Caroline trying to limit your visitations? What's her reason for keeping the two of you apart?''

A muscle in Josh's cheek jumped and tightened, and the blue of his eyes froze. "Because she's remarrying and planning to move to California with her new husband, a computer whiz with a six-figure earning potential. I think she believes that it will be better for Zack if I'm out of his life. That way, Patrick can move right in as the new daddy.''

The pain in his eyes made Quinby wish she hadn't asked and she reached out, laying a hand on his forearm. ''I'm sorry. She's wrong.''

Josh smiled, the usual impact of his sexy smile dampened by his sadness. He patted her hand and then slid out from beneath her touch, sitting back and resting his arms along the back of the booth. Quinby glanced away, her heart tightening against the disappointment of his gentle rejection of her attempt to comfort him.

''Enough about me. What about you? How'd you end up in foster care?'' he asked.

''Oh, so now I get the third-degree, huh?''

He nodded. ''Turnaround is fair play.''

Quinby reached up and peeled a piece of melted wax off the side of the Chianti bottle. It was still warm and soft, molding itself to the tip of her finger.

''My mom wasn't able to take care of me.'' She glanced up, concerned Josh would get the wrong idea. ''She was a very caring person. She just wasn't very good at mothering. I think she was too busy growing up herself.'' She flattened the piece of wax against her napkin and went back to peeling several more pieces off the wine bottle. ''She meant well, but I was a headstrong kid, and by the time I was twelve, I had gotten involved with a group of pretty wild kids.''

''Wild how?''

Quinby paused. She liked Josh. Really liked him. But trust was another issue. Did she tell him all the stuff about her lousy past? What if it drove him off? Made him believe all the stuff people like Tripp were saying about her.

But then as quickly as she worried about it, she dismissed it. Josh was her partner, and partners shared information like this. It was the stuff that created the glue that bonded them together. The cement that made their partnership all the more powerful.

"I saw the inside of Family Court more than a few times by the time I was thirteen. Nothing major—just stupid kid stuff. My mom was pretty sick by then—cancer. Hospice was coming to the house every day, but there really wasn't anyone to look after me. My probation officer finally recommended that I be put in foster care."

"Your father didn't visit at any point during that time?"

Quinby shook her head. Tears prickled the corners of her eyes and made her afraid she'd burst into tears. If there was one thing she didn't want to do, it was to cry in front of Josh Reed.

"Did he know what was happening?"

Quinby took a sip of water. "I don't know. We never really talk about the past. Mainly we talk about what I'm going to do with the rest of my life." She shrugged. "I assume my probation officer talked with him back then. Tried to see if he'd take care of me. But he must have been busy with his own problems—he didn't need to be saddled with a troubled teenager."

"Why do you make excuses for him?"

Quinby tilted her head. "I'm not."

Josh leaned forward. "But you are. Brad Tennison is your father, and he's never stepped forward to accept that role. Ever."

Quinby shifted uncomfortably. "Funny. I thought you and my father were good friends."

"We are. But that doesn't change my opinion of how he's acted. And knowing your father as well as I do, it's a given that he's feeling some kind of guilt over how he's treated you."

Quinby swallowed against the tight knot in her throat. "Somehow I've let him down."

"You've let *him* down?" Josh's shoulders bunched and shifted beneath his shirt. "Your father is the one who never acknowledged you. Never stepped forward to help his own daughter who needed him."

"But I've let him down by being a lousy cop. Whenever he talks about being a cop this unbelievable sparkle leaps into his eyes." Quinby sighed. "And we all know how much I've messed up my chance to be a cop."

Josh shook his head and sat back, running a hand through the dark strands of his hair. "Don't you see that if you want to be a cop that all you have to do is focus and believe in yourself? It's all about what you want—not what your father wants."

Unsure of how to respond, Quinby continued to peel wax from the bottle. Josh reached across and covered her hand with his own, stilling her senseless shredding of the candle wax. The warmth of his hand seemed to engulf her, surrounding her with a heat that was almost unbearable. She lifted her head to meet his gaze just as Vince Gill's smooth, sweet voice spilled out of the jukebox singing, "When Love Finds You."

JOSH SMILED REASSURINGLY, recognizing how close Quinby was to breaking down completely. He hadn't planned on that happening. He hadn't meant to get so close.

The evening had been going so nicely—almost blissful, in fact. Then they had to ask all these silly personal questions, which put them both on edge.

He needed to get things back to where they were a few minutes ago, before they'd stepped over the imaginary boundaries they'd created to protect themselves.

He nodded in the direction of the jukebox. "That's one of my favorite songs. Any chance I can get you up to dance?"

He watched a flash of indecision flicker across her face and then disappear behind a wide smile. It was quick action on her part. Apparently she had decided to push the thoughts completely out of her mind and concentrate on other things. Better for both of them. A pleasant dance, finish their coffee and then he and Zack would leave for home. Nothing to it.

They stood together and moved over to the tiny dance floor.

Quinby stepped into the circle of his arms, and Josh felt a small shudder ripple through her frame as she reached up to put her arms around his neck. Her thumb grazed the warm skin at the back of his neck, and his body reacted with its own shiver.

The first few bars of the song drifted across the dimly lit room. He moved, and when she tried to follow, the tip of her sneaker came down on his toe. "Sorry," she mumbled, not lifting her head.

Josh pressed his hand against the middle of her back, pulling her closer, his fingers tracing the line of her spine. "A little less distance between us might help, Parker," he said. "Relax. This is a dance, not a police drill."

She nodded, but didn't look at him. He figured she was too nervous, her attention glued to her feet, trying to keep count. Her movements were stiff and jerky. They moved together for a few minutes, almost seeming to get the rhythm, but then she stumbled again. She swore softly against his shoulder, and her fingers tightened, her movements becoming even more wooden.

Josh was amused. She was totally out of her element. Discomfort seemed to radiate off her in giant waves of panic. He paused and stepped back, forcing her to look up at him. "Are you okay?"

Her face was flushed, a pinkness visible even in the mute lighting at the back of the restaurant. She seemed to sense his amusement, and her mouth tightened, a glint of grim determination entering her eyes.

"What?" she demanded.

Josh laughed. "Are you always this tense? I thought you were the proverbial lighthearted soul." He rubbed his hands up and down her arms like a trainer preparing his fighter for the ring. "Relax, will you? I could snap you in two you're so uptight."

"Might save me from having to do this," she said. "I'm not a very good—"

He stopped her in midgrumble by pulling her up against him, plastering her long, luscious curves down his entire length, nudging his pelvis up against hers and allowing her to feel his heat. She attempted to look up, a protest on her lips, but he simply touched the back of her head, his fingers threading through the soft curls and pressing her cheek gently to his shoulder.

"Close your eyes, Quin," he said. "Let yourself go. Don't think. Don't move unless I move you. Let me do everything."

And so they moved, a gentle swaying motion of two bodies pressed tightly together as one, and Quin found that she could barely breathe, let alone speak. A strange heaviness came over her, flooding her limbs and weighing down her eyelids.

Her heart raced and she held on tighter. It was his scent that got to her. His scent and the graceful glide of his muscles beneath her fingers. It was like stepping off the edge of a cliff and suddenly finding that you can fly.

He seemed to sense the liquidness that had overtaken her limbs and he pulled her closer, the warmth of his hand radiating through her shirt seeming to burn an imprint upon her hot skin.

"Whatcha doing?" a small voice asked.

They both looked down to see Zack standing next to them, his eyes wide with wonder.

Quinby felt as if she was molded to Josh, but Zack's appearance brought her back to earth. She stiffened and started to pull away, but Josh stopped her by tightening his arm.

"Relax," he whispered softly.

He leaned down and scooped Zack up, nestling him

in next to them, and suddenly, they became an interesting circle of three.

"We're dancing," Josh said, "and there's nothing more important for a man to learn, Zack, than how to dance with a beautiful woman."

The three of them continued to move as one to the smooth notes of the jukebox, and the flickering wall lanterns surrounded them in a warm, yellow glow.

It was a strange sensation. Exotic and comforting all at the same time. A mixture of Josh's power and strength moving beneath her hands, and Zack's tiny frame wedged against her side.

Zack had laid his head against his father's chest, his thumb stuck firmly in his mouth. His head was turned toward her, and he watched her with a child's seriousness.

"Daddy?" Zack asked.

"Yes, Zack?" Josh said.

Zack's blue eyes stared into hers, and above her, Josh rested his cheek against the top of her head.

"Quinby's pretty, isn't she, Daddy?"

Quinby held her breath.

"Yes, Zack. Officer Parker is a very pretty lady." As he spoke, Josh lifted his head off hers.

Quin released the air trapped in her lungs. With the use of her official title, Josh had neatly replaced the invisible barrier between them. The spot on top of her head where he'd rested his chin was cold.

Even if he felt the strong pull—the delicious possibility of something more, Josh was making it perfectly clear that he wouldn't allow it to happen. He had relegated her back to the position of partner.

8

THE NEXT MORNING the temperature soared into the mid-forties. Unusual for the month of January in the North Country, a place accustomed to the deep freeze.

Josh arrived at the station a little earlier than usual, aware that this was the day he had promised to meet with the chief to report on his daughter's progress.

He pulled into the lot and backed in next to Quinby's piece of junk truck, still stalled from last night. He'd help her tow it to the garage down the street after work. All it needed was a new battery.

Climbing out, Josh paused next to Quinby's truck. He ran his hand along the frost-encrusted tailgate. Last night had been a mistake. A major mistake. One that he had committed with his eyes wide open. But when he'd finally stumbled out of his stupor and realized what he was doing, he found his arms wrapped around Quinby's lithe, athletic form.

When Quinby had stepped back out of his arms last night, there had been a few uncomfortable moments. Both of them had scrambled to fill in the uncomfortable awkwardness that followed and ended up stumbling over each other's words. But finally, after a few minutes, Josh managed to thank Quinby for a wonderful evening. He shifted a sleepy Zack higher up onto his shoulder and left.

For a moment, he had thought that Quinby was going to follow them out to the truck, but in the end, she didn't. Instead she stopped at the doorway, wrapping her arms around her upper body in a useless attempt to ward off the night air. She watched as he buckled Zack in.

Finished, he turned toward her, their eyes meeting wordlessly. She had smiled and leaned a shoulder against the door frame. The soft light from the restaurant haloed her lush body, outlining her long legs and wild curls. She waved and Josh raised his hand. A small voice in the back of his head had whispered, *Fool.* But Josh ignored it and walked around to the driver's side. The decision hadn't been an easy one, but it was the one Josh believed was right.

Shaking off the sentimental thoughts, Josh made his way to Brad Tennison's office, stopping off to pour two cups of black coffee. When he entered the chief's office, Brad Tennison sat hunched over a thick computer print-out; Josh figured it was the stats for the past month. Brad Tennison might be close to retirement age, but he was a cop who believed in modern policing. He insisted all his officers be proficient in the use of computers, and he included himself in that dictate.

In response to Josh's entrance, Brad sat back, pulled off his reading glasses and rubbed his eyes. "Punctual as usual."

Josh nodded and set one of the mugs of coffee down at the top of Brad's desk blotter. "We don't have much time because my shift starts in about twenty minutes. I'd prefer Quinby didn't see me in here. Lack of confidence is her biggest problem." He sat in the chair opposite the desk. "I'd like her to believe that I have enough faith in her skills that I'm not in here reporting on her every time she turns around."

Brad raised an eyebrow. "Does this mean you've had an unexpected change of heart in regards to her candidacy as an officer in this department?"

Josh took a sip of the hot coffee, allowing the strong brew to shoot a jolt of caffeine through his system before answering. "I believe that Officer Parker has the skill and intellect to become a fine officer in this department. If that's what she wants." He set his mug on the edge of the desk and shrugged "Your guess is as good as mine."

"What's that supposed to mean?"

"It means that I think she's doing this because on some level she believes it will please you."

Brad frowned and sat forward in his chair, the padded back snapping forward in response to his sudden movement. "Did Quin tell you she felt that way?"

"Quinby wouldn't admit to it even if someone was shoving hot bamboo shoots under her fingernails. On some level she truly believes that she wants this."

"But you don't believe her?" Brad sat back, a look of disappointment crossing his face. "You think she's simply going through the motions to please me?"

"That's not what I said." Josh stood up and moved to the window overlooking the parking lot. "Quinby is drifting. She knows that she wants to please you because you're the only family she has left. Deep inside she believes that by being a good cop, she'll gain your respect—" he turned and faced his boss "—and possibly force you to accept her."

Brad scowled. "That's ridiculous. I respect Quinby. And I accept her, too... What the heck does that mean anyway—accept her?"

The chief's scowl deepened, and Josh knew he was treading on dangerous ground, but something prevented him from backing off. "It means do you really accept her as your daughter—your flesh and blood?"

Brad's complexion paled a bit, and he sucked in a deep breath. He avoided eye contact with Josh, concentrating on polishing the lens of his eyeglasses. "Of course I do. Why would I assign my best officer to work with her if I didn't?''

Shaking his head, Josh folded his arms and leaned against the window frame. "You're not getting this, Brad. It isn't about Quinby passing her field training. It's about her father accepting her and recognizing her as his daughter.''

A heavy silence settled over the office as a myriad of emotions played across Brad's face. He laid his eye-glasses on the blotter and allowed his gaze to connect with Josh's. "You never were one to mince words, were you?''

"Not when I see you doing something you normally wouldn't condone in another person.''

"You're saying that I've failed her, aren't you?''

Josh sighed. He hadn't wanted to stick his nose into the chief's business—especially business that was of such a personal nature. In fact, it was the last thing Josh wanted to do at this point in his life. He had enough of his own stuff to deal with without going out and looking for more to wade through.

He raked a hand through his hair and glanced out the window again. As if on cue, a taxi pulled up, and Quinby climbed out, laughing at something the driver said, before reaching back into the car to pay the fare. She slammed the door shut and waved before hurrying up the walkway.

Her extravagant hair streamed out behind her, the curls spilling across her collar in a cloud of warm color. The simple act of seeing her stride up the walkway with her long legs forced Josh to lean forward to catch a final glimpse of her as she disappeared through the front door.

Brad drew his attention back to the conversation at hand. "Are you saying that Quinby feels as though I've rejected her—failed to recognize her as my daughter?''

"Have you?" Josh asked.

"We're both busy adults—we don't have time for much, but we go out to dinner occasionally."

His glimpse of Quinby gone, Josh turned back toward Brad. "When you're out, do you introduced her to people as your daughter?"

Brad's eyes shifted away. "There really hasn't been a chance."

"That's bull, and you know it." Josh rounded the desk and sat back down. "I've been out to dinner with you a thousand times and there isn't a time that someone hasn't stopped by the table to talk."

Brad held up a hand. "Okay, I've been dodging the issue of Quinby's parentage for some time now. I figured that she was an adult and it wasn't that important. That helping her find and keep a career was more important."

"If you believe that, Brad, then you're a bigger fool than I thought."

Brad sat back in his chair, the creaking of the springs splitting the heavy air. "How so?"

"Come on. Did you really think that Quinby wouldn't be hurt by your refusal to recognize her publicly as your daughter."

"No. I knew it was hurting her even though she tried to hide it." Brad rubbed two fingers between his eyes as if trying to relieve some tension. "She's never said anything or complained, but I knew it bothered her. I was just too cowardly to come out and admit it."

"Then I guess I don't need to explain it to you anymore, do I?" Josh glanced at his watch and stood up. "I need to get going. I hope you're able to sort this out, Chief."

He headed for the door, stopping once to glance back. Brad sat with his hands folded loosely in front of him, his broad shoulders slumped beneath the heavy weight of the knowledge he was trying to absorb. He looked up and smiled apologetically, his handsome features composed into a pensive expression.

"Thanks for setting me straight, Josh. I'll make things right," Brad said, before looking back down at his hands.

Josh nodded and left.

QUINBY SIGNED IN, changed into her uniform and wandered into the briefing room looking for Josh. She was glad to see Paige and her partner sitting at one of the tables, conferring in front of one of the computer screens and finishing up some end of shift paperwork. When Paige glanced up, she smiled and motioned Quinby over.

"Where's the Iceman?" she asked, a small smile of amusement playing around the corners of her lips. She nudged her partner with her elbow. "Bull here was just telling me about some of the Iceman's lesser advertised accomplishments. I told him that if I could bribe you, I was switching partners as of Monday."

Quinby glanced over at Bull Michaels, wondering how nervous the guy got at the thought of her stepping in as his new partner—even if Paige was joking.

But he seemed unfazed, smiling benignly as he henpecked out another line on the keyboard before commenting, "And I told Paige that any partner of Josh Reed's was welcome to partner with me. At least you probably know how to fill out the paperwork in a timely manner."

Paige laughed and elbowed her partner again, only a little harder this time. "Watch it, Ace. You've misspelled perpetrator three times already. You should be thanking the report writing gods that you're partnered with Mrs. Mason's third-grade spelling bee champion."

She leaned over and tapped the screen, pointing out three spots on the report.

Bull scoffed, "What do you think a spell check is for, Paige?" He clicked on the spell check program and quickly corrected the errors.

Paige looked at Quinby. "Sit down. Talk to me for a minute. I hardly see you anymore. Are you ready to qualify at the range in two weeks?" The concern in her voice was obvious, and a small frown popped up between her perfectly plucked blond brows.

Quinby pulled out a chair from the table in front of the two and sat down. "As ready as I'll ever be," she said wearily.

"You need more practice. Going into this exam cold isn't going to help the situation," Paige warned.

Quinby nodded. Lord knows how much more practice she needed, but things had gotten complicated—the two lousy performance evaluations, and the assignment of a new training officer. She hadn't been over to the practice range in what seemed like eons.

It wasn't that she was a bad shot. Quite the opposite. At the academy, Quinby had actually been at the top of her class in weapons, but her recent difficulties seemed to have so affected her confidence that she had performed pretty badly on her last check. This next one needed to come in at a near prefect level if she wanted to keep her job.

"Relax. I have a little over a week to practice."

"Practice for what?" a voice asked from over her left shoulder.

Quinby jumped and looked up to find Josh standing directly behind her. How did he manage to sneak around like that? He seemed to tower over her, and it only took her a second to see that he was in his Iceman mode. His chiseled features were frozen in place and carefully composed into supercop mode.

She weighed the advisability of letting Josh in on her upcoming weapon evaluation and quickly decided it would only muddy their already murky partnership.

After last night, Quinby wasn't sure where she stood with him. One minute she was wrapped up warm and tight in those strong arms, and the next time she looked, he was all stiff and unresponsive. People might call her wacky and indecisive, but they needed to get a look at Josh Reed.

"Practice what?" he repeated, the cool blue of his gaze hitting her like a splash of ice water.

"Nothing important," Quinby said, shooting a warning glance in Paige's direction before standing up.

As usual, Paige ignored the warning. "Quin's worried about qualifying at the range. Any chance you can give her a few pointers?"

Josh shot a sharp look in Quinby's direction. "Why didn't you tell me you had this coming up?"

"Because I wasn't aware that I was required to report every aspect of my life to you. I have an appointment with my dentist on Tuesday for a cleaning—I didn't tell you about that, either."

Her sarcasm gave her little comfort. It wasn't Josh's fault that she messed up on her last evaluation. She had only herself to blame for that.

But darn it all, the man had her all tied up in knots. Last night had been wonderful. Sweet music. A strong, male body holding her tight and stirring up those delicious, aching feelings she'd worked so hard to ignore these past few months. One minute things had been great and the next they were gone. It was enough to leave any red-blooded woman dazed, confused and begging for more. But Quinby wasn't the type to beg—sarcasm had always worked so much better.

Before Josh could respond, the phone rang at the back of the room, and one of the other officers picked it up and called, "Judge Banner's office on the phone for you, Josh."

Josh gave Quinby a look that told her their conversation wasn't over and walked to the back of the room. He took the phone and talked quickly, nodding his head and jotting a few things on a piece of paper.

Quinby dug her nails into the center of her palm. How did he manage to look so calm? Didn't it bother him to face her this morning after last night? Was she the only one affected by what had happened?

Who did he think he was kidding? She had been pressed up against him. He couldn't deny his desire for her. His need. Heck, his *need* had almost drilled a hole right through her upper thigh on the dance floor.

Her cheeks burned hot, and she glanced away, embarrassed that she couldn't stop thinking about him. Another minute and she'd be foaming at the mouth. She really needed to get over this silly infatuation. Otherwise, work was going to become impossible.

She glanced up to see Josh hang up the phone.

He walked back over. "We need to get going. I have to stop by Judge Banner's office and then we can head over to Oscar's house."

Quinby remained silent but gave a quick nod. Further clarification wasn't needed. Talking to him was hard enough especially since he seemed totally unaffected by last night.

"Change back into civilian clothes," Josh said. "There's no need for us to attract any more attention than we have to. I'll meet you out at my truck in fifteen minutes." He turned and left.

"Whew. Talk about abrupt. Does the man ever smile?" Paige asked.

"Rarely," Quinby said wearily. Of course she didn't bother to comment on the fact that Josh's rare smile tended to curl her toes and shoot electricity up her spine.

Quinby glanced at the door and chewed on the inside of her cheek. Something was up, and it must be something big. Although she had been working with Josh for a relatively short period of time, she was adept at reading his moods. He was obviously distracted from what was going on around him. But the hard glint in his eyes told her he was focusing on something internal. Something important. Something that didn't have anything to do with baby-sitting Oscar or patrolling a retirement community.

A wave of excitement washed over her, and she gave Paige a quick nod before heading back to the locker room. No sense in keeping the man waiting, especially since her curiosity was about to get the better of her.

WHEN THEY ARRIVED AT Judge Banner's office, Josh ran in, leaving Quinby to wait in his truck. He was back out ten minutes later, stuffing the warrant he'd asked for earlier into his inside jacket pocket.

The chief might have thought he'd taken Josh off the Zander case, but Josh had never actually handed the file over to anyone else. He'd worked too long and too hard to give it up. Zipping up his jacket, he climbed into the truck and headed for Oscar's condo.

The sight of Oscar's nurse standing outside the condo, her coat blowing open in the stiff breeze, her iron-gray hair whipping around her head, told Josh that as usual things were not destined to go smoothly.

He coasted to a stop beside the curb, and Quinby rolled down the window.

Bea Crandall leaned down. "He gave me the slip again. How he got past me, I have no idea." Her breath came in short, angry huffs. She yanked her coat shut, holding it closed at the throat.

"Any idea where he might have taken off to?" Quinby asked.

"Probably over to the flea market—something about wanting something to wear to the wedding Saturday. He said Sergeant Reed promised to take him there today." Bea scowled. "I guess he got impatient."

"He thinks he's going to find something to wear to a wedding at a flea market?" Quinby asked, incredulously. "I know I'm not known for my fashion expertise, but even I know not to shop there."

Mrs. Crandall sniffed. "Well, wherever he is, I've had enough. You can just tell Mayor Pepper I quit." She whirled around and stomped off in the direction of the garage.

"Oscar's gonna be all broken up about that," Josh said, putting the truck into gear and heading for Madison Circle and the giant flea market.

A few minutes later, Josh drove through the gates of the Bonanza Bazaar, the local flea market. Josh knew from experience that the market was run by an odd collection of characters.

The largest group of sellers was an army of young women, housewives mostly. They occupied the front, filling their stalls with children's clothes and equipment, toys and household items. Nothing was priced very high, and they ran it like a giant swap meet.

A few of the other stalls were run by small-time antique dealers. But the group of sellers Josh knew on a much more personal basis were the ones who ran the stalls at the back of the flea market. Josh and his fellow officers were usually most interested in them—a few skirted the edge of the law, fencing things for some of the more desperate local thieves who needed a couple of quick bucks.

Pulling into an empty spot, Josh turned off the ignition and glanced over at Quinby.

She shifted in her seat. "So what's the plan?"

"To find Oscar."

Quinby raised an eyebrow. "And what about the warrant you've got tucked in your pocket?"

Josh glanced over at her and laughed. "You don't miss much do you?"

She shrugged. "I try not to." She waited a beat and then asked, "So what's the warrant for?"

Josh rubbed the palm of his hand along the upper edge of the steering wheel. He wanted to present this in a way that didn't alarm Quinby but instead, gained her cooperation. "I'm pretty sure that the guy who pulled the Zander robbery is a petty thief by the name Kenny Drake. Kenny's girlfriend runs one of the stalls here at the flea market. She knows me so I can't go over to her booth without alerting her."

"What's her name?" Quinby asked.

"Cindy Robinson—she deals in antique jewelry and has a small stall called Gems By Cin. Most of it is pretty much junk—costume jewelry. But this girl knows her gems, and once in a while, she gets a hold of a fairly good piece and sells it for a decent profit. We're pretty sure that a lot of the stuff she handles is stolen, but we've never been able to prove anything."

"You think she handled the Zander jewelry?" Quinby asked.

Josh shrugged, trying without much success to hide his frustration. "I can't say for sure. I've never caught her with anything. And believe me, I've looked." He shifted in the seat, turning so that they were face-to-face. "It would make sense if she did. Cindy would know how much they were worth, and she has the contacts to sell them."

Frowning, Quinby tilted her head. "But there's no way she'd have them sitting out on display for any Tom, Dick or Harry to take a peek at, right?"

"No. She's too smart for that. Even Kenny, who is

pretty challenged in the brain power department, wouldn't make that kind of mistake.''

"So you're looking for me to just snoop around and see what's cookin'—maybe get a peek at her *special collection* should she be so inclined.''

Josh reached out and touched her shoulder. "Now you're thinking like a cop.''

"Any hints on what I'm looking for?''

"Funny you should ask.'' He shoved a hand into his side pocket and pulled out several sheets of paper. He passed them to Quinby. "These are copies of the pictures the insurance company had on file. It gives you a pretty good idea of the pieces in the Zander collection.''

Quinby studied the pictures and whistled softly through her teeth. "Quite an array of pretty stones.'' She sifted through them a second time. The intense look in her eyes told Josh she was imprinting the pictures on her memory.

Finally she looked back up at him. "Drake and his girlfriend have had more than enough time to break the collection up—disassemble it so to speak. What makes you think you'll find anything left? Anything recognizable?''

"Kenny Drake is small-time stuff. But he's got an ego the size of the state of Texas. He'd have to keep something around—he wouldn't be able to sell the whole package off without keeping a souvenir. This was his biggest job ever. It put him in the big league.''

"Okay. I'll take a look when we get in there.'' Quinby glanced toward the entrance. "Might be better if we don't go in together.''

Josh nodded. "My feelings exactly. I'll hang back a few minutes, and then come in through one of the exits in the back. You go on in. If you see Oscar, leave him to me. You go check out the booths in the back.''

Quinby handed him the pictures. "What's the signal

if by some slim chance I actually see anything that looks like it belongs in the Zander collection?''

Josh reached up and lightly nudged the bill of her Mets cap. ''Pull off your hat and slap it against your leg. That'll tell me that it might be helpful for me to come take a look. I don't want Cindy to have the chance to dump anything.''

Quinby grinned, the flash of amusement in her eyes and the quick arch of one dark brow irresistible. Her teeth flashed white between lush pink lips and created quite a stir low in his belly. Josh was surprised at the intensity of the sensation. It made him wonder when this silly attraction was going to wear itself out. Soon, hopefully. He wasn't sure he was going to be able to ignore it much longer.

''Why the sudden trust in my abilities to pull this off?'' Quinby asked, her grin switching to a frown of suspicion.

''It's all that jewelry store experience on your résumé that convinced me.''

She shook her head. ''You don't give up with the jabs about my frequent job changes, do you?''

''Hey, don't complain. This time it was to your advantage.'' He resisted the urge to reach out and stroke the ponytail of cinnamon-brown curls that poked out the back of her baseball cap. They looked almost alive with color against her leather jacket.

He shifted around to face forward again. For pity's sake. He was mooning over his partner like some lovesick high schooler when he was supposed to be teaching her how to act like a true professional. Good thing she wasn't able to read his mind.

It was time to get a grip. Quinby seemed oblivious to his predicament, her frown still in place as she opened the truck door and climbed out.

"I'll meet you inside." She slammed the door shut to cut off any further comment from him.

He watched in the side mirror as she came around the rear of the truck and headed for the main entrance. The frown had been replaced by a look of grim determination. She'd jammed her hands into her side pockets and hunched her shoulders against the wind whipping across the parking lot.

Obviously he'd again said the wrong thing, making her all the more determined to show him that she was cop material. Little did she know that he'd already started to believe in her.

QUINBY OPENED ONE OF THE heavy glass doors that lined up across the front of the flea market and stepped back to allow a pretty blond woman pushing a stroller to come through first.

The baby, sitting like tiny royalty in among the stroller's cushy padding, smiled up at Quinby and grabbed at her pant leg with one cracker crumb embedded hand. His mother smiled apologetically and leaned down to hand her little prince another chunk of brown cracker. He shoved one end into his mouth and gummed it happily. His mother nodded to Quinby and headed off.

Quinby stepped onto the main floor of the market. It was laid out like a giant warehouse. She had only been out to the market a few times, usually with one of Mama's daughters, who were always on the lookout for good deals on baby clothes or baby furniture.

The stalls stretched from one end of the building to the other. Simple wooden partitions separated each stall from the next. Some of the renters had dressed up their individual spaces with carpet, hanging plants and tablecloths. Others focused on selling minus the frills. It made for an odd collection of tiny neighboring store-fronts.

To the right of the stalls, lining the far wall, was a fast-food bonanza. The smell of sautéed onions, popcorn and fry vats hung heavy in the air. Quinby took a minute to get her bearings.

It wasn't hard to spot Oscar. He stood in the middle of the aisle halfway down the second row of booths. He'd stripped off his pants and stood there in a pair of red plaid boxers. His pasty legs stood out like two skinny toothpicks with hair.

Quinby shook her head. What next? A naked Oscar swimming in the local YMCA pool during the ladies' water aerobics class? As she watched, he glanced up and waved, motioning her over.

Although Josh had told her to ignore Oscar and head right for Cindy's stall, Quinby figured she'd better see what he wanted. Otherwise, the guy would probably end up following her around and blowing her cover.

She walked over to stand next to him. "You've been a bad boy again, Oscar."

He grinned. "I live to be bad. Where's Josh? He making you come in and do his job again, I suppose."

"I work with Josh. Unfortunately you're my responsibility, too."

Oscar grabbed a pair of hideous green, knit pants off the top of a pile of clothing on the table in front of him and proceeded to put them on. The flaps on his bomber hat swung back and forth as he teetered on one foot like some kind of stork, pulling them on and up. It looked as if he buttoned them somewhere up around midchest. The bell bottom hem stopped just above his bony ankles.

Oscar lifted his arms and turned around in a full circle. "Well, what do you think? They'll look mighty nice with my electric-blue blazer."

Quinby swallowed hard, unsure of how to answer.

The owner of the stall, a large woman dressed in a kind of Hawaiian flowing dress, leaned over the pile of clothing and gave Oscar the once over. "Honey, you look good enough to eat in them trousers."

Oscar preened and then winked at his new admirer. She giggled like a fifteen-year-old and brushed back several strands of rooster-red hair mixed with gray. Quinby figured she was somewhere in the neighborhood of her late fifties.

Quinby blinked, trying to clear her vision. Was she seeing right? The stall owner's eyebrows were penciled in using two different colors, one a dark brown and the other a dark blue. The blue one extended a good inch longer than the brown one.

"How much are you selling these for, sugar pie?" Oscar asked, whipping off his cap and smoothing back several wisps of hair on his bald dome.

"For you, cutie, two-fifty. And the name's Mimi. Mimi Cauley. What's yours?" Mimi pushed one ample hip forward and her chubby cheeks flashed a coquettish smile.

Quinby rolled her eyes. But Oscar seemed truly smitten. Or at least as smitten as Oscar got with all the women he tried to hit on. Poor Mimi had no idea what she was in for.

"Oscar. Oscar Pepper. And may I say that you're one fine-looking woman."

Quinby could only guess what he'd look like at the wedding tomorrow if he was left too long on his own to shop the stalls. But at the moment, she had more important business. "Why don't you two chat a bit, while I take a look around."

Quinby figured now was a good time to leave. At least Oscar would be less inclined to follow her and blow her cover while he was trying to make time with the lovely Mimi.

Oscar nodded without looking over and waved her off, already leaning over the pile of clothes to chat with Mimi. Quinby made her way toward the back of the market, careful to pause and examine the merchandise in the different stalls as she went. It wouldn't look good to head straight to the back of the building. Quinby knew that a true flea market browser took her time, eager to locate that one buried treasure among all the junk. As she moved, Quinby kept on her target, the booth in the far corner.

blow her cover while he was trying to make time with
the lovely blond.

Oscar nodded without looking over and waved Ben
off, already losing any couple of chance to chat with
blind. Cubby made his way toward the back of the
market, careful to pause and examine the merchandise
in the different stalls as he went. It wasn't bad, good
instead straight to the back of the building. Quinby
Kenny was there.

9

THE REAR OF THE FLEA MARKET overlooked a large
marsh. A few pickup trucks and trailers were parked
near one of several back doors, an area designated for
unloading and loading. As Josh came around the end of
one large trailer, he spotted two men sitting at a red-
wood picnic table situated at the edge of the pavement.

They sat hunched over against the stiff breeze coming
in off the marsh, smoking cigarettes and chatting. It
didn't look terribly comfortable, but they nodded amicably to him and then returned to their conversation.

Assuming a casual air, Josh strolled over to the back
door and stepped inside. The rear storage area was filled
with stacked boxes and wooden crates. The hum of
voices out front filtered through the curtained wall separating the storage room from the main floor.

No one was in the back, leaving Josh free to maneu-
ver himself into an area directly behind the Gems By
Cin stall. A stack of crates hid him from view should
anyone come in through the back exits. He fished his
penknife out of his jeans and cut a small hole in the
heavy curtain.

After Quinby had left the truck, Josh had called for
backup. Two patrol cars were en route—just in case
they needed the extra manpower. On the way in, he had
checked for any sign of Kenny Drake's silver car. It
wasn't parked out front, and there was no sign of it
behind the building, either. That meant they had some

time to look around without Kenny poking his nose into things.

Peering through the hole, Josh spied Quinby making her way down the aisle toward Cindy Robinson's booth. He smiled, enjoying the studied expression of nonchalance Quinby had adopted. She was taking her time, trying not to alert anyone to the focus of her mission. He settled in, wedging his shoulder against one of the crates, determined to provide her with backup should she need it.

QUINBY WALKED DOWN THE back aisle, Gems By Cin stood directly ahead. It was the largest booth along the back wall, a corner stall with its own private entrance in the back. The actual setup was a little fancier than the others. Cindy apparently had the money to invest in something a little classier than your run-of-the-mill flea market stall. She had standing glass cabinets and velvet-lined display cases.

Without glancing around, Quinby wondered where Josh was hiding. She didn't doubt that he'd gotten inside. The skin on the back of her neck tingled, telling her that he was somewhere nearby.

A young girl with short brown hair and a dimpled smile sat on a high stool behind Cindy's main showcase. Quinby estimated her age to be around sixteen or seventeen. Definitely not Cindy Robinson, unless Kenny was robbing the cradle.

The girl leaned forward, her dimples deepening as Quinby approached. "Hi. Can I help you?"

"Just browsing," Quinby said, concentrating on the items in the case. "I'm not sure what I'm looking for. But when I see it, I'll know it."

The display was mostly costume jewelry, with a few more expensive pieces scattered in among the cheap stuff. Quinby knew it was an old salesperson's trick to separate the ignorant from the more savvy shopper. If a person went right for the *good stuff*, then the salesperson knew they had a knowledgeable buyer.

Quinby pointed to a small cameo. "Could I look at that, please."

"Sure thing! Isn't it gorgeous? It's one of my favorite pieces." The salesgirl used a key to unlock the case and slipped out the tray with the cameo on it. She set it on top of the case and handed the brooch to Quinby.

Quinby examined it for a few minutes and then laid it back down on the tray. "It's nice, but not quite what I was looking for."

"Can you give me a little hint of what you're interested in?"

Quinby smiled at the girl and shrugged. "I'd love to, but as I said, I'm not really sure what it is."

She walked along the length of the case, sighing heavily as she perused the different pieces. Out of the corner of her eye, Quinby noticed a woman stand up from behind a computer console. An attractive woman with long wheat-colored hair and a shrewd look in her green eyes. Hellooo, Cindy Robinson, Quinby said to herself. She concentrated on the case, pretending not to notice that Cindy had motioned for the young salesgirl to step aside.

She moved further down the counter, finally, pointing to a small gold ring with several nicely cut rubies set in the band. It sat regally in among a trayful of less glamorous silver rings. "That one. Let me see that one."

"Certainly. It's lovely isn't it," Cindy said, reaching into the case.

Feigning surprise, Quinby looked up and raised an eyebrow.

Cindy smiled smoothly and handed her the ring. "I'm the owner, Cindy Robinson. I overheard you talking to Katie and thought I might be of more assistance."

"Lovely," Quinby said, hoping that Josh was somewhere nearby in case this went down quickly.

She glanced around, trying to be unobtrusive about it, but wishing she could see a familiar long, lean figure with midnight black hair lurking somewhere nearby. Just a glimpse would have soothed her tense stomach.

She turned back to Cindy. "I'm looking for something unique. A gift for a close friend. She's—she's getting married this weekend."

"May I ask in what price range?"

Quinby shifted her weight to her other foot. "Cost really isn't an issue. It's more important that I find the right piece." Quinby knew that how she came across was going to determine whether or not Cindy bought her story. She wondered again if Josh was somewhere nearby.

"I have a few pieces that I don't put out in the case because of their value. Would you be interested in looking at them?"

"Definitely."

Cindy stared at her for several seconds, the assessing glint in the depths of her eyes telling Quinby that she was trying to decide if this was a setup or not. Quinby gazed innocently back at her.

Finally Cindy nodded and moved to the back of the stall. She disappeared from view for a moment, and Quinby took the chance to glance around again. Still no Josh. A tiny twinge of anxiety tugged at her insides. What if he had gotten tied up?

"What's going on?" a familiar voice asked at her elbow.

She looked down to find Oscar standing next to her. The acid sensation in her stomach went up another notch.

"Get lost, Oscar," she ordered.

He frowned. "Hey, I thought you were supposed to

be keeping an eye on me? Josh know you're off fooling around?''

She glared at him, wishing him to disappear in a puff of smoke before Cindy Robinson came back.

Oscar smiled, wiggling his upper dentures. "I need five bucks to pay Mimi."

Quinby grabbed a wad of cash out of her jeans pocket and peeled off a five.

Oscar grinned and said, "Make it a twenty, and I'll stay clear of you for longer than five minutes."

Quinby snatched off a twenty and shoved that into his hand. "Here's twenty-five. Now shove off."

Oscar wandered off in the direction of the lovely Mimi just as Cindy reappeared with a metal attaché case. She swung it up on the counter and unlocked the combination lock.

"I keep a few really nice pieces with me all the time." Cindy slid a tray onto the top of the counter and set the attaché case on the floor beside her. The tray contained an exquisite collection of rings, brooches and necklaces.

"Maybe something here will catch your eye," Cindy said.

Quinby quickly assessed the collection. Nothing that belonged to the Zander collection. Or at least none that she recognized. But from the top-notch quality of the gems and the fact that they were sitting in a showcase at the local flea market, Quinby was pretty sure they were from someone else's collection. Perhaps the result of other jobs Kenny had pulled.

"They're lovely." Quinby picked up a few of the rings and tried them on. As she set them back in their respective resting places on the posh black velvet, Quinby affected a bored, uninterested look. "But not what I was really looking for."

A flicker of impatience flashed across Cindy's face, but she quickly hid it behind a cool smile.

Quinby set the hook with her next question. "Actually I was looking for something along this caliber of workmanship, only with rubies. Do you have anything like that?"

Cindy bit her lower lip. Quinby could almost see the gears turning. Cindy shook her head. "No. Sorry. This is my best merchandise at the moment. But leave your name and number. I'll give you a call if anything like that comes along."

Disappointment shot through Quinby. Cindy had thrown the hook. Or perhaps she really didn't have anything remaining from the original Zander collection.

Swallowing her frustration, Quinby watched as Robinson leaned down to pick up the attaché case on the floor beside her. A flicker of red and gold spilled out over the top button of her sweater, and a jolt of excitement shot through Quinby.

The eye of the tiger in the Zander collection. A beautifully cut ruby pried out of its original setting and carefully laid into another. It hung on the thin, gold chain around Cindy's neck.

Josh had been right. Cindy Robinson couldn't let the whole collection go when she sold it off for Kenny. She'd kept a small but significant piece for herself.

It was time to bring in Josh.

JOSH LEANED CLOSER to the hole he cut into the curtain, watching Quinby work Cindy. He smiled. She was a natural. If nervous, she didn't show it. He could hear the confidence in her voice, and her calm demeanor seemed to put Cindy Robinson at ease.

And then, everything seemed to change. He could see Quinby stiffen, and her hand went to her cap. Cindy swept the tray she'd laid out on the countertop into the open metal case.

"That's a beautiful necklace you have. May I see it?" Quinby asked as she slipped her hat off her head.

"Uh...it's just a clever imitation. Nothing important," Cindy snapped the latches shut on the briefcase.

Quinby slapped her cap against her thigh just as a man sidled up to stand next to Cindy. Josh straightened, his fingers tightening on the curtain. Kenny Drake had made an unexpected appearance, coming in through one of the side entrances.

"What's up, Cin?" Drake asked, a tinge of suspiciousness colouring his voice.

For the first time since they'd started this game, Josh felt a twinge of apprehension. Trying to trap Cindy Robinson was one thing. Playing cat and mouse with Kenny Drake, small-time hood, was an entirely different matter.

"Kenny! I didn't expect you until later." Cindy spun the dial on the attaché's combination lock. "I was just showing a customer some of our new items."

"You know you're not supposed to show the private stuff without checking with me first," Drake scolded, his hand gripping Cindy's upper arm.

"She's okay, Kenny," Cindy protested.

"Yeah, I'm okay, Kenny," Quinby said, smiling pleasantly.

Josh saw it for what it was—a solid attempt to put Drake at ease. Josh knew Quinby was giving him time to make an appearance. He flipped open his badge and slipped it into the top pocket of his jacket. As he moved along the back wall, he slipped the safety strap off his gun.

A few seconds later, Josh stepped through the opening in the curtain. Drake saw him and started for a side exit, but Josh pulled his gun and shook his head. "I wouldn't do that if I were you, Drake."

Drake skidded to a stop, a sullen expression sliding across his weasely face. "You ain't got nothin' on me, Reed. I don't own this place. And you have no right to just come in here and hassle us."

"Oh, but I do," Josh said. He pulled the warrant out of his pocket and shoved it into Drake's hands. "Read it and weep."

Quinby hopped over the counter and moved to take the attaché case away from Cindy, motioning for her to take a seat.

Drake crumpled up the warrant and threw it on the floor. "You're on a fishing expedition, Reed."

Josh threw his cuffs to Quinby. "Cuff our friend, Mr. Drake."

Drake stiffened. "What's the charge?"

Josh smiled. "I think we'll go with obstructing the execution of a warrant. We'll see what develops after that."

Quinby cuffed Drake's hands behind his back and led him over to one of the chairs next to Cindy.

When the two were seated side by side, Josh asked, "Okay, Quin, what did you find?"

Nodding, her expression stone serious, Quinby reached over and gently lifted the gold chain out from beneath Cindy's sweater. The stone caught the light and glittered blood-red. "Sergeant Reed, meet the tiger's eye from the Zander collection."

Josh whistled softly. "Exceptional, Officer Parker, I'll never say another word about your extensive job résumé again."

Quinby nodded, a sparkle gleaming in her eyes. For the first time, Josh realized how much a compliment from him meant to her.

He liked the effect it had on her. But before he could

consider the possibilities, the flea market around them seemed to come alive. Patrons pushed their way to the back to see what all the commotion was about, and the two backup units arrived to provide support. Within a few minutes, they became engrossed in the details of arresting Drake and Cindy for possession of stolen property.

QUINBY BARRELED OUT of the locker room and checked her watch. It was already 4:50 p.m., and she knew the garage down the street closed at 5:00 p.m. If she didn't get down there before five, she'd be stuck without her truck for another day.

She was still high on the adrenaline from arresting Drake and Robinson and essentially busting the Zander robbery case wide-open. Quinby knew she'd handled herself like a seasoned veteran. The compliments and teasing praise from her fellow officers was wonderful, particularly in light of their recent ridicule and jabs about her competency as a rookie.

But it was the quiet praise and recognition from Josh that hit home the hardest. The sweetest. It made her feel all warm and tingly inside. He never said anything other than the one compliment at the site of the arrest, but all during the booking procedure, Quinby soaked up his vibes of quiet pleasure and support.

Quinby nodded to the desk sergeant and headed for the front door. Although bumming a ride from Josh had a definite appeal, Quinby knew she'd be pushing her luck if she asked again. He was bound to misunderstand and see her as pushing herself on him after he'd made it painfully clear last night that he wanted to keep their relationship strictly professional. She had no intention of hurting the new alliance they had forged today.

"Need a ride, Quin?" Josh called from behind.

Quinby grabbed the door handle and tried to gather

the strength to turn around and tell him thanks but no thanks. Her fingers tightened on the cool metal. All she had to do was smile politely and tell him she preferred to walk, that the exercise would do her good. Oh Lordy, it was hard to be strong.

"Thanks, Josh, but I think I'll walk. It's pretty mild out, and I need the exercise." There, she'd said it, and it hadn't hurt a bit. Like hell it hadn't. It felt like someone had punched her in the gut.

Josh strolled over to the desk and dropped off a handful of reports on the countertop. Pete handed him a clipboard and pointed to a section he wanted Josh to review. Josh nodded and then glanced over his shoulder at her. "You sure? I'm headed in that direction anyway."

Quinby stuck her hands into her jacket pockets, trying to look casual. "Yeah, I'm sure."

She had to ignore the sudden urge to kick herself. Who was she kidding? She'd go with him anywhere if he'd only see her more than just his burdensome partner.

Josh shrugged and made a few notations on the clipboard. He leaned over the counter and shoved it onto the shelf. He threw the pen to Pete and walked over to her.

"I don't have Zack tonight so it's not as if you'll be holding me up."

Quinby opened her mouth to refuse one more time, deciding that she'd give in if he pressed the issue any more after that. A woman could be only so strong— have only so much pride.

"Quinby! I'm glad I caught you."

She looked up to see her father stroll across the lobby. He nodded to Josh and stood by quietly as if waiting for her to finish up with Josh. At least his arrival would give her an excuse not to take Josh's offer for a ride.

But surprisingly, Josh stood rooted where he was, turning to nod agreeably in her father's direction. Now what? Did everyone stand around looking pleasant while never discussing the real issue—the fact that her father had fostered her on Josh and that now he was saddled with her for the near future.

"Afternoon, Chief," she greeted softly.

"Am I interrupting anything?" her father asked, looking back and forth between the two of them.

"No, Josh was just offering me a ride." At the question in her father's eyes, Quinby explained, "My truck broke down last night. It's down at the station getting a new battery put in."

Her father grinned and rubbed his hands together with relish. "Excellent. How about joining me for dinner?"

Quinby shifted restlessly and glanced around the lobby nervously. Had anyone overheard? A few other officers stood in a small group at the other end of the lobby, but other than that no one else seemed interested in what they were doing.

It surprised her that her father would be this open in his acknowledgment of her. He usually kept the personal stuff for after work, calling her at her apartment if he wanted to invite her to dinner or meet for coffee. After all, she was a lowly rookie, hardly someone the chief of police would know on a first-name basis, let alone make an offer for dinner.

"I—I was going to put in a few hours at the restaurant," she said.

"Come on, you can take a night off. It'll be my treat," he coaxed with a smile. "I have a few things I need to discuss with you."

Quinby darted a look of suspicion in Josh's direction. But he stared back at her, an innocent little grin playing around one corner of his mouth. Quinby frowned, and her suspicions deepened. Perhaps her father had gotten an update from Josh on her performance and was going to gently ask her to resign. It didn't matter that she'd done well today at the flea market. The writing was on the wall, and she wasn't Brackett City Police Department material.

She shrugged and nodded. "Sure. That sounds great. Do you mind giving me a ride over to the garage to pick up my truck?"

Her father grinned. "Great. Let me get my coat." He turned and clamped a fatherly hand on Josh's shoulder. "You're welcome to join us, Josh. We're going to stop over at Wrigley's, nothing fancy."

Josh shook his head and backed up a bit. "No, thanks. I've got a few things to do. But you two have a good time." He glanced at Quinby. "You might want to try the chili. It might be an improvement over lunch."

Quinby rolled her eyes, but didn't bother taking the bait. She watched her father cross the lobby in the direction of his office before turning to confront Josh. "I thought you told me that I was doing well?"

"You are."

"Then why is my father asking me to have dinner with him?"

"He's hungry? And he'd like to eat with his daughter?"

"Very funny. You know as well as I do that no one here knows I'm his daughter. Why would he take me to a restaurant where we're bound to run into a load of cops—off and on duty?"

Josh's smile stretched even wider. "Maybe he likes to live dangerously. Personally I think you're getting too paranoid."

Quinby scowled. This wasn't getting her anywhere. "Are you sure he isn't going to fire me?"

Josh grabbed a handful of her jacket and pulled her closer. "Will you please relax. You're doing fine. In fact, I've decided that tonight we'll get together and do some target practicing. Get you ready for your qualifying exam.''

Quinby resisted the urge to lay her cheek down on his hand. She could feel the heat from his fingers soak through the leather of her coat. It took all her concentration not to reach up and cover his hand with her own. The man made her crazy, and he didn't even know it.

The blue of his eyes stared into hers, wreaking havoc on her insides. ''You don't have to do that. I'll get some practice time in, don't worry.''

''I'm not worried,'' he said. ''That's why I'll pick you up at your apartment around nine tonight. You'll be back from dinner by then, and you'll be able to concentrate on improving your aim.'' He took his hand off her shoulder and zipped up his jacket. ''If we spend a couple of hours tonight, you'll be ready to pass the weapon check on Monday.''

''But I—''

''Just be ready at nine, Quin.''

He turned and walked out the front door, leaving her standing alone in the middle of the lobby. She watched him stride down the walkway, his long, powerful legs eating up the pavement effortlessly. And as much as Quinby didn't want to admit it, she couldn't wait until nine o'clock rolled around.

10

FOUR HOURS LATER, Quinby watched as Josh pulled up outside her apartment. He blinked his lights when he saw her standing at the window. She grabbed her coat and knapsack and headed for the front door.

A tiny voice in the back of her head whispered that she was making a mistake for taking Josh up on his offer to go to the shooting range. It meant being alone with him. And Quinby wasn't a fool. She was too attracted to Josh—too taken in by his dark good looks and quiet intensity. It was a dangerous combination. One guaranteed to cause problems.

Quinby zipped up her jacket and flicked off the apartment lights. Well, so much for listening to her own warnings. She ran down the hallway and took the stairs two at a time. There was no way she was missing out on this opportunity.

Once outside, Quinby opened the passenger side door of Josh's pickup truck and slid onto the front seat.

"How was dinner?" he asked.

"Surprisingly good," she said. "The chief wasn't in his usual lecture mode. We actually talked." She paused, reflecting on the dinner and her father's uncharacteristic behavior.

"You look surprised."

"I am."

"Why?"

"Something strange happened. While we were eating,

Tripp and a few of his cronies stopped by the table. Tripp had that smarmy smile on his face. You know— the one that makes your skin crawl.''

Josh nodded. ''Yeah, I know the one. What did he want?''

''Oh, he made some comment about my father *robbing the cradle*. The idiot assumed that my father was on a date with me—like he'd date one of the officers under his command.''

''So, what was your father's response?''

''That's the strange thing. He just smiled one of those steel smiles of his, and then introduced me to Tripp and the others as his daughter.'' Quinby burst out laughing. ''You should have seen Tripp's face. You could have knocked him over with a feather.'' She shook her head. ''Truth be known, you could have knocked me over with a feather.''

''First time he's ever done that?''

Quinby nodded. ''He'd always introduced me by name to people, but never as his daughter. I think the embarrassment was too much for him.''

''So, how'd it feel when he finally did the right thing?''

She glanced over at him, a bubble of pure happiness pushed against her insides and made her feel as if she'd burst. ''It was pretty much okay with me.''

Josh shot her a grin. ''Just okay?''

''No, it was wonderful.'' Quinby frowned and glanced down at her hands. ''You didn't by any chance have anything to do with getting him to do that, did you?''

''Who me?'' Josh asked innocently. ''You asked me not to interfere, didn't you?''

''Yes.'' She looked up at him. ''So did you interfere?''

He shook his head. ''Nope.''

Satisfied with his answer, Quinby settled back in her seat. "Are you sure you're up to doing this? I mean, it's really not your problem. It's silly for you to take all this time to help me learn how to do something as simple as how to sight down the barrel of my gun properly."

Josh turned the key and the engine rumbled to life. He sat silent for a moment, his face pensive in the dim light of the dashboard. Quinby pulled her hands up into the sleeves of her coat, seeking warmth.

When he turned back toward her, the clean lines of his face were crisp and clear, his gaze steady. "I can't think of anything more important than helping my partner learn to shoot properly." He slipped the gear into Drive. "Who knows, it might be my life on the line someday, and I might find myself relying on you to get me out of a tight situation. I'd like to feel confident that you know what you're doing."

A crazy warmth swept through Quinby. *I might find myself relying on you.* He'd said it as if she really was his partner and not some probationary nerd he'd been stuck with due to a sense of duty. She nodded, sure that if she tried to say anything it would come out sounding geeky.

Josh pulled away from the curb, and they rode in comfortable silence for a few minutes, until Quinby thought she could trust her voice. "So where are you taking me to practice?" She figured that he must have access to a private club, but she didn't care if he was simply planning to take her up to the town dump to shoot rats.

"My house," he said.

She almost got whiplash turning to look at him. "Your house?" she squeaked out.

"I've decided you need privacy. If no one's watching, maybe you'll have a chance to really focus. Hopefully that will help to get your confidence up.''

''You think I lack confidence?'' she asked.

He glanced in her direction as he pulled onto the expressway heading out of the city. ''Yeah, I think you definitely lack confidence. You have a problem with that?''

Quinby considered this. But even as she considered it, she found herself thinking about the possibility of seeing where Josh lived. Where he woke up each day and stretched that long, lean body. Where he showered and shaved. Ate breakfast. Spent his weekends. And all her concerns evaporated. This was too good to pass up.

''Nope, no problem here,'' she said, sitting back.

He didn't live far from the city, but it might have been on the other side of the earth considering the amount of privacy he had. They drove for twenty minutes on the Northway and then took one of the exits leading to Enders Landing, a small village on the outskirts of Brackett City.

The nice thing about Enders Landing was that it existed outside the crowded streets, multiple dwellings, grit and grime of the city. It was rural, but only a short trek from the city. The thick woods bordering the Adirondack Park kept it blissfully secluded.

Josh lived on a dead end street, on the opposite end of the tiny village. They passed a few other homes before they turned onto Josh's street, large, rambling homes set discreetly back from the road. But once on his street there were no other dwellings.

Josh pulled up next to a mailbox shaped like a miniature log cabin. The uniqueness of it made Quin wonder if he'd made it himself. A small wreath with a red ribbon and tiny bells hung from the post. Nice decorating touch. Quinby had an anxious moment when she wondered if maybe he had a girlfriend who had a Martha Stewart flair for decorating.

Seemingly oblivious to her silly insecurities, he rolled down the window, reached out and grabbed his mail, and then dropped it on the seat next to them. All she could see of his place was towering pines and a neatly paved driveway leading somewhere.

Gunning the engine, he drove up a driveway. Quinby tried not to hold her breath in anticipation, but there was no denying her excitement. She was actually going to get to see where he lived.

The driveway ended in a small clearing, and when the house came into view, a small sigh escaped from between Quinby's lips. It was exactly as she'd expected. A large rambling log cabin with a huge front porch set in among a snow-covered clearing. Tiny white lights were strung across the front edge of the roof, giving off a warm, festive glow. On one end of the porch, a swing swayed gently in the evening breeze.

Quinby realized that Josh had stopped a few yards away from the house, his head turned toward her, waiting. It wasn't hard to tell that he was looking for her reaction to the house.

"It's beautiful," she said softly, leaning forward to get a better look out the windshield. The defroster blew hot air against her face.

Josh grinned, obviously pleased with her response, and Quinby realized that Josh, the Iceman had disappeared. Puff! Gone completely. In his place was the same man who had danced with her last night. She liked this Josh, and she silently welcomed him back.

"I'm glad you like it. I built it myself...well at least I helped." He pulled up next to the front porch and turned off the engine. "Come on in. I'll show you around."

As they climbed the front steps, a deep bark filtered through the heavy oak door.

"My dog, Mercury. He gets pretty lonely staying by himself all day." Josh pulled out a key and unlocked the front door.

He barely got the door open when a chocolate lab squeezed through the crack and bounded out onto the porch. He paused for a brief second to nose Josh and then wiggled his way over to Quin. He pushed his soft muzzle into Quin's hand, and she smiled as his wet nose skittered across the center of her palm.

Quinby crouched down to give the dog's velvety ears a scratch and almost landed on her behind as Mercury took a quick lunge to lick her face.

"Down, boy," Josh said, grabbing her arm and pulling her back up.

Quinby stumbled and brushed up against him. She touched his arm in an attempt to steady herself, lifting her head to gaze up at him.

He stared down at her. An unfamiliar expression flickered across the clean lines of his face. His light eyes seemed to darken around the edges, and his lips parted as if he was going to say something. Something tender. Perhaps intimate.

Quinby glanced away, struggling to dismiss the silly thought. If she didn't stop trying to analyze everything, she was going to be sincerely sorry. Josh was her partner. Nothing more, nothing less. And it didn't matter how much she wished it was otherwise, things weren't going to change simply because she wanted them to.

"Sorry," she mumbled, regaining her balance and attempting to hide her own confusion by pretending to brush off her jacket. "It's been a while. Living in an apartment limits one's pet options."

"No problem." Josh opened the door again and leaned in. A few seconds later, light flooded the inside of the house. He stepped back and motioned her inside. Mercury deserted them, bounding off the porch and into the woods.

The inside of the house was as warm and inviting as the outside. Hardwood floors covered with colorful throw rugs dotted the large entry hall. Josh stepped around her and led the way into a cathedral ceiling room that served as a combination living room, dining room and kitchen. A massive fieldstone fireplace dominated the room.

The furniture, made of heavy, rich brown wood, dotted the room. It was neat, but Quinby was relieved to see not compulsively so.

Quinby turned to smile at him. "Beautiful place."

He nodded and walked inside, turning on lights as he went. "Want a cup of coffee or something?"

Shaking her head, Quinby moved over to stand in front of the patio windows overlooking the backyard.

Josh strolled over and flipped on the floodlights, watching her face as the pond came into view. She leaned forward, pressing her hands against the glass as her expressive eyes widened in surprise.

A smile of amazement curled the corners of her lips, and a sparkle touched her dark eyes. "You have your own pond?"

Josh nodded. "It's Zack's favorite spot when he's here. It doesn't matter what time of the year, he always wants me to be out there with him puttering around. We built a little warming hut down there so that we can unfreeze our toes when we're skating." He walked over to turn on the hall light. "You'll have to come out one day and skate with us."

Quinby nodded. "I'd like that."

He walked over to the fireplace and grabbed one of the ten-inch matches sitting in the brass canister off to the side. Moving the grate aside, he struck the match on the rough stone and touched it to the paper and kindling stuffed beneath the stacked logs. Flames flared upward, consuming the paper in a flash as the kindling crackled and caught.

Josh pulled the screen back into place and stood up. "Come on, we'll go practice while that gets going."

"We're going to need it after standing outside trying to shoot in this cold," Quinby grumbled.

Josh laughed. "A little discomfort will force you to find your focus and keep it." He pushed open the patio door and stepped out onto the deck. "If you concentrate, then your marksmanship will improve."

"Oh goody. My two worst skills—focusing and concentration."

Josh turned around slowly and faced her head-on. She stopped in the doorway, her grin fading at the expression on his face.

"What?" she asked.

"It's your belief or lack of belief in yourself that is going to make the difference between passing or failing, Quin." He pulled her out onto the deck and shut the door. "You keep making negative comments like that and no amount of practice is going to make a difference. Understand?"

Quinby blinked, her thick lashes shuttering and then opening to reveal the depth of her insecurities. He'd thrown her off balance with his bluntness. She had expected teasing, and he had surprised her with seriousness. She swallowed and hunched deeper into her jacket.

He waited, not willing to let her off the hook. "Do you understand what I'm saying?"

She nodded, but didn't look up, apparently unwilling or unable to meet his eyes. "I hear you. You want me to can the negativism, right?" She knocked a closed fist against her forehead. "Think positive. Think positive. Got to get it through my thick head."

Josh reached up and grasped her wrist. Her pulse beat hard against the pad of his thumb. "Be gentle. You'll begin to believe in yourself once you have some success."

The warmth of her brown eyes drew him in, and Josh felt himself falling right into her gaze. Quickly, he turned and led her off the deck and down toward the pond. The snow crunched beneath their feet, and a light breeze blew across the field, stinging his cheeks.

Josh stopped next to the tiny warming shack to flick on the skating lights. The pond glistened white and blue. A sheen of water covered the top; the result of the warm day.

He pointed to the targets set up to the right of the pond. Three separate stacks of hay with the figure of a man tacked on them. He never used his gun when Zack was around, too risky. But sometimes, the lonely days and nights of no family...no Zack got to him, and he went out to practice to pass the time.

He used the tip of his boot to clear some of the snow off the ground in front of them. "Stand here," he said, pointing to a spot marked off with a piece of wood sticking out of the snow. "I measured the distance to match the length of the department's range."

Quinby stepped forward and dropped her knapsack on the ground. Bending down, she rummaged though it and stood back up with her police revolver in her hand. She pulled off her gloves, grabbed a clip out of her jacket pocket and loaded her gun, working swiftly and confidently.

"Ready when you are." She stepped forward, her gun hanging at her side, the safety on. He handed her a pair of ear protectors, and she shoved them over her hat and onto her ears, leaving one slightly off center so she could listen to his instructions. He did the same with his own pair.

"Now get into your stance and sight on the target," Josh said. "But don't shoot until I tell you." He wanted to get a feel for how she stood—her level of comfort when handling a firearm.

Quinby nodded and planted her feet firmly in the snow. She brought her gun up, using a standard two-handed grip. She held her concentration, never glancing over at him.

Removing his gloves and dropping them on top of her knapsack, Josh reached up and placed his palm beneath her hands. The warmth of his hands met hers as he tested the steadiness of her grasp. "Nice grip, Quinby. Now open up your stance just a bit more."

She nodded silently, a tiny frown of concentration wrinkling the smooth skin between her light colored brows. She moved her long legs a tad further apart and sighted on the target. Her top teeth gnawed impatiently at the corner of her lower lip.

Josh leaned down and touched the sweet spot at the back of her knee. It was an attempt to test her stance, to get her to loosen up a bit. But instead, he seemed to distract her, and she stiffened, shifting her weight restlessly.

"Relax," he said. "The more tense you are the less apt you are to hit anything."

He straightened up and brushed his hand across her shoulders, seeking to square them with the target. She didn't move this time, but when he glanced at her face, he was surprised to see her eyes shut for a moment, as if trying to regain something lost.

When she opened them again to glance at him, there was a small smile playing with her lips. "Then stop touching me like that or I'll never be able to concentrate."

He laughed. "Sorry. But the better able you are to ignore distractions, the more focused you'll be." Although tension seemed to radiate off of her, she didn't turn around. Josh leaned forward and whispered softly in her ear. "Am I distracting you now?"

Quinby lifted the one shoulder as if brushing away a gnat. "Not a bit."

He parted her hair and trailed his finger along the back of her neck, right above the collar of her coat. She shivered, but kept her eyes focused on the target.

Smiling, he leaned in closer, inhaling the sweet scent of soap and something light and fragrant. He could tell she was holding her breath. He kissed her nape, and his lips moved against her soft skin, tasting her. Her breath hissed out from between her teeth.

"Go ahead," he whispered. "Start hitting those targets." The words were barely out of his mouth before she dropped down into a deeper stance and squeezed the trigger.

The shots came in quick succession.

Loud.

Powerful.

Each bullet hit the target with a muted thud. Within seconds, the silhouette was covered with small, dark holes, all clustered around the upper left side of the man's chest.

The clip empty, Quinby stood up, pulled the clip out of the gun and dropped it on her knapsack. She put the safety on and then, glanced back at him. "Was that focused enough for you?"

"Admirably so," Josh said, unable to keep the surprise out of his voice. "Are you sure you really flunked your last qualifying exam?"

She grinned. "Maybe I need someone nibbling on the back of the neck in order to qualify." She turned around and stood toe to toe with him. "Do you think maybe they'd let you do that for me?"

Josh cleared his throat, feeling as though she had

turned the tables on him. She stood close, too close. The toes of her boots nudged his, and the breeze lifted the ends of her hair, blowing her curls forward. The end of one brushed against his cheek, and Josh resisted the urge to reach up and capture it between his fingers.

"I think you'll do just fine without me."

Without looking away, Quinby stuck a hand into her pocket and pulled out another clip. He watched as she reloaded and then handed the gun over to him.

"Now let's see how you do," she said.

He nodded and stepped up to the mark.

Quinby disappeared behind him, and Josh tried to ignore the tiny flicker of apprehension that licked the back of his neck. What was she up to? But then he grinned. What the heck, turnaround was fair play. Whatever she had planned for him, Josh had no doubt he'd enjoy it.

QUINBY STOOD BEHIND JOSH and pressed a hand to her mouth. It was hard to keep from bursting out in nervous laughter.

She looked up and down his long, lean body. Now what? He was too tall for her to nibble on his neck without climbing up on him. And as delicious as that sounded, it wasn't part of the game.

"Okay, Josh, get into your stance and sight on the target," she ordered, using the same commands he had used on her a few minutes ago. "But don't fire until I tell you."

He did as she asked.

Quinby reached up and touched the lobe of his left ear. Josh stood rock-still. No reaction.

Biting her lower lip, Quinby bent down and ran a hand down the back of his left thigh. Her nails rasped along the worn cloth of his jeans. "Relax," she said. "If you're too tense you won't hit anything."

His muscle jumped beneath her fingers. She enjoyed the feel of power over him and ran her fingers lightly over one taut cheek up to his belt. She pressed herself against him from behind and felt his body shift slightly beneath her.

"How's that concentrating, Josh?"

"Still focused," he said, his voice strained.

"Well, then, I guess I'll have to try a little harder."

She skimmed both palms along the sides of his hips and around to the front.

"Can I shoot now?" he asked, his voice a strangled whisper.

"Steady, cowboy." As she spoke, Quinby slid both hands across his flat belly to the zipper of his jeans. She pressed her fingers over his hardness and nudged him from behind.

"Son-of-a—" He shot the entire clip in a matter of seconds.

As soon as the clip was empty, he dropped his hand, clicked on the safety and shoved it into her knapsack. When she tried to step away, he grabbed her wrist and pulled her to him.

"Not so fast," he said, lowering his mouth onto hers. She lifted her head and accepted his lips on hers eagerly, sliding her arms up around his neck.

His lips were hard and silky hot. His tongue stroked the inside of her mouth, sliding along the length of her tongue, caressing it. She leaned into him, feeling his hands move magically over her body, his hands slipping up under her jacket. He tugged at the hem of her shirt, pulling it out of her pants.

Cold air hit her warm skin as he slipped his palms up along the length of her back and around to the front. He pushed aside her bra and cupped her breasts, the rough skin of his fingertips rasping across the nipples. They stumbled backward and landed up against the side of the warming shack with a dull thud.

Quinby pulled her mouth off his and gasped for air. Josh continued to kiss the corner of her mouth and then down along the side of her neck. His teeth scraped lightly along her skin, sending a jolt of pleasure up her spine. He moved closer and nudged his thigh between hers, resting it against the apex of her legs. Without saying a word, he shifted forward, leaning into her and applying pressure.

Quinby turned her head sideways and rested her cheek on his chest. Her breath came in short, little pants. She clutched the nylon of his coat between her fingers as he moved against her. His muscular thigh was creating a most interesting and exquisite pressure.

She gasped for a breath of cool air. She knew one of them was going to need to show some restraint. Sadly, she knew it wasn't going to be her. At this point, she would have to fling off every stitch of clothing and slide on the ice in order to cool the fire burning inside her.

She lifted her head and moved her lips up against the side of his neck. "If you don't stop, Josh, we're both going to be sincerely sorry."

He sucked her earlobe between his lips and nibbled. Quinby groaned, feeling her insides go to liquid mush.

"I don't plan on feeling sorry about anything," Josh said as he whipped his hands out from beneath her jacket. But before she could protest, he leaned down and scooped her up in his arms.

She struggled to get down, but he held her tight, bending down to swing the knapsack over one shoulder and starting back toward the house.

"Put me down," she demanded, even as she leaned closer to lay down a series of kisses along the side of his jaw.

The two of them might be nuts, but Quinby was honest enough to admit to herself that this was exactly what she had wanted from the moment she had climbed into Josh's truck. Heck, from the very first time she'd seen him in the lobby of the Brackett City Police Department, and he had smiled at her.

He carried her across the yard, and when they reached the porch, Quinby tried to grab the railing. "Come on, Josh. Let me walk up the steps before we both land in the snow."

"No way. You might take off on me."

"Not even if you tried to run me off with a rifle," Quinby said, laughing.

He lifted her up higher and threw her over his left shoulder. Her head flopped down against his back, and she started giggling even harder. Hopefully none of his neighbors were out for a walk. If so, they were getting an eyeful.

He clamped one hand over her legs and reached up to pat her behind. "How's this for distraction?"

Quinby was laughing so hard now that she was hiccuping. "Let me down, Josh. You're going to get a hernia."

"I've got an ache in that general area. But believe me when I say that it has absolutely nothing to do with a hernia."

Her arms hung limp, and her chin bumped against his back as he climbed the steps. She was weak from laughter.

Within seconds, they were inside the house, and he slid her down off his shoulder.

Her feet hit the floor, but when she moved, he shook his head and held her in place.

"Not so fast, lady."

She lifted her head to protest, and he stepped in close, backing her up across the room until her knees hit the couch. She fell over backward onto the pillows, and he followed, dropping down on top of her.

"Are you sure this is what you want?" she asked.

He shrugged out of his coat and threw it on the floor, shaking one arm up and down when the sleeve caught around his wrist. "Are you kidding?" he asked, practically falling off the couch in an attempt to get the coat off. It fell in a heap on the hardwood floor. "There's no way we aren't going to finish this."

"I was hoping you'd say that."

Quinby squirmed around beneath him, trying to get out of her own coat. Recognizing her plight, Josh yanked it over her head and dumped it on the floor.

His clever fingers were immediately at her waist, sliding up beneath her striped shirt, skimming over her ribs as he helped her out of it. It barely hit the floor before his hands were on the snap of her jeans.

"It might be a teeny bit easier if we both undressed ourselves," Quinby said, her breath coming in short pants as one hand worked the rivet of his jeans and the other unbuttoned his shirt.

"Yeah, but then we'd miss all this fun."

"Wouldn't want that." Quinby impatiently shoved Josh's shirt off his shoulders, laid down a series of kisses along his shoulder blade and then returned to work on his jeans.

He urged her to lift up off the couch and yanked her jeans down around her knees, while at the same time, Quinby tugged his down. In the rush, their legs tangled, and they teetered on the edge of the couch, tumbling off and hitting the floor with a grunt.

"Forget the couch," he said.

"Floor's too hard."

Josh lifted his head and glanced around. "The rug," he ordered, his fingers already working on the fastener of her bra.

Clutching her to him, Josh inched along the floor. Quinby used the heels of her boots to scoot along with him. They were both breathing so hard, Quinby worried that they'd pass out before they managed to get to the real fun. She wondered if it had been as long for Josh as it had been for her.

When they reached the thick rug in front of the fireplace, Josh grabbed her arms and rolled over, taking her with him.

When they came to a stop, Quinby stared up at him, drinking in the fringe of dark lashes sheltering his gaze and brushing the clean line of his cheekbone with each blink.

She slid a palm across his flat abdomen, taking satisfaction in his sharp intake of breath. ''Just be careful that in all the excitement we don't end up rolling into the fire.''

''Don't worry. I plan on making our own fire right here.'' He bent his head and lightly touched his lips to her breast, sucking gently as his hand slipped between her legs and started to caress her with a sweet, primal rhythm.

Quinby moaned, and turned her head from side to side as he sucked the tip of her nipple, his tongue circling it with slow easy strokes. She shifted beneath him and lifted herself to meet his hand. The sensation was exquisite. Wickedly delicious.

She hooked one leg over his slim hip, trying to make the connection deeper, but Josh whispered for her to wait. He reached over her head and started fumbling around.

Slightly dazed, Quin lifted her head, straining to see what the holdup was. ''I don't mean to sound pushy here, but I seem to be on the brink of something wonderful here.''

Josh laughed and brushed her lips with his. ''Put it in Park for a minute, sweet stuff. We need to cover all the bases.'' He strained to reach something, his skin sliding over hers with a delicious shimmer of sensation. His knee nudged her in the most interesting way as he hitched himself up higher.

Quin tilted her head back. ''Are you losing interest here, Reed?''

''Hardly.'' With a triumphant smile on his face, Josh pulled a foil packet from the pocket of his discarded jeans.

Quin smiled. "Guess someone was pretty sure he'd get lucky tonight."

Josh settled back over her, the foil packet between his teeth, "A guy can only hope," he mumbled around the foil.

Quin reached up and grabbed the packet and tore it open. She sat up and reached down to slide it on him, taking great satisfaction at the hiss of air slicing between his teeth as she touched him with a sure, confident hand.

Quin wanted him deep inside her. Part of her. Now. She lay back, wrapping her legs around him and guiding him into her.

Shifting his weight, Josh sunk himself into her warmth. He sensed the quickening of her need and watched with satisfaction as her eyelids fluttered and a soft moan slipped between her lips.

"Easy, Quin," he said, easing himself deeper and filling her with his hardness. Her fingers tightened on his back, her nails scraping slightly across his bare skin. He felt her satiny legs tighten around him, holding him to her as he moved deeper.

He buried his face in the wild spray of hair spread out on the pillow next to her head, inhaling the heady smell of vanilla. Nothing had ever felt so good. So right.

Beneath him, Josh felt Quinby shudder and call his name. He quickened his rhythm, holding her close as she tumbled over the edge into sweet bliss. He lifted his head and settled his mouth over hers as the bottom dropped out for himself, sending him plunging over the same edge of pure ecstasy.

A short time later, Josh eased himself down next to Quinby and sighed, reluctant to move, to pull himself from her. He savored the feeling of being buried deep inside her. Near her. Part of her.

She lay quiet with her eyes closed, a fine sheen of sweat peppering her upper lip. Beneath the palm of his hand, cradling her left breast, Josh could feel the crisp, clean beat of her heart. He reached up and gently brushed back several damp curls stuck to her cheek.

Without opening her eyes, Quinby touched the tip of her tongue to the middle of her top lip and released a shuddering sigh. "That was wonderful." She rolled up on her side and snuggled against his side, her head coming to rest on his chest. "Do you treat all your partners this well?"

"Always." He chuckled softly and twisted a strand of her warm, brown hair around the tip of his finger.

He leaned in and kissed the top of her head while silently berating himself. How had he gotten himself into such a mess? What could he have been thinking?

Josh shook his head. He knew very well what he'd been thinking. He'd lost himself in thoughts of a wild mop of hair and soft laughing eyes. And he'd been bowled over by the glorious smell of vanilla and the delight of just being with her.

But in spite of the niggling regret pulling at him, Josh couldn't deny the unbelievable pleasure and joy he'd felt making love to her, losing himself in her. Nothing had ever felt more right. More perfect.

But Josh was a professional, a man who played by the rules. And he knew that his only option was to make things right. Either he was Quinby's partner or he was her lover. He couldn't be both.

Reaching over Quinby, Josh pulled the heavy quilt off the back of the couch and tucked it around them. As she slid a hand down the center of his, her nails creating the most delightful sensations along the surface of his skin, Josh felt himself harden with renewed desire. He quickly decided to put it out of his mind until tomorrow—it would come soon enough.

11

A LIGHT SNOW AND ICE mixture started to hit the pavement and the hood of the car. Obviously the warming trend was over.

Quinby held the steering wheel in a relaxed grip and smiled serenely. Not even the thick clouds pressing down low over the city or the impending threat of an all-out ice storm could put a damper on her spirits.

Waking up next to Josh earlier that morning had been as close to a revelation as Quinby had ever experienced in her lifetime. A tingle of unadulterated pleasure zinged through her body, traveling from the tips of her fingers down to the tips of her toes.

Last night and this morning had been a seemingly endless taste of ecstasy at the mercy of Josh's clever hands and mouth. And she'd been able to keep up. As a result, Josh hadn't skimped on his words of appreciation.

The memory of waking up and finding him staring down at her, his hands gently stroking her awake, brought a heated blush to her cheeks. They had romped and rocked until she wasn't sure she'd ever be able to walk straight again. Spending a single evening with Josh Reed more than made up for her recent dry spell.

Breakfast was a box of cereal—Zack's Cookie Crisps, fed to each other while lounging on their backs in bed. They shot the little, tasty circles into the air and dodged and weaved to catch them in their mouths. Most of the cereal hit the bed rather than their mouths, but it sent the two of them into silly hysterical laughter. The kind of laughter two people experienced right after making wild, passionate love—it was a celebration of life.

After Josh had dropped her off, Mama had never once said anything about Quinby not coming home last night. As much as Mama tried to deny it, all of the kids knew that she slept restlessly in her worn armchair by the window, watching for them all to get home. But in spite of Mama's self-enforced reserve, Quinby wasn't fooled. She could see the question in Mama's ancient eyes. Quinby knew that there would be no dodging a relentless interrogation from Mama later that night when she returned home.

Quinby leaned forward and turned up the truck's heater. She glanced out at the dull, gray sky. Not the kind of day one would wish on anyone for a wedding. Josh's ex-wife had to be disappointed. The sky told Quinby that they were in for a nasty storm.

Josh had dropped her off at her apartment to change for the wedding. Quinby tugged at the hem of her single decent cocktail dress, a simple sheath that clung to her in all the right places. Josh had decided that going in uniform would distress his already uptight ex-wife.

One of her standard pantsuits might have been a more appropriate selection considering that she was still on duty and might have to run Oscar to the ground, but after last night, Quinby didn't have the heart to wear anything so drab. She was determined to knock the Iceman's socks off at the reception and cause a major and much more permanent thaw. This guy was much too good to ever give up without a fight.

Ten minutes later, Quinby entered the Brackett City Police Department lobby. She garnered a few wolf whistles as her long coat flapped open and the two desk officers got a look at her extreme hem and the smooth expanse of legs beneath.

"Stuff it, you two," Quinby said, breezing by the desk and heading for her father's office.

"Your father's busy, Quin," Anderson called after her. Obviously Tripp and his cronies hadn't wasted any time letting everyone else know her relationship to the chief.

"No problem. I'll wait," Quinby said without turning around.

Waiting wouldn't be hard. Quinby knew she still needed to get her head screwed on straight before facing her father. At their dinner together last night, Brad Tennison had thrown down a challenge. A challenge that had hit Quinby harder than she would have ever expected. *For once in your life, Quinby, finish what you started.*

At the time, Quinby had gotten her nose out of joint. She had considered his challenge a bit presumptuous. But when she had taken the time to think things over, she had realized he was right. She did need to finish what she started. It wasn't difficult to see that no matter what happened on her final evaluation, she would feel better about herself if she gave it her best effort. No quitting this time.

The outer door to her father's office was open a crack, and Quinby could hear the rumble of voices inside. The secretary's chair in the small waiting room was empty, a plastic cover over the screen and keyboard. Even Evelyn insisted on getting her weekends off in spite of Quinby's father's obsession that he could only keep the city running by working seven days a week.

Willing to wait, Quinby perched on the edge of one of the waiting room chairs nearest the open door and reached down to smooth out the shimmering material of her dress.

She hadn't seen Josh's truck when she had pulled into the parking lot, so she figured that Oscar was holding him up. It would give her enough time to talk to her dad. To tell him that her decision to become a cop had been the right decision after all. That she'd finally found her place. The thing she was meant to do.

Her father's voice filtered through the crack in the door. "Nice finish to the Zander case. I didn't realize you were that close. The D.A. tells me that with the necklace and the girlfriend willing to testify against Drake, a conviction is essentially assured. Good work."

"Quinby was the one who spotted the necklace. She's got a cop's eye."

Quinby sat forward. There was no mistaking that voice. Like warm whiskey poured over cold ice, smooth and rich. Josh was the other person in her father's office.

She crossed her legs, trying without much success to ignore the answering ache deep inside her. How was it possible that just hearing his voice was enough to throw her body into sexual overdrive? If it kept up, it could get embarrassing.

"What was so all-fired important that you needed to see me today?" her father asked.

"Quinby is supposed to meet me here in about fifteen minutes. I'm here because I needed to talk to you alone for a few minutes—before Quinby gets here."

Quinby dug her fingernails into the arms of the chair, her body tensed. What was this all about? There was no getting around the queasy feeling that she was eavesdropping, but how was she supposed to get up and walk away after a comment like that?

"I hope you're not here to tell me that she's not going to make it," her father said.

"Not at all." She could hear Josh clearly now. He was obviously pacing the room and it had brought him closer to the open doorway. "She's doing just fine. I have no doubt she'll qualify at the range next week."

"Then why do I hear some hesitation?"

Quinby stayed tense, agreeing with her father's assessment. There was no missing the wariness in Josh's voice, and it worried her.

What if Josh was hung up on the fact that she'd fallen into bed with him? Maybe the fact that she'd made love with her field training officer counted against her in Josh's book. She swallowed hard. Could he suspect that she'd done it in an attempt to wrangle a favorable evaluation out of him?

"I came in to tell you that I want off this assignment effective tomorrow."

Quinby's stomach tightened as a sick feeling crept over her. Had she heard him right? Was he really asking for her to be reassigned to someone else?

"Why the change? I thought the two of you were getting along famously?" her father asked, his voice mirroring Quinby's own confusion.

"Look, Brad," Josh said. "You knew going into this that I wasn't happy about this assignment. Well, Quinby's doing fine. She has another week of field training. It will solidify the work she's done this week on getting her confidence up." His voice moved closer to the door, and Quinby sat on the edge of her chair, ready to flee.

"Why not another week with you?" her father asked.

"Because I need things back the way they were. You know how much I hate having a partner."

Quinby swallowed hard. *I need to have things back the way they were...I hate having a partner...* The words slashed at her like tiny knives, piercing her skin and driving their way straight into the center of her heart. He was dumping her. Getting rid of her while he could and running in the opposite direction.

She bent forward, her breath coming in tortured little gasps. Her elbows hit the tops of her thighs, digging into the tender flesh and making the pain of his words all the more real.

What had possessed her to believe that he might actually like her…even love her? The pain of finding out that he still thought of her as a burden—a favor to her father that he couldn't dump quick enough—hurt more than Quinby had ever thought possible.

What made her think she, Quinby Parker, could affect that cold, lonely heart beating inside that magnificent chest? Better to just believe that she was lucky to get out of the partnership with her skin slightly scorched but in one piece.

She got to her feet. Time to get out of the waiting room before Josh came out and found her standing there like some fool with a broken heart and hurt feelings.

There was no way she'd ever give Josh that kind of power over her. No way that she'd let him know the extent of her hurt. Better to wait for him out in the lobby. That would give her time to steel herself. To shore up the boundaries and put on a show that demonstrated nothing was wrong.

She wobbled slightly on her heels as she walked out the door, feeling all the world like a new colt treading out into the big, bad world.

JOSH STEPPED OUT OF BRAD'S office, quietly closing the door behind him. He paused beside Evelyn's desk, reaching down to take a peppermint sucker out of the small jar she kept next to her computer. He threw it in the air and caught it in his mouth, tucking it into one corner as he smiled and thought about this morning.

Popping Cookie Crisps in Quinby's mouth had been more than fun, it had been downright erotic. Who'd have thought eating a kid's cereal would be so darn indecent? It could mean a whole new market for the cereal industry if word got out. He made a mental note to stop at the Grand Union on the way home to see if he could order them by the crate.

Quinby's final week of training would go quickly. Josh didn't doubt that she'd do fine. The problem was going to be getting her to understand the need for a change in training officers.

Josh knew without question that Quinby needed to do the final week on her own, without him standing over her. It was important that she find her own confidence without feeling as though she needed to rely on him. Their relationship had changed last night, and Josh didn't want to take any chances that he might stand in her way of becoming the cop she was capable of being.

But first he needed to convince her of this. Straightening his tie, Josh strolled out into the lobby. He found Quinby standing in front of the reception desk, her elbows propped beneath her chin as she talked to the officer on duty. She hadn't seen him yet, engrossed in the conversation she was having with the young man stationed in front of the computer.

She'd pulled her hair back away from her face, a silver band laced through the thick strands. He liked the warm gold color shimmering on the tips and the curve of the curls.

The brilliant color of her earrings winked in the light as she smiled warmly at the officer. An unfamiliar twist of jealousy ripped through Josh. Funny. When had he gotten so taken with her that he couldn't stand her smiling like that at anyone but him.

She seemed to sense his presence and looked up. The smile disappeared, replaced with something else—a flash of anger? Disappointment? For the first time since he'd met Quinby, Josh sensed a closed wall around her. A wall meant to keep him out.

Before he could speak, she turned away and went back to talking to the guy standing behind the counter. Surprised at the snub, he walked over. What had brought about the sudden change?

"Are you ready?" he asked, his voice more brusque than he'd intended.

Quinby shot him a withering look, but whether it was for the gruff tone or something else he wasn't sure.

"See you later, Pete," she said, bestowing another prize-winning smile on the desk officer.

"Don't forget your purse, Quin," the kid-faced cop said, practically scrambling over the top of the counter in an effort to hand Quinby her beaded bag. "And when you're finished with your shift, come on over to the Station House Bar & Grill. A few of us are meeting there after work."

Quinby plucked the purse from Pete's hand with a flourish and nodded, her hair swinging forward to brush against her cheeks in a maddening way. Maddening to Josh because it reminded him of last night and the feel of those soft strands brushing his own face.

"Thanks," she said. "I just might take you up on that." She turned and cocked an eyebrow in Josh's direction. "Are we all set then?"

"I am. But you seemed to be tied up filling in your social calendar," he said.

She shrugged. "Unlike you, I happen to enjoy the company of others."

"What's that supposed to mean?"

"Take it to mean whatever you want, Josh. I'll meet you outside." She turned and walked out, her long legs eating up the walkway. The distance between them widened and seemed to magnify the chasm which had opened up between them.

Sighing, Josh followed.

When he reached the cruiser, Josh found Quinby sitting in the driver's seat, the engine running, her eyes focused straight ahead. He could tell from the set of her jaw that she wasn't in any mood to discuss who was driving and who was sitting in the passenger's seat. He climbed in next to her.

They rode in silence for a few miles until he couldn't stand it any longer. "Are you ready to tell me what's wrong or am I supposed to guess?"

Her knuckles whitened on the wheel, but the smile she turned on him seemed pleasant enough. "Nothing's wrong, Josh. Everything's just peachy." She pulled into the driveway of the Whispering Pines Retirement Community and slowed to allow the guard to wave them through. "We're finishing up our assignment. I have one week left in my training, and then you'll be free to work your cases. Unencumbered and blissfully alone. What could possibly be wrong?"

"Then why am I sitting here feeling like the ax is about to fall?"

"I don't know, Josh. Guilt maybe?"

She hit the brakes so hard in front of Oscar's condo that Josh had to wedge his palm against the dashboard to keep from going headfirst through the windshield.

"I'm not—" Josh stopped when he saw Quinby staring, her eyes wide with shocked surprise.

He turned to see Oscar coming out the front door, turning to regally offer a hand to Mimi. The two ambled down the walkway arm in arm. Oscar in his pea-green trousers and electric-blue blazer under his wool coat and bomber cap, and Mimi in one of her brilliant, multicolored Hawaiian dresses under a floor-length, fake leopard fur coat.

Josh swore softly under his breath and hit the door handle, climbing out. "What's going on, Oscar? Didn't you get the tuxedo your son sent over?"

Oscar grinned. "Of course I did. But Mimi and I decided to go in our own creations."

"What's—Mimi doing here?"

"She spent the night. We're engaged. And she's going to the wedding as my guest." Oscar stepped around Josh to open the back door, handing Mimi into the back like she was a delicate flower. "The invitation said I could bring a guest. You have a problem with that?" He didn't wait for Josh's response, climbing in after Mimi and snuggling up against her like a contented cat.

Josh shook his head and slammed the back door shut. "No, I don't have a problem, but Caroline is sure going to have one." He slid into the front seat and nodded for Quinby to go. With the two lovebirds in the back seat, the conversation about Quin getting a new training officer was going to have to wait.

12

SIX TEDIOUS HOURS LATER, Quinby leaned up against the back wall of the reception area, lifted one leg and tried to unobtrusively rub her calf muscle. Wearing heels hadn't been one of her more brilliant decisions. So much for wanting to look sophisticated and chic for Josh. He'd barely glanced in her direction since they'd reached the reception.

Josh had recommended that they split up on arrival, cover all the exits. But Quinby knew it was hardly necessary. Oscar wasn't going anywhere. He was having too much fun tearing up the dance floor with his new girlfriend. So in her heart, Quinby knew that Josh's plan was one to keep her at a distance. To keep her at arm's length. The seduction was over and now onto business. It hurt, and hurt bad.

But in spite of it all Quinby couldn't help smiling when she glanced at the dance floor. The two lovebirds, Oscar and Mimi, had a conga line going, Oscar in the lead and Mimi bringing up the rear. The line weaved in and out among the tables, a zigzagging line of wiggling hips, shaking derrieres and jiggling bosoms. In spite of the late hour, things were definitely not winding down. After uncountable trips to the open bar, the majority of the guests were feeling no pain.

Quinby had a moment of panic when it looked as if Oscar and the line was headed in her direction. But the D.J. slipped a ballad on, and the conga line broke up.

Considering the amount of panting and gasping going on among the conga line participants, his decision was probably a good one. From the looks of things, another few minutes and the hotel would be calling 911 for the rescue squad.

Quinby made her way over to the massive wood and brass bar and waited for the bartender to notice her. Although she was about ready to float out of the building due to the number of sodas she'd downed over the past three hours, Quinby figured she needed something to occupy her hands. Simply standing against the wall like some type of pathetic wallflower just wasn't going to cut it.

She cocked an elbow on the smooth wood and glanced out at the dance floor. Couples. All couples snuggling up and moving like one person. Quinby scowled. It reminded her of the night at the restaurant when she'd danced with Josh and Zack. Obviously she had read that situation wrong—Josh wasn't interested and probably thought last night was a major mistake. At least he could have had the decency to tell her to her face rather than just avoid her.

She glanced around, wondering where he had slunk off to. Oscar was in clear sight, but no Josh. She craned her neck, trying to see over the crowds. Finally she spotted him, leaning up against the wall directly across from her, half in the shadows, half out.

As she stared, Quinby realized he was staring right back at her. Her heart beat a little faster. How long had he been there?

Strange as it seemed and as mad as she was that he'd essentially dumped her, Quinby was relieved to finally see him again. There was no denying the sense of calm that seemed to settle over her whenever he was close by.

Quinby straightened up, prepared to amble on over

and simply apologize for getting all huffy and temperamental earlier in the day. Maybe if she told him that she wouldn't pressure him for anything other than a professional partnership, he'd stick it out—help her finish her training.

But then, just as she was working up the courage to walk over, Josh's ex-wife stepped out of the crowd and moved to stand in front of him. Her delicate hands smoothed the satin, hand-embroidered gown spreading out from her willowy figure, and she tilted her head to one side as she spoke to him.

One of the silver spotlights overhead shone on the diamonds and pearls threaded through the elegant twist of wheat-blond hair artfully arranged at the back of her head. Quinby tried to push aside an uncomfortable pang of jealousy. Without breaking a sweat, Caroline managed to look like a full page ad for *Modern Bride* magazine.

As she watched, Caroline threw her head back and laughed at something Josh said. For a moment, Quinby wished she was a tiny fly on the wall behind the two of them. Then maybe she'd figure out what was so darn funny. From the way they were laughing and carrying on a person would get the idea they were good friends rather than a divorced couple.

Of course, knowing that Caroline was bestowing a little good humor on Josh should have pleased her, especially since she knew the type of pressure he'd been under lately with regard to Zack. Perhaps his appearance at the wedding had done something to improve that situation. She couldn't complain about that.

Out of the corner of her eye, Quinby noticed the bartender move up to her. "What can I get you, miss?"

She tore her gaze away from the mutual admiration party going on across the room and faced the bartender. It was on the tip of her tongue to tell him to set up five shots and a chaser, but instead, she ordered another soda.

The bartender filled a glass with ice, shot the soda in from one of the fountain taps and set it in front of her. Before she could thank him, he moved off to serve someone else. Quinby took a long sip and then turned back around to see if Josh and Caroline had gone back to their neutral corners.

She almost choked. Caroline was now in Josh's arms, and they were skimming along the dance floor. They looked so good together that other couples seemed to fall back and give them more room, a few pausing to watch. Caroline's full skirt dipped and swirled on the floor, looking like creamy froth.

Quinby took a fortifying gulp of her soda, and set her glass down. This was more torture than she was willing to suffer right now. She glanced at her watch. Her shift was up. She was going home.

Slipping around a group of guests clustered at the end of the bar, she made her way out to the main hall and over to the cloakroom. What she needed right now was her coat, a cab ride home and two extra-strength pain relievers to take the edge off the dull headache that had taken up permanent residency right between her eyes.

Quinby slid open the cloakroom door and started pawing through the collection of coats jammed into the huge closet.

"Leaving?"

Quinby didn't bother to look up, she knew it was Josh. "Things are winding down, and I've had enough for one day. I'm sure the mayor won't begrudge me leaving a few minutes early."

"Guess you need to get over to the Station House Bar & Grill before the group breaks up."

"Yeah, whatever." Quinby shrugged and ran a hand across the coats, trying to figure out which was hers.

How did a person forget what her coat looked like? Frustrated, she yanked a heavy mink aside, trying to find something that looked vaguely familiar.

"Nice ceremony, wasn't it?" Josh asked, moving closer. She could feel the warmth of his body press in on her. The light, clean scent of his aftershave invading her nose.

Quinby gritted her teeth. She wouldn't beg, and she wouldn't plead. Josh had shown her exactly where she stood when he'd dumped her this morning, talking to her father without ever letting her in on his game plan.

Well, he'd gotten what he wanted. And if she was willing to be honest with herself, Quinby knew she'd gotten what she wanted, too. A chance to be held in those powerful arms and kissed by those magnificent lips. A taste of what could have been. And now she couldn't complain. She'd walked into Josh's arms with her eyes wide-open. He'd already made it clear once that he wasn't interested in romantic entanglements.

"You okay?" Josh asked, leaning forward, trying to catch her attention.

"I'm fine," she said, pawing through the coats. Darn it. Where was the stupid thing? If she didn't find it in another few seconds she'd leave without it. She was so hot anyway that it would feel wonderful to hit the cold evening air without a coat.

"You've been in some kind of snit all day. Have I offended you in some way?" Josh reached out and smoothed his hand across her shoulders. "Are you regretting last night?"

Quinby stiffened and tried to shrug his hand off, but he tightened his fingers, the tips seeming to burn into the bare skin beneath the straps of her dress. *Regret last night?* How could anyone regret something so wonderful?

"Quin, you need to tell me what's wrong," he said.

Quinby shook her head, determined to ignore the soft, coaxing quality of his voice. "Nothing's wrong. I'm just tired. It's been a long week, and I'm glad it's over."

His hand lightly stroked her shoulder, the skin tingled beneath his touch. "Making lame excuses doesn't cut it. For once in your life, don't run off without facing your problems."

His comment of *running off* sent a jolt of anger sizzling down the length of Quinby's spine. She whipped around, knocking his hand off her shoulder. Her reaction must have surprised him because he dropped back a step.

She jabbed a finger into the middle of his chest. "Me? You're accusing me of running away?" She poked harder, but it seemed to have absolutely no effect on him. "I'm *not* the one who dumped my partner like a piece of useless garbage. And I'm definitely *not* the one who was so eager to work solo again that he couldn't tell her the truth."

Quinby turned back to the coats and started to savagely push them aside. It only made her angrier. Hot tears spilled down her cheeks and onto the backs of her hands. Oh, for pity's sake, this was ridiculous. She wasn't the crying type. Now her mascara would run, and she'd end up looking like some kind of raccoon.

"Quin, I—"

She whirled around again. "And another thing, don't hide behind that line about liking to work solo. You're dumping me because I got too close, and that makes your skin crawl. Didn't it, Officer Iceman?" She fairly spit the words out, tears washing over her lips as she opened her mouth. "What a perfect name for you. I used to think it had to do with the way you were so cool, calm and collected while on patrol. But now I know what it really means—that you have a heart of ice!" She reached up and impatiently swiped the back of her hand across her cheeks. Her breath rasped in the back of her throat.

Josh reached out and pulled her into his arms, pressing her up against his chest and wrapping her in a circle of warmth. "Aw jeez, Quin. You shouldn't listen at office doors and not expect to overhear things that you don't want to hear."

She froze, her sobs becoming a giant lump in the back of her throat. So it was true. He wasn't even going to try to deny it.

"I'm sorry if last night meant more to me than it did you," she said, her voice muffled against his shirt.

"Do you really believe that?" He used a finger to tilt her head back and gazed down into her eyes. "Do you really think that last night meant nothing to me?"

Quinby took in a shaky breath. "Sure seems like it from what I overheard you say in my father's office." She stepped back almost tripping over the track of the cloakroom door. "Your rush to get rid of me was quite an eye opener."

Josh shook his head. "You don't understand. I didn't dump you to hurt you. I didn't even know you were out there."

"Obviously."

Even in the subdued lighting, Quinby could see a sliver of regret enter Josh's eyes. It was mildly reassuring. At least he hadn't intentionally wanted to hurt her. Even Josh Reed wasn't that cold and cruel.

He reached up and grasped her upper arm, his hand firm. "I'm sorry you heard it that way. I wanted to explain things to you myself—in person and away from the station house."

"Oh, yeah, right. Let me down easy, right?"

Quinby tried to pull away, but Josh held her fast, his big frame pushing in on her, crowding her in the small space.

She forced a smile. "Don't sweat it. I really understand why you did it." She ignored her quivering upper lip and pushed on. "Hell, I'm actually kind of grateful. It makes changing to a new partner all that much easier."

She tried to move around him, but Josh didn't budge or loosen his hold. "You're not leaving until we've settled this."

She laughed, surprised and pleased that it actually sounded real. "I thought things were settled. I'm going home."

"You're running again, Parker."

Anger rocked through Quinby. "Don't play benevolent mentor with me, Josh Reed." She stepped back and folded her arms. "You've been effectively relieved of that responsibility at your own request. Besides, you're the one who is turning tail and running like a scared rabbit."

Josh frowned. "How's that?"

"You were the one who couldn't handle us being partners and lovers at the same time." She lowered her voice a tad as a couple strolled by, glancing at the two of them with ill-concealed curiosity.

Josh reached out to cup her chin, his thumb gently stroking her bottom lip. "Actually, Quin, I rather enjoyed both. But you know as well as I do that we can't have it both ways—it isn't professional."

Quinby batted his hand away. So what if what Josh said was true. It still hurt. It cut into her like a knife, reminding her that he was thinking about his damn job while she was thinking about how it felt to be held in his arms and kissed long and deep.

"I thought that you'd at least finish out the two weeks. That you wouldn't be so afraid of getting close to me that you'd run the first chance you got," she said.

Josh stepped closer, forcing her back against the row

of coats. Before she could protest, he caught her up against him and slanted his mouth across hers. His lips sent a sizzle of fire shooting through her. A fire so hot that it scorched her insides.

Quinby tried to pull away, determined to keep the sweet sensation from overwhelming her. But Josh, seeming to sense her withdrawal, tightened his hold. His breath mingled with hers, warming and stroking the heat within her heart.

Josh lifted his head and asked softly, "Tell me, am I acting like a person who is afraid to get too close?"

"Kissing doesn't count—that's just physical closeness. You're afraid of letting me close enough to get under your skin. To mean something to you—something more than your partner on the beat."

Josh paused, looking down at her, the dim light shadowing one side of his classically handsome face. "You mean something to me, Quin. Something very special. And I'm not sure I can describe it, but it's there."

Her heart stilled, and she looked up. Was he admitting that he cared for her? That she held a place in his heart that had nothing to do with being a cop?

"Then why are you doing this to me? Why are you pushing me away?" she whispered.

Josh reached up and trailed the tips of his fingers along the side of her jaw. Quinby shivered and reached up to slide her hand over his. But Josh shook his head and stepped back, his hand slipping out from beneath hers.

She tried to still the flutter of panic that swept through her. His eyes lost their gentleness, hardening as she watched.

"You need to finish this for yourself. You don't need me or anyone else to help you do it."

Quinby clenched her fists. "That's not right. I need

a training officer. I can't complete my training without one."

"You need a partner who will act professionally. That's not me. I stepped over the line."

Quinby fought to stay steady. She needed to convince him how much she needed him to get through the next week. "It wasn't you. It was me. I knew exactly what I was doing. I wanted you and went after you. I promise to behave. We'll both behave. We'll be the most upstanding, politically correct partners the department has ever seen."

Josh shook his head, a fan of thick hair falling onto his forehead. He reached up and impatiently brushed it aside. "Go home, Quin. I'll finish up here." He turned away.

"Josh, please don't do this."

"Good luck, Quin. I'll see you around the station." He walked away without looking back.

Quinby bit her bottom lip as her heart shattered into a million pieces.

A WEEK AND A HALF LATER, Quinby ran up the stairs at the station house, taking the steps two at a time. When she hit the first floor landing, she pressed the release bar on the door with two hands and burst out into the back hallway. She was ready to burst—to explode wide-open.

Looking both ways up and down the hall, she swore softly. Empty. Not a soul around. No one to share in her excitement. Paige had already started her shift, and her father was across town at an administration meeting. Her new partner had left at the end of their shift to attend his daughter's ninth birthday.

She smiled and shrugged. So what? This win was for her, and savoring the sweet taste of it alone wasn't as bad as she'd thought. Heck, she'd won it all on her own, might as well celebrate it the same way.

She peered out the back door and checked the parking lot. A few cars. Twenty or so trucks, and a dark green van. As good a place as any to let loose. Pushing open the door, she stepped out onto the icy pavement. It wasn't as cold as earlier, but a cool breeze blew gently. The sun was setting behind a row of apartment buildings off to the west.

Quinby sucked in a deep breath, jumped up and let loose with a wild war whoop.

"So, I guess that means you passed?"

Startled, Quinby whirled around to see Josh leaning up against the side of his truck, his arms folded and one leg propped up on the side running board. He smiled, a slightly crooked smile. The breeze lifted several strands of his hair and blew it back off his forehead, and the fading sunlight hit his eyes, turning them brilliant blue.

Seeing him sent a jolt of longing shuddering through Quinby's bones. It was a feeling so strong and so sweet that she almost doubled over from the shock of it.

Instead Quinby straightened up and smiled tightly. It was too soon. She thought she'd have more time to recover before he started popping up in her life again.

But she wasn't going to kid herself. She knew Josh worked at the same place, walked the same halls and punched the same clock. So the fact that their paths would cross again wasn't any big surprise. But somehow, Quinby thought she'd have a little more time to regain her equilibrium.

It was a surprise that he'd even shown up. After his comment at the reception about her needing to make it on her own, Quinby had figured he wouldn't come around for a while. That he'd let her deal with it on her own. After all, Quinby didn't doubt that the look in her eyes and the expression on her face had been so pathetic that he'd run to get clear of her.

"How's it going, Josh?" she said, hoping against hope that it came out sounding casual.

"Going just fine," he said.

Quinby nodded, waiting to see what happened next. It was critical not to make a fool out of herself. It wasn't who she was anymore. She had a real reason to be proud of herself. She'd just aced her final weapon check as a field trainee and passed on into the ranks of a full-fledged, full-time employee of the Brackett City Police Department. She was kick ass ready to take on the criminal element of Brackett City. Her smile widened. She was even prepared to take on the legend of the department.

Josh pushed himself off the side of his truck and grinned. "I gather that congratulations are in order."

"You gather right. I passed both my weapons check and my final week of field training."

"Never doubted it for a minute."

"Well, I did," Quinby said, finally able to laugh, surprised when it came out sounding so free and easygoing. Her insides didn't feel that way. Her stomach was in a knot. She wanted him so badly it hurt.

Josh walked over to stand in front of her, and she wondered if he knew what she was feeling. She couldn't tell from his expression. It remained closed. Private.

"Your doubts were the main reason I left you to finish on your own."

He had moved so close she could smell the crisp scent of his aftershave.

He smiled and reached out to touch several strands of her hair, his fingers brushing her cheek. "You needed to build your confidence, Quin. To really believe in yourself. I figured being a cop would mean more to you if you did it all by yourself."

Quinby shook her head in exasperation. "So you're

saying you dumped me because you thought I needed to do some kind of crazy, trial-by-fire thing?''

He laughed. ''I guess you could call it that.''

''That's ridiculous!'' She grabbed the front of his jacket in her fist and tried without much success to shake some sense into him. ''Admit it. You did it because you were scared I was getting too close.''

Josh gently pried her fingers off his jacket, and before she could step back, he gathered her into his arms. ''Actually I rather liked having you close. Liked it a little too much because it wasn't the right time for us to be together.''

''Oh, and a week later it is?'' Quinby scoffed.

He leaned down and kissed her, only lifting his head when she was breathless and hanging on to him to stay upright.

''Definitely. And to prove it, I've got an interesting proposition for you.'' His voice was deep and seductive, striking a warmth deep inside of her. ''A proposition I've never made to another partner I've ever had.''

''What?'' Quinby asked, her hands seeming to move of their own will, sliding up around his neck and tunneling through the thick hair at his nape. She tugged gently pulling his head back down to hers.

''Oh, you'll find out,'' he said, kissing her again.

He lifted his mouth off hers and placed it next to her ear. He sank his teeth lightly into the lobe before saying, ''You wanted to know if I was afraid of intimacy. It's actually one of my favorite things to do—especially when it's you I'm being intimate with.'' He started to suck gently, his tongue hot and insistent against her skin. ''And I plan on being intimate with you a lot.''

''Oh, yeah?'' Quinby said. ''Do I have any say in this?''

''Oh, most definitely,'' he whispered in her ear. ''After all, you could always say no when I tell you.''

Quinby tilted her head back. "Tell me what?"

"That I love you."

Her hands stilled. "You mean that? I—I mean really, really mean that?"

He grinned. "Yeah, I really mean it."

Quinby threw back her head and laughed with joy. Then smiling, she asked, "You ready to take me home, cowboy? I've got this wild hankering for some of your very special shooting lessons."

He nodded and swung her up into his arms. "No big surprise here, but I've had the very same urge."

Quinby leaned her head against his chest and smiled with contentment when she felt the strong beat of his heart beneath her ear as he carried her to the passenger side of his truck. As she slid onto the front seat, Quinby reached out and touched Josh's cheek. A thrill of happiness raced through her as he turned his head and pressed his lips to the center of her palm. It was then that Quinby understood that she'd found a partner for life—someone who would give over to her as much as he would ask of her. And as much as it was frightening, it was also wondrously glorious. Beautifully freeing. Lovingly so.

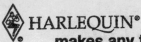

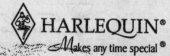

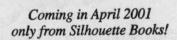